VIOLENCE IN THE VOID

Published by Inderton Press LLC.

Cover by Fantastical Ink

Map illustration by Laura Andrews

Formatting by Alice Stanco

Violet and Xander portrait by FlashFryed

Proofreading by ZaBrina Houston

Developmental Edits by Taryn Deirmenjian and Melissa Erickson

Line Edits by Tiffany Grimm

Contents

To anyone out there who has lost a part of themselves to their trauma.
You may find it again someday, or you could build something even better.

Never stop fighting.

AUTHOR'S NOTE

The differing societies within this fictional universe each have their own dialects, which are reflected in cultural differences, word choice, line delivery, and–most glaringly–the spelling. You will find that some chapters have American English spelling and others have British English.

These are not typos or errors and have been constructed intentionally.

If the only reason this book has found its way into your hands is that you know me in real life, and not because you genuinely enjoy this genre, I highly recommend you reconsider.

Read the trigger warnings and do your research on dark romance before proceeding.

Finally, and most importantly:
This book was born from a lot of pain and trauma. For that reason, it may be triggering at times. The story touches heavily on struggles with mental illness and suicidal ideation, and I fear that it could have a negative impact on some readers' mental health.
If you ever find yourself slipping—because of this book, or otherwise—*please* seek out help.

United States Suicidal Crisis Support
Call 988 or text 741741
UK National Suicide Prevention Helpline
Call 0800 689 5652

You are never as alone as you may feel.
There is always hope, and new beginnings waiting for you.

I hope you enjoy my story.
The Astrales await.

This story contains...

Death of family members, house fire, murder, trauma responses, PTSD episodes, depression, depressive episodes, mentions of suicide, suicidal ideation, struggles with appetite, disordered eating habits, captivity, assault, physical torture, mental torture, choking, blood, explicit language, explicit sexual descriptions, light masochism, light sadism, safeword usage, edging, breath play, marking, biting, physical restraint, sexual coercion, magic play.

ℙRONUNCIATION GUIDE

5 Cores

- Astrolite [Ă-stro-lite] – stars
- Hydroseis [Hi-dro-seize] – water
- Mistral [Mĭ-strull] – wind
- Terrala [Ter-ah-la] –earth
- Soothsayer [Sooth-say-er] – mind

Names

- Archibald [Arch-e-bald]
- Astrale [Ah-straw-lay]
- Amelia [A-meal-ia]
- Batskii [Bat-ski]
- Mr. Berger [Bur-ger]
- Chelsea [Chel-see]
- Dana [Day-nah]
- Dhan [Dawn]
- Dmitri [Dme-tree]
- Eloko [E-low-co]
- Imani [E-mah-nee]
- Jax [Jacks]
- Laura [Lor-uh]
- Lilliana [Lilly-ah-na]
- Marj [Marge]
- Manakoar [Man-a-core]
- Neerah [Near-ah]
- Nygaard [Nye-guard]

- Pehliah [Pah-lie-ah]
- Ren [Ren]
- Roslyn [Rah-sah-lin]
- Sensinor [Sen-si-nore]
- Shaed [Shade]
- Violet [Vio-let]
- Xander [Zan-der]

Places

- Armantrea [Are-mahn-tree-ah]
- Barlo [Bar-low]
- Bedruke [Bed-ruhk]
- Bosquera [Boss-care-ah]
- Callieso [Kah-lease-oh]
- Cavell [Kah-vell]
- Inderton [In-dur-ton]
- Myrana [Myr-ah-na]
- Sarehm [Sare-um]
- Serrant [Sir-aunt]

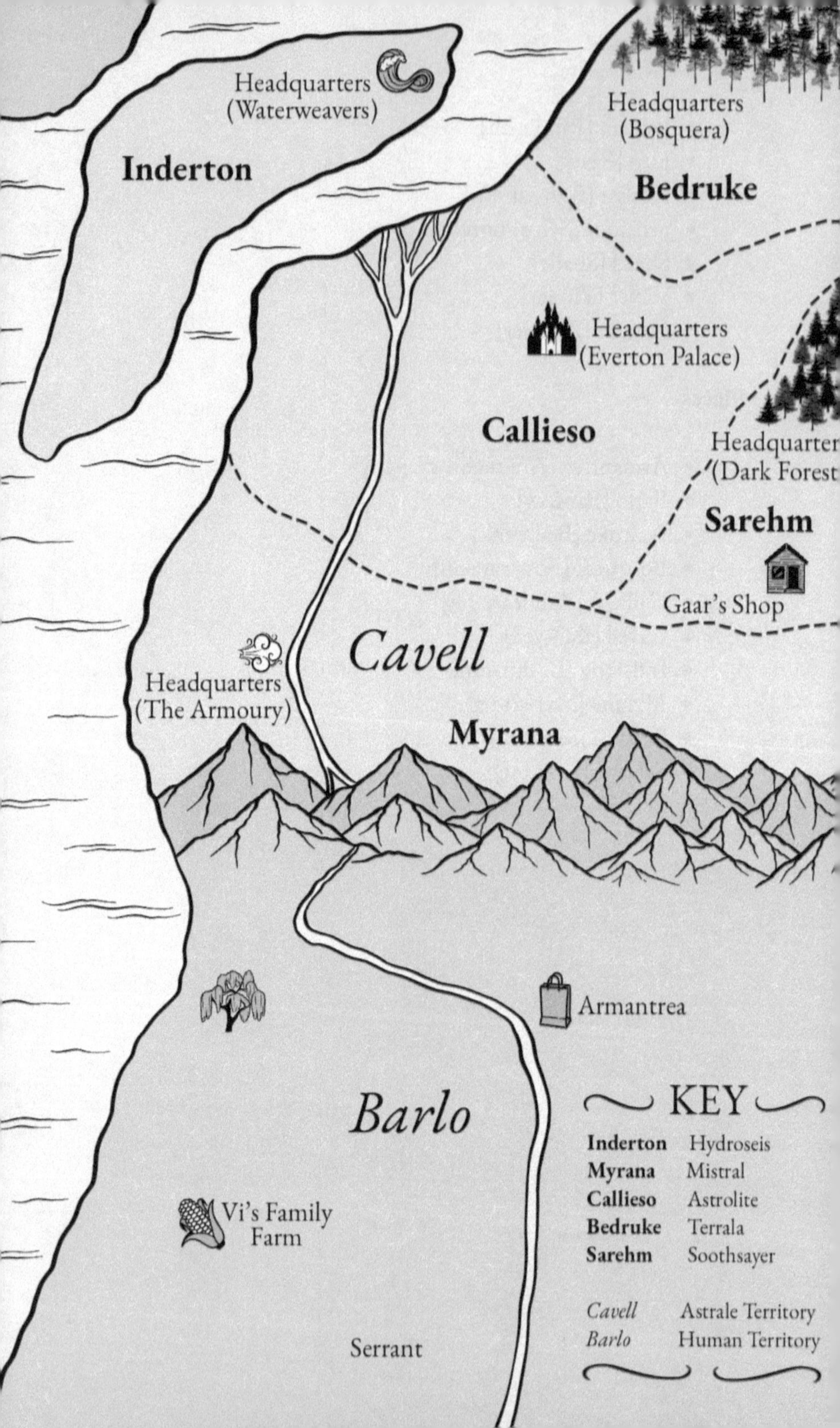

Headquarters (Waterweavers)
Inderton
Headquarters (Bosquera)
Bedruke
Headquarters (Everton Palace)
Callieso
Headquarter (Dark Forest)
Sarehm
Gaar's Shop
Cavell
Headquarters (The Armoury)
Myrana
Armantrea
Barlo
Vi's Family Farm
Serrant
KEY
Inderton   Hydroseis
Myrana   Mistral
Callieso   Astrolite
Bedruke   Terrala
Sarehm   Soothsayer
Cavell   Astrale Territory
Barlo   Human Territory

"SHE WAS TRAPPED IN THIS
WORLD WHEN HER SOUL
LIVED ELSEWHERE."

— *RINA KENT*

PROLOGUE

So, what do you do when Death appears on your doorstep, and you've entirely accepted that you're going to die, but then suddenly, Death concedes—and your miserable little heart decides to keep on beating?

At first, proceeding with gratitude seems like the best way to go. Be thankful that you get to see another sunrise, that the air is still filling your lungs and the birds are still singing. Don't think about the *'what ifs'* or the *'I wishes'*. Staying positive will work because they tell you it will.

That is, until you realize that the numbness burning inside of you is only growing because of it. That the forced smiles and false optimism are only accentuating the gap where a piece of your soul used to be.

You can also try yielding to the Void, letting it consume your every waking second until you are nothing but vacant expressions and glazed-over eyes; until eating and drinking and getting out of bed take as much effort as running a mile used to.

Some people say talking helps. You could spend minutes and hours and days trying to find a way to articulate the frustration that comes from not wanting to be dead, but not particularly wanting to be alive either, because you don't *feel* alive.

All you feel, since that day, is an in-betweenness in life; a crossroads that can never be crossed.

The truth is, none of these options are viable in the long run.

The only thing you can do is accept that a small part of you, deep down, died that day. Because Death doesn't make a visit and then leave empty-handed. If It realizes It can't take you in your entirety yet, It still leaves with a fragment of your soul, forcing you to wake up every day and feel a certain undistinguishable lacking within yourself. It forces you to wonder, on a repeated loop, when It will be returning to claim you.

And in that way, It already has.

This is the story of my stolen fragment, and how I stole it the fuck back.

Part One

THE VOID

CHAPTER ONE

VIOLET

"You son of a *fucking bitch!*"

I sighed heavily and repressed a scream as I looked down at the rice scattered all over my apartment's wooden floor. I was already running late for the market and, in a rush to grab my keys, knocked the jar of uncooked rice off the counter.

Checking the clock and seeing that I should have left ten minutes ago, I quickly grabbed the broom and began to sweep up the mess I'd made.

"Violet?" Archi asked as he emerged from his bedroom, the fact that I'd woken him up clear in his voice. He must've been deeply asleep to be using my given name and not his usual nickname.

I winced. "Sorry, Arch. I was trying to be quiet and get out of the house on time, but apparently the universe had a different plan for me today."

I finished sweeping up and emptied the dustpan into the garbage. When I turned, I saw Archi resting against his door frame on one shoulder, his arms crossed, wearing his blue flannel pajama pants and a white shirt.

He shook his head, making his short red hair catch the light. "It's no big deal. I just worried that you fainted when I heard the crash."

That made something catch in my chest. He knew me so well. I mean, it would've been hard for him not to, seeing that we'd lived together from such a young age–but still.

"You are the best. You know that?" I asked, walking over to him and giving him a quick hug.

I pulled back and looked at him, finding a familial warmth in his eyes.

But then I remembered how late I was, so I hurried to the foyer to get my shoes on.

"I'm probably going to be back around eight or nine tonight," I said. "You know how the market usually goes late on Saturdays. Plus, we need every mark we can get for next month's rent."

Archi nodded, grimacing slightly. "I know. I'm sorry that I haven't been able to contribute as much recently. I did find someone who is interested in buying my 'Pocketful of Daisies' piece, though. I'm meeting with her today."

"Arch–that's great! You know I get it, though. It's not like selling my pottery is any more stable than you selling your paintings."

It had its issues–both of us surviving off of our art. The pay was extremely unreliable and insufficient most of the time, but we were born to create.

What's the point of living if you aren't doing what makes you happy?

"Okay," I said, reaching for the door handle. "I really need to go. There is always a line to get into the storage cubes when I get there after nine-thirty. See you tonight. Good luck with the meeting!"

I heard Archi's thanks echo off the stairwell as I closed the door and began racing down the flights of stairs.

The market square was about a fifteen-minute walk from our apartment building, so I only had a few minutes to spare before the other sellers would swamp the storage facility to retrieve their goods. Every vendor received their own locker when they registered with the official Armantrea market so that they would be able to set up their stalls without the hassle of carting merchandise and tents across the city.

As I bustled down the sidewalk of a high-traffic road, I took a deep breath and felt myself relax a bit as the cold air filled my lungs. The streets were busy this morning; people of all natures coming and going.

This was what I loved about Armantrea–it was the capital city of Barlo, making it home to a wide variety of people, cultures, cuisines, and so much more.

Archi and I had dreamed about making a life for ourselves here for so many years. It still felt surreal sometimes that we had actually done it. Those moments–when I took a step back to bask in how amazing our life here was–were too few and far between.

When I was sixteen, we were living in a tiny cottage in the middle of nowhere. It was our first permanent residence, and we were young and naïve, but we'd gained some hope for what our future could look like.

One night, Archi and I sat at our kitchen table and mapped out a ten-year plan:

Year one: find steady employment

Year two: fix-up the cottage to make it more comfortable for two people

Years three and four: save every mark we could for moving to Armantrea

Year five: make the move and find an apartment to rent

Years six and seven: establish a customer base in the city

Year eight: meet the loves of our lives

Year nine: buy our own homes

Year ten: start living the lives we were always meant to

It was a surreal feeling, reminiscing about the plans we'd made and how much things had changed. I felt rather proud as I entered the storage facility and reached into my pocket for my key.

Here I was, living in my dream location, pursuing my passion, and thriving because of it. Even though the exact timeline of events hadn't panned out, we'd still made the move when I was only twenty–an entire year before we thought we would.

I had yet to solidify my clientele, but I was only twenty-two. And I had gained many more important things. Friendships, a sense of belonging within the community, but most of all–*experiences*. I had time for the rest of the plan. Right now, I just wanted to enjoy my life and spend time with the people who made me feel whole.

So, I slid the key into the door of my storage cube and smiled at the way my life was turning out. Everything was exactly how it was meant to be.

Right?

☽

"Mr. Berger, I'm sorry, but four copper marks really is the lowest price I can do," I said, trying to keep the annoyance out of my voice.

Mr. Berger was a regular customer, which I appreciated. In fact, I liked the man...for the most part. His kind eyes and familiar smile were always a welcomed sight.

Except for the days when he tried to haggle me down to the last copper mark. On those days, I felt like throttling him.

"Oh, c'mon, Violet. This can't have taken you too long to make. It's just a simple mug!" Mr. Berger responded, squinting his eyes while inspecting the mug in question.

It was glazed with a deep shade of purple and had a perfectly symmetrical oval shape. This, along with the intricate grooves along the bottom, took me about five hours to make.

"Again," I started with a sigh. "I make everything here by

hand, so I set the prices accordingly. If you want a two mark mug, you are welcome to go buy one someplace else."

The man chuckled in response and shook his head. "Alright, alright. I'll take it. My granddaughter is going to love it. Purple is her favorite color, you know."

I repressed another sigh. "Mhm, I know."

I suspected Mr. Berger had some memory issues—he was constantly repeating himself to me.

"Let me wrap it up for you," I offered, noticing someone looking at a bowl on the other side of the tent. I called over my shoulder while reaching for the paper, "I will be right with you!"

As I wrapped the mug in white paper, I noted how many people were bustling through the different stalls.

The traffic today was much higher than usual. I'd sold my pottery at this market almost every day for the past two years, and early Saturday mornings were usually a lull as people tended to sleep in. This happened even more so now that it was winter, so I wondered if there was an event happening today.

I was still able to get my things out of storage quickly and set up my stall easily enough, though. I had only been open for about an hour and already made twenty-six copper marks, so it seemed like my day was picking up.

I put a rubber band around the mug to secure the paper and passed the wrapped bundle to Mr. Berger. "Thank you for stopping by. I hope she likes it."

He smiled kindly while passing me the money. "She will. I'll see you soon, Violet. Be safe."

I smiled at his departing comment–the same one he always made–while I walked over to the man, who was now looking at one of my favorite pieces. A vase with a swirling shape and a glaze that was never the same color, shifting as the light hit it from different angles.

The man holding it, though...*strikingly beautiful* were the only two words that came to mind.

For starters, he was over a head taller than me. That was really saying something, considering I was already taller than the majority of men I knew.

His full cheekbones were pronounced, arching upward toward a crown of unruly black hair. It was the kind of black that seemed all-encompassing; as if every other color existed only to emphasize its own achromatic being.

"That piece is one of my favorites," I shared as a way of greeting. "It took many days of curing in between layers to get the glaze right."

He didn't respond–only put the vase into a ray of sunlight and looked more closely at the coloring.

Well, okay then.

"Can I help you find anything in particular?" I tried again.

He set the vase down carefully and looked at me headlong. I blinked twice in response to the color of his eyes. I had never seen such a pure and bright green before, and it was slightly unnerving.

"Yes, Violet, actually you can."

I felt my entire body stiffen.

First, at the fact that he knew my name. Secondly, because of how *familiar* his voice sounded. I knew I had never met this man before in my life. I would have remembered him.

I didn't have much time to dwell on the thought, though. He snapped his fingers, and the entire world exploded into color before I was whisked away into darkness.

CHAPTER TWO

VIOLET

I landed softly on a cushioned surface and had to blink several times to clear away the disorientation. Once I recovered, I looked around to see that I was in a large, brightly lit room.

What in the holy fuck.

Floor-to-ceiling windows showed a magnificent view of an unfamiliar city, allowing natural light to flood the room. On the stark white walls hung massive works of art–a grand waterfall, a beach I didn't recognize.

There was only one beach in my city, and it looked nothing like that.

"Not to worry, Angel," that accented voice called from my right. "Your tent has been packed up with care and is in a safe place."

My head whipped toward the man sitting in an armchair across from the couch I was on. The couch that *he* somehow transported me to.

He crossed his right leg over his left, his ankle resting on his knee, as he inspected the fingernails on his right hand, as if he was bored.

"Um, do you care to tell me what in the actual *fuck* is going on?" I asked, looking around incredulously.

His eyebrows shot up. "Well. You've got a sharp tongue on you."

There was some sort of accent to his voice that I couldn't

discern. A certain lilt to his words–a harsher finality to the consonants and more emphasis on the vowels.

"Ask nicely, and maybe I'll tell you."

I scoffed and stood up, walking across the room to one of the windows to try and get a grasp of where the hell I was. I didn't recognize anything about the city I beheld. Even Armantrea didn't have this many buildings, and they were so much taller than what I was used to. How could they possibly build them up so high?

What really caught my attention, though, was that everyone I saw wore light and short clothing. The sun was beaming.

Where in the fuck am I?

It was the dead of winter in Armantrea. That, and the obvious dialect differences happening, told me we were very, very far away.

"Where the hell did you bring me?" I asked, rounding on him. "Who are you?"

"You are unusually unafraid," he remarked as his head cocked to the side in observation. "Feisty and volatile, sure. I must admit, though, I expected *some* terror out of you. Maybe even a tear or two." His tone suggested that he was more than slightly disappointed, as his lips tugged down in a pout.

"I'm not afraid of you," I said between my teeth.

I probably should have been scared, but all I could feel was deep-rooted anger simmering over my confusion.

He laughed, but the coldness of it sent a shiver down my spine.

"Okay, Violet," he said with a resigned sigh, leaning forward. "My name is Xander. I'm Madame Lilliana's apprentice, and I was given the order to bring you here so that we can discuss your...art."

Confusion struck me again. Who was Lilliana? And what could these people possibly want with my art?

More importantly...

"How exactly did you bring me here?"

"Oh, you know, this and that." He waved a large hand through the air before crossing his arms.

Son of a bitch.

"Where even *is* here?" I asked.

Xander groaned dramatically. "You can stop with the questions now. It's rather irritating."

"Well, maybe if you didn't fucking kidnap me," I countered, "you wouldn't have to deal with my questions."

He laughed again, his unnervingly green eyes twinkling with amusement. "Mmm, yes. You're a feisty little thing."

Resisting the urge to scream, I opened my mouth to respond, but a reproachful female voice cut me off. "Xander. You wouldn't be antagonizing our guest now, would you?"

I turned and saw a short and slim middle-aged woman entering the room. She wore a loose-fitting, black dress that went down to her ankles. She carried an air of unbreachable authority with her. In fact, it seemed a bit like the air itself was parting to allow her passage.

"I wouldn't dream of it, Lilliana," Xander said, still smirking in my direction.

The woman rolled her eyes but smiled anyway. Her wavy blonde hair swayed as she walked straight toward me, and as she got closer, I saw the freckles splattered across her cheeks and nose. She had warm brown eyes, the color so light it almost looked like honey.

"Hello, Violet. My name is Lilliana. How are you?" she asked in a pleasant voice that held the same accent as Xander's.

Were these people genuinely, certifiably *insane?*

"Oh, I'm just peachy. Those mid-day kidnappings always put you in the best mood, don't you think?"

Lilliana's jaw tightened, and her smile strained but stayed in place. She spoke in a bright voice. "Xander, dear, I'd like to speak with Violet alone. There's an errand I need you to run anyway. Go on and ask Roslyn–she knows all about it."

Something shifted within his eyes, and his gaze flicked to me before quickly sliding back at her.

He cleared his throat. "Surely it can wait, Lilliana?"

Her lips tightened, and she shot him a look over her shoulder that I could only assume was a glare.

"Alright then. I'll be back in a bit."

His green gaze shifted to me one more time before he got to his feet, and even though I didn't know him well enough to know his body language yet, I could have sworn that there was something rigid about his posture as he walked out of the door.

☽

Once Xander left, I followed Lilliana through a set of double doors that led to an office. The space was bright and airy, similar to the first room, but much smaller. Floor-to-ceiling bookshelves were the backdrop to a large desk, both made from the same lightly colored wood.

We sat on opposite sides of it now, her in a plush-backed chair and me in an uncomfortable wooden one that was much lower. Even though I had many inches of height over Lilliana standing, she sat two inches higher than me now. And, as I sat across from her, I couldn't help but feel like a rabbit that a fox had cornered.

While she was putting on a good show of looking casual with her movements, I noticed that her eyes never quite left me. After adding sugar to her tea, she settled in the chair across from me, stirring it slowly with a small silver spoon.

She took a small sip before putting her floral teacup down on a matching saucer.

"I imagine that you have many questions, but if you don't mind, I would like to say my piece first."

Her tone was too sweet—the kind of patronizing superiority that set my teeth on edge. I subconsciously clenched one of my hands into a fist to refrain from snapping at her, but realized my mistake when I saw her eyes track the movement.

She must've taken my silence as agreement, though, because she continued. "I would like to start by apologizing for the methods we had to use to get you here. I don't particularly like the fact that you had no choice in the matter, but unfortunately, it was a necessary evil.

"It is imperative to the safety of my people that I speak with you." Lilliana's voice was assertive, and when she finished, she brought her hands together, interlocking her fingers on the desk.

I wondered if it had ever crossed her mind that it is impossible to know if something is a *'necessary evil'* without having attempted the alternative. Then again, if Xander had just randomly asked me to come with him to his boss's office, I would have said no in a heartbeat. So maybe she did have a point, but it didn't change the fact that I was still confused as hell.

How could I have anything to do with the safety of her people when I didn't even know where I was?

"I have absolutely no idea what you are talking about or who 'your people' are. How far are we from Armantrea?" I asked, doing my best to keep the annoyance out of my voice.

This woman was a complete stranger, and I learned long ago not to assume the best in people. Especially, you know, considering the fact that she'd just had me kidnapped.

Lilliana's amber eyes widened. "You truly have no idea where you are?" she asked. "Not the slightest inkling?"

I looked around, wondering if I had lost my mind and was now inside a hallucination.

"How in the hell would I know where I am? Your lackey showed up to my booth, snapped his fingers, and now I am in this...whatever this place is." I let out a breath. "So, no. I truly have not the slightest fucking clue where we are."

So much for keeping your cool.

Lilliana blew out a long sigh and shook her head, resting her forehead on two fingers for a moment.

"Perhaps it was a lapse in judgment sending Xander to retrieve you. He does love making a dramatic scene." She rolled her eyes. "Regardless, you're here now, and that's what matters. I am the governess of Myrana, which is a sector of the continent Cavell."

I wasn't highly educated by any means, but I knew a fair amount about the geography of our continent from my travels with Archi, and I had never heard of either place.

She reached below the desk to grab a binder and pulled out a thick piece of cream-colored parchment from it. When Lilliana turned it toward me, I realized it was a map and immediately pitched forward, trying to get a sense of where I was in relation to Armantrea.

There was one small problem with that. Absolutely nothing about the land on this map looked even remotely familiar.

A small laugh left her in response to my eagerness. She assured me, "I have nothing to hide from you. But you won't be able to conclude much from this map on your own. Our land is not something you will have seen before, my dear."

I clenched my jaw as the endearment made my frustration jump up a few notches. Lilliana seemed heedless of my reaction, though, continuing seamlessly.

"This," she announced, circling the entire continent, "is Cavell. We are here."

She pointed at the oblong district that spanned the southernmost point of the continent, bordering along an expanse of mountains. I squinted to find the name of them and pulled back once I saw it.

The Edithian Mountains—the same ones that bordered my lands in the north.

"If you were to follow this river south on foot, you would reach home in about three weeks," Lilliana explained as she pointed to the map again, breaking my focus. "Though you could never hope to do so without someone of our kind with you."

It would take three *weeks* of walking to make it back home?

Wait.

"What exactly do you mean by your kind?" I asked.

"I truly expected you to have at least some knowledge of this, but I guess I'll have to start with the basics." Lilliana cleared her throat and looked very uncomfortable. "Xander and I are not exactly human. That is, at least, in the way that you think of the word."

She flattened her hands against the desk, almost as if she was trying to come across as peaceful.

"We are of a bloodline called Astrales. Essentially, we are able to draw on higher powers that give us magical abilities. Our life-span is also very different from your kind."

She stopped talking, gauging my reaction.

I blinked a few times, wondering if her tea consisted of the red flowers people made a fortune off of in Armantrea.

Surely she couldn't be serious.

I thought about ignoring her, not even dignifying any of this with a response, but decided to play into her little joke. Anything to get the hell out of here as soon as possible.

"What kind of abilities are we talking about?" I asked with mock interest. "Can you fly? Turn invisible? Make people do your bidding without a second thought?"

The thing that I struggled with on a daily basis happened then–I sold my sarcasm too well, my tone too dry to come across as jeering. When this happens, the person I am talking to always thinks I am serious, which totally negates the sentence in the first place.

Lilliana seemed surprised and pleased by what she thought was my immediate acceptance of her revelation.

"Yes, essentially!" She nodded enthusiastically, and my mouth dried out.

Case in point.

"The gifts that manifest as we age are different for each indi-vidual, but some people in our history have been known to harness those you mentioned.

"For instance, Xander is a Whisken, meaning that he is able to move freely between two points in space by his own will. That is how he was able to bring you here by snapping his fingers. Though, that last part was entirely for show. So dramatic."

She rolled her eyes again and tossed her golden waves over one shoulder before looking at me intently. "I'm going to get right to the point though, Violet. I don't know to what extent yet, but you are, without a doubt, connected to our world."

Lilliana opened the binder again and began flipping through the pages until she found a painting. When she turned it to me, I saw a tall woman holding an object above her head. There was a crowd of people before her, kneeling with their heads bowed.

Pointing to the woman, Lilliana said, "This is Katerina Avalong, the first of our kind. Two thousand years ago, she was born an ordinary human. When the world around her erupted into chaos and war, she was visited in a dream by the Mother."

Lilliana pulled out another painting that showed the same woman, only this time she was sleeping on a bed of moss and flowers, and her slim face was cast into an expression of deep concentration.

Lilliana explained, "In this dream, the Mother shared that it was time for a new race to be born. One that would focus its efforts on cultivating the land and appreciating it, as opposed to destroying it with their hatred and unrest." Her eyes blazed with passion. "Katerina was instructed to gather her family and friends to make the trek–"

I cut her off. "Sorry to interrupt your fable, but can we skip to the part where I have absolutely anything to do with this?"

My patience was wafer-thin, and I didn't have it in me to pretend to buy any of this bullshit anymore.

Lilliana's lips curved into a tight smile, her eyes narrowing slightly. "As you wish, Violet."

My name sounded sharp on her tongue in a way I hadn't heard from her yet, ringing a warning bell in my mind.

"Katerina and her followers set out to cross the Edithian mountains with the aid of the Mother guiding their passage.

When they arrived in Cavell, she saw a single pillar raised at the top of a hill in the distance. Once she finally made her way there, she saw a clay Chalice sitting upon it."

Lilliana handed me another painting that showed a cream-colored wine glass with an intricate, swirling pattern of metallic gold along the rim and stem. There was an instant blossom of recognition in the back of my mind when I saw that pattern, but I couldn't figure out where it came from.

Her voice broke my focus.

"The Chalice is how Katerina and her followers became the first Astrales. Katerina simply had to fill it with water while it sat upon the pillar, drink, and the change would begin."

She leaned back in her chair, clearly finished with her story. I blinked again and tried very hard to suppress the urge to laugh at the ridiculousness of it all.

Lilliana stood and walked around the desk, stopping at my right.

"Does this look familiar to you?" she asked, gesturing to the painting I was holding.

I opened my mouth to deny it but closed it as that familiarity struck again.

After a second, Lilliana pulled an image out of the binder and set it down on the desk next to the painting. If not for the fact that the image was clearly taken with a camera and was physically more preserved than the painting, I would have thought they were the same. I felt my brow furrow in confusion as I looked between them.

Finally, Lilliana broke the silence.

"Six months ago, this photo was taken and slowly traversed over the mountain, coming to my attention through a colleague of mine. It is showing a chalice that *you* made."

Lilliana stepped behind my chair, coming around to stand on the other side of me and leaning her hip against the desk.

"I, for one, am very curious as to how a young, human woman like yourself, who clearly knows nothing about the

Astrales' existence, was able to perfectly replicate our most cherished relic."

I looked closely at the photo that was undoubtedly taken at my stand. If the flashes of my other pieces in the background weren't indicators enough, the ring I wore every day on my second toe was visible in the corner of the image.

It made my skin crawl to imagine when someone took this photo, and how I didn't notice it. Was I that oblivious to my surroundings, or would it have been impossible for me to notice? Were there other photos as well?

But, regardless, even if my design mirrored one of their relics, it didn't automatically mean that they were related. Maybe I had just seen this painting before. I said as much.

Lilliana shook her head. "No, Violet. That is simply not possible. I assure you that you would never have had the opportunity. Astrales dating all the way back to Katerina's time have gone to extensive lengths to ensure that our world remains hidden from your people. The only overlap that occurs is in the very few spies we have in the human lands, who are there for this very purpose." She gestured to the photo and painting again.

Then Lilliana stopped speaking, looking contemplative as she cocked her head slightly, staring just about as deep into my soul as possible.

I raised my chin slightly and maintained eye contact.

If she wanted to make me cower, she'd have to try a lot harder than that.

"You're a stubborn girl, aren't you?" she asked.

I couldn't hold back my smirk, and her gaze turned even more calculative.

Lilliana seemed to make some final decision as she stated, "I believe that you are the one we have been waiting for. The Mother has chosen you to Create once more."

And that was my final straw.

"Okay, look. I've tried hearing you out, but clearly you are out of your fucking mind."

I tried standing, but only made it a few inches before invisible hands roughly shoved me back into the chair—the unforgiving wood bit at the backs of my thighs and calves from the force of it.

"What the hell?" I exclaimed. "So one of my pieces looks similar to some super special–"

"It doesn't just look *similar*." In the span of a second, her voice had gone from silk to stone. "It is absolutely identical."

"But–"

"I'm curious," she cut in. "How did this nick along the bottom happen? Was it a mistake, or did you add that in by design?"

Lilliana pointed to a notch along the base of the piece. It took me a minute, but I remembered. After I had finished constructing the clay, I was smoothing the surface and my hand twitched, causing the tool to carve a small indent. I'd begun to repair it but then decided that, for some reason, it looked better that way.

Lilliana didn't wait for me to answer before pushing on.

"And this pattern along the rim of the Chalice? What inspired that?"

My heart began thundering in my chest. "I had a dream. I was walking in the art district, and every canvas had the same design, over and over again. I couldn't get it out of my mind for days."

She leaned back against the desk with a smug expression on her face, crossing her arms.

"Okay, I'll admit they're the same. And that vision-dream thing is weird. But that doesn't mean that I am some *'Chosen Creator'*. Even if I were, I want absolutely no part in that. So..." I drew out the word. "Now that we cleared that up, I think I'll be going."

A cold laugh left her, betraying the sunny persona that she'd taken on at the beginning of our conversation.

"Even if you could leave that chair, which I think we've established that you can't, you have zero hope of returning home without help."

I swallowed thickly as panic began to seep in.

She continued, "I would be happy to have Xander escort you home, just as soon as you tell me where the Chalice is."

I spoke as calmly as possible. "Hate to burst your bubble, but I can't. I sold it."

I'd sold it so many months prior, it was shocking that I even remembered it. The only reason that I did was because it had been Mr. Berger who purchased it.

Her nostrils flared, and as she stood up straight, I thought for a second that she would legitimately strike me. But after a few moments and exhaling heavily, her expression cleared.

"Well, you will simply have to retrieve it and bring it to me."

I scoffed. "I'm not going to run around town tracking down a cup. And I sure as shit am not going to take orders from you."

The words had hardly left my mouth when a crushing pain came down on both of my legs, beginning in my toes and spiraling through my thighs and up my spine.

I cried out as it felt like a fire had ignited in my bones, all the while not being able to move at all. A few more seconds of agony and screaming, and then the pain was gone.

Lilliana leaned forward so that her face was mere inches from mine. She spoke in a tone that was far too quiet, sending chills up and down my entire body.

"I think you'll find that you will want to do as I say. I was hoping that this would be more civilized, but hear me when I say that there is *nothing* I won't do to protect my people."

I tried moving again and found that I could, but only a few inches.

What options did I have? I could refuse, but based on the past two minutes, that wouldn't go very well for me. I could go find Mr. Berger and get the damn cup. Or, I could pretend to go along with this insanity, get Xander to bring me back to Armantrea, and split the first chance I got.

Using every scrap of willpower I had, I kept my face blank.

"When do we leave?"

CHAPTER THREE

VIOLET

I sat in a puffy red armchair with my arms crossed, glaring out of the large window across from me. I was in what was clearly a spare bedroom, on the verge of losing my shit from restlessness. At least five hours had gone by without a word from anyone.

The small square room was minimally decorated, with everything I desperately tried to avoid in my own. The walls were painted a stark white with few adornments: a body-length mirror was hanging by the door, and a simple painting of the moon against a starry sky hung above the small fireplace. There was a decently-sized four-poster bed in the center of the back wall, with a door nearby that led to the adjacent bathing room.

At least they put me in a comfortable room with the necessities, as opposed to the concrete cell I was expecting.

Lilliana had briefly explained what needed to happen, and then a woman named Roslyn brought me to this room. As annoyed as I was, I couldn't help but like Roslyn. I instantly recognized her *'I don't give a fuck'* demeanor. That, paired with the fact that she apologized for the situation and didn't try for small talk afterward, made me feel a sort of kinship toward her. It occurred to me then that I hadn't even checked to see if she had locked the door behind me.

I immediately got up and tried the knob, but it stayed in place.

Goddamnit.

I ran my hands down my face and began pacing the room, biting my right thumbnail as I tried again to process what was happening.

Lilliana said that Xander and I would be leaving today to begin looking for the Chalice. I'd sold it five months prior, to Mr. Berger, but I had no intention of bringing him into this mess. These Astrales had proven their brutality to me very quickly, and I didn't want to endanger him. I would just have to find a way to stall Xander and then escape.

Maybe I could go south to Serrant and open a little studio to sell my pottery. I would have to find time to go home and get some essentials to last the journey. And to somehow explain to my roommate and best friend, Archi, that I'd be moving and beg him to come with me. Well, *fleeing* was more like it.

How did this happen?

Only a few hours ago, I was still dredging through the early morning mind fog and working at my stall. Somehow I ended up on some unknown continent, being accosted and semi-tortured by people of some sort of magical species, and forced to set out on a search for some random cup I made.

I took a deep breath, attempting to calm down, desperately wishing that I had some of my Kava grounds. I could really benefit from the way they let me hit pause, slowing my erratic heartbeat and allowing me to dissociate for a minute.

Instead, I stepped in front of the mirror by the door and looked at the eyes that were so much like my mother's. The soft brown irises and upturned shape were an identical match, the only difference being the small blue segment within my left eye. My mother always said it was something I was born with and that, from the first time she saw it, she knew I would be entirely unique.

It wasn't my only birthmark, though—not by a long shot.

I cast my eyes down to my left hand to look at the faint patch of brown peeking out of the black long-sleeved shirt I wore. It was several shades darker than my olive skin tone, but I hardly ever registered it anymore. There were nine or so scattered around my body—all varying in size, shape, and color. I had become desensitized to them after so many years, only thinking of them when my mother came to mind. She'd loved them so much, always emphasizing how beautiful they were and how lucky I was to have them.

My chest squeezed at the memory of her. No amount of time would ever stop these sudden moments of grief, when all I could think of was the phantom feeling of her arms around me and the fact that the exact melody of her voice had been long since forgotten.

A sudden knock at the door jolted me out of the mental spiral I was in, bringing me back to the reality of being locked in a room by a bunch of supernatural freaks.

The knocking sounded again, more impatiently this time.

A burst of frustration coursed through me, making me clench my hands into fists and shout, "I don't know why you are knocking as if I could *open the fucking door!*"

The doorknob jangled, and a familiar, low-pitched voice grumbled, "Really?" He sighed loudly. "She locked you in there?"

After a moment, there was a screeching metal noise before the door swung open, and Xander was there, taking up almost the entire doorway. His green eyes were glowering down at me with a look of contempt on his face.

"Did you actually just break the doorknob?"

He shrugged. "I didn't feel like tracking Roslyn down to get the key."

Brushing past me, he walked over to the fireplace and leaned against the mantle on one elbow, keeping his eyes on me the entire time.

Back in the lobby area, I hadn't felt anything but annoyance and some potentially homicidal anger toward this man. Now that I had somewhat adjusted to the situation, I realized how...*not* human he really looked.

Besides those brilliant green eyes and the fact that he was enormous, there was just something transcendental about his overall presence. That, paired with the disdain I could feel radiating off of him, left me feeling a little unnerved.

But I couldn't help but notice how the hard cut of his jawline was more pronounced in this mood. How it perfectly framed his chin, which tilted down as he glared at me. He really was striking, and this whole angry vibe was only working in his favor. It was all slightly distracting me from the fact that he was some sort of wizard and was currently aiding in my captivity.

Regardless, I willed myself to remain impassive and maintain eye contact.

"Is it time to go already? I totally lost track of time with all of the entertainment offered." Sarcasm dripped from every syllable.

Xander scoffed and pushed off the mantle, standing up straight. "You humans can't even last a couple of hours without something tangible to occupy your mind. It's pathetic."

"If you think I am so pathetic, why agree to come with me? Why not make someone else do it?" I asked, bristling at the way he said 'humans', as if the word disgusted him.

"This was a direct order from Lilliana. I didn't have a choice. I'm about as happy about going on this little mission as you are, Angel. Let's just get it over with so we can get back."

"Fine, whatever."

I began walking to him but stopped in my tracks once his words sunk in. "Wait, get back? What do you mean? Lilliana said that I would be free once I found it."

I didn't miss the fact that something shifted in his expression before he cleared his throat. "Well, you'll have to bring it back to her, won't you? Now, come on. I'm losing my patience."

I rolled my eyes in exasperation. "You act as if I'm the one with the ability to bring us across the mountains."

I shook my head and took a few steps, closing the gap between us. Xander's eyes flashed as they tracked down my body, taking in the fitted long-sleeved shirt and baggy jeans I wore, ending on my worn trainers, and moving up again slowly.

There was a thickness to his voice when he spoke. "Where should I be whisking us to get this Chalice then?"

"Why the hell would I have been locked in this room for hours if I knew where it was?" The annoyance was clear in my voice.

He let out a low laugh. "I am so incredibly sorry for the dire mistreatment. The comfortable furniture, fireplace, and private bathing room must've made for an absolutely *dreadful* afternoon." There was a gleam in his eye and the slightest of smirks on his lips. "Now, can we get going?"

"Didn't we already establish that's up to you?"

He stepped into me completely, and I felt my breath catch as I looked up at him. This close, it was easy to see why his eyes were such an intense color and how they seemed to reflect his mood.

While the overall color was a dazzling sort of emerald, there were vines and shoots of seafoam and chartreuse that seemed to be constantly shifting and moving. For whatever reason, they had an immediate calming effect on me, and I found myself not wanting to look away.

Xander's eyebrows bunched together, and his Adam's apple bobbed on a swallow.

"You'll do well, little human, not to look at me that way."

And, yet again, before I had the chance to respond, that kaleidoscope of color and blink of darkness engulfed my vision and swept me away.

☽

THE FIRST THING I NOTICED AFTER BEING WHISKED back into Armantrea was how clear my head felt. The second was that nothing hurt, even though I was thrown roughly onto my ass in a deserted alleyway. I may as well have landed on a cloud.

In fact, it was so comfortable that I exhaled and let my body fully relax for the first time in hours. How many had it even been? Seven? Eight?

Then a deep, clipped voice returned and ruined everything.

"Do you plan on basking in the sun all day? Get up. We have people to interrogate."

I bristled and stood, brushing the gravel off of my pants and shaking out my shoulders.

"Where the hell did you dump us? And we will not be *interrogating* anyone. Stop being so dramatic."

He gasped and put a hand on his chest in mock shock. "Me? Dramatic? Hardly."

I rolled my eyes and looked around, trying to get a grasp of where we were when I noticed the building in front of me–the black-painted bricks and the scent drifting out of the exhaust.

I whirled on him and gaped openly. "Clarif's? You whisked us to *Clarif's*?"

Clarif's was my favorite restaurant in the entire city. The interior was decorated in a warm and cozy manner, with stained glass lamps casting a multi-colored hue over the entirety of it. I always felt a shift in my mood the second I stepped into its atmosphere.

I came so often that the chef–Imani–and I had become very close over the years. Archi and I had spent countless hours sitting by the fire with her after closing, playing whisky games and eating her freshly made cream puffs until we were ready to vomit–the cause of which varied depending on the night.

Imani was one of the few true friends I had, and I treasured her with every scrap of my soul.

Xander's brow furrowed. "I don't know what that is, but I did aim for the food district. Lilliana sent me straight to you upon my return and I haven't had the chance to eat since this morning."

I narrowed my eyes at him. He seemed a bit off-kilter, repeatedly straightening the collar of his button-down linen shirt, bouncing on his heels, his eyes skirting toward the alleyway opening and back.

"The fuck is wrong with you?" I asked him bluntly.

Not only was it annoying that he was whining about his lack of food when none of them had thought to bring me any over so many hours, but he wouldn't stop acting like *I* was the reason we were there. As if I wanted to prance around town with this enormous, ignoramus motherfucker.

He looked exasperated at my question. "Nothing is wrong with me. I'm trying to get my Glamour into place, but it takes a bit more concentration over the mountains. I usually do it beforehand."

I didn't know what the hell a Glamour entailed, but I wasn't really interested in finding out firsthand. I opted for a safer route instead.

"Okay," I drew out the word. "Is there anything you don't eat? I can go inside and order us something while you deal with... that." I finished, gesturing his entire body in a circle with one open hand.

"No, anything is fine. I should only be a minute." I turned toward the street but was halted by Xander borderline shouting, "Wait! No cabbage! I *detest* cabbage."

"Um. Okay? No cabbage."

Weird thing to feel so strongly about, but whatever.

I moved to the street and rounded the corner toward the main entrance of the restaurant. With every step I took toward the door, more and more tension left my shoulders as the familiarity began to sink in.

The cobblestone road of the food district wound down the row of mismatched buildings, and the very human assortment of people walking down it. The sign hanging above the door had a big, swooping 'I' that created a base for the rest of the letters. I cherished the soft sound of the chimes ringing as I entered the haven this building had become.

I was immediately greeted with the smell of baking bread and rich spices as I entered the front door. The sound of Imani yelling at someone behind the counter was so familiar and welcomed that I almost sagged to the floor with relief.

"How many times do I need to say it? It's not that fucking hard to remember. Metal *never* comes into contact with my pans. That happens again, and you will be out on your ass without a job."

I heard a muffled, male protest coming from further back in the kitchen as I stepped up to the counter, and Imani came into view. She wore her black curls swept back from her face with a green and blue scarf that matched her blouse and emphasized her long neck.

She yelled back, still facing the opposite direction from me, "I don't care if you're my nephew. I will still fire you without so much as a second thought."

She broke off as she turned around and saw me, her expression quickly changing from shocked to relieved to angry. Having seen the result of being on the receiving end of that glare many times before, I was slightly nervous but also confused. I couldn't have possibly done anything to piss her off since I saw her two days ago. Right?

"Violet Willow. Just where in the fuck have you been?" Imani asked as she ducked under the counter's door and came to stand in front of me.

Underneath her obvious anger, I could see concern etched into her features through the slight narrowing of her dark brown eyes as they combed over me and the way her full lips were tilted downward slightly.

"Woah! What the hell are you double-naming me for?" I couldn't imagine why she was acting this way. It had only been two days since I was last here, and I had gone far longer than that in the past.

She raised her chin and looked down her nose at me, even though she was four inches shorter.

"You have had Archibald going out of his mind with worry over you. I hope to god you have been home before coming here. You have, haven't you?"

God, Archi. That overbearing mother hen had come here looking for me after only being gone for a few extra hours?

"No, Imani, I haven't, but I'm going straight there from here. Look, it's a really long story that I definitely don't have time to tell you right now, but I'm going to need your help."

Deeper concern settled into her features, making her look much older than she was. Well, actually, I didn't know how old she was–she would never tell me, no matter how much I begged or how drunk I got her. After a full two years of trying, I had finally given up.

I brushed the useless thought aside and leaned in closer to her. "Look, Imani. There is this man that is going to be coming in here in a few minutes, and he cannot know that I said anything to you. Or that we know each other at all. I need you to act like we are just two random customers and that everything is normal. But I will be coming back here, hopefully within the next day or two, and I will need food. Enough to last three or four days, and that will keep well. I will explain everything to you then."

Imani cast that violent look my way again, but this time I knew it wasn't directed at me. It was *for* me.

"Violet," she murmured low and quiet, a warning stitched into every syllable. "Are you in danger?"

Now how the fuck was I supposed to answer that?

"No–well...yeah, kinda. Okay, I don't exactly know, but–" At that second, I heard the chimes on the front door ring and immediately began speaking, hoping that Imani would catch my drift. "Thank you for showing that to me! We'll just get the two chicken wraps, but I will make sure to try the special next time."

I made a show of looking at the board hanging on the wall behind Imani's head that read:

Chef's Special: Brown sugar glazed fish with greens

"Oh, and please make sure those have no cabbage," I finished with a smile and widened my eyes at her slightly before turning back to Xander.

He was glancing around the small restaurant, his eyes flicking between the ten or twelve empty tables with an unreadable expression on his face.

I narrowed my eyes. He looked exactly as he had in the alley. His staggering height was the same, as was the intensity of his eyes and that other-worldly quality he had.

What ever happened to this so-called Glamour he was getting into place?

I began walking toward my regular table in the back corner but decided that I didn't want to tarnish that bubble of happiness with this titan, so I sat rather abruptly at one in the middle.

Xander slid into the seat opposite me with a grace that should have been impossible for someone his size.

"Well, this is a cozy little place, isn't it?" he asked, still taking in the room with that wandering gaze.

When I didn't answer, he looked at me and tried again. "Do you come here often?"

I maintained eye contact–the first rule of lying well–and flatly said, "No."

The corner of his lip quirked up slightly, and some sort of humor that I didn't understand danced in his eyes.

Which reminded me...

"Just so you know, whatever Glamour you tried to put on most definitely did not stick. You look the exact same as before."

His brow furrowed, and I stiffened as he quickly reached into his pocket to grab something. That smirk returned as he opened his hand to show a small, circular object, popping it open to reveal a mirror. He actually carried a fucking *mirror* in his pocket.

"You didn't think I was reaching for a weapon now, did you?" Xander asked in that jeering tone he loved to use.

"What man carries a mirror?" I asked as he tilted his chin from side to side, looking at his reflection.

"What *person* doesn't care about their appearance enough to ensure that they will be able to check the status of their hair at any given moment?"

I wasn't really sure how to respond to that.

He snapped the compact shut and replaced it in his pocket. His jaw ticked as his gaze flickered around my face.

"Interesting."

I opened my mouth to ask him what the hell was so interesting, but two water glasses were placed rather harshly on the table, interrupting me.

I looked up to see a tall and slim man who appeared to be in his early twenties, and noticed the family resemblance immediately. The high cheekbones and deeply set eyes were identical to Imani's, though his skin tone was a shade lighter brown.

When he spoke, the deep pitch was completely at odds with his slender frame, and I hoped I hid my surprise well.

"Your chicken wraps will be ready in just a couple of minutes. Can I get you anything else to drink besides water while you wait?" Imani's nephew glanced between Xander and me, waiting for one of us to answer, but I was waiting for him to jolt at Xander's appearance.

He didn't show any sign of shock or alarm at the giant man sitting across from me, which just annoyed me further.

I swallowed my indignation. "No, thank you. We are fine."

After he walked away, I reluctantly looked back at Xander to find him observing me the same way he had in Lilliana's office, like I was some puzzle he was trying to figure out.

"May I help you?" I asked crossly.

He was undeterred. "You can see past my Glamour. Clearly, it is in place because that boy would have shown a reaction if it wasn't. Trust me, they always do."

"So, I can see past it. Why does that matter?" I muttered, crossing my arms and looking toward the unlit fireplace.

Xander didn't answer, but I felt too distracted to listen anyway. That last bit he'd said sat heavily in my gut. People oftentimes stared at me as I bustled through the city to get to the market. Whether it was because of my height or my leisurely clothes and usually unpampered hair giving me away as lower class, I didn't know.

I had noticed early on that if I wore clothes that showed my birthmarks, it was inevitable that I would feel many sets of eyes on me. That happened to be why I preferred the colder months. It was also why I didn't like that Xander experienced that judgment as well, which was stupid because I didn't even know him. And he'd only ever been irritating and condescending as shit.

After a few minutes of silence, where Xander continued staring at me and I therefore pretended he didn't exist, Imani's nephew–Pehliah, I learned–returned with our food and promptly rushed back to the kitchen after delivering it to our table.

The food was amazing, as it always was when Imani was behind the stove. The perfect combination of crunch from the vegetables and seasoning on the chicken was delicious, and after a few bites, my temper leveled out enough for my brain to function more logically.

In between bites, I said, "Okay, if you're done staring at me like I'm a science experiment, I'm going to need you to fill in some gaps for me. Lilliana was the actual definition of vague and abrupt in her lesson on Cavell, and I have some questions. Well, a lot of questions, actually."

Xander's pupils constricted briefly, but then he nodded and took another bite of the wrap. Taking that as the closest thing I would get to an agreement, I continued.

"What does Lilliana want with this Chalice?"

He continued chewing–pretty quietly, I noticed–and swallowed before he answered, "I'm not at liberty to tell you that."

I blinked. "Seriously?"

The deadpan expression told me everything I needed to know.

"Okay...well what about the different—what did she call them? Sectors? What can you tell me about them?"

He looked at me from beneath his brow and continued chewing, ignoring my question entirely. I waited until he was done, but he stayed silent.

My temper swung back around again in a second.

I swallowed the words on my tongue and tried again. "Lilliana mentioned that she was the governess of Myrana. What does that actually mean?"

This, apparently, he could answer.

"She is the official leader of the Mistral sector, Myrana. And before you ask, she was elected by the people. She holds court and listens to testimonials of all sorts, as well as appointing those who uphold the law. We don't have many laws, but those that we do have are absolute."

When he finished, he plopped his napkin onto his empty plate and leaned back in his chair, crossing his arms. The movement caused his biceps to swell and strain against his fists, something I definitely didn't need to be noticing because I *had* just been wondering if their leaders were elected, and I couldn't figure out how the hell he could have known that.

Unless...could he read minds?

Realizing that he was finished eating and I was only half done, I waited until I had taken a few more bites before asking the next question.

"Who is Lilliana to you?"

"She is my mentor," Xander responded in a guarded tone, one that piqued my attention.

I couldn't really explain how, but the dynamic between them seemed to run deeper than that back at Lilliana's office. Something wasn't adding up.

"Does she happen to be a mentor that you are also fucking?" I asked, only half joking.

His jaw tightened impossibly, and his eyes turned to ice as he leaned forward slowly, placing his large hands flat on the table and speaking clearly.

"Listen, *human*." He practically spat the word. "Why don't you focus your energy on figuring out how to find this Chalice instead of asking me pointless questions about a world you have absolutely no hope of surviving in?"

I swallowed thickly at the truth in that statement.

His voice turned soft in a way that made my blood still in my veins. "As for Lilliana, if you ever suggest anything like that again...I have ways to ensure you won't be able to speak for a week."

CHAPTER FOUR

VIOLET

Xander stared at me for a few seconds with an unmistakably authoritative glare, making sure his threat sunk in before he pushed back from the table and stood up.

He blinked, and his expression leveled out. His voice returned to normal when he said, "We're leaving in two minutes. I'll be back."

He grabbed both of our plates and cups, bringing them to the counter and leaving me more than a little perplexed.

Clearly, suggesting that he and Lilliana were an item was a sore subject, and I was dying to know the baggage that could've caused such a reaction. On the other hand, said reaction also had me feeling things that were definitely inappropriate, considering my current situation. The way his hands had flexed as he said 'if you ever' was...alluring.

I wasn't about to sit there and pretend like he wasn't the most attractive man I had ever met in my life, either. I'd never been the type to lie to myself, and he was extremely nice to look at. That, paired with the dominance that seemed to roll off him in waves, undeniably affected me.

What can I say? A girl's got needs.

I had a good mix of routine and spontaneous partners in Armantrea, but nothing ever stuck. I constantly found myself getting bored with the way they looked, how they touched me, or annoyed with the way they spoke. Plus, people often assumed that fucking me entitled them to answers to personal questions about me or my past. That was an immediate turnoff and usually resulted in me cutting them off or ignoring them until they got the point.

Xander didn't strike me as the type to pry into unwanted territory. Even though he was particularly rude and obnoxious, he did have that going for him.

"Are you daydreaming again already?" Xander's voice cut in as he approached the table. "It's time to go."

Yep, definitely obnoxious.

"You're pretty fucking annoying. Anyone ever told you that?" I asked as I got up from my chair.

"Oh, yes," he quipped chipperly. "Plenty of people." Xander put his hands in his pockets and began walking toward the door.

I locked eyes with Imani as we made our way past the counter. There was no way I could talk to her again without Xander knowing, so I did my best to communicate with my eyes that I'd be seeing her again soon. She gave me a slight nod before turning her gaze to Xander's back.

My plan was to stall Xander long enough for an opportunity to get away, then go home and tell Archi everything. I hoped he would decide to come with me. Maybe it could be a new adventure for us. A chance to repeat history, but use our knowledge and experience to make it even better this time around.

"Okay, little human with the magical hands, will we begin at your flat?" Xander asked as he stepped out onto the sidewalk and looked around at the people bustling up and down the street.

I scrunched up my face and followed him out.

"First of all, let's never call me that again. Secondly, my what?"

Xander's lip kicked up into a smirk as he leaned back against the brick wall on one foot and reached into his back pocket, drawing out a black cigarette tin. He pulled one out and held it between his teeth, bringing his pointer finger up to the tip.

A few small, green sparks shot from his fingertip and my eyes widened as he lit the cigarette; the smoke instantly billowing in the winter air. I could tell by its scent that it was tobacco and some sort of herb combined, the distinctly floral undertone complimenting the richness.

"What's with the face, Violet?" Xander asked after taking his first drag, the smoke in his lungs making his voice sound full and strained at the same time.

I hadn't realized I was making any sort of face and quickly cleared my expression before I shrugged.

"You just don't really seem like the smoking type to me."

He stared down at me with a bemused expression on his face as he blew the smoke out through his grin.

"And why is that?"

I didn't really have a solid answer for that, so instead, I said, "I guess I figured that you otherworldly beings have better things to do than engage in our human habits."

"Oh, on the contrary, Vi. We quite like some of your extracurricular activities–the self-debilitating ones are particularly enjoyable."

"Why do you talk like that?" I asked, unable to hold it in any longer.

I mean, seriously. The guy sounded like he was starring in a mediocre play showing beneath a bar.

"Like what?"

"Well, obviously, there's the whole accent," I remarked, unimpressed by Xander's cocky grin. "But it's also the words you use... dreadful, basking, not at liberty, flat. They're just unusual."

He laughed at that, a deep, rich sound that echoed off the street and sent a confusing shot of warmth through my chest.

"All this, coming from the woman who is capable of making magic pottery without even realizing it. I would say that qualifies as unusual, wouldn't you?"

I rolled my eyes at his absurdity. "Mhm, sure I am."

He smiled, his lips curling around the cigarette resting between them. "I believe your people call flats apartments. I just refuse to do so because it is an idiotic use of the term. It literally means 'a separate place'."

I didn't understand his logic—if you could even call it that.

"Isn't that the point? It is a collection of separate homes."

Xander smiled again and pushed off the wall, stepping toward the sidewalk.

"Debating the proper term for your home makes for riveting conversation, but shouldn't we be heading there?" He looked down at me with a glint in his eye as he put his cigarette out on the top of the garbage can and threw it inside.

I didn't miss the fact that he ended the debate right when I was about to win it, but I let it go. I had much more important things to focus on.

"No. I have to get a few things before we go back to my place. I need to see my herbalist, and she is the closest to us now, so we can start there."

I turned to the right and began walking toward the city center. I didn't necessarily need to go see Mikkie right now, but I was running low enough on my Kava grounds to warrant a visit. What I really wanted was to get to the most populated part of the city so I would have a better chance of slipping away from Xander.

He stuck to my side as I careened down the sidewalk, and I realized he was keeping his stride slow so that we were walking at the same pace. This was entirely foreign to me. I was used to having to do that for other people because of my height.

I kind of enjoyed the reversal of roles for once.

"So, is it normal for Astrales to be so tall?" I asked him while glancing his way. "Or are you just a special kind of magician?"

He looked amused by my question but continued staring ahead. "First off, never call me a magician again. They pull rabbits out of top hats and wear white gloves. That's tacky."

I surprised myself by laughing, and he looked over at me, the lighter green in his eyes churning.

"Astrales are purely elemental beings that draw on the essence of nature, allowing them to siphon magic. And secondly, no. Astrales are not inherently tall."

I was hoping for more of an explanation than that.

"What makes you different then? I mean, you have to be at least six-foot-five."

His face lost its grin, now showing a guarded expression. "Just about, yes."

I let a few seconds of silence go by before deciding that he wasn't going to give me any answers about that. I didn't need to push him on that, especially when I knew how annoying it could be. People constantly asked me questions about my birthmarks and my sectoral heterochromia.

It got old really quickly.

We rounded another corner and continued on, only a few minutes away from the market square now. As the chill in the wind bit my cheeks, I cursed myself for not asking Xander to grab my jacket from whatever 'safe place' he'd apparently put my things from the market in. I was only wearing a long-sleeved shirt and jeans that were not cutting it in the winter air.

I noticed that he was wearing a similar outfit but didn't seem cold at all, making me wonder if he was somehow impervious to the cold.

"Where is Cavell in relation to Armantrea?" I asked, changing the subject.

I was shocked that he didn't hesitate before answering. "Geographically, it is just on the other side of the Edithian Mountain range, but–"

"Wait." I saw Xander's eyes flash when I interrupted him, but I was undeterred. "Is that why so many people go missing or lose their minds when they try to cross it?"

One of the first things that Archi and I learned in our travels was that we were *never* to attempt crossing the Edithian Mountains. As far back as our history goes, no person has ever successfully made it there and lived to tell the tale. They either go as far as they can and return mad, or–more frequently–don't come back at all. I'd heard rumors that the peaks go so high into the sky that it makes your brain explode, but I never thought for a second that they were true.

Xander grimaced. "Yes. There are Wards in place to prevent any human from crossing over. Those that try to push their way through either lose their sanity or die."

My stomach felt like it had been filled with lead as I thought about all of the widows and orphans who lost their loved ones to the journey.

"That is so fucked up. You don't know how many people's lives you have affected by doing that."

He seemed unaffected by my accusation. "We can't risk the exposure of our kind. I don't like that it has to be this way, but maybe if those humans had the sense to stop trying it, they would stop hurting themselves and their families. Besides, it's not like I cast the Wards myself, Violet."

A fresh surge of rage pressed its way into my chest, and I had to clench my jaw to keep from screaming at him in the middle of the street. We were only a few blocks away now, but I realized that I had slowed my pace down in my anger, and Xander hadn't.

"If it's so important that your race stays hidden, why even come into our territory at all?" I asked with a bite in my tone. "Don't you worry that humans will find out and try to, I don't know, exploit your magic or something?"

As I finished, Xander led us on another right turn, bringing us into an alleyway that served as a back entrance to the city center.

How the hell did he know where to go?

"Well, that is precisely why we don't come into your territory very often," Xander quipped, giving me a sidelong glance.

Why the fuck did everything out of his mouth have to sound so *prickish*?

"Then why do you know your way around so well?" I squinted my eyes at the back of his head. Apparently he was done slowing down for my benefit.

"I travel here occasionally doing favors and the like for Lilliana. Sometimes it is unavoidable." His voice gained that arrogant fucking tone again, and I swallowed the snicker that rose to the back of my throat. Clearly, he thought it was some great honor to be working under Lilliana.

"And that happens often enough for you to know the city this well?" I asked skeptically.

Xander didn't answer, opting for a shrug instead. It was enough to make my pulse spike with annoyance.

"What is up with that, anyway? You just run around town doing whatever she asks you to do?"

He ignored me and continued walking, picking up his pace so that I practically had to speed walk to keep up with him. It was so infuriating that the question shot from my mouth before I could think twice about it.

"What did you do to become her bitch boy?"

Xander stopped walking so abruptly that I nearly crashed directly into him. Slowly, he turned his head to the side, looking down at me with a withering glare that made my mouth dry out.

"If I were you, little human, I would refrain from talking about things you don't know the first thing about." The usual air of loftiness and teasing vanished from his voice, giving way to the same steely coldness he had exhibited in the restaurant. He leaned forward, closing the gap between us, and spoke so softly that a chill ran down my spine.

"Especially when you have absolutely no idea what this *'bitch boy'* is capable of."

CHAPTER FIVE

VIOLET

I'd be lying if I said that Xander's words hadn't rattled me. It wasn't just the fact that he had inadvertently threatened me, it was the way he said it.

The thought of it caused a dual reaction.

On one hand, I was feeling the familiar surge of lust that came from very specific displays of dominance. On the other hand, a painful awareness that I had absolutely no idea who I was dealing with settled in my gut, leaving behind a sense of unease.

I knew next to nothing about his capabilities as an Astrale, or what direction his moral compass pointed. He could literally murder for sport, for all I knew. Judging by the fact that his boss had threatened to torture me, I guessed that wouldn't be entirely out of the question. What I was most concerned about was what that meant for a human like me.

Did he even view us as equals?

Considering his tone every time he called me out on my race, I would guess not.

But, underneath the fear and unease, there was a sense of excitement at the unknown possibilities that Xander could bring. I had been thinking lately that I was beginning to crave the occasional, unorthodox sexual activities I'd experimented with more and more over time.

I physically shook my head and shoulders, trying to rid myself of that train of thought. Why in the hell was I even putting any energy into thinking about sex with a man I was actively trying to escape from? I chastised myself for the senseless direction my thoughts were gravitating toward. I needed to get my shit together.

I spotted Mikkie across the street from me. She was sitting on a stool behind her table, one of the smaller booths in the market today, with a book in her hand. As I got closer, I realized it was actually a ledger she was writing in, which made a lot more sense.

Mikkie was the kind of woman who didn't understand having a love for reading books. She didn't judge it by any means. She would just much prefer to be out in the world experiencing things instead of reading about them.

Sometimes I would go a full two weeks without seeing her, just to find out she had taken a spontaneous trip hiking across the continent or jumping from city to city, partying until her body physically gave out. I respected her ambition and desire to fit everything that she could into her life, even though I didn't relate to it at all.

If anyone was ever searching for me, they knew they'd find me on my couch with a cup of coffee, a Kava cigarette, and a good book.

"Well, well, well," Mikkie greeted as I approached, her voice raspy as ever. "If it isn't our missing link. Where have you been hiding out, and why didn't you invite me?" She pouted. "You know I love a good bender."

Mikkie looked good. The purple eyeliner she wore made her gray eyes pop against her fawn skin, which had paled from lack of sun. In her typical fashion, Mikkie's scarf perfectly matched the plum shade, but contrasted with the white and black swirling pattern of her thick sweater. Where the hell she got her clothes, I would never know. They seemed to get more and more eccentric by the day.

"Bitch, please," I chastised. "You know if I was going on a bender, I would have called you." I rolled my eyes aggressively. "Did Archi seriously come crying to you, too? I really need to talk to him about codependency. It's starting to kill me."

Mikkie laughed, a low and throaty noise that brought a smile to my face.

"I'm not touching that one," she said, shaking her head.

"Yeah, fair enough."

I smiled wider, the easy banter making me feel the same relief that walking into Clarif's had.

"What can I get ya today, sweets? You running low on K? Or have you finally decided to listen to me and give Cerro a go?" Mikkie wiggled her eyebrows in invitation.

I scoffed. "If you don't stop trying to push that shit on me, you're going to lose a loyal customer."

Both of us knew the threat was nonexistent. I would never stop buying from Mikkie, even if she hadn't become a close friend of mine. Her product was too fresh, and her prices were too low. She grinned knowingly, likely thinking the same thing I was.

However, it was getting on my nerves that she kept badgering me about trying Cerro when I had already told her so many times that I wasn't interested. It was a new herb that was circulating Armantrea, one that caused feelings of euphoria and amusement. Many people had taken to the altered state of mind it brought them, but I wasn't interested in anything that brought my guard down like that. I just wanted a light herb that would slow my heart rate a bit and help me relax.

"I am just running low on my K, and I'm about to go on a little...excursion. I will buy a double bag this time just to be safe."

Mikkie began her process of scaling out the grounds, grabbing an opaque black pouch with an airtight seal and filling it with the brown powder. As she worked, she asked, "So, where are you headed? Any place I know?"

The warmth inside of me seized and shrank as her question brought me back to reality. I didn't know when I would see her next or how long it would take for me to return to the city. The thought threatened to bring tears to my eyes, and I blinked rapidly to keep them at bay.

"I'm not quite sure yet," I answered truthfully, before shifting into the lie. "I've been feeling low on inspiration lately, so I'm hoping that a little unorganized getaway will spark something in me. You know, artist's block and all."

She nodded and made a noise of agreement. "That'll be three copper marks, V."

"Absolutely not, Mikkie," I replied back immediately. "I'm all for a friends and family discount, but that is excessive."

Typically, just one bag would cost three copper marks. I'd ordered two, so my purchase today should be at least one silver mark. Knowing damn well how unreliable living off of market sales could be, I was not about to accept that.

I fished a silver mark out of the emergency stash in the hidden compartment of my right shoe, annoyed that Xander hadn't returned any of my belongings yet. I realized then that I wouldn't see any of those things again. They'd be lost once I escaped from Xander. My wallet and hundreds of marks worth of pottery, and my tent—gone.

Motherfucker.

Mikkie took the silver mark I handed her, only to give me back two copper marks in return. I started to protest, but she cut me off.

"Let's call this a compromise and leave it at that." She grabbed my hand and folded my fingers over the coins, holding my closed fist in her hand and squeezing. "I know how expensive traveling can be, Violet. And I'm doing well right now, really. Please, just take it and shut the fuck up about it."

I couldn't stop the ear-splitting grin that hit my face, and I pulled her into a tight hug.

"Thank you," I whispered, finding it hard to bring my voice any higher than that.

I couldn't think about the fact that this was the last hug we would have for an unknown amount of time. I needed to keep it together.

"Anytime, sweets," Mikkie responded, the shock clear in her

voice. I had never been an overly touchy person, so this hug must've seemed entirely out of the blue.

I pulled away and put the coins into my shoe, making sure the latch clicked into place and was secure. Mikkie returned to her chair behind the table, settling down and grabbing her ledger.

She smiled at me. "Be safe out there. Hope you find what you're searching for."

"I will be, Mik. See you soon."

I had to turn around and get my feet moving to avoid the searing pain in my gut.

I had *finally* found my place here. My people. And now I had to leave.

Truth be told, though, I wasn't entirely surprised. Life had a tendency to uppercut me just when things started working out.

Freshly irritated and feeling melancholic, I began scanning the crowd for Xander, realizing I hadn't seen him since I went up to Mikkie's stall. This had to be some sort of test. Surely he wouldn't have just left me, trusting that I would stay put.

I wove through the different stalls, saying hello to familiar vendors and shoppers that I came across, looking for that crown of black hair towering over everybody else.

The dumbest surge of hope I've ever felt in my life started to creep its way into my chest.

Had this plan actually worked? Would I actually be able to get away?

I did a final sweep around the center of the market, having stepped into one of the smaller offshoots, and–when I still couldn't spot Xander–decided this was my best shot.

I spun on my heel and sprinted, the activity causing my hip to scream after only a few meters, my old injury rearing its ugly head.

I made it to the end of the alley I had escaped through and took a sharp right turn, knowing that this backstreet was heading in the direction of my apartment. I kept running even though my joint was begging me to stop, and I knew that I would be paying for this later, but I didn't care.

I was getting away. Every pump of my sneakers against the concrete brought with it the jangling noise of the coins in the sole. With each metallic ring in the air, my chest felt lighter and the pain subsided more as relief washed over me. In less than ten minutes I would be safe inside my apartment, hugging Archi and reprimanding him for the fuss he'd caused.

At that moment, a creeping sensation ran along my shoulder blades, indicating that I was being followed. I whipped my head around quickly to see the road empty, save for an employee bringing trash to the dumpster. With wide eyes, she looked at me, clearly confused by the fact that I had just been sprinting through the backstreet at full force and now stood still, staring at her.

I gave an excruciatingly awkward half-wave and continued on my way, wondering if this whole ordeal with the Astrales would cause more years of glancing over my shoulder continuously.

God, I hope not.

I had just recently shaken that particularly long-lasting effect of my trauma, and I definitely didn't want to go through the process of stopping it again.

I forced myself not to think about it because I have learned throughout my life that intrusive thoughts only occupy as much space in your brain as you allow them to.

Fuck that.

I came to the end of the buildings that formed the alley I was in and peered around the corner, seeing that the street was mostly empty. I turned back the way I came, leaning against the wall and taking a deep breath to gather myself before running across the street to the next alleyway. I did one more inhale–to the count of four–and then sprang on my toes toward the street.

Thump.

My teeth clanked together so hard that my ears rang as I ran full force into Xander's chest. I tried to jerk back, but his arm banded around my back, trapping me against him.

A whirlwind of emotions ran through me. Annoyance at myself for even thinking I could get away to begin with, irritation at Xander for toying with me, and an unwanted surge of heat through my core from the way he was crushing our bodies together.

"Well," Xander said with a smirk. "That was fun. Are you ready to actually start this mission, or do you want to play a little more?"

I growled low in my throat, thrashing to get away from him and failing miserably.

Xander gasped dramatically. "So you *do* want to play! How fun. If I let you go, will you run?" he asked, the hope clear in his voice.

While I was gaping at his statement, my brain decided to take notice of the very distinct, very *large* bulge digging into my lower stomach.

I gulped.

"I haven't gotten to chase a pretty little thing like you in a long time," Xander continued, oblivious to where my thoughts had gone. "That would be lovely."

My jaw dropped. "Let go of me, you fucking freak!" I exclaimed, banging my fists against his chest.

"Gladly." He laughed again and released me abruptly. "But, for future reference, I have a solid track on your scent, and can hear you from much farther away than you realize. There is nowhere you can run and hide from me that I won't find you. Ever."

I took a step back as his words sunk in. Obviously, his sense of smell couldn't be at a human level, meaning his other senses were likely heightened as well. There would be no escaping him unless he was incapacitated.

Fuck. Imani would be expecting my return, but there was no way I would be able to now.

Oh god. Did that mean he could hear everything I'd told her when I first entered Clarif's, too?

Xander regarded me with amusement written all over his face, clearly enjoying watching the helplessness and panic set in. It pissed me off, but I didn't want to give him any more satisfaction than he was already getting.

So, I started walking to my apartment without so much as a glance in his direction. He stepped into stride with me immediately.

"Where are we going?" he asked.

"Do you have memory loss?" I snapped. "I need to get a few things from my apartment. There is also a letter there with Mr. Berger's address on it. Hopefully, he will be there with the Chalice, and we can conclude this mission by the end of the day."

I really was hoping for that to be the solution, but it seemed unlikely. I would need to prepare to be gone for a few days, just to be safe.

"I hope so as well," Xander added, "but mostly for your benefit. Myrana's Mistral Festival is coming up, and I will not be happy if I miss it because of you and this mission."

I gave him a side-eye. "You can stop acting like it's my fault your psychotic boss forced us to do this. You're literally holding me against my will, so your lack of logic regarding this '*mission*' is getting really old."

Xander stopped walking abruptly and grabbed me by the elbow in an iron grip, keeping me in place. He leaned down so that our eyes were level and squinted slightly.

"You need to stop speaking about Lilliana that way. I won't stand here and tolerate you disrespecting her. You don't know the first thing about why she needs the Chalice, so stop fucking acting like you do."

"Uh..." I cocked my head. "Is that supposed to be my fault? Because I'm pretty sure you're the one with the ability to clue me in."

Xander didn't speak, but his expression turned even more murderous as the pressure of his grip increased.

Good god.

"Alright, relax," I said, exasperated and tugging on my arm. He let it go and straightened but continued glowering down at me. "I will keep my thoughts to myself, but that doesn't make them any less prevalent."

We walked in silence the rest of the way to my building. Xander was clearly irritated, huffing every now and then and clenching his jaw. In all honesty, the sight made me a little happy.

If I was miserable, then at least he was as well.

I pulled open the front door, not bothering to hold it open for Xander, and walked across the small entryway to the steep and skinny staircase. It was old and rickety, but in a way that promised character, not danger. After two flights up, we were finally standing outside the wooden door to my apartment. I realized that I didn't have my key, so I tried the handle and found the door to be unlocked.

What the fuck, Archi?

It irritated me beyond all hell because Archi knew how important it was to me that our door remained locked at all times. Even though it currently worked in my favor, it still bothered me that he and all of our belongings were left vulnerable. All of that melted to the background, though, as I opened the door and stepped through the threshold.

"Willow? Is that you?" My heart thumped in my chest at the sound of Archi's voice bouncing off of the walls. It felt like home and warmth and everything good.

Xander ducked under the door frame as he entered. I closed and locked the door behind us and, after taking off my shoes, walked around the curve of the foyer and into the kitchen.

"Yeah, Archi, I'm home."

Archibald has been the closest thing to family I've had since my parents died when I was twelve. My orphan status and his outcast identity instantly bonded us through our shared self-pity and loneliness, and we haven't let go of each other since.

I caught a quick glimpse of his cropped red hair and freckled cheeks before he bound into me and squeezed me tightly in his arms.

"What is wrong with you? You've been gone for three days

without a word. I was about to start sweeping the woods for your body." He pulled back to scan my face and body for injury.

I swatted away his hands and stepped to the icebox to grab a fruit bar.

"I'm fine, you drama fiend. And have you been on those damn shrooms again? I've only been gone for like nine hours."

His delicate features were set in concern now as he regarded me from behind a raised chin. "No, you haven't. You've been gone for like eighty hours." The blue of his eyes was barely visible now as he squinted at me. "Have *you* been eating my mushrooms?"

I rolled my eyes and began devouring the strawberry frozen fruit bar. The instant the tangy taste hit my tongue, my saliva glands spasmed, and I had to swallow a moan.

"Right. That's probably something I should have explained," Xander drawled as he sauntered into our apartment.

Archi's head whipped around, and he took a small step closer to me as he regarded the unearthly man from head to toe. Xander's eyes were sweeping around the small room with interest.

It was a quaint and cozy space, one that emphasized how huge he really was. The ceilings were low and only cleared his head by about a foot, if that.

I chose the neutral beige color for the walls so they wouldn't offset the various colorful paintings we'd hung. They were mostly Archi's creations, but a few were from random artists we'd come across during our time at the market.

The couch, crafted from tattered black leather and worn from years of use, still remained one of my favorite places to be in the entire city. Sitting in the middle of the room, it faced the small cobblestone fireplace and was only a pace or two away from the dining table. Most of the items in our home were secondhand, found at the market, and I loved them all the more for the nicks in the wood and the small tears in the fabric.

Looking at the space filled my chest with the warmth of being home, and I couldn't bear it for too long, knowing I had to leave again.

Xander seemed to be satisfied with his examination because he returned his gaze to mine and finished his earlier statement. "Time moves a little differently between our two regions. It goes much faster here."

Archi's eyes flicked between us rapidly. "Willow. Do be a dear and explain who this mammoth dredging mud into our apartment is. And what is he talking about?" He looked directly at Xander. "What region are *you* from?"

Xander looked down to see that he had, in fact, left boot prints of mud on the wood floor. To his credit, he took a small step back toward the foyer before opening his mouth.

"Well, that's a complicated–"

I cut him off before he could get out whatever condescending thing he had been about to say. "Trust me, Archi. He's not even worth the breath needed to explain. Besides, I don't have time to right now. I only came back to grab a few things, but I'll be back soon, and I promise to tell you everything then."

As per usual, Xander looked amused by this. Archi, on the other hand, looked like he was about to object, but I didn't give him the chance.

I moved to my bedroom and grabbed a duffle bag, shoving clothing items in it at random. It didn't take long to pack all of my toiletries, but when I looked in the mirror, I groaned at the tangled mess my hair had become. I ran a brush through it and put that in my bag as well.

Before I went back out, I made sure my folding knife was still in the pocket of my jacket as I slid it over my shoulders. Not that I thought it would be all that effective against the supernatural giant acting as my watchman, but it couldn't hurt to be safe.

In case I didn't have time to go back to Clarif's, I went to the kitchen and grabbed some hearty food. I brought some dried fruit and meat, almonds, and apples. As I was packing them up, I noticed Xander staring intently at the only image of my parents I had left. I stormed over to him and ripped the frame out of his grasp before stashing it in my bag, safely tucked between a sweater and leggings.

Meanwhile, Archi was standing a healthy distance away from Xander, observing his movements with his arms crossed and disdain written clearly across his face.

Xander, noticing this, narrowed his eyes and coolly asked, "Did you need something?"

"You are, like, genuinely enormous. And pretty strange looking, no offense. I mean, don't get me wrong—you've got that whole *'I am a broody giant'* thing going for you for sure."

A surprised laugh bubbled out of me at Archi's haughty impersonation of Xander, and the latter's head shot around to glare at me.

Archi began slowly circling him, and I stifled another laugh at how uncomfortable Xander looked. He finished the lap and came to a stop in front of Xander, cocking his head to the side.

"I've never seen anyone resembling you in the slightest." Archi's tone had changed from skeptical to intrigued. I recognized the somewhat vacant expression on his face and the softening of his voice as indicators that he was envisioning his next painting.

"Archi, no," I interjected before he got too far into the vision and went into full-on hyperfocus mode. "Trust me; you don't want to paint him."

"Ah, on the contrary, Willow. I do very much."

"In any case," Xander interjected, taking a step backward and putting his hands in his pockets. "If you've gotten everything you need, we must be going now."

After shoving my journal into the bag and zipping it, I walked over to Archi and hugged him tightly.

"I'll be back as soon as I can, I promise." Lowering my voice to a whisper, I added, "Do not let anyone into the apartment that you don't know well. Things are really fucked right now, and I'm not sure who we can trust, but I'll do my best to find out."

I kissed him on the cheek and made to pull away, but he gripped my shoulders and spoke softly. "I have no idea what's going on...but I'll be careful. Be safe and hurry home, Willow. I love you."

"You too, Arch. I love you."

Xander clearing his throat behind us made me roll my eyes and head for the door. I put my shoes back on and reached for the doorknob, but Xander grabbed my elbow to stop me. I jumped at the small electric shock I felt when he touched me, presumably from my socks on the rug, but it was quickly forgotten the second he spoke.

"There is still one more thing to take care of."

Apprehension instantly filled my gut. "What the hell do you mean by that?"

Instead of answering me, he simply turned toward Archi. Not willing to risk anything, I moved as fast as I could, jumping in between them and drawing the knife from my pocket. In a blink, I had it pressed against Xander's throat with my thumb braced on the dull side, ready to apply pressure.

So much for keeping the element of surprise.

"You even think of touching him, Xander, and I will cleave your head right off of your fucking body."

Behind me, I heard Archi say, "Woah...*kinda* feel like I missed something here."

Xander had the nerve to look amused. The right side of his lips curled up as he looked down at the four inch knife pressed to his jugular.

"Seems a bit small for cleaving, no?"

"Why don't you try me and we can find out?"

This elicited a small chuckle from Xander, boiling my blood and making me press the knife in slightly, just enough to draw a drop of blood.

"Stay. Away. From. Him."

"As much as I'm enjoying this..." His eyes flicked down to my hand and lingered for a second before returning to my face, the green in them flaring intently. "You're going to want to get out of my way."

When I didn't move, he dipped his head–seemingly unconcerned about the knife–and said, "Violet, I'm not going to hurt him."

I leaned closer as well, not backing down for one second. "Yeah, well, if you think I'm going to give you the opportunity to, you're delusional. Turn around and leave."

He let out a closed-mouth sigh, making his nostrils flare, and stared at me for a few seconds, his eyes tracking the features on my face. When he spoke, it was soft and steady in a way that had my pulse jumping inside my throat.

"Last chance, Angel. Step aside, put your precious little blade away, and we can move past this with no issues or dramatics."

There would be no convincing him to leave Archi be, so I had no choice.

The second the thought cemented in my mind–before my muscles had even received the signal to slash the knife–my hand spasmed. I heard the clank of the metal hitting the ground, but it was a background sensation.

All I could feel was pressure, like the air around me was pressing in on my entire body and keeping it in place. It wasn't necessarily painful–nothing like what Lilliana had done to me in her office–but it was the most constrained I had ever felt in my life, and panic began to take force in my mind.

Images of my hand tugging, tugging, *tugging* on the window latch sprang forth. The sound of the hinges creaking but not giving way to my efforts. Finally giving up and sprinting back to the door on the floor, hoping that something had changed since my last attempt to open it. Pulling at the handle, hitting the door, kicking it, throwing my entire weight against it—nothing would work. The exits had been sealed.

Trapped. Trapped. Trapped.

I snapped back to the present to see Xander walking toward Archi with his hands flexed in front of him as if he were taming a wild animal. I could tell by the way his head was moving that he was speaking, but I couldn't hear anything at all.

NO, I tried to scream, but nothing came out besides a pathetic little gust of air.

Archi faced me, but his eyes were locked onto Xander's, holding an expression I had never seen before. They were wide with admiration, practically shining with the need to placate and satisfy. Utter devotion was flowing out of his entire presence, and it made my scream roar inside my head. There had to be a way I could break this spell. I couldn't let him brainwash Archi.

I tried to thrash, to kick and scream, but nothing was happening. My body felt as though it were bound by cement.

I flinched internally when Xander brought his fingertips up to Archi's temples, causing his eyes to slip closed.

No! Let him go, you maniacal piece of shit!

Suddenly, an opaque black mist seeped out of Xander's fingers, wrapping around Archi's head in a sort of halo. The sight of that is what finally unleashed me.

There was no way in hell I would sit and watch while this lunatic took over the mind of the only family I had. Not Archi.

I tried to scream again, tried to thrash, but the mystical force was holding strong. The last words my mother ever spoke to me came rushing back at that moment, and I thought for a second that this might have been the exact reason she had voiced them.

'The world will try to make you believe that the depth of your emotions is a weakness. Do not listen to them, Violet. Your intensity will be your saving grace. Use it, always.'

I did something then that I had never done before–I intentionally called forth the memories of that night.

The night of her and my father's murder.

The sweet sound of my violin rang through the air as my father swung my mother in a twirl, their dance carrying them all around the living room. We'd pushed all the furniture to the walls to allow for a makeshift dance floor. I was sitting on the couch, my wrist aching with the effort to continue playing after so many songs.

Right when I was bringing the bow down on the strings to begin playing my favorite ballad, the loudest, most destructive sound I had ever heard exploded into the air. I remember intense heat and a bright white light that seemed to be coming from everywhere and nowhere all at once. It was that light I saw when my body went flying. The terrible noise of my violin shattering against the wall filled my ears as I was slammed into a wall, and a scream escaped my throat.

"Violet! Violet, where are you, my baby?" my dad bellowed, but I couldn't see him through the white crowding my vision.

I heard the sound of many footsteps approaching at a rapid pace, men and women alike shouting.

"Where's the girl?" one shouted.

"You have nowhere to go. Just give her to us now, and no one gets hurt," said another.

"Don't you fucking touch her, you weasely little bitch!" I heard my mom scream, her voice closer to me than the others.

The pain of that night erupted in my chest tenfold, the memories just as vivid as they were the day it happened. That was the day I was left alone in the world, the two most important people to me–dead.

I called on that pain, used every scrap of my will to pull it to the surface until I *became* it. It was a tangible force, the kind that was capable of taking out anything and anyone in its path.

A scream poured out of me, beginning in the pit of my stomach and gaining momentum as it crawled up and out of my body and forced itself upon the world. Xander whipped around to face me, the surprise written all over his face, causing his fingers to drop from Archi's head. His jaw was slack, his eyebrows raised, and his body perched like it was ready for a fight.

I looked behind him toward Archi, my neck and head finally moving as I broke out of the spell. His eyes were still closed, but he remained standing completely still, almost resembling a statue.

The voice that came out of me was gravelly and unrecogniz-able. "What the fuck did you do to him?"

Xander was still staring at me in shock, which made me think that I could take advantage of his distraction. When I went to take a step toward Archi, though, the apartment around me began to swim and swirl, blackness creeping in around the edges of my vision. I had the sensation of air filling my head to the brim, and I swayed on my feet, realizing that I was about to pass out.

Xander was there in a second, his arms wrapping around my waist just as my knees gave out. My muscles felt entirely slack, his firm body created a wall that I melted against. I felt my eyes roll to the back of my head, but before the darkness took over completely, I heard Xander speak with a quiet voice that was somewhat awe-struck.

"Just what kind of marvelous little human are you?"

CHAPTER SIX

VIOLET

Through the haze of an early-morning fog, I looked out on the meadow and saw two young girls chasing each other, laughing while their parents watched from a sitting position on a blanket nearby. I had no idea who they were or how I even got there, but I had an overwhelming pit of dread pooling in my stomach.

Whatever reason brought me here, I knew it wasn't good.

Out of nowhere, I was moving forward so quickly that everything blurred around the edges of my vision, and–

I woke in a rush, my hands braced against the bed at my sides as I gasped for breath. It felt like the air was too thin–too little– inside my lungs. The feeling only got worse when I looked around and found myself in a completely foreign room.

The walls displayed a rich shade of green, and the single window had matching drapes. I didn't know if it was the disorientation from the dream or if the room really was that small, but the wall seemed impossibly close to the bed.

I had to close my mouth as nausea swirled in my gut. Just like all of my other dreams, it was incredibly vivid and made me feel as though I was actually there; no matter how far-fetched it was.

"Bad dream?"

I shrieked–actually shrieked–at the shock of Xander's voice, and whipped my head to the right to see him lounging on a chaise, his hair dented slightly on the side as if he had been sleeping.

"What time is it?" I asked, my voice raspy from how dry my throat was.

"Probably about four AM," he replied, sitting up slightly and readjusting by pushing his body up with his knuckles. "We got here at about half-past-six last night, but you've been asleep since you fainted. It was quite a hindrance getting your body in here, by the way. I had to put a Soothe on the clerk, which was not easy to do while I was carrying you." Xander gave me a drab look.

My heart began to race as everything that had happened rushed back all at once. The way Archi looked frozen and in a trance.

"What did you do to him?" The voice that came out of me was level and held an idle threat. Xander had the fucking *nerve* to roll his eyes.

"Your friend is perfectly fine. I told you I wasn't going to hurt him, so I didn't."

I swung my legs off the bed and faced him. "If you didn't hurt him, then what was with that black mist?"

"All I did was Soothe him into forgetting about everything to do with this mission. No harm done–except that which you inflicted upon yourself."

That made me angry enough to get me to my feet.

"Inflicted upon *myself?*" I asked, my voice raising with each word.

Xander rested his head back on the chaise with a bemused expression on his face as he looked up at me. "Yes," he stated simply. "Had you just listened to me, I wouldn't have had to glaciate you, and we could be back at the Armory right now, far away from each other and in our separate quarters."

Well, damn. I mean, it's not like I wanted to be near him, but what reason did he have for that comment?

I was perfectly pleasant to be around.

"Oh, please. That shit wasn't necessary. Archi wouldn't have mentioned anything about this to anyone–he is as loyal as they come."

Xander laughed under his breath. "Well, pardon me for not taking any chances."

Irritation aside, I did feel better knowing that he had just altered Archi's memory. If I had it my way, he wouldn't have touched him at all, but that was far better than what I'd been imagining.

But that thing he'd done to me, the way my entire body was frozen and locked...it made sense for them to call it 'glaciating'. I'd never felt so trapped in my entire life.

I scowled at him with the thought, still annoyed that he'd actually blamed me for that. He gave me a pleasant smile and a slight tilt of his head that was a little unnerving now that I'd gotten a glimpse at the kind of power he possessed.

I crossed my arms and looked around the tiny hotel room. It wasn't as small as I'd thought upon waking up, but there was little room to move around the bed and the chaise.

"Where even are we right now? Still in the city?" I asked.

"Just on the outskirts, near Perlington Street. I wanted to be as close to Mr. Berger's apartment as possible so that we can get this over with tomorrow morning."

Wait a damn minute.

"Did you go through my fucking bag?" My tone took on a chill as the realization of Xander's invasion of privacy set in.

I began to do a mental checklist of what he could've seen in there, but he cut off my train of thought.

"Don't flatter yourself, Angel. I wasn't looking for anything more than an address. Although..." His lips curled up on the right side. "There *was* a little lacey number in there that caught my eye."

I threw my hands up. "You're intolerable."

Xander shrugged and put his hands behind his head, closing his eyes. "You can't fault a man for what he unintentionally finds. Now be quiet. I need some more sleep before we leave."

I bristled but moved to the adjoining bathing room after grabbing my bag, knowing I wouldn't be able to fall back asleep.

It was a bit dingy, but had a functional shower, so it was fine by me.

Something about taking a shower always allowed me to reset. Like the warm water beating down on my scalp forced the incessant nature of my thought process to pause, and I can just be.

I reached in and turned the knob, jerking back before the stream of water hit my sleeve. After stripping off my clothes, I put them on the counter and grabbed my toiletries.

Within moments of stepping directly into the warm water, I felt much more grounded.

For a few seconds, at least.

What in the hell was I going to do if Mr. Berger didn't have the Chalice anymore? I could see no reason that he wouldn't, but something about this whole situation was really strange. The more I thought about it, the more my memories from that day resurfaced, and it all felt...off.

There was usually a reason for every purchase he made. Either it was something his granddaughter would like, or it was an item he'd been missing in his kitchen. But the day he bought the Chalice, he was unusually curt and brisk with me. I'd chalked it up to him having a bad day, but what if it was more than that?

Was he actually an Astrale? Or was he working for whoever Lilliana was trying to keep the Chalice away from?

I slathered my legs in cream and picked up my razor, beginning to shave.

I couldn't find it in myself to truly doubt Mr. Berger. I mean, maybe I didn't even know his first name, but I still felt like we'd bonded a lot over the past months. He always seemed genuinely interested in my success and well-being, and had become a constant presence in my life.

I needed him to be home, and I needed him to have the Chalice. I couldn't fathom the idea of being away from Archi for an undetermined amount of time.

What did he even think I was doing if Xander had erased our entire visit from his mind?

My movements sped up in turn with my thoughts, and the razor caught on my ankle, nicking the skin and causing blood to swell immediately.

"Son of a bitch." I sighed in irritation and went to bring my foot into the spray of water, but ended up knocking over the shampoo bottle in the process. Sighing, I bent down to pick it up, but jolted when I heard the doorknob jangle as Xander tried to open the door.

"Violet? What's happened?" Xander asked, his voice sounding worried, even through the door.

"Um, *excuse me*? Did you seriously just try to get in here?"

"You're bleeding, and I heard a crash," he said, still sounding off.

I crinkled up my nose, his elevated senses still rattling me.

"I just nicked myself shaving. Go away, you super-smelling freak."

Xander laughed, but the sound was cut off abruptly. There was a slight pause.

"What exactly are you shaving?"

I made an incredulous face at the porcelain shower wall; as if it could join me in my exasperation.

"There is absolutely zero chance I'm answering that, you perv. Now fuck off. I'm showering."

His laugh echoed off the walls and slowly faded as he moved away from the door.

I thought he was supposed to be sleeping. Why would he have even cared that I was bleeding anyway? It couldn't be that he was worried about me; I knew that much. It was probably just the fact that he didn't want anything getting in the way of our plans tomorrow.

Finishing up, I took a deep breath and turned the water off.

Resting my forehead against the wall, I felt my thoughts speed back up and my anxiety settle back into my chest.

I didn't know what the hell was coming. All I knew was that I was going to do whatever I could to get this over with quickly.

And that the only person here I could trust was me.

CHAPTER SEVEN

VIOLET

About three hours later, I looked up at the rundown terracotta apartment complex and confirmed one last time that we were at the right address. I pulled open the front door and walked in, Xander fresh on my heels.

We hadn't spoken much since he got up. After I showered and dressed, I found him deeply asleep on the chaise, so I decided to go down to the lobby. I sat at the table closest to the fireplace with my journal and began to write down the events of the past day, which quickly transitioned from an entry to a lengthy list of questions.

After contemplating them for a while, I mapped out a few ways I could casually slide them into conversations with Xander in the event that this mission wasn't over today.

If I was going to be involved in maintaining the Astrales' safety, the least Xander could do was answer a few fucking questions.

Rounding the corner of a hallway and continuing on, I found the apartment marked *1H* and stepped up to the door. Feeling uneasy, I halfway turned and looked back at Xander. He was staring right back at me with an expectant look on his face.

"Well?" he asked. "What are you waiting for?"

"You need to promise me that you aren't going to hurt him."

Xander sighed and looked up at the ceiling, which was only a foot higher than his head. "Why is it that you think I am always out to hurt people? Do I give off a threatening aura?"

"Um." I gave him a doubtful look. "Sorta, yeah."

His face split into a feral grin, and he leaned into my space. "Good. Keep trusting that instinct, little human."

Xander booped a finger on my nose, making me lean back and scrunch my face up.

Fucking weirdo.

He leaned over my shoulder and raised his own fist, seemingly done waiting for me to do it. But on the first knock, I heard the hinge creak as the door pushed open on its own. I turned my head and felt all of the air rush out of my lungs as I took in the scene in front of me.

Complete destruction ravaged the entire apartment. The couch lay flipped upside down, its cushions strewn across the floor, each one torn open with slash marks. Among the feathers was what seemed to be an impossible amount of shattered pottery, the shards of countless pieces littering the ground everywhere I looked.

I made a small sound of hurt at seeing my art displayed in such a way, but it was quickly brushed aside by the growing sense of dread for Mr. Berger's safety. I went to step forward, but Xander's arm shot out and stopped me in my tracks.

He stepped around me and crossed the threshold slowly, keeping an arm back to signal me to stay put. His boots made loud crunching sounds on the glass as he moved through the living room. When he looked to the right, toward a room I couldn't see, his hand dropped to his side and closed around the handle of a short sword holstered in his belt.

What the fuck?

Where had that come from? I definitely would have noticed earlier if he was walking around with an eighteen-inch blade.

Xander's expression was pained as he turned to look at me, and I couldn't handle the suspense anymore. I walked toward him and felt my stomach bottom out as I looked at the kitchen.

"No," I breathed.

The same destructive pattern had affected everything within

the room, mirroring the devastation seen in the living room, but that wasn't what had my knees wobbling. It was the words written in rough letters across the open wall.

Bring us what we seek or he dies.

Silent sobs began to wrack my chest as I read the words over and over again. This couldn't be happening. Mr. Berger was hurt, and his entire house was ransacked, all because he was trying to support my business. The feeling of guilt only intensified as I took a few steps closer to the wall and saw what the table had been blocking from my line of sight.

Beneath the writing, the ground was completely engulfed by a pool of blood, spanning a diameter of at least five feet. I brought a hand to my mouth to hold in the bile that rose in my throat as I looked up at the letters again, realizing they were written in blood.

"Violet," Xander uttered, his voice the gentlest tone I'd ever heard him use.

I looked back at him, seeing his figure blurred slightly by the tears that had filled my eyes.

"What do we do?" I forced out, my voice barely above a whisper.

He ran a hand through his hair and sighed. "I don't know." He took a few steps forward and looked down at the ground before shaking his head. "With that amount of blood...he could very well be dead already. I don't know if there is anything we can do to help him. We must continue on our mission."

"*What?*" I asked, aghast. I couldn't be hearing this right. "You want to abandon him to whatever savages did this because of the amount of blood? What, are you some sort of expert in the amount of blood loss it takes to kill a person?"

"Well," Xander drawled. "I actually kind of am."

That made me pause.

Well, alright then. We'd be circling back to that later.

"I don't give a shit what you think you know. I mean, that

could be pig's blood, for fuck's sake! We don't know that he's dead, and we are not giving up on helping him until we know for certain that he is!"

Xander was looking at me like a puzzle to be solved. *Again.* I was so frustrated and felt so helpless that I wanted to scream until my lungs collapsed. He deepened his gaze on me even more, so I stepped forward and shoved him roughly on the shoulder, which took more force than I expected because of his height.

I narrowed my eyes at him and spat, "Cut it the fuck out and help me look for some sort of clue. We need to know who did this."

That stupid little grin flashed onto his face again momentarily before he seemed to remember the situation we were in. It disappeared just as quickly, and he glanced back at the wall. "I think I already know. I'm going to go in the hallway for a moment and check with Lilliana. You stay here and start looking in case I'm wrong."

My brow furrowed. "What? Lilliana is in the hallway?"

He laughed under his breath. "No, little human, she isn't. We have means of speaking over long distances. It is called Inmind communication."

My brain spun at the concept, unable to imagine what he meant. But as he walked toward the door, I quickly forgot my curiosity. I looked back at the carnage of the living room and felt my shoulders slump.

This is all my fault.

When I heard the door shut, I took one step toward the couch but stopped in my tracks and gasped.

"Uhhh...Xander?" I called out.

About five feet away from me was a tiny, red orb of light floating in the middle of the air. It was slowly expanding into an ovular shape, doubling in size every second, getting bigger and bigger. The red in the center was the deepest in color and pulsing visibly.

"Xander!" I yelled, frozen in place. "There's a fucking portal or something in the air! I repeat, *there is a portal FLOATING IN THE AIR!"*

Xander opened the door in a rush, looking around frantically. I saw his eyes widen in shock as he looked at the orb before they shot back at me.

He spoke calmly and slowly. "Don't move."

"What the hell is it?" I asked.

"I have no idea," he responded, making me tense up.

How wouldn't he know what this was? Clearly, it was a spell of some kind, which was supposed to be his territory.

"What kind of Astrale are you?" I asked. "How do you not know what this is?"

He squinted at me. "Keep running that mouth of yours, Angel, and we'll see where it gets you."

What was that little twist in my gut from his words?

It couldn't possibly be excitement.

Xander took a very measured step forward, but the second his foot crossed the threshold, the orb blinked out of existence. Stunned, I continued staring at the air, waiting for it to reappear, but it didn't.

"Okay now, what the fuck." My head was struggling to keep up with everything that was happening, and for the first time in weeks, I felt the Void creeping its way up my spine.

Not now.

I dug my fingernails into the fleshy part of my palm until I felt the skin give way, using the pain to keep the Void at bay. I couldn't deal with that right now on top of everything else.

"Well, this is odd," Xander remarked matter-of-factly. His nostrils flared as his eyes shot down to my hand. There was no doubt he could smell the blood I drew, but he didn't comment on it.

"*Odd?*" I asked, my voice pitched an octave too high.

Instead of responding, he took a step backward, drawing out the moment his foot passed the doorway. Almost instantaneously, the red pulse was back and had apparently finished growing. It was roughly two feet long, suspended in the air right at the line of my eyesight. The center of it was flashing at a consistent pace, almost as if it was trying to lure me to it.

With knots twisting my stomach, I turned toward Xander to see him leaning against the doorway with his arms crossed, observing the flashing light before me.

He jerked his chin. "Walk towards it, slowly."

"Oh, yeah, that's a great idea!" I blurted out, my voice raising. "Go *toward* the blinking death portal that only shows itself around me. I'll get right on that!"

He rolled his eyes. "It is clearly some sort of message only intended for you." He paused briefly, looking contemplative. "Seems Mr. Berger isn't just a common elderly human after all."

Message or no, I didn't want to just blindly approach this thing. I had absolutely no idea what the parameters of the Astrales' magic were. For all I knew, it would swallow me whole the second I was in its grasp. I reached for any reason I could to avoid going toward it.

"You just told me to stay still." I inwardly cringed at the fact that I'd even said that.

Xander straightened fully, his voice and expression gaining an irritated edge. "Well, now I'm telling you to walk towards it."

I looked at the pulse doubtfully before glancing back at Xander.

He sighed at the ceiling before looking back at me. "Look, if something happens, all I have to do is step into the room, and it will disappear. Just trust me. There's nothing to fear."

I huffed out an annoyed breath but faced the pulse fully, his words having registered with me.

It can't hurt you.

I took a timid step, and the pulsing seemed to intensify, like it was getting what it wanted. This continued with every step I took until it stopped throbbing and stayed a steady, deep red.

When I was only a foot or so away from it, Xander's voice softened. "That's it."

Strangely enough, something in my gut eased at those two words.

"Now just reach your hand out slowly, and we'll see what happens."

I raised my left hand, unsurprised to find it shaking. It was a common occurrence, sometimes brought on by the smallest of things–bright lights, seeing couples dancing, loud crashes. Anything that triggers my mind to that night brings an onslaught of symptoms, both physical and mental.

I intentionally shoved the thoughts away, unable to think about that, on top of everything else happening in my head.

"I'm right here with you." Xander's voice was soft and comforting in a way that surprised me.

Inching forward, I came into contact with the light, gasping at the way it felt against my fingertips. It was what I imagined touching a cloud to be like. The red substance was soft and airy as my hand passed through it. I stayed still for a moment, making sure that nothing bad was about to happen before I continued pushing my way forward. Once my entire hand had disappeared, I felt something solid brush against my fingers, and my pulse spiked in response.

"There is something in here," I called over my shoulder to Xander.

"Go on then," he replied impatiently. "Pull it out."

I did as he demanded, feeling a thick piece of paper with a hard circle in the middle of it. Once it was in my grasp, I pulled my hand out quickly and blinked as the portal vanished from the air. Xander was at my side in less than a second, making me jump. The speed at which he could move was going to take some getting used to.

I glanced up at him, but he was staring at my hands.

I looked down to see a cream-colored envelope with a red wax seal in the shape of an emblem I didn't recognize. Turning it over, I recognized Mr. Berger's handwriting immediately from the customers' slips he'd signed so many times.

With a trembling hand, I popped the envelope open and pulled out the letter.

Violet,

There are many things you need to know, but I don't have much time. I am sorry that you have been brought into all of this; it is the last thing I ever wanted for you.

There is a tile behind the toilet that is a slightly different color than the rest. Pry it open, and you will find a key and an address. This will lead you where you need to go.

Be safe.

Be safe.

The words stayed printed in my mind in his signature looping scrawl. It was the farewell he left me with every time I saw him.

I staggered out of the apartment, unable to look at the carnage any longer.

Be safe.

What the fuck did any of this mean? Did he know what it was when he bought the Chalice? If he did, why the hell did he think it would be a good idea to keep it in this dingy apartment?

Who had taken him? What was his involvement in this?

The note told me one thing for certain—Mr. Berger was still alive.

And I was going to find him.

CHAPTER EIGHT

VIOLET ~ AGE TEN

My giggles bubbled out of my chest as I ran through the field, my puppy Arley following close behind. I loved when he chased me through the corn stalks. It felt like we were the only two people in the world when we were whipping through the maze.

"You're not gonna get me!" I yelled back at him.

He barked in response.

I took a sharp right, heading back toward the house. I was getting tired. We had been running for a while, and I wanted a snack.

What's that smell?

I stopped running and sniffed the air.

I turned around and screamed when I saw what was behind me. There was a wall of fire coming at me through the stalks. It looked like a strange kind of fire, but I didn't think about it for too long. I needed to run, or it was going to burn me.

"Arley! Come on!" I yelled at him, making sure he was following as I began to sprint.

We raced forward, the fire getting closer and closer, until we finally made it out of the field and ran into the yard. I turned back around and saw flames everywhere.

All of the corn was going to burn!

I tied Arley up to the tree quickly and ran back to the edge of the cornfield, remembering how Poppa always stomped on the bonfire to make it go away. I tried to do it to the corn, but the fire bit my ankles. I kept trying, but it wouldn't work.

"Violet!" Momma screamed as she sprinted toward me. "Get back from there!"

I leaped away from the fire and hugged myself, my cheeks wet with tears. Momma came up to me quickly and knelt down, her eyes darting all over my body.

"Momma, I'm sorry. I'm so sorry. I don't know how it happened! One second, I was running with Arley, and then it was all on fire. I tried to stop it. I tried to stomp on it the way Poppa does, but it wouldn't work. It just kept biting my ankles. I–"

"Darling, *shhh*," she soothed, running her hands down the sides of my head and along my arms, grabbing my hands and clutching them between hers. "It's okay. It doesn't matter."

"Yes, it does! What about the corn? What about the money it would have made us? It's all gone now," I ended as a sob rocked my chest.

"You listen to me, Violet," Momma demanded, her voice turning firm, and she clutched my cheeks and held my gaze to hers. "None of that matters, okay? Not the crop, not the land, and certainly not the money. There are always new seeds to be planted, there is always more money to be made. But there will never be another *you*."

I continued whimpering but tried to listen to what she said.

"Do you understand, baby?" she asked.

I nodded, and she smiled softly, pulling me into a tight hug.

"Now then, let's head upstairs and get you in the bath. You are absolutely filthy!"

Momma picked me up and walked over to the tree, untying Arley to bring him inside with us. I sniffled and laid my head on her shoulder as she walked to the house, looking back at the stretch of ashes where our cornfield used to be.

CHAPTER NINE

VIOLET

I sighed. "It's not going to work if you keep manhandling it, you fucking dingus."

Xander drew away from the gate he was just assaulting and passed me the key with a confused expression on his face.

"Dingus? I'm guessing that's not a term of endearment?"

I brushed past him, unable to stop the small smile from playing on my lips. "You could say that."

After Xander dug the tile out of the wall in Mr. Berger's apartment, he came back into the hallway with a key and a piece of paper that had an address written on it. Before we left, though, he wanted to confirm with Lilliana that it was leading us where he had suspected.

Seeing their form of communication in action was a strange experience. I stood there uncomfortably, watching as Xander stared blankly at the wall, wondering what the fuck was going on. About a minute later, he perked up and grabbed my elbow, warning me that we were about to whisk over the mountain.

Then, in a blink, we were standing in front of a black, iron gate that spanned as far as I could see. I had no idea what time it was there when we arrived–I only knew it was night because of the darkness engulfing my surroundings. It was quiet as well... unnervingly so.

I put the key into the slot and gently prodded it to the left a few times. It clicked open immediately, causing me to shoot a smirk at Xander.

He huffed. "That was purely luck."

While reaching over my shoulder to push the gate open, his elbow brushed against me lightly, and I felt that tingling rush of awareness again. Ignoring it, I walked through the gates to find a deserted-looking property with pine trees riddling the land. There wasn't a house or person in sight—just trees upon trees.

I took one more step, and Xander grabbed my elbow and pulled me back harshly. "Must you insist on acting without hesitation?"

"Must *you* insist on manhandling me like a ragdoll?" I asked, yanking my elbow out of his grip.

Xander's eyes flashed. "There could be Manakoars or any night-roaming creatures in these woods waiting to get their hands on a pretty little thing like you."

I stopped in my tracks. First at the fact that he called me pretty, which was admittedly vain. But also...

"That is the second time you have called me little. I don't know if you are just spatially unaware or what, but I am five-foot-ten. Decidedly quite large."

In a blink, he had my back pinned against a nearby tree, his hands on either side of my head, creating a cage. Xander leaned down slowly so we were eye-to-eye, emphasizing our size difference. I swallowed thickly at his closeness; just an inch separated my mouth from his full, pink lips.

"Still feel so big and tall now, little Vi?"

His breathy words were a caress that traveled down my neck and sent a shot of heat to my core.

I took a deep breath that went nowhere. We were so close that the movement made my breasts graze his chest, oh so lightly. His pupils dilated with the contact, but he smirked and pulled back, as if he had somehow won. I opened my mouth before I really knew what I was going to say, but something behind his shoulder grabbed my attention.

Deeper into the woods, about two hundred feet away, there

was a pinpoint, white light shining brightly. It was unwavering, hanging midair between two trees and beckoning me to it.

"What is that?" I asked him, our weird interaction entirely forgotten.

He turned around and followed my gaze, squinting his eyes even though his vision had a longer range and sharpness than my own. "A tree? You humans do have trees, don't you?"

I scowled at him. "I meant that light over there, dickhead."

I pointed to it, and he looked again before turning back to me with his brows raised. "I'm beginning to think that this is a deflection method. Did I shake you that much?"

Wow.

I rolled my eyes and brushed past him, walking toward it, and he surprisingly didn't try to stop me. He just followed close behind as I did my best to tread quietly between the trees.

I kept getting that shivering sensation down my spine, feeling like somebody was watching us. Xander, apparently sensing something too, circled his hand around my wrist and slowed his steps. I stopped and looked at him as he scanned the woods around us, those green eyes of his flaring intently.

"Something's not right here, Violet. Let's go."

"I'm not leaving until I see what that light is. Every second we waste is another minute that Archi is alone, paying my share of the rent, and Mr. Berger is somewhere having fuck-knows-what done to him."

Instead of waiting for his protest, I wrenched my wrist from his grasp and moved forward. He swore under his breath behind me, but it was only fifty feet away now, and glowed more intensely with every step I took toward it. As I came right up to it, I slowed my approach to make sure this wasn't some sort of trap.

Contrary to whatever he might think, I did actually have some common sense.

The arrangement of the trees surrounding the hovering light created an eerily perfect semicircle, and I scanned the ground for any tripwires. Not finding anything, I looked at the gaps in the forest and came up blank again.

As I began to step forward, a strong hand on my arm brought me to a sudden stop.

"I don't like this," Xander admitted with his head lowered so that he was looking into my eyes.

I flashed back to what it felt like to have that face within inches of my own and immediately cursed myself for the thought.

"Is the big, bad Astrale *scared*?" I asked, my voice full of mock surprise.

He clenched his jaw, the muscles and tendons there doing wonderfully fascinating things, and his eyes glittered as he let go of my arm and clicked his chin forward in a 'go on' type of gesture.

I timidly stepped forward until I was directly in front of the light. Reaching my hand out, I touched it, and for a second, I thought that nothing would happen. But then the light expanded and exploded, casting my entire line of vision into a blinding white light so bright I could still see it after I closed my eyes.

There was a soft *thud,* and I opened my eyes to see a small, silver box had fallen to the ground.

I bent down to pick it up, and when I turned it over, I saw that it was entirely smooth and sealed around the edges.

What the hell was I supposed to do with this?

Suddenly, a strange, screeching growl came from the woods to our right.

Xander exclaimed, "Shit. Violet, get behind me. *Now.*"

I had never heard his voice this serious and commanding before, and it shook me into submission. I scrambled to stand behind him, making sure the cube was zipped safely in my pocket.

"Alright, you little pest. Come out and play then, if you're so eager." As he spoke, Xander was doing something with his hands that I couldn't quite see from my position. It almost resembled the motion of making a snowball but was more compact.

He let out a low, sinister laugh. "I'll bet you're hiding some-where, thinking of how you could still win out in this scenario."

The arrogant lilt was back in his voice now, and strangely enough, it calmed me that he was teasing whatever monster was lurking in the trees. As he continued moving forward, he was still twisting his hands and a soft green glow began emanating from them.

After a few more turns, he stopped the movement and drawled, "I know that you Manakoars are typically only interested in ravishing females, but you have to admit, it's not every day you encounter all this." Xander gestured to his large body with his hand, ending with a circle around his face.

The green light seemed to be seeping out of every pore of his hands, creating a brilliant light, and his face was truly majestic in its wake. The color matched his eyes perfectly, and it only seemed to make his hair blacker, as if it was absorbing all of the light around it.

We both stayed quiet and strained our ears to listen, but about thirty seconds went by without a single sound. With a sigh, Xander turned back to me.

"I don't know about you, but I'm feeling a bit impatient. Do you care to speed this along?"

Not knowing what that meant, I said, "Uh, sure?"

He prowled to me and took my right hand in his much larger one, palm up. My skin was entirely cast in his green glow, all the way up to my elbow. Xander's light shining on my birthmarks made them appear much darker, almost black in color.

At the touch of our skin, I felt that damn tingle shoot up my fingers and through my arm more intensely than it ever had before. My gaze shot to his, and I was about to ask if he felt it too when I noticed him staring down at the small knife in his hand.

Where the fuck did he get that from?

"It doesn't need to be deep. It just needs to draw blood." His voice was soft and comforting, and something deep in my gut told me to trust him.

Apprehensively, I nodded, unsure where this was going.

There was the strangest expression on Xander's face as he brought the knife down to my palm, and I couldn't drag my eyes away from it. He almost looked...revered by it? His charcoal lashes swept downward, and his round lips were slightly parted as he took a breath.

My breath caught as the blade nicked my palm, a brief stinging sensation. The pain was swiftly swept away as the growling noise returned, much much closer this time. It was raw and guttural and so disturbing, I knew I would be hearing it again in my nightmares.

Through my pounding heartbeat, I heard Xander scoff.

"So predictable," he said. "Once you have them marked, you can't resist their scent, even when you're clearly walking into a trap."

The growl morphed into an ear-piercing shriek as the Manakoar tore through the treeline behind Xander and came charging at us.

No, charging wasn't the right word.

It was *slithering*.

The beast itself was contradictory to the deep noises that were coming out of it a second ago. Its body was tall and spindly, and it would have been somewhat humanoid if not for the countless limbs protruding from all over its body. The skin, if you could call it that, appeared thick and dry, the cracked texture making me want to vomit on the spot. Its body ended in a single, thin appendage that was moving like a snake, propelling it toward us at a rapid speed.

I inched backward, circling the ring on my pointer finger to confirm it was there. Not that it would do anything against this thing, but it reassured me nonetheless.

"Don't move an inch until it is dead," Xander warned me in a low voice. "You will never outrun this creature, and your movements will only make it faster."

I couldn't find my voice, so I signified my agreement by remaining still.

The beast was close to us now, and I wanted to scream at Xander to do something. Why the hell was he egging it on just to stand like a statue when it attacked?

"Time to die, bastard." He said it in a cheerful, sing-songy voice that sent chills over my entire body.

Xander raised his hands in a collective fist, the green energy inside of them screaming to be let out. As soon as he opened them–in the direction of the Manakoar–it opened its mouth and let out a sort of screeching howl.

I hardly even noticed the electric stream of green power shooting across the clearing. All I could see were the rows of the Manakoar's teeth staring me in the face. They were jagged and lined the entirety of its mouth, giving me a visual I would never be free of.

My voice found me then, jumping out of my throat in an involuntary scream that rattled me so deeply, I turned on my heels and ran instinctively.

I barely made it five feet before my arm was in a scaly vice grip, and my ears were ringing with the sound of the Manakoar's howl directly in front of my face. I kept my eyes screwed closed, knowing that the sight of its mouth that close would scar me beyond repair.

The noise was cut off in a second, though, flipping into a wounded sound before disappearing completely.

When I opened my eyes, I saw the thing on the ground.

In *pieces*.

The body that was once whole now lay scattered on the ground between me and a seething, infuriated Xander.

He stood with his legs shoulder-width apart, his regularly-colored hands in fists at his side. Xander's undivided, homicidal focus was directed at me, his chest rising and falling rapidly with each heavy breath.

"I thought I told you," he growled, emphasizing every word. "To stay. The fuck. *Still.*"

I took a tiny step back, letting out a small noise when Xander stepped over the Manakoar's head to eliminate the space I had made.

"Run," he let out in a loud whisper, his green eyes flashing with predatory intent. "I dare you."

I turned on my heel and moved as fast as I possibly could, slamming my feet into the ground like it was my lifeline.

What the fuck?

Pieces. That thing was in *pieces.*

How in the hell did he even manage to do that?

I hooked right after a tree, doing my best to avoid a straight and predictable path. A branch snapped across my face as I passed it, but I hardly even recognized the sting.

All this time, Xander was capable of *that*? I'd slept next to a being that was capable of tearing apart a monster in a matter of seconds.

My feet moved even faster at the thought, and I heard Xander's laugh echo through the woods in response. I turned again, feeling frantic but knowing I had no true endgame here. I was in an entirely foreign land, in the middle of nowhere. I had nowhere to run.

Suddenly, a large hand clamped over my mouth as I was jerked roughly back into a hard body. I screamed against it, but it was no use; his hand easily spanned the sides of my jaw, which he was gripping roughly.

"You know what?" Xander let out a slow, relieved breath. "Thank you for that. It was very needed. But you're not off the hook yet."

And with that, the familiar flash of color enveloped me before we were back in the same room inside the Armory.

Xander released me with a shove, so that I fell back onto the bed. I bounced on my side and sat back up with a scowl that made him step forward. His eyes twitched slightly around the corners as he glared down at me, and I felt something leave my body on an exhale.

I opened my mouth to speak, but nothing would come out. My brow creased with the effort to make my tongue move, but no matter how hard I tried, nothing would come out of my mouth. It felt like a nightmare where the connection between my tongue and brain was severed, but it was much worse because I was distinctly and undoubtedly awake.

Xander let out a long breath between his teeth and leaned down so we were face-to-face, grabbing my jaw roughly.

His eyes flashed with irritation. "That is three times now that you have blatantly disobeyed my command—and it *will not* happen again. I won't allow you to put yourself in danger just because you think you know what is best in every situation."

As if the words frustrated him even further, his grip on my face tightened, and his eyes scanned my face, looking for something.

"That thing nearly killed you, and it won't be the last time an encounter like that happens. You are navigating a world you know very little about, so you will listen to me from here on out; unless you are in favor of me keeping this leash on your wicked little tongue. Because I will."

He released my chin and his hold on my voice in the same instant, standing to his full height and glaring down at me. His eyes rested on my right hand for a few seconds before they slid back to mine.

"Don't test me," he warned, giving me a final once-over before turning around and stalking out of the room.

CHAPTER TEN

XANDER

For as long as I can remember, violence has been the single, stagnant presence in my life.

In the beginning, it was the sort of companion that chased after me incessantly, even when I may not have favoured it.

It was relentless–coming back to cling to me day after day.

Violence became such a frequent visitor that I began to overlook its downsides at times, and actually enjoy its company.

Until one day, it stopped altogether. It never visited me again.

After so many years of its continuous presence in my life, it was as if I couldn't function properly without it. So I learned to seek *it* out.

And that, as it turned out, fit very nicely into my lifestyle.

"What the bloody hell is wrong with you today?" Roslyn demanded as she put up an arm, barely blocking the hit I'd just sent her way.

Usually, I would hold back a bit while sparring with her, but I needed to expel the pent-up energy a certain little vixen had given me.

I ignored her, sending another jab to her face, camouflaging the kick that was coming next. She knew my patterns too well, though, and grabbed my foot with her left hand, bringing her right elbow down onto my shin.

I grunted at the contact, cursing myself for not seeing it coming.

"You're being *sloppy*," she hissed out, shoving me with two hands. "You don't do sloppy, so tell me right now—what's happened?"

"Fuck off, Ros. I'm not in the mood."

I came at her with all the speed I could muster, knocking her off her balance and gaining the upper hand. Landing a punch on her face, I took advantage of my advance and pummelled her in the side.

While we continued our little dance, my mind wandered to the human girl who was sleeping just one level down. I felt my rage pulse to the surface at the mere thought of her after that stunt she'd pulled with the Manakour.

The insolent little brat. Who the fuck did she think she was to continue to disregard my advice?

Time and time again, she didn't listen—acted however she pleased—even though it should be obvious that I would know what was best when it came to my world. It made me want to tie her up in a pretty little bow and shove her to the back of my closet, where no one and no thing could ever find her again.

My head kicked back from an uppercut to the jaw by Roslyn, making me bite my tongue. I tasted the coppery tang of blood and laughed, spitting it out on the floor.

"That's all you've got?" I laughed, wanting more.

Hit harder. Kick faster. *Make me forget.*

What was frustrating me the most wasn't actually that Violet disobeyed me. It was the fact that I fucking cared whether she was hurt or not. Because there was no denying that I did.

That fact alone made me want to level a building.

Who was she to elicit emotions and urges out of me that I had yet to encounter in my sixty years of existence?

She was just a human girl. One that had disrespected my people countless times in the span of the past few days we'd spent together, at that. She was crass, careless, and infuriating, not to mention insignificant.

So why the fuck was I ready to kill her over her lack of regard for her own safety?

The only people I ever cared to protect were Lilliana, Gaar, and the spitfire that was pounding her fists into my ribs. They all played a part in my assimilation into society, and therefore, I would kill for them. I *had* killed for them–plenty.

Not that they fully knew that, but it didn't change the facts.

But even then, that only extended to situations that threatened their lives. I truly couldn't care less if someone hurt them in a superficial manner. Healing themselves–or receiving healing, if they were not a Sensinor–was easy enough.

Violet, on the other hand, had done absolutely nothing except for rile me up. So why was I so damn bothered by the look of horror and despair in her eyes when she first walked into Mr. Berger's apartment? Why couldn't I shake the pull inside of me to go to her, lock the door to her room, and fuse the keyhole with my Corefire?

Maybe then she would learn a thing or two about doing whatever the fuck she pleased.

The thought filled me with renewed energy that made me go at Ros faster, blocking her advances and sweeping my foot to knock her on her arse. I brought my elbow down on her tiny neck, applying just enough pressure to cut off her breathing.

She bucked and tried to disrupt my stance, but there was no use with me in that position. It would take a much larger person to counterattack when I had this sort of advantage on them.

I wondered if the little Angel would be able to. She was, after all, not as tiny as Roslyn.

The fuck?

Where had that thought come from? It's not like I would ever have that jagged human under me, anyway.

Roslyn tapped her hand three times on the mat–her signal that she was forfeiting. I smiled smugly before removing my elbow and standing fluidly, letting her get to her own feet.

She massaged her throat and glared at me. "Remind me to never spar with you when you're in one of these moods."

"Hmph."

"You're lucky I'm a Sensinor," Ros said, wincing and poking gingerly at her side. "I think you cracked a fucking rib."

"You'll live," I replied, shrugging.

Ros was a Sesnsinor–an Astrale with healing abilities–and a damn good one at that, so it would only take her a minute or two to heal that injury.

Plus, things like cracked ribs don't tend to phase you when you've experienced the sort of atrocities I have. When you were brought up the way I was.

I felt it then, the little Inmind ping alerting me that Lilliana was attempting contact. Dread hit my gut, not because I didn't want to talk to her but because that likely meant my assignment had awoken.

Duty calls.

I opened the door in my mind to her and immediately responded. *Yes, Lilliana?*

The human girl is awake. She is in my office, demanding that I find someone new to complete this mission with her.

I laughed aloud as Lilliana continued.

I don't know what happened, and frankly, I don't really care. But this girl needs to get it in her mind that she is in no position to be making demands. I've had it with her attitude. Take care of it, or I will.

That made my laughter die down instantly. I knew Lilliana's version of 'taking care of it', and let's just say...it never turned out well.

I'll handle it.

I broke the Inmind connection after sending the message and moved towards the exit of the studio.

"Oh, don't worry, dickhead! I'm totally fine!" Roslyn hollered at me from her position, hunched over on the bench.

I threw a certain finger over my shoulder on my way out the door.

Making my way towards the stairwell, I realised that I could probably do with a shower, but–for a reason I couldn't quite place–I wanted to get Violet out of Lilliana's vicinity immediately. Maybe it had to do with the threat hanging over my head, but it felt more likely that I just wanted to get my hand wrapped around that little wrist again and feel her erratic pulse. To see those long, purple nails curl into her hand when I did.

I enjoyed the spark in her eyes whenever I touched her–partially fear and something else that was hard to pinpoint.

Excitement? Or hatred?

Whatever it was, it made me want to bring it to the surface so that I could stomp all over it and crush it, just to summon it again.

I smiled to myself as I reached Lilliana's floor.

The little Angel truly had no idea just how fucked she was.

But she didn't need to...not yet.

☽

VIOLET

I SAT IN THE RED ARMCHAIR INSIDE MY ROOM AT THE Armory with my arms crossed over my chest, tapping my foot on the ground. Staring out of the window was my way of pretending that I was unaffected by Xander's presence here, but I wasn't sure if I was selling it or not.

He stood across the room, leaning against the small desk with one ankle crossed over the other, staring at me with unnerving focus. He hadn't spoken a word to me yet, which made me wonder what was going through his mind.

Was he still as upset with me as he was last night?

A chill ran down my spine at the memory of his rageful expression that was zeroed in entirely on me. The anger in his eyes was definitely alarming, but what was bothering me more was my reaction to it.

Although my survival instincts had me running for dear life

immediately after the incident, I couldn't get comfortable last night. After he disappeared from my room, I went through the stages.

At first, I was furious. How dare he treat me that way, as if I am required to listen to every little thing he says? Who does he think he is to order me around?

I even walked the halls for about an hour trying to find him and give him a piece of my mind before giving up and returning to my room.

Once the initial shock of what Xander was actually capable of wore off, I started to think about the fact that if I had listened to him and stayed put, that first shot of his magic–or whatever it was called–probably would've taken out the Manakoar right away.

And maybe, just maybe, he was a little bit right about me thinking that I know best in every situation.

So, after realizing that he wasn't *totally* in the wrong, even though his methods were barbaric, my mind shifted back to the other aspects of the night.

Like how he tried to stop me from entering the circle when he felt that something was off. Or when his fingers circled my wrist, holding me close to him.

And yes, even when he looked at me with that lethal rage. His eyes were shining such a vibrant green it almost hurt to look at him. There was so much power behind that single look...it still caused a physical reaction when I thought about it.

But most of all, I couldn't stop remembering the feel of his hand clasped around my jaw, tilting my face up to him to give him a better look. Against my better judgment, my body was singing the entire night to be in that position again. I hardly slept at all– just tossed and turned in an uncomfortable and thoroughly both- ered state.

So what did I do?

The moment I was awake, I quickly showered, got dressed, and found my way to Lilliana to request–politely–that I get a new partner for this escapade. At least, that's how I meant for it to happen, but it came out of my mouth as more of a demand.

I should work on that habit one of these days.

She denied me with a laugh, and a few moments later, Xander was strolling in and clutching my elbow to whisk us back into my bedroom.

He released me as soon as we landed, and I immediately moved across the room, sitting down and turning my chin to avoid looking at him.

As the minutes ticked by, I became more and more stubborn about the fact that I was not going to be the first to break this silence, even if I might've been the one in the wrong.

Just a little.

"Anything on your mind you'd like to say, little Angel?" Xander's voice was soft and menacing, but it carried to my ears as if he had spoken loudly.

My chest fluttered a bit at the nickname, regardless of my attempts to stop it.

God, my head was in the wrong place. No, the wrong *universe.*

Mr. Berger was missing, Archi was alone back home, and I was sitting there getting butterflies over a supernatural man calling me 'Angel'?

Get it together.

Instead of addressing our confrontation, I reached into my pocket and grabbed the little silver cube I'd found in the woods, lobbing it Xander's way.

"This is what the light was leading me to yesterday."

He caught it, and his eyes widened when he saw it, but he looked back to me and narrowed them once more.

"That's all? There's nothing else you'd like to say?" he asked, pushing off the desk and walking toward me.

I lifted my chin and maintained eye contact. "Yes, that's all."

His jaw moved side-to-side momentarily as he ground his teeth together, but that was the only reaction it elicited from him.

After a few more seconds of the intense stare-down, he finally broke it and looked down at the cube, tossing it in the air and catching it. "I know what this is, but we will need a viewing vessel to be able to gain anything from it."

"Okay, well what is it? And what's a 'viewing vessel'?" I asked, annoyed that he was being so vague.

"Wouldn't you like to know." Xander smirked.

What a child.

"How fucking old are you?" I meant it as a rhetorical question, but maybe Astrales didn't have those.

"I have about forty years on you, Angel."

I literally felt my eyes bulge at the fact. This man was over sixty years old?

He chuckled at my shock, the sound secretly warming a part of me that had been cold since the encounter with the Manakoar last night.

"Our kinds age very differently. In the relative positions of our lifespans, you and I are closer in age than we may seem to you."

I struggled to think of a response to that, but evidently, I didn't need one because Xander moved on.

"I'm going to check about retrieving the vessel for this." He held up the cube, giving it a shake. "In the meantime," he started, his eyes gaining a light that made me both nervous and slightly mesmerized.

"You are going to stay in this room..." He reached down, grabbed my right hand, and placed the silver box in it. My blood rushed a bit at the feel of his calluses against my skin. "Not speak to anyone..." His thumb grazed over the fleshy part of my palm once before he closed my fingers into a fist. "And prepare a beautiful and winding apology to deliver to me once I return to release your leash."

"My wha–"

My words were abruptly silenced as Xander seized the small presence within my chest and lifted it out, his sadistic eyes gleaming with delight at my complete helplessness to speak.

You sociopathic fuck! I shouted at him internally, hitting my fists against the arms of the chair in protest.

He tipped his head up and laughed, deep and sound, before turning around and striding to the door with a fucking pep in his step, the psycho.

Did he get off on this? Was that it?

"Enjoy your contemplation, Angel," Xander called out in a sweet tone before he closed my door behind him, the sound of the lock clicking home echoing in the room and leaving me with a deep-rooted feeling of helplessness.

Well...*fuck*.

CHAPTER ELEVEN

XANDER

The bell ringing above the door as I walked through the threshold was a familiar and piercing noise that would never lose its annoyance. I pressed my tongue to the roof of my mouth, willing myself to push past it.

The sound was so similar to that bell from my past life that I had to fight the urge to rip it off the wall and crush it every time I walked through the door.

The dim lighting of the approaching sunset cast the apothecary into a golden hue as I stepped around the clutter of shelves and towards the desk.

Honestly, I'm not even sure why Gaar called it an apothecary when most of his dealings included selling illegal goods and information. I would say that it was his 'cover' but it's not like he needed to worry about repercussions from the authorities.

I *am* the authorities, and I was there all the time.

For this case, though, I'd done everything in my ability to avoid coming to Gaar. Even though I knew it would be extremely difficult to track down Memorium goggles, I didn't want to bring him into this. So I exhausted every other avenue possible, making sure to Soothe any memory of my inquiries. But every person I asked turned me away. One had even laughed in my face.

I made sure he would have a long-lasting headache that he couldn't remember the cause of.

I knew after that visit that I had no choice but to come here.

"Gaar," I sang, knowing the bastard was lurking in here some-where. "Your favourite recluse is here."

"Xan," the deep, gravelly voice made my arm hairs stand on end as he greeted me and walked out from the backroom.

Gaar was dressed in his typical blacked-out ensemble: the shirt, jacket, and trousers all blended into the suit of armour designed to mask what was going on inside his head. He thought it made him seem approachable. If anything, it only emphasised that he was a demon walking this planet.

His long, salt-and-pepper hair was pulled into a low bun today with a few loose strands framing his face, emphasising his perpetually pinched brow and strong nose. The warm lighting of the shop at this hour made his skin glow in a deep hue as he observed me behind a cool expression, and I had to actively remind myself why I was there in the first place.

"I need your help securing a vessel," I explained, settling down into one of the chairs opposite him.

"And what kind of vessel would that be?" Gaar asked with an edge to his voice.

He never liked it when I skirted around the point, preferring for things to be cut and dry and, essentially, over before they even started.

"Memorium goggles," I responded, conscious of my eye contact and keeping a nonchalant tone to my voice.

He let out a low chuckle. "Memorium goggles? Do you have any idea how difficult those are to secure?"

"Why do you think I came to you?" I asked, flashing him a charming smile that I knew he secretly loved.

He confirmed that fact when he scowled, his face consistently showing the exact opposite of his actual reactions.

"You know," Gaar drawled, "sometimes it seems as though you think I am at your beck and call." He rounded the counter, coming to stand in front of my chair and looking down at me. That was when I noticed his irises were entirely black.

Fuck, he needed to feed.

"Is this true, Ponce?" he asked, breaking that train of thought. "Because I haven't received payment from you in a long while."

My entire body flushed with the intent of his words, making my blood rush to the surface and my heart pump faster in response.

"No," I let out in a choked voice. "No, that's not true. I've been busy."

"Busy with missions," he sneered. "As if those are more important than *me*."

"That's not what I meant," I retorted, standing up so I was positioned above him, needing to move before his tone got the best of me. "You will get your payment, but I need to complete this mission first. It is important and time-pressing."

"Hmm," Gaar mused, feigning contemplation and toying with me. "I'm not sure I can take your word on that. I do have an interest rate, you know, and your charges have accumulated very quickly."

I grabbed the lapel of his jacket in my fist. "Don't fuck with me, Gaar. This is important."

His black eyes flashed and slowly–too slowly–moved down to my hand on his jacket before narrowing and moving back up to mine.

Fuck. I knew that look, and it wasn't good.

"What an interesting turn of events," he sneered, gripping my wrist and pressing in on the exact pressure point that made my fingers spasm and release his jacket. He continued to hold it in his grip, making the tips of my fingers tingle as he pressed roughly on the nerve. "Please, do share what has you in a big enough tizzy that you think you have the right to fucking *touch* me."

I swallowed my reaction to that and instead answered his question.

"It is a big responsibility, bigger than any Lilliana has given me before. And considering what she has said, not addressing it in a timely manner could lead to dire repercussions."

I left out the part about Violet and how I needed to get her the fuck out of Cavell before she ingrained herself into me permanently.

If she hadn't already.

I felt like punching myself in the throat when my stomach clenched, and my cock hardened at the memory of that sweet little helpless expression on her face before I left this morning.

How did my feelings towards her change so quickly?

"This isn't about Lilliana," Gaar concluded, piercing through my façade with one look. "Who is she."

A statement, not a question.

Fuck. How did he always see right through me?

"What's that now?" I asked, feigning confusion.

"You know better than to play dumb with me," he snapped in the tone that made my spine straighten reflexively.

"Who is the woman causing that smitten fucking expression?"

"I don't know what you're talking about."

He stared at me for three long seconds, seemingly deciding what he was going to do. My stomach dropped when a devious grin crept its way across his face, the infrequent sight both beautiful and deadly.

Shit. What was he plotting?

"I will see what I can do about securing the vessel," Gaar advised, turning around and walking to the back room. Without a glance, he added, "I'll be in touch," and disappeared from view.

With a muttered curse, I whisked myself back to the Armoury to brief Lilliana on what had happened. Before heading there, though, I needed to deal with a certain little vixen.

I smiled as I dug in the pocket of my pants for the key to Violet's room, looking forward to hearing what she'd decided to say once she had her voice back. I sincerely hoped she had come to her senses and was ready to admit that she was in the wrong.

As I rounded the corner of the hallway, I flipped the key in the air and caught it before putting it into her keyhole. As soon as I applied pressure, the door popped open. I was about to wonder how she got the lock open when a small fist collided with my gut.

Hard.

I bent slightly and grunted, the unexpected attack taking the breath out of me.

"Give her back her voice. *Now.*" Roslyn demanded, her voice firm and eyes shining.

I chuckled down at her and ruffled her brown hair, knowing that would rile her up even more. "Why do you think I was coming in here to begin with? It's not like I would have left her like that forever." My tone was teasing and light, getting too much enjoyment out of Ros's reaction to this.

"This isn't *funny*, Xander," she hissed out in a low whisper. "Look at her," Ros said, glancing over at Violet, who was sitting by the window in the same red chair I'd left her in this morning. I'd thought it was pretty amusing that she was stewing here the entire day without the ability to speak, just like I told her to.

But my smile died, inside and out, when I stepped forward and got a clear view of her face. The expression lying there hit me harder than Roslyn's punch.

Vacancy.

She was looking out the window, hugging her knees to her chest with her cheek resting on them, making her head tilt to the left. There was nothing on her face. None of the usual scepticism, judgement, anger, or passion was to be found, having been replaced by a faraway look that clouded her eyes. The fire wasn't within them as it should be, making even the spot of blue within her brown irises appear flat and hollow.

"Violet?" I prodded in a quiet voice.

She didn't show any sign that she'd heard me, just continued staring.

"Little Angel," I voiced a bit louder, lowering myself to one knee next to the chair.

When I put a light hand on her right forearm, she flinched

visibly and jolted into an upright position. I winced, the sight twisting a knife in my gut before her gaze shot to mine. It was still hollow and disconnected, but at least she was showing signs of life.

Without any other words, I released my hold on her tongue, allowing her voice to flow back into her. I saw the moment she felt it register, her chest caved on an inhale and her eyes closed briefly. When they opened again, they locked on my gaze immediately but still held that vacant look. A few moments passed before she muttered, "I'm sorry."

That was it; her voice gravelly and dead. The sound made panic rush to my throat and guilt weigh on my chest.

She wasn't supposed to react this way. She was either supposed to get on her knees and grovel, or put up more of the fight that drove me insane. She wasn't supposed to space out on me and turn into some sort of hollow, apologetic shell of herself.

Her eyes returned to their original position, directed unseeingly towards the city below us. I got to my feet and walked out the door, ignoring Roslyn's hollers at me as I whisked myself across the city. I was more shaken than I would've liked to admit and needed to get the fuck away from that...*thing* that had taken the place of my Violet.

I paused. When in the fuck had I begun to think of her as mine?

Well, truth be told...I had been since the first time I laid eyes on her and saw that awe-inspiring expression. The feeling only grew with her little outbursts and glares–the shields she wielded to cover up the fact that she was drinking me in with her eyes. I'd seen through them this entire time, but that didn't mean I didn't enjoy them and the way they made my heart hammer inside my chest.

She made me feel things that I'd previously thought to be impossible. And while that frustrated the hell out of me, it also made me feel more alive than ever before.

But that girl sitting by the window? That was *not* her.

Suddenly, talking to Lilliana was the farthest thing from my mind. I wanted to do everything and anything I could to revive my Angel. My vixen.

And I had just the idea.

$$\mathbb{)}$$

VIOLET

Every so often, I enter what I call the Void. A sensation of numbness overcomes me—my thoughts slow, my emotions ebb, and I become a shell of myself.

It started the day my parents were killed. That first time, I was in such a panic-ridden state that I hyperventilated for over twenty minutes. I could feel my heart beating its way up my throat, as if it was trying to escape my body. I didn't know what to do, so I called out for anyone, anything to help me.

Suddenly, like a tidal wave, the Void rushed over me.

Everything came to a standstill. I didn't feel much of anything, so I was finally able to breathe again.

It came and went with the days. I enjoyed the little breaks from grieving and remembering that It gave me, but as time went on, I began to feel a deep sense of dread after It left. What if one day It didn't go away, and I remained in the in-between state for the rest of my life?

The problem was, after so many years of experiencing it, the fear that I would feel after the fact slowly slipped away. I began to *crave* the Void. So much so that I almost became it.

That was, until I met Archi.

Archibald Henry Quiver. He was my absolute saving grace.

But now he was hundreds of miles away. Wait...was it hundreds, actually? Thousands?

It didn't matter. He was nowhere to be found, and after the events of the past few days, the Void was particularly strong.

As I stared unseeingly at the view from Roslyn's balcony, I

clutched my steaming coffee cup to my chest, hardly noticing the way my skin was protesting.

You would think that with all of the fucking magic these people possessed, they would have mugs that didn't conduct so much heat.

I blinked forcefully, trying to get my eyes to see again, but it was no use. There was a thick screen between me and my surroundings, and I wasn't sure if anything could break me out of it.

So I stopped trying.

Right after Xander took away my voice, everything that had happened since he showed up at my stall crashed down on me at once, overwhelming me until I reached out and welcomed the Void with open arms. I knew, without a doubt, it would have happened regardless of what Xander did.

It was all just too much.

The day passed in a hazy blur, and before I knew it, the sun was setting and Xander was there, kneeling next to me with a look of concern etched deeply on his face as his eyes scanned mine. It was almost enough to make me smile because it reminded me so much of Archi in our early days, when the Void would come out of nowhere and my entire demeanor would shift.

How precious, I'd thought.

And then he gave me back my voice, and I remembered one of the last thoughts I had before bottoming out–that I needed to apologize for running in the woods. I endangered us, and didn't want to be the kind of person who was too proud to apologize when they should. So I did my best to convey that in the state I was in, and then he was gone again.

Some time later, Roslyn came into my room with coffee and muffins, making me realize that the sun was up and I hadn't slept. She chatted with me, and I pretended to listen, even though it was a bit beyond me. Just like my eyes, I couldn't get my ears to focus, even if I wanted to. She had to have realized that, but she kept talking regardless, and I appreciated the gesture.

One thing she said grabbed my attention enough for me to engage for a few minutes, though.

"Can you repeat that?" I asked, grimacing at the way my voice came out. It sounded strained from disuse.

"Repeat what?" she responded, seeming shocked that I'd spoken.

"You mentioned something about having a different Core? What does that mean?"

Her brown eyes skirted downward briefly. "Well, I don't think I'm supposed to tell you..." And then she smirked, leaning toward me conspiratorially before she whispered, "Good thing I've never really cared for being told what to do."

Roslyn explained to me that there are five elemental Cores that serve as a source for the Astrales' magic.

"The five Cores are Mistral, Terrala, Hydroseis, Astrolite, and Soothsayer. Each person only has one, meaning their powers lie within one realm of siphoning."

Did that mean their magic drew directly from the elements?

"Mine, for instance," she interjected, "is the Terrala Core, which is rooted in the land and nature's essence."

So, yes to the elements, then. I wondered what her capabilities were, but she didn't share, so I didn't ask. I wasn't sure if that was considered rude, and didn't want to overstep when she was showing me so much kindness.

Roslyn continued, "But we are currently in the Mistral sector–Myrana. I deserted from my home sector many years ago."

"Oh," I murmured, surprised. "What does that mean?"

She looked uncomfortable, fidgeting with her brown curls, and I immediately regretted asking the question.

"I had some issues with my family and needed to get away. Lilliana offered me asylum, and that is how I became an Enforcer. My story is similar to most of the Astrales' living here, actually."

I nodded, trying very hard not to pry, regardless of how badly I wanted to know more. I did, however, want to learn about

Xander, and this felt like the first real opportunity I'd gotten. So I went for it.

"Does Xander have the Terrala Core as well?" I asked as casually as I could.

Her round face remained carefully blank. "Xander doesn't really...fit in a single box."

That was all she said about it before changing the subject, and I took the not-so-subtle hint that it was as far as she'd go. As her voice drifted out again, I tried to put two and two together.

My best guess was that Xander was somehow able to have more than one Core, meaning that he also had access to more than one kind of magic. I wasn't sure whether to feel unnerved or impressed by that fact, probably because of the very little information I was running off of.

Which was getting pretty old.

After we'd both finished eating the muffins and drinking our coffee, Roslyn told me that she had some jobs to do and left me with a stack of books to read. I appreciated that even more than the fruitless conversation and wondered if she could somehow sense that I was a reader, or if she just gave me the most accessible form of entertainment available.

Two days later, I sighed at the view of Myrana. Xander remained absent, sent on another mission by Lilliana. Apparently, since we were stuck waiting on the vessel to arrive, she saw fit to get some more work out of him in the meantime–which confused the hell out of me.

Didn't Lilliana make it seem like she wanted him to drop everything to find this Chalice to begin with? Surely there was some way to get what we needed faster.

Five days. Five full days of this mission, and we still had no result.

I also couldn't stop wondering what could've been so important that she sent him away for this long. Maybe there was some sort of uprising he needed to help with? It made sense why she kept him so close, considering that–if my theory was correct–he seemed to have access to multiple Cores when everyone else was limited to one.

I wondered how often she took advantage of that–how often she forced him to do things he wouldn't otherwise do.

Not that I was worried about his happiness or anything. I was just...curious.

I took a sip of coffee and sighed contentedly as I felt it blaze a path of warmth from my throat all the way down to my stomach.

I've always loved that feeling.

I had no idea what time it was, but judging by the sun's position in the sky, it was sometime in the early evening. I'd already finished the last remaining book from Roslyn's stack a bit ago and saw no real reason to fight the exhaustion battering my eyelids, so I grabbed the book and my empty mug before making my way out of her room. She'd invited me to use her balcony and get some fresh air, which I appreciated.

Our rooms were on the same level, the walk between them winding through a long hallway. This place felt like a maze, which made me wonder how big it actually was. I had yet to be shown around–if they even intended for me to be.

One thing I'd learned was what the Armory actually was. Roslyn explained to me that it served as living quarters to many of the continent's law enforcement, or *Enforcers,* as she called them. She'd said most of them live their lives in solitude, but that those who had spouses and children were allowed to live in homes of their own, so long as it did not disrupt their work habits.

I was very curious to see what these living quarters might look like, and to meet some of the so-called Enforcers, but had not been given the opportunity to yet.

There obviously had to be some sort of kitchen here, but because I didn't know where that was, I just brought the mug to my private bathing room and rinsed it in the sink. I made quick work of washing my face and neck as well, applying my cream and brushing my teeth before wedging the desk chair under the door-knob and crawling into bed.

As I slowly slipped into the peaceful cushion of sleep, I only had one thought. The same thought that had been returning to my head relentlessly the past two days.

I wish I was back under that weeping willow with Archi.

CHAPTER TWELVE

VIOLET ~ AGE TWELVE

After my parents died, I had no idea what to do.

I spent the first week up in my treehouse, too afraid to even open the door. What if the bad people who killed them were still down there hiding and waiting for me to come out?

Luckily, my momma was smart and had a pack of food stored up here for emergencies. That, along with the canteen of water, was enough to hold me over for a little bit, but not forever.

I could see from my view in the treehouse that our entire house was gone. The fire that the bad people lit burned it all down like kindling. Everything I owned, except for the small bag momma gave me that night, was lost.

So, I went back and forth from the treehouse to the well, filling up my canteen whenever I needed to. I tried to avoid looking at the huge pile of white ashes where our house used to be while I was on those trips, and I definitely avoided thinking about my parents' ashes being there too.

It was a good thing we used to be farmers because I was able to harvest the crops that were left for myself to eat, but that wouldn't last forever. They'd run out soon, and I didn't know how to make more grow. Momma had only taught me how to pick the produce so far, not how to plant it.

So, after about a month, when the crops started to run out, I knew I had to leave. I found the strength to finally sift through the ashes of our house, hoping to find any remnants of our life there, but there was nothing left.

After packing up the big basket in the treehouse with every last fruit and vegetable I had left, some blankets, books, and my canteen, I left behind our land and started walking.

I didn't know if there was a certain place I should go. Poppa and I hadn't gotten to the land in our studies yet, so I knew nothing about my surroundings. I just started walking.

A few days later, I was in the middle of nowhere. It wasn't getting too cold at night yet, so I'd been doing okay, but I knew that wouldn't last, either. I would need to find a town and someplace to sleep pretty soon.

I'd gotten tired from carrying my basket and backpack, so I decided to lie down underneath a tree for a while, figuring it was safe because there were no people around. And I liked how its branches were swooping down, creating a little pocket that I could hide in.

"Hi there!"

The voice was unexpected and made me startle into a sitting position.

I looked up to see a scrawny boy with bright red hair staring down at me with a huge smile. Not wanting to talk to him, I scooted away and turned around, hoping he would realize that I wanted to be alone.

"My name's Archibald," the skinny boy announced, ignoring my hint and sitting down next to me. "What's yours?"

I glared at him over my shoulder before turning back around and grabbing a book out of my basket.

"UGH!" He groaned loudly. "You like reading? My sister likes reading, but I always tell her she should stop. Why would you read when you could be outside making your *own* adventure?"

I rolled my eyes at the boy, not wanting to talk to him even more after hearing that.

"What else do you like besides reading?" he asked.

When I didn't answer, he continued in his one-sided conversation.

"My favorite thing to do is ride my bike, but I don't have it anymore. I also like when my mom gets out the craft stuff, but that only happens every once in a while. Did you know that paints are really expensive? She always tells me that when I ask her to do crafts and says that I should stop pestering her about it. I don't really know what pestering means, but it doesn't sound very good."

A few seconds went by.

"You should really tell me your name, you know. We're going to be friends, and it will be hard to be friends if I don't even know your name."

I glared at him, but it was only half-heartedly. I kind of liked this boy and his annoying rambling. It was nice to not be alone and only have my thoughts to listen to anymore. Besides, he kind of reminded me of another friend I used to have.

"How old are you?" he asked, but didn't wait for my response. "I'm thirteen. Mom and Dad told me that I'm a big boy now, so I had to leave. They said that they can't afford me anymore, so I needed to go find someone who could or learn how to take care of myself. I don't really want to find anyone to take care of me. I want to take care of myself and buy all the paints I can find."

Archibald puffed out his chest like he was proving that he was, in fact, a big boy. If anything, I thought it made him seem even younger. It was sad that his parents kicked him out. They didn't seem very nice.

I reached into my basket and pulled out an apple, passing it to the boy.

"Ohhh, thank you!" he exclaimed, greedily grabbing the apple and tearing into it with his teeth.

He must've been very hungry.

"Did you know this tree is called a weeping willow?" he asked around the apple in his mouth.

I made a face at the noises he was making, talking with his mouth full. Gross. He didn't seem to notice, though, because he was staring up at the branches.

"Dad said they are called weeping willows because it looks like the branches are crying. Usually, tree branches are sticking out, but these ones seem all droopy and sad." The boy perked up, leaning over and nudging me with his shoulder. "Hey! That's kind of like you."

I narrowed my eyes at him, regretting giving up one of my apples now.

"Are you *suuure* you don't want to tell me your name? Last chance," he taunted, poking me in the side.

I changed my mind. This boy was just annoying.

"Okay, fine, you give me no choice. Hmm," he mused, rubbing his chin dramatically. "I could call you 'apple girl', but that seems too long. It would be a pain to say."

I rolled my eyes and opened my book, leaning back against the tree's trunk to read it.

"I know!" Archibald exclaimed as soon as I found the line where I'd stopped reading before. "Willow!"

Archibald extended his hand for me to shake, and when I didn't extend mine, he pried it off the book and put it into his.

"Willow, I'm Archibald. And we are going to be the best of friends."

I had no idea at the time just how right he was.

CHAPTER THIRTEEN

VIOLET

The next morning, I woke to the sound of someone knocking harshly on the door to my room. I groaned, not wanting to wake up yet, but the sound was insistent and gaining frequency.

Making a dramatic effort out of getting up, I stomped over to the door, removed the chair, and swung it open. Xander was standing just outside with his fist still raised and a smile on his face.

"Well," he drawled. "Someone's not a morning person."

I noticed his smile fall away slightly as his eyes swept down to the long t-shirt and small sleeping shorts I was wearing. His gaze intensified as he reached my bare legs, but he didn't seem to linger over the large birthmark on my left leg like most people do.

"Did you need something?" I asked with a bite, still annoyed that he woke me up this early.

Well, I actually had no idea what time it was. But it *felt* early.

"Yes," he replied, regaining his composure and looking at my face again. "We are leaving. Gather your things and get ready. I'll be back in twenty minutes."

And with that, he was gone.

I bristled and closed my door again, moving to the bathing room to shower.

Who did he think he was, ordering me around all the time?

'Listen to me, Violet.'

'Don't move, Violet.'

'Stay locked in your room for two fucking days, Violet.'

It wasn't that I was upset about him leaving me here while he was on his mission. It was the fact that he still hadn't told me anything about the situation I was in. I didn't even know what it was we were waiting on, only that it had to do with the cube I'd found. The little information I did have was given to me by Roslyn, and that was probably just because she felt sorry for me while I was in the Void.

I jolted, realizing that I'd woken up in my base state. I wondered if that had to do with Xander waking me so abruptly, or if my brain had enough of a rest that it was finally ready to re-enter society.

I was glad to have come out of it now that we were finally doing something, whatever that was.

After showering and quickly brushing my teeth, I applied a light coat of makeup: some mascara and bronzer. I liked the way it pulled my features up, but more so than that, I wanted to feel put together today.

I wasn't really sure what one was supposed to wear in Cavell, or wherever we were going, so I opted for a thin, long-sleeved shirt over a tank top and leggings. Xander didn't mention how long we'd be gone–because of course he didn't–so I emptied my bag and repacked it with enough clothes for two nights.

Before leaving, I figured that I should probably return Roslyn's books. I checked the clock to make sure I still had a few minutes to spare and grabbed the stack, holding it to my chest as I opened the door. I stopped short, though, because Xander was standing in the hallway leaning against the wall on one foot.

"Where are you going with my books, Angel?" he asked with a smirk.

"Your books?" I asked incredulously.

"Yes, *my books.*" He whispered the two last words mockingly, titling his head to the side and widening his eyes.

God, he was annoying.

"I thought they were Roslyn's," I grumbled, shoving the stack at his chest.

I would never have guessed these books came from Xander. Not because I didn't expect him to read, but because of the *selection*. A few were just your typical fiction romance, but the others were depraved and degrading *smutty novels*.

In other words, my kind of shit.

The thought of Xander reading them–let alone enjoying them–did things to me that I'd rather not pay attention to.

"What did you think of the selection?" he asked, the smile clear in his voice.

I shrugged, doing my best to give off a casual reaction. "It was decent."

"Decent enough to pull you out of your state?"

I narrowed my eyes at him, appraising him from head to toe and not saying anything.

"What exactly happened, anyway?" he asked nonchalantly, clearly trying to disarm me into giving him an answer.

"Nope," I stated, turning on my heel to grab my bag.

He followed me into my room and put the books down on the desk. "You're really not going to tell me what that was?"

The way he said it implied that he was owed an answer, which really set me off.

"Oh, really?" I laughed humorlessly. "Because you're so forthcoming about yourself?"

Xander looked thoughtful for a second before shrugging. "Fair enough."

I gave him a look of over-the-top appreciation. "So relieved you agree."

He didn't react to my sarcasm the way I'd expected. His expression turned somber and serious in a way I hadn't seen yet.

"They were supposed to be an apology." His voice sounded... off. Choppy and unsure.

"What?" I asked, entirely confused.

His eyes scanned my face. "The books. I hated seeing you that way, and the fact that I caused it. I thought they might help fix it."

I observed him for a moment. He looked genuine–albeit slightly uncomfortable and out of sorts, but I felt like he was telling the truth.

After a single nod, I tried to lighten the mood. "At least you're self-aware enough to realize when you've acted like a colossal piece of shit."

He let out a low, rumbling laugh that traveled straight to my clit.

Fucking hell.

"Charming as always, Angel," Xander quipped. He walked to my bed and grabbed my duffel bag before extending an elbow my way with a charming grin.

"I can handle my own bag, you know," I remarked, reluctantly placing my hand on the crook of his arm.

"Nonsense," he responded before lobbing the bag into the air.

"Wha–" I started, worried about my glass cosmetic bottles breaking, but then the bag vanished out of nowhere.

"Why carry something that can sit happily in a pocket dimension?"

"Is that pocket dimension also where you have my entire collection of pottery? And all of my money?"

"Your belongings are safe," Xander assured me. It wasn't lost on me that he didn't answer the question, though.

As he whisked us somewhere new, I wondered if there would ever come a day when he would answer one of my questions without a vague, no-meaning response.

☽

XANDER

I CHERISHED THE LOOK OF SHOCKED WONDER ON MY little Angel's face as we walked down the main trail in Bosquera. Her eyes were wide with admiration as she took in the timber town for the first time.

The path curved its way through a mossy forest that was home to hundreds of thousands of redwood trees, spanning from one hundred-fifty to three hundred feet tall. The trees themselves weren't all that far away from each other, so their leaves formed a canopy to block the strong sun that this district got. Seeing that it was the northernmost point of our land, it was typically hot this time of year.

I smiled down at Violet as she continued staring up at the villas in admiration. She seemed to love the little houses that were built high up in the trees. Each tree had one or two stories of living space, depending on how many people it housed. The houses all had suspension bridges hung between them, connecting the families the same way sidewalks would in a typical neighbourhood. Some of the bigger trees held multiple houses with staircases built into the tree, winding up the trunk like a coil.

The light was so bright in her eyes, lifting a weight off my chest that I hadn't fully realised was pressing down on me the past few days.

As I was tracking down the rogue Astrales Lilliana sent me to take care of, my mind kept returning to that vacant look on her face and the fact that I might have been the one to cause it. Maybe I was being narcissistic, thinking I had that sort of power over her, but I couldn't help it with the timing of it all.

Regardless, the change in her demeanour was significant. And haunting.

Actually, it reminded me of a quote I read in a book once. One of the books that I just so happened to give to Violet.

'She was trapped in this world when her soul lived elsewhere.'

That is exactly what it had looked like–as if her soul had escaped to some unknown and unreachable place.

Fuck whatever it was that took her away from me. When I told her there was nowhere she could run and hide that I wouldn't find her, I meant it. I just didn't realise at the time that there was a way she could hide without moving her body an inch.

That was the real reason behind our little trip here. I figured she could use a change of scenery and would enjoy learning about this harmless corner of my world. I didn't tell her that, though, coming up with the excuse of running an errand for Lilliana before we went to check on the Memorium goggles.

I didn't love the idea of bringing Violet to see Gaar, but I hated the option of leaving her at the Armoury even more. I didn't trust Lilliana with her, and while I didn't have a choice the past two days, I did now.

This girl wouldn't be leaving my side, whether she liked it or not.

The Astrales living in these timber towns are mostly arboreal, but there are many Terrala that live in ordinary houses as well. The residents of the Terrala sector, Bedruke, all contain the Terrala core, which draws on the essence of nature and plants. For that reason, the citizens here are responsible for most of the farming and agriculture for all of Cavell. Many individual sectors have their own source of supplemental food and have developed unique cuisine practices over time, but the main source of produce comes from here.

"What is this place?" Violet finally spoke, that wonderstruck look on her face bleeding into her voice.

"This is Bosquera. It is one of many timber towns in the Redwood Forest, but this one is the largest. A sort of capital, if you will."

"It's amazing," she responded, turning around in a circle and looking up at the trees. "I've never seen trees this big before."

"They're a rare species," I told her, forcing my gaze ahead so I wouldn't continue staring at her. "As far as I know, this is the only sector they have been discovered in."

"And which sector is this?"

"Bedruke. The citizens here are called Terrala. They live harmoniously with nature, drawing on its essence to perform their magic."

Violet looked up at me with those big, round eyes, and I decided that if she was going to give me that look every time I answered one of her questions, I would be making a habit out of it.

"What kind of magic do Terralas possess?"

I looked up at the network of houses, trying to find the right words to describe it.

"There really isn't one answer to that question. While each Core draws on different elements, there are a wide variety of gifts that manifest within them."

I put my hands on each side of Violet's hips, and she let out a small noise in surprise as I hoisted her over a tree that had fallen in the path. The sound was like a choir to my ears and had my chest filling with air at the thought of all the things I could do to hear it again.

When she was settled, she looked up at me with an expression that made my hands linger for a second too long before I pulled them away.

I continued walking and speaking before my intrusive thoughts got the better of me.

"For example..." I grinned–*again*–as she practically lunged to fall into step with me, not wanting to miss a single word.

"I have seen a Terrala capable of bringing a field of dead crops back to life after they'd withered from the sun. I have also met some that are only able to raise a single flower from the ground."

Violet nodded, her eyes skirting from side to side as if she was cataloguing the new information in her brain.

"Generally speaking, we do not judge people according to what their abilities are. They may have different jobs and responsibilities, but that doesn't mean that they have a lesser standing in society. That is more so determined based on their personality traits and the typical hierarchies that come with social interaction."

Violet looked thoughtful, but I was eager to get up to the top and witness her face when she realised what we were doing here.

"Okay, now," I started leaning up against the base of the tree I'd been leading us to and grabbed a cigarette out of my tin. I lit it, enjoying how she watched my Corefire, and took a drag. "We need to do something about that accent of yours. It's a dead give-away, and no one here can know that you are human."

She scrunched her nose up in that way that made my stupid fucking chest swell.

What is this girl doing *to me?*

"And how exactly do you expect me to get rid of my accent? There is no way I can just put yours on."

"That isn't what I was thinking, though I would love to hear you try."

I held back a smile when she scowled at me. I really did love getting under her skin.

"I'm going to put a Soothe on you," I explained. "It will make everyone hear your voice with the Astrale accent."

She took a small step backwards and pulled her shoulder blades back slightly, as if that would protect her.

"It's not going to be anything like it was with Archi." I noticed her tensing up at the mention of his name. "It looked intense because I was altering his memories. I will just be changing your articulation. It will hardly take a moment."

Violet looked up at me with contempt, reminding me of our first few days together. She nodded, though, and stepped closer to me. I reached my hand out and lightly grazed the side of her neck with my fingers, cherishing the way her eyelashes fluttered closed.

Noted.

I zeroed in on the memory of her voice, calling on the darkness deep inside me to force my will onto her. This was the process I underwent every time I placed a Soothe on another person. I'd dig into the depravity of human nature, focusing on it until I felt the distinct tingle underneath my skin.

After sending out my signal, I felt the moment it took root and pulled away from her.

"Well? Let's hear it."

"You're an asshole," she quipped sweetly, smiling at me.

"True." I smiled right back at her. "But that sounded exactly the same to me. Try again."

Her eyebrows pinched together. "It definitely sounded different to me."

"Nope. You sound human as ever."

"There is something wrong with your ears," Violet dismissed, brushing past me and starting up the stairs with a giddy energy. "I sound so cool like this! Almost like I should open a tattoo studio and change my name to 'Astrid' or something."

I followed behind her more slowly than I needed to, stalking her like a predator does prey.

The dots started to connect in my mind.

The way I was immediately protective of her after we met, not wanting to leave her alone with Lilliana.

Altering my path to bring her to a restaurant after hearing her stomach growl once.

Clouding her landing in Armantrea–by instinct–so she wouldn't hit the ground too harshly.

The way she saw past my Soothe when I changed my appearance.

My reaction to her putting herself in danger when I usually didn't give a damn what happened to other people, let alone a practical stranger.

The fierce desire–no, *need*–to protect her every time I saw fear shining in her eyes.

The slight spark I felt when we touched, the same one I knew she felt as well.

The small shift I felt inside my chest every time she looked at me with that serene expression.

The moment I accepted the truth, it was like a shifting of the planet's axis. She was *mine*.

As I followed her up the winding staircase, I looked at the back of her head, her short brown hair bouncing as she eagerly climbed to the top.

This little Angel had no idea that she was stuck with me now.

For life.

CHAPTER FOURTEEN

VIOLET

I heaved a breath, regretting the extra energy I expelled by skipping up the stairs in the beginning. I was too excited by my new voice to realize how many damn stairs there actually were, and now I needed to sit.

After coming around a curve, I realized we were almost at the platform and turned around to find Xander stalking behind me in slow, measured steps. His gaze was piercing and focused entirely on my face, as if he was trying to evaluate my thoughts.

"Um," I started. "Is there something I can help you with?"

"Not at the moment."

I couldn't read his tone or his response.

"Then would you stop hovering behind me like a stalker?"

Something indecipherable crossed his face before a smile swept it away. Xander climbed up to the step below mine and stopped, but he was still taller than me by a long shot.

He stood close enough that I could smell the fresh tobacco on his breath and see the different shades of green within his eyes. The smile on his face faltered slightly, replaced by a more intense expression. Those eyes shifted down to my lips and lingered there before he shook his head slightly and looked behind me.

"Are you ready to see why we are here?" Xander asked me.

"What do you mean? I thought you had to run an errand for Lilliana." I couldn't resist my tone being a little snarky at the end of that sentence.

The narrowing of his eyes filled me with amusement.

He needed to learn not to react to my taunts if he ever wanted them to stop.

"There is more to it than that," Xander said, his shoulder brushing against mine as he moved past me toward the platform.

I followed him, confused by this turn of events, and stopped dead when I saw what was before me.

There were people spread all around this level of the sky, their chatter filling my ears. Some were standing, others were lounging on the platforms jutting out of the trees at various heights. There were a few other people on the same level as us–which was much, much larger than it seemed from down below.

That wasn't what had my jaw hanging to the floor, though.

There were a multitude of thick, winding vines hanging between the trees, and a few of them were occupied by an Astrale or two as they hung onto them and swung through the open air.

My mind spun as I watched them shoot across the space. It seemed that we were on the lowest platform because there were also people on the vines above us, laughing and shrieking as they carelessly gripped an organic rope that was swinging hundreds of feet in the air.

True to my line of thought, someone shrieked as their hand slipped from the vine, and they freefell down quickly.

I gasped and rushed forward, but Xander halted me with an arm and bent down to whisper in my ear. "Don't show a reaction. This is normal for everyone here and you don't want to alert your-self as an outsider."

"This is *normal?*" I whispered harshly.

I mean, yeah, they're supernatural beings, but surely they can't survive a fall from that height, right?

"Take a look," Xander suggested, nudging me forward.

I walked to the edge of the platform and looked out to find the woman who had fallen lying in the air with a smile on her face.

Yes, lying *in the air*. It was almost as if there was an invisible bed floating beneath her with the way she was sprawled out on her back.

"What the…how in the hell?" I muttered under my breath.

How was this possible? And why didn't I see it when we were walking down below?

Another person fell, seemingly on purpose this time, and I watched in awe as he bounced in midair when he reached the same level as the lounging lady. The new guy did a double backflip before landing and springing up again. The movement made his shoulder-length blond hair glint in the sun as it moved all around him. His efforts didn't seem to affect the first woman at all, or the other people I noticed in similar positions.

"It is a magic barrier," Xander explained softly, leaning down so that his head was close to mine. "It stops people from being hurt if they slip and allows others to fall for fun."

"For fun," I repeated slowly, not understanding what would be fun about plummeting down like that.

"You'll love it," he assured me, hooking an arm around my waist and steering me to the right.

"Are you insane?" I hissed as he forced me to walk toward a vine at the edge. "I am not doing that!"

"Sure you are."

"I've never done anything like this before!" I squeaked out as he continued pushing me forward. "How am I supposed to do it alone without making it obvious that I'm an outsider?"

"Who said anything about you doing it alone?" Xander asked suggestively.

Oh.

"I guess I just figured…" I tried to decide how to phrase it, but he cut me off with a mocking gasp.

"What? You mean you assumed what was going to happen? I'm absolutely astounded."

I scowled at his sarcasm. "Fuck off."

Xander laughed as we reached the vine, and he grabbed it before pulling me to his side.

"Well?" he asked. "What would you rather hold onto? Me or the vine?"

I contemplated it for a second before deciding that I was better off relying on the one with supernatural strength. I went on my tiptoes and wrapped my arms around his neck. Xander's eyes flared in response, the color deepening and locking in on mine.

I felt my breath hitch at our closeness. But when he wrapped an arm around my lower back and effortlessly lifted me, I stopped breathing altogether.

The position forced me to wrap my legs around his middle, eradicating any space left between us. A tingle shot through me as I felt his abs constrict against my center. The friction intensified when he reached for the vine, and I felt my muscles clench, desperate for some undivided attention.

"Are you comfortable, Angel?" Xander asked, his tone implying that he knew what I was struggling with.

"Yep," I said, feigning obliviousness. "I'm perfectly fine."

He smirked and wrapped the vine around his hand before tightening his embrace and shifting my body up and down once, subsequently grinding my clit against his hard muscles.

I gasped as heat rushed to my face and through my body.

"That's better," Xander confirmed with a nod. "You just needed a little adjusting."

Prick.

Before I could curse him, we were jumping and flying through the air.

I tried to hold in my scream before I remembered that the others were as well, so I let out a small one and scrunched myself against Xander's shoulder, tightening my hold on his neck.

The tree bark and leaves were a blur as we swept through the air, their colors mixing and mingling to create a beautiful swirling view. As we moved, the wind whipped against us, and it was surprisingly peaceful.

It felt like the breeze was wiping away the stress of the past few days and all thoughts along with it, leaving me feeling centered and serene.

"Just land on your back when you want to stop bouncing," Xander said into my ear over the wind.

That was the moment I realized my mistake in trusting him because of his strength. I should have thought of his *brain*.

"Wait! No–"

Xander let go of me and easily separated the grip of my hands with one of his.

I was too stunned to even scream as I dropped like a sack of bricks, falling through the air at a fast speed. My stomach rose and rose until it felt like it was in my chest, and then sank to my toes when I looked down and saw the ground approaching quickly.

I panicked, scrambling in the air to grab onto anything I could, but then my feet collided with a plush surface, and I was shooting upward again. A shocked laugh left me at the sensation, and I watched in fascination this time as I fell again and bounced off of the invisible barrier.

If I didn't know any better, I would think that I was in a drug-fueled dream.

I continued bouncing and giggling, feeling more carefree than I had in a long time. I looked to my right and noticed Xander lounging on the barrier. He was sitting and leaning back on his hands with his ankles crossed, watching me with an easy, closed-lipped smile that lit up his eyes.

I was slightly nervous about this whole landing procedure, but I did my best to angle my body so that I would end up on my back and not my head. It went surprisingly well, and I sighed happily as I settled into the cloud-like surface and looked up at the trees above us. It was plush and comfortable, erasing any idea I had about getting up to talk to Xander. Apparently, I didn't need to, though, because he moved to my side.

"So?" he asked. "Did you enjoy it?"

"Yes," I happily replied. "I can't remember the last time I felt so..." I couldn't find the right word.

"Free," Xander suggested, a strangely vulnerable tone to his voice.

I nodded and looked over at him, hoping to catch a glance at what was causing his demeanor. His face was closed off and guarded, though, not giving me a clue.

"Do you want to go again?" he asked.

I nodded and sat up. "I want to try it alone this time."

He chuckled. "But I thought you were so comfortable last time."

"Whatever, dickhead," I shot at him before turning around and moving toward a tree.

I made it one step before Xander picked me up and legitimately chucked me ten feet into the air, as if I weighed nothing at all.

I was still openly gaping when I landed on my back and saw him glaring down at me.

"I'm becoming very tired of your fucking *tongue*, Angel."

I didn't even know what to say, but at that exact moment, a slow, sensual laugh approached us. I turned to see the same man who was doing backflips earlier coming our way.

His face was angular and sharp, spearheaded by his sweeping, aristocratic nose. The blond color of his hair was so bright that I thought it might be artificial, but I couldn't be sure. As he got closer, I noticed the small mole beneath his left eye, and something about it struck a familiarity within my gut.

When he finally reached us, the dark blue eyes only added to that sensation.

"Xander," the man greeted cheerfully. "Please introduce me to this beautiful woman that is so miraculously skilled at getting under your skin."

Where Xander's voice was deep and rich, this man's was unmistakably warm and flirtatious. I have never trusted anyone who radiated that much sunshine–it usually meant they were covering up a plethora of issues within.

"Shaed," Xander acknowledged, his voice closed off and cool as he shifted forward so that he was between me and the newcomer. "What are you doing this far from home?"

Shaed's eyes crinkled with a charming smile that was so big it made my insides sour. "I'm just off having a bit of fun today. Dom and Neerah claimed that they were in desperate need of better company, but it seems that they don't need me here after all." He nodded behind us at a couple that was lying on the barrier together, kissing passionately.

I turned back around quickly to find Xander still staring Shaed down as if he was his newest opponent.

"And Daddy dearest was okay with that, was he? No galas to attend today, golden boy?" Xander asked in a provocative tone, confirming my suspicions that there was some bad blood between these two.

Shaed remained smiling, but it was cold and edged now as he shot knives at Xander with his eyes. He turned his gaze to me, and everything about his face warmed again. "Would you like to introduce yourself, since the ogre you are with is too rude to do so?"

I felt Xander glance at me, but I was busy examining my nails in mock boredom.

"I'm okay, actually," I uttered in a cool tone, still wiping imaginary streaks off of the dark purple paint.

I peeked up at Xander when a little laugh left him. He looked at me with amusement, surprise, and something else I couldn't put my finger on. I knew that I wanted to see it again, though.

When I looked back at Shaed, he was glancing between me and Xander with a guarded expression.

"Well, if that'll be all..." Xander trailed off and grabbed me, throwing my body over his shoulder effortlessly.

I laughed as he whisked us to a faraway platform and plopped me down on my feet in front of him.

"Who *was* that tool?" I asked breathlessly, still not used to his methods of traveling.

"Just a little toff, filled with self-importance. His father is a wealthy leader of the Astrolite sector—Callieso—and he likes to make sure that everyone knows it. Especially when he is bending the rules about mingling between sectors." Xander was looking downward in distaste, presumably in the direction of Shaed. His lip curled up so extensively that I had to hold back my laugh.

"So is that not a law that you enforce? Like, as an Enforcer, I mean."

Xander leaned down to whisper in my ear, each word sending its own gust of air skating down my neck. "I'm a bit put out, honestly, that the Soothe isn't working for me. The idea of hearing your human phrases with the Astrale accent is quite amusing."

"Like what?" I felt his smile against my cheek.

"Like, '*like*,'" he said mockingly.

"I don't say it *that* much," I insisted, crossing my arms between us.

"Oh, but you do."

I gave Xander a dry look. "Don't think I missed that diversion."

Ignoring it for now, I pulled off my long-sleeve shirt over my head. I'd broken a sweat with all of the jumping and silently thanked myself for deciding to wear a tank top underneath it.

I looked up and smiled inwardly at the way Xander's eyes had darkened. They were focused on my breasts, which the low neckline now accentuated.

"Take care of that, would you?" I asked, tossing him my shirt before running straight at the edge and hurling myself off of it.

I took pride in the shocked curse that left Xander's mouth as I fell.

Not even bothering with the vine this time, I just let myself fall and dropped my arms so that they were floating alongside me. All of the tension left my body, and I checked to make sure that the coast was clear of other Astrales before closing my eyes. I wanted the bounce to be a surprise this time.

I continued jumping on the barrier for a while. Xander was nowhere in sight, but I didn't mind that at all. I was enjoying a little bit of time to myself, and the landscape was breathtaking to see. Plus, I couldn't possibly remember all of the burdens on my shoulders while bouncing like a child on a bed.

Until Shaed approached and ruined everything.

"Hello," he greeted, lining up his jump perfectly so that he dropped down next to me and sprung up at the same time.

"Uh. Hi," I responded, immediately falling on my back so that I would stop.

He did the same and stood up, offering a hand to help me.

I declined and stood on my own, turning to move to the closest tree. Shaed stopped me with a hand on my arm.

"I've never seen you around here before," he commented with a leading tone.

"Oh? Is that supposed to mean something to me?"

"Pe–perhaps not," I narrowed my eyes as he stuttered. He didn't strike me as the type to do that often.

"Okay, well, if that's all..." I said, looking pointedly at his hand still on my arm.

He removed it and stepped back. "Xander is not good company to keep. Come and find me when you realize that for yourself."

I scoffed. "Not fucking likely."

At that moment, Xander dropped down forcefully and somehow landed on his feet without bouncing, crashing into the barrier and steadying himself with one fist on the ground. He straightened to his full height and straightened the sleeves of his shirt, towering over Shaed, who raised his hands in innocence and stepped back further.

"I was only hoping to learn her name. She is quite fascinating, after all."

"You don't need to learn *shit* about her," Xander growled in a possessive tone that caused my toes to curl.

Where did that come from?

Without another word, Xander grabbed my hand and whisked us away, turning the beautiful forest into a colorful blur.

We landed in a desolate area. The ground was relatively

barren, made out of packed dirt that was so dark it almost looked black. There were no trees or plants in sight. In fact, I could only see a small building that seemed to be constructed from black-painted wood.

"Where the fuck are we now?" I asked, getting whiplashed by yet another foreign surrounding.

"This is Sarehm, the Soothsayer district." His voice was cold again. Distant. "We are going to check on our vessel and see if it is ready."

Xander walked past me without looking back, clearly expecting me to follow. I did just that, a little bit shocked that he was including me in this. When we reached the door of the small building, Xander turned back and looked down at me with blazing eyes.

"Okay, this is one of those times that you are going to listen to my advice," he asserted in a condescending tone as he rested a hand on the door handle. "You are to stand quietly by my side while I do the talking and not draw any attention to yourself. Understood?"

I narrowed my eyes. "Would you like me to bow at your feet as well?"

I really did like my voice with the Astrale accent. It sounded mysterious and deeply feminine, like I was a woman who had been around the block.

"If you please," he teased pleasantly, seemingly liking the idea.

My eyes rolled so far back into my head that I wasn't sure they would ever return, but I followed him into the shop and did as he said. I noticed a slight tightening in his shoulder blades when the bell above the door chimed and wondered what the cause was.

The shop itself was a cozy little space. A deep red color coated the walls, offsetting the black shelves scattered throughout. Most of the walls had built-ins, but there were also a few free-standing ones in the middle of the room, creating a winding layout with many nooks and crannies.

Standing behind a counter at the back of the room was a man.

He was tall–not *Xander* tall–but I'd guess he was about six-foot-two. With his face tilted downward, the few streaks of white hair hanging around his face stood out starkly against his bronze skin and blacked-out suit. The rest of his hair was dark brown and pulled back into a bun. I was just forming thoughts of how attractive he was when he looked up, and I felt my soul leave my body.

The irises of his eyes were red. And not 'a brown so rich it borderlines on red'.

They were a deep and pure red, reminding me of the color of blood. They were also framed with a thick fringe of dark lashes and eyebrows, making the color stand out even more.

"And who might this be?" the man asked without greeting, his deep, raspy voice sending chills over my entire body.

"A new colleague of mine," Xander responded casually, keeping his answer vague.

"And does this 'new colleague' have a name?" He directed the question to Xander, but his unnerving eyes remained locked on me. They swept all around my body, skipping between the different birthmarks that were visible in this outfit. The two on my arms and the one peeking out of my tank top near my collarbone were in the clearest view.

I steeled my spine, refusing to shrink under his observation.

Xander's tone sounded guarded and measured when he spoke in my direction, but for some reason, I couldn't look away from the man in front of me.

"Violet, this is Nygaard, but you may call him Gaar. He is an advisor of mine."

I nodded and greeted him with a simple, "Hello." With Xander's warning at the forefront of my mind, I didn't want to say too much.

Nygaard didn't respond, just continued looking at me with a cocked head. I shuffled on my feet, not sure what to do with myself under his scrutiny.

He finally spoke, but it was in Xander's direction. "I will go check on your shipment."

He turned around and walked through a set of doors at the back of the shop.

As soon as Nygaard was out of sight, I whipped around to Xander in shock. "Okay, what in the *fuck* is up with his eyes?" I whispered.

Xander's face was closed off. "Gaar is a very...particular kind of Soothsayer, Violet. I wouldn't recommend getting on his bad side."

"Yeah, no shit," I retorted incredulously.

I wasn't sure why anyone would want to get on his bad side, considering his off-putting demeanor and demon eyes. I really wanted to know what made his eyes red, but figured this probably wasn't the best time to push Xander on it, considering Gaar was just in the other room.

After a few seconds of silence, I asked, "Are you ever going to tell me what this vessel actually is?"

"You remember the cube you found–yes?" he asked, stepping around a chair to come and stand at my side.

"Obviously," I said dryly, earning a glare from Xander.

"Well, inside that cube lies a memory," he started. "It is very rare, but there are some Astrale–called Memora–that are capable of encasing a memory into a physical form. But there is no way to know who it belonged to, or what it contains, without the proper viewing vessel.

"Enter Gaar." Xander gestured as he looked in the direction of the doors he left through. "Memoras have slowly died out over time, causing the remaining few to have their practices exploited and abused by others. It became such an issue that we were forced to ban all use of the Memora practice commercially. For that reason, the vessels are nearly impossible to procure today."

My mind marveled at the prospect of encasing memories. Forgetting things is a common trait of mine, especially while in the Void, so having that skill would seriously come in handy.

If only I were an Astrale.

And an extremely rare one on top of it.

"But not too impossible for Nygaard to find?" I asked.

"There are not many things that are impossible for him." Xander's words felt like they were laced with a double meaning.

"So, can somebody be a Memora without–"

A fluffy-tailed creature bounded through the swinging doors and barreled into me, cutting off my words and knocking me on my ass. A shocked laugh left me as he panted in my face and pawed at my shoulder, begging to be pet.

"Hello, little guy," I greeted, stroking his head.

My mood immediately brightened in response to this surprise. I've always adored animals in general, but dogs hold a special place in my heart.

"Or girl?" I asked, looking up at Nygaard as he re-entered the room, assuming the dog belonged to him.

I noticed then that both men were staring down at me in bewilderment, where I was still lying on the ground from the furry attack.

"What?" I asked.

"This has never happened before," was all Nygaard replied, cocking his head to the side as he continued observing us.

I was getting really sick of how the people here insisted on looking at me like that.

"Briella is a female, and she does not take kindly to people," Xander said, finally answering my question. "Ever. Quite the opposite, in fact."

Briella snarled in Xander's direction, pulling back her lips to show sharp incisors. I grinned down at her and scratched her behind the ears, making her relax and climb even further into my lap.

"Well, maybe it's the quality of the company that's been lacking. She seems to have good taste."

Briella barked in response, wagging her tail eagerly. A small laugh bubbled out of my chest when she licked my arm. I hadn't pet a dog in far too long.

I looked up to find Xander staring down at me with an

intense gaze that caught my attention, until Nygaard spoke and broke the connection.

"What do you think you're doing," he enunciated slowly, swinging his red gaze to Xander's green one. "Bringing a human into my shop?"

☽

XANDER

My heart stopped dead in my chest at Gaar's words.

I did my best to mask my reaction, taking a casual step towards a shelf with apparatus stones and pretending to look at them so that I was positioned between him and Violet.

"I'm not sure I know what you mean," I finally responded.

Gaar scoffed. "As if your pathetic little Soothes would actually work on me." He rounded the chair that was between us and made to step around me towards Violet, but I blocked his pursuit with my body.

He looked me up and down with an appraising glint in his eye. "Have you forgotten your place already, Ponce?"

"No," I replied with a casual tone, even though my stomach was in a knot because of what was unfolding. "My place has merely shifted."

Gaar regarded me heavily for a moment until I saw the realisation dawn in his eyes. He looked between me and Violet, who was rooted in place with confusion written all over her beautiful face. The slight frown and furrow between her brows made her look adorable.

Fuck. Since when do I find people adorable?

I looked back at Gaar, and my insides froze at the hunger I saw on his face as he looked down at Violet. To anyone else, he would have appeared catatonic and bored. But his interest was evident in

140

the constriction of his pupils and the way he raised his chin, assessing his newest conquest.

Having been on the receiving end of that look, I knew exactly what was going through his mind.

"*No,*" I growled, shoving him back a step by his chest. "You stay the fuck away from her."

His red eyes flared along with his nostrils, rage overcoming him in a second.

There were a few moments of heavy silence before he spoke, both of us staring each other down.

"Are you drawing a line in the sand, Xander?"

I was thrown off guard by two things: his cool tone and his use of my full name. It was always either 'Ponce' or 'Xan', so I knew that meant our dynamics were shifting.

I felt a pull inside me–much stronger than I expected–to fall back, to submit to him. But I couldn't do that.

Not anymore.

The time had come for things to change. We both knew this would happen eventually. It just happened a lot more abruptly than either of us expected.

"Yes," I replied in a firm tone. "This is my line."

Gaar looked at me for a moment longer, and I saw something flash across his eyes that I never had before.

Sadness.

The sight broke something inside of me, but it was gone in a second, and he went back to his typical stone-faced expression.

"Your vessel will be here within the next day." Gaar's voice was detached and dismissive. "Next time, wait for me to contact you before showing up on my doorstep."

And with that, he was walking through the doors at the back of the shop. I looked down at Violet, who was staring up at me with an open and questioning expression, likely wondering what the hell had just happened. Briella was still sitting between her legs; the sight making my skin crawl.

I had seen that dog tear a child's arm off in a blink, but here she was, cuddling up to my Angel as if it were her favourite activity.

"Briella! Here!" Gaar hollered from the back in an annoyed tone.

The dog sent Violet a longing look and nuzzled her with her snout one last time before sprinting to her owner.

The man who brought me back from the brink countless times and taught me how to manage my particular traumas. The one who rescued me in more ways than one and knew me better than anyone else alive.

The man who slowly weaselled his way into my heart by teaching me how to channel my demons. I never thought he had one himself until just a moment ago, when I saw the pain flashing in his eyes.

As I led Violet by the hand out of Gaar's shop, I looked back towards the doors and couldn't shake the feeling that this was an unofficial goodbye.

CHAPTER FIFTEEN

VIOLET

My hopes were not very high for our accommodations for the night as I looked at the outside of the inn. It was a small and old crumbling building made out of slabbed stone. But truthfully, after the day I'd had, anything with a bathing room and a bed would do.

Maybe even just the bed.

Xander hadn't spoken since we left Nygaard's shop. I asked him if he was okay, but he was uncharacteristically somber and demure. I didn't like the slight hunching of his shoulders and the faraway look in his eyes, as if he was deep in thought. It kind of made me want to wrap him up in a hug and not let go until he was acting like himself again.

I knew within a few seconds that there was something going on between Xander and Nygaard. It was written all over the lingering glances and loaded words they exchanged. Where my understanding stopped was when my name entered the conversation.

'Have you forgotten your place already, Ponce?'

'My place has merely shifted.'

What was written between the lines in everything they said?

Xander wordlessly whisked us to this inn once we were outside the shop. Judging by the look of the dark and vacant village we were in, this was still the Soothsayer sector, but there was no real way for me to tell.

Xander opened the door, holding it for me to enter first.

The space was surprisingly homey, run-down as it was. There was a large fireplace made out of the same stone as the building, with a few tables and chairs filling the small room in front of it. Along the back wall toward the left was a wooden counter with a small, hunched man standing behind it, writing in a notebook.

He looked up upon hearing the door close and immediately straightened.

"Hello there. How can I help you two tonight?" His voice was high-pitched and weasley.

Xander spoke in that refined way of his, weaving a subtle hint of mockery into his tone. "We will be needing two of your finest rooms, please."

The man, Darin, according to the small sign on his desk, shook his head.

"Unfortunately, sir, we only have one room available tonight. I am terribly sorry for the inconvenience."

Despite his words, Darin was clearly trying to figure out why we needed separate rooms as his eyes flicked between us.

"There is not a single person in here. How is it possible you only have one room?" I asked, a little annoyed with the prospect of having to share a room with Xander.

Not that I cared about sharing a bed with him—although the giant probably would take up the entire thing. I was just craving some time alone to digest everything that had happened.

He cleared his throat. "Well, mi lady, we have only four rooms in total, and three of them are already occupied. The guests have already turned in for the night."

I looked at Xander, exasperated, but quickly lost sight of why when I saw the blood-chilling expression on his face. His chin was turned down, mouth firmly set, and jaw clenched. But more so than any of that, were his *eyes.*

The entirety of his irises had turned black. The stark contrast to his usual vibrant green was absolutely harrowing as his gaze bore into Darin, who suddenly became impossibly still.

Xander spoke, and his voice was full of shadows; somehow bold and a whisper at the same time.

"Tell the truth."

The man was still unmoving, but his eyes carried the same look of admiration that Archi's had when Xander put a Soothe on him. "I am, sir," Darin confirmed in a strained voice. "There truly is only one room."

"Whaaat the fuck," I let out under my breath, rocking back on my heels slightly. Watching the mind control in action was extremely unnerving.

Xander straightened and blinked. When he opened his eyes, they were back to their normal color, and I openly gaped.

"What?" he asked casually, as if he hadn't just morphed into what I imagined a prince of Hell to look like and then back to normal in the blink of an eye.

"Your eyes...just turned...black," I uttered incredulously.

"They did?" he asked, and for a second, my heart clutched– until he smirked.

Xander looked back at Darin. "If there is only one room, then that's what it'll have to be."

Darin led us through an archway by the fireplace to our room. It wasn't anything special, but it would more than suffice for one night. The bed was bigger than expected, and there was actually a two-seater sofa adjacent to it. The one door in the room led to a bathing room with a toilet and a tub–no shower, but at least there was running water.

As soon as Darin left, Xander retrieved our things from what-ever pocket dimension he was storing them in and immediately went to freshen up. I was still a little caught off guard by his mood, but I used the opportunity to think of all the questions I wanted to ask Xander.

Starting with his eyes turning fucking *black*.

I was sitting on the couch with my mental list, and a cup of peppermint tea Darin brought when Xander emerged from the bathing room.

I couldn't stop myself from staring at him. His hair was damp and messy from being towel dried, forming a tumbled crown around his head. He wore loose pants and a black long-sleeved shirt that hugged the swell of his biceps, leaving little to the imagination.

"I told you once already. Don't look at me like that, Violet," Xander warned with a husky voice, glowering at me from across the room.

I blinked and stopped my ogling. "I don't know what you're talking about."

"You're going to pretend that you're not over there practically undressing me with your eyes?"

Arrogant prick.

I rolled said eyes. "You have a majorly overinflated sense of my attraction to you."

I tried to be as convincing as possible, but I worried my thundering pulse would give me away. I still wasn't sure if he could hear it with his elevated senses or not. Judging by the way his gaze snagged on my neck, I guessed the answer was probably yes.

"Is that so?" he asked, raising his chin slightly, causing his jawline to flex.

I did my best to cover up the way my stomach did a little flip, forcing my face into a mask of indifference.

"Yes."

He smirked, and his green eyes twinkled intensely as he teased, "Keep telling yourself that, Angel."

He walked toward the door and spoke over his shoulder. "I'll be back in a few hours. You should rest; tomorrow will be a long day."

And then he was gone. I continued staring at the door with my questions on the tip of my tongue, feeling unmistakably alone.

Isn't that what you wanted?

I groaned at my internal contradictions and moved to the bath, making quick work of washing away the day's sweat and dirt.

I really enjoyed the time we'd spent in the...what had Xander called it? A timber town? Regardless, it was a lot of fun—even though I sweated my ass off in the process. I was glad to have finally bathed, feeling much more grounded now.

I climbed out of the tub, eager to get into my night clothes and into bed. I never understood how people could enjoy soaking in the tub for extended periods without showering first.

Why would you want to float there like a carrot in a stew of dirt?

I shook myself at the thought, moving past it to more important things. Like when the fuck I was going to get home.

Even though I was growing a *little* attached to Xander, I ached to be back in Armantrea, where things were familiar and I could see Archi's face again. I wanted to know how this time difference worked–how much longer I'd been gone to him.

A week? Ten days?

I plopped into bed, irritated that Xander ran off without letting me ask him any questions. Although, it was probably for the best because I wouldn't have been able to hold off asking him about Nygaard. I didn't think now was the best time for that, considering that they'd just had a falling out.

Or was it a breakup?

Whatever it was, it really wasn't any of my business. Even though the thought of Xander with that burly, intense man caused multiple reactions inside my body–

Nope. Not going there.

I rolled over in bed and tried to bring my mind back to the mission. I was worried about Mr. Berger and his safety, of course, but I still felt a sense of dread at how easy this could have been if he were just home that day. I could have gotten the Chalice immediately and been done with it.

How selfish can you be?

Instead of thinking about how his absence inconvenienced me, I should only be worried about his well-being. And I was–I had thought about it many times in the days since, but the deeply rooted sensation of homesickness I was feeling took over everything else.

I just couldn't look past the desire to get back to Archi and our little home. I missed his company, his laugh. The way the corners of his mouth twisted down when he was concentrating on a painting. I craved his freshly baked sourdough bread so badly–I could practically taste it.

The phantom taste remained as the day's exhaustion caught up with me and I finally drifted off to sleep.

☽

THE WIND WHIPPED AGAINST MY FACE BEHIND THE deep hood drawn over my head. I was standing in an unfamiliar, dimly lit alleyway between two dilapidated brick buildings.

I didn't have any control over my limbs–they were moving entirely of their own accord. Crumpled in my right fist was the collar of a woman's jacket. I lifted a shining metal object–a knife– that glinted in the moonlight.

An expression of terror crowded her slim face, with tears shining behind her brown eyes as she pleaded, "Please, I will do anything! Have mercy, please! I am pregna–"

Her words sputtered out into a wet, gurgling noise.

The last thing I saw was the black knife handle as it protruded out of the woman's neck and blood beginning to gush out around the hilt.

I shot out of bed, gasping to get air into my lungs. It took a second to remember where I was, but as I looked around the room, reality slowly started to set back in.

You are in Cavell, at an inn.

You were just dreaming.

You didn't do anything to that woman.

As I tried to reconnect with myself, images from the dream

kept flashing in my mind. The crumbling brick wall. The tears streaking down the woman's golden skin.

The blood.

Bile rose in my throat, and I sprinted to the bathing room, barely making it in time. After I emptied my stomach into the toilet, I leaned my back against the wall to my right, braced my elbows on my knees, and put my head in my hands.

I breathed in slow and deep for a count of four, and out for a count of six. The calming mechanism Archi taught me shortly after I met him immediately began to do its job, slowing my heart rate and bringing me back to reality. The knife flashed in my mind again.

'Please, I will do anything.'

I leaned over the toilet again, and suddenly, there was a large, warm hand gathering my hair at the nape of my neck and another rubbing soothing circles on my upper back.

Once I was sure it was over, I sat back and looked at Xander. His beautiful black hair was tousled from sleep, making him look kind of...adorable.

He reached out and tucked a strand of hair behind my ear, brushing my cheek lightly with his thumb. His eyes scanned my face for a few moments before he disappeared and returned in a second, handing me a damp washcloth that smelled of lavender. I blotted my face with it, desperately trying to cool my cheeks down as they began to heat with shame.

He seemed to sense my embarrassment, though, and admitted, "I used to have night terrors almost every night. For years."

He spoke very softly and openly, inviting me to trust in him and what he was saying. I had never seen him look so genuine or vulnerable. The sight pulled heavily at my heartstrings, and that's when I knew I was entering dangerous territory.

I needed to get my shit together before I started to care too much.

"What were yours like?" I cringed at how my voice came out– all weak and wobbly.

He grimaced and shifted so that he was sitting with one leg up, his arm hanging loosely off of it by the elbow. "Oh, absolutely horrendous. Sometimes they would replay the worst things that have ever happened to me, repeatedly. Others were my biggest fears. Most often, though, they reminded me of the worst acts I've committed in my life."

I wondered what he could have done that was so horrible that it plagued his nightmares.

"I still get them sometimes," he admitted hesitantly, like he was cautious of revealing too much.

My heart rate was slowly returning to normal with the living, breathing distraction in front of me occupying my thoughts.

He was so ridiculously beautiful that even sitting on the tiled floor in his night clothes, he may as well have been wearing a tailored suit. Illogically, his disheveled hair only made him look more decadent, making me wonder how it would feel to run my fingers through it.

The moonlight coming through the window made the green of his eyes stand out against his pale skin as they focused intently on my face. I could see the pain in them, and I suddenly wanted to know every struggle, every hardship that made such a brilliant color so sad.

"I know that I should be distancing myself..." His voice was barely a whisper. "But *fuck*. You keep looking at me like that, and it's getting harder to remember why."

The breath I took didn't seem to go anywhere.

I should not have asked the question, the situation being what it was, but when has that ever stopped me?

"Why should you distance yourself?"

Because the reality of it was, even though I knew that there were roughly twenty-eight million different red flags about this man–namely the kidnapping and constant threats–I couldn't find it in me to listen to them. I was intrinsically attracted to him, regardless of the things he'd done and the shit that constantly spewed out of his mouth. And the fact that he had been intentionally keeping space between us meant something to me. I just wasn't sure what yet.

Xander spoke in a bitter, self-loathing tone. "I'm not good, Violet. I've done things so terrible that I don't think your beautiful human mind could even begin to dream them up." When he finished, Xander looked into my eyes again, as if he could see directly through them, into my brain and soul in a way no one else ever had.

"You have absolutely no idea what things I've seen. Don't project your idea of a typical human life onto mine because, I swear, it doesn't even come close to reality."

He regarded me from head to toe and back again, before saying, "You're right. I don't know what you've been through. What I do know is that being with me would only bring you more darkness and hardship–that is a fact. If you were smart, you would take that warning seriously."

I squinted my eyes, picking over everything he'd said. Nothing he had done thus far indicated that he was the type to care about me getting hurt. So, either he was lying about his motivations, or it was something else.

I shouldn't even care if he wanted me or not, considering that as soon as we found this Chalice, I would never see him again. But I couldn't shake the feeling that he *did* want me and was just trying to pull some martyr bullshit.

I was having absolutely none of that.

Plus, he was outrageously sexy, and it had been too long since I had taken anyone to bed.

"How about we say, for argument's sake, that I'm *not* smart?"

Xander was silent for a few moments, looking at the night sky through a small circular window with his jaw clenched tightly. He apparently came to a conclusion because he stood and helped me up before guiding me back to the bed with a soft hand on my lower back. After I sat down, I couldn't stifle the small disappointment that I felt when he walked back across the room and sat down on the couch.

He didn't speak for what felt like a long time, and when he did, it came out sounding strained. "There is still a lot you don't know, Violet. About how my world works, yes, but also about me. It wouldn't be fair to you."

"So just fucking tell me!" I breathed in a quiet tone. "You want to talk about *not being fair to me?* How about being dragged on this stupid dead-end mission against my will and still not knowing most of what's going on?"

He gave a resigned sigh and ran a hand down his face. "You're intolerable, you know that? Lilliana will have my head for this."

I should have realized it sooner–I still knew so little about him, about this society, because he was under gag orders from that frigid wench. The immediate spark of anger I felt toward her was cut short by Xander speaking.

"There was a time when all of Cavell was united under one territory. There were no separate sectors; everyone lived in harmony with each other. But, shortly after our creation, a plague spread throughout Cavell. No one could figure out the cause of it for over 40 years."

I was hanging onto every word, absorbing any and all information Xander was giving me.

"People slowly started losing their magic all across the continent. It always started small, being unable to cast protection wards and the like. Eventually, they would become entirely cut off from their magic.

"But you see, that is one of our life sources. "

Xander stopped talking and clenched his right fist so tightly that I worried his nails would puncture the skin, but then he opened it and an iridescent green fog floated upward out of it, molding into a figure eight shape. The mist flowed from one point to the next in a glistening, never-ending cycle that I couldn't look away from.

He continued talking while following the movement of the life source paradigm with his index finger. "Magic cannot exist without us, and therefore, we cannot exist without magic. When one is cut off..." He sliced a finger directly through the middle of the loops, separating them. "The other dies."

The once-flowing symbol deflated without any sort of shape, filling the air with limp and purposeless smoke.

Xander continued, "The Astrale population was already so small to begin with that our numbers were dwindling dangerously low. But, when Katerina reached her one hundred and fourteenth year, she finally figured out what was causing the curse–the Commixing of different elemental Cores."

He merely looked at it, and the smoke in front of him warped into five separate glowing orbs, each made of a different swirling color: celeste blue, evergreen, brilliant white, pearly iridescent, and, the most captivating of them all, an ever-changing black. Some streaks within the darkest orb were pure, all-encompassing black, while others varied to a deep gray.

This was true with all of the globes. As the smoke ebbed and flowed, the colors morphed, never to be the exact same shade again.

I opened my mouth to ask what the different Cores were and which color they correlated with, but he swept a lazy hand through the demonstration, making it disappear completely, and spoke before I could get the chance.

I swallowed my frustration so that I could at least absorb the information he *was* giving me.

"When two Astrales are in love and together for a significant length of time, their very souls begin to meld together. So, if they have different elemental Cores, it creates chaos and confusion in their ability to siphon.

"In the early days of our existence, Astrales didn't always know what true Cores they possessed. Life was very different then, and it wasn't always obvious what source of siphoning presented with which abilities. Katerina sacrificed all of her power, therefore her life, in order to create a tool to distinguish one basic Core from another, so that we could establish a society that would prevent the plague from ever returning."

Xander shifted, sitting up straighter. "So from there, they drew the lines, created provinces for each Core, and filled them accordingly, which have remained so to this day. We still communicate and collaborate with one another, but we now keep things much more separate."

My head was spinning like a top, and it took a few blinks before I even began to process everything that he had explained. Meanwhile, Xander was regarding me coolly with an unreadable expression on his face.

After a few moments, I asked, "So basically, it's outlawed to marry somebody outside of your sector?"

He nodded in confirmation.

"That's pretty fucked up," I stated blankly. "I mean, even if differing Cores were the cause of the plague, couldn't they have found some other way around that?"

Xander's lips slipped into that annoying smirk, and his eyes twinkled. "Yes, little human, that's exactly what they did."

He leaned forward, resting his elbows on his knees and clasping his hands in front of them. The sleeves of his shirt were pushed up to the elbows, exposing his forearms, and my eyes snagged on the slightly protruding veins running from his knuckles all the way under the sleeves of his shirt.

Xander's voice broke the slight trance, bringing my gaze back to his face.

"If someone falls in love with an Astrale of a different sector, they may marry and live together, but only if one renounces their true Core entirely, cutting off that part of their soul forever. A ritual is then performed between the couple in which half of one's magic is transferred to their partner. The couple emerges from the ceremony bound together emotionally and magically, but, as a whole, they only have half of their original access to magic.

"Because of that, and the pain that comes from casting away your true Core, it is done very rarely."

I scooted forward so that I was sitting on the end of the bed.

"Okay, that makes sense, I guess. But what about their family? And their friends? Do they get to see them again?"

"That is yet another reason why it is performed so infrequently. The non-native Astrale may communicate with their family and friends and have them visit on occasion, but it is highly frowned upon that they ever return home permanently. Even if they did, it isn't likely that their community would welcome them back. Deserters are not highly regarded by their home sector."

His tone gave me a good idea of what horrors that entailed.

"So even if the couple wants to get divorced or the nonnative's spouse dies, they can never return home?" I asked incredulously.

Xander gave a solemn nod. "I'm not saying that I agree with it. But the argument is that if it weren't that way, if anyone could desert and then return as they please, it would create chaos. The governors fear that it could even cause the curse to return."

There were a few moments of silence while I tried to wrap my head around a society that worked this way. To have to choose between home and love, knowing that you could never return for fear of being persecuted by your former peers or government...it seemed so archaic. And unnecessary. If this plague was simply caused by mixing Cores, it seemed that there had to be a better solution to preventing it.

Why do I even care?

"I appreciate the lesson on your society's dynamics," I started, and for once, I wasn't being sarcastic in the slightest. I truly did feel like I had a better grasp of the way things work in Cavell, which was something that had been sorely lacking.

"But what does this have to do with us?" I asked, utterly confused about how this conversation had turned into one of marriage and magical sacrifice.

Xander cocked his head to the side and raised his eyebrows. "I won't speak for you, but I'm not particularly fond of the idea of slowly losing my magic until my body starts feeding on itself." He made a distasteful face. "Doesn't seem all that enjoyable."

"Right, well, as you love to point out–I'm human. So I still don't see how any of that relates to what you said before."

He laughed under his breath and stood up, walking toward me slowly. "Oh, yes, you certainly have the most human characteristics of anyone I have ever met."

He stopped walking and stood before the bed, absolutely towering over me, and placed the tip of his pointer finger on the wall of my sternum, right above my cleavage. The contact sent a little jolt through me.

"But, in here?" Xander tsked. "No, I don't think you are human at all."

CHAPTER SIXTEEN

VIOLET

"I mean truly, Violet. You couldn't have expected a *human* was randomly chosen to create artifacts with magical abilities."

Not wanting to give Xander the satisfaction of making me angry, I attempted to keep a neutral expression. But try as I might, I felt my face redden against my will.

"It's not that I have anything against humankind in general," he admitted with a softer tone, pulling a scoff out of me. "It just isn't possible that someone without any Astrale blood could do what you can."

I sat there trying to wrap my head around what he was implying, but every time I imagined my parents as Astrales, my mind capped out.

They were so ordinary. Xander had to be wrong.

What if they weren't actually–

Nope.

I cut my own thoughts off, unwilling to open that door. It wouldn't do me any good. Plus, Xander's claim was baseless and didn't make any sense. If I were a magical being, I would have discovered it by now.

"Okay, whatever. So you think I'm not human." I threw my hands up in a 'why not' gesture, emphasizing its absurdity. "But I still don't see how it explains why you have to keep your distance. Or why you won't just get in the bed. It's not like I'm going to fucking jump you."

I saw every part of Xander tense up, his shoulders tightening and his jaw working overtime.

His voice dropped an octave when he spoke. "If I get in that bed with you..." His eyes flicked down to my exposed legs. "It's already taking everything I have not to come over there and make you forget about every single thing except for the feeling of my lips against you."

I swallowed thickly as the intent of his words sank in.

"Besides." He shrugged. "I don't have to sleep every night."

"What?" I asked, entirely distracted from his earlier statement. "How often do you sleep?"

He chuckled at my shock. "Every two or three days, depending on how much energy I use."

Um, wow. Okay.

"Is every Astrale like that?" I asked in wonderment, thinking of how much more I could get done if I only slept that much.

"No, that's just me," he said, smiling with bitterness. "I'm special."

"Why are you special?" I asked carefully, trying to get him to admit to me that he had access to more than one Core.

After hearing his explanation of the different Cores, I was even more curious about how in the hell he was able to use more than one magic.

Maybe he was a child of two runaways from different sectors?

"Trust me, Angel. You don't want to know the answer to that question." His voice sounded so flat and far away, his eyes gone to whatever memories flashed in his head.

I intentionally kept my voice from rising when I asserted, "Maybe you should stop assuming what I do and don't want."

Xander looked at me fiercely before he stood and prowled to the bed. He sat down to my right, against the headboard, and kept his distance.

"I do know something you want for certain," he purred with a sultry tone.

I spun around to face him, still sitting at the end of the bed. "And what might that be?"

"Three questions," Xander offered with a smirk. "I will give you three questions that I have to answer, no matter what."

I felt a rush of excitement, thinking this was too good to be true. Instead, I forced myself to take a moment to contemplate which questions were the most important, not wanting to waste this opportunity.

"Take your time," Xander remarked with amusement. "This is a very serious decision."

I threw up a middle finger in his direction.

Ignoring Xander's mocking smile, I finished up my decision. "How does the time difference work between Cavell and Armantrea?"

"Nice," Xander nodded with a smile in response to my question.

"Thanks," I said, flipping my hair behind my shoulder jokingly. "I pride myself on practicality."

Xander let out a small laugh, the sound warming me within. I hadn't heard that since we were jumping on the barrier.

God, was that only yesterday?

"The answer to that is pretty simple. For every hour here, there are eight hours there."

"What?!" I asked shrilly, my heart beginning to pound. "Time moves eight times as quick–"

"Careful," Xander interrupted. "You just used your second question. Are you ready to use all three?"

He had a shit-eating grin on his face that made me scowl. The goading bastard thought he was *so* clever.

I bristled and tried to refrain from doing the mental math of how long I had already been missing from Archi's life. I had to focus on using my last remaining question wisely. I decided to go for something that I couldn't see Xander answering willingly anytime soon after what went down in Nygaard's shop.

"Why are Nygaard's eyes red?" I asked, noting the way his smile fell away completely.

"What do you understand about Soothsayers, Violet?" Xander asked me in return.

"Um, nothing," I said incredulously.

I mean, seriously, did this man want me to stab him?

"Oh, come now," he goaded. "Don't speak so carelessly. You know that they are able to control the minds of others. You saw it in action just last night with the innkeeper. What you don't know is *how.*"

"You're so annoying," I muttered, sick of his technicalities and suddenly exhausted. I lay down on the bed, looking up at the ceiling as he spoke.

"And you're repetitive," Xander shot back, but there was a smile in his voice as he spoke. "Each Core draws on the essence of something that is naturally occurring. The Terrala channel nature and its produce–trees, plants, the soil, and so on. Astrolites' magic is a function of the stars. The Hydroseis possess water magic, and the Mistrals, wind.

"Soothsayers are different. They are the only Astrales that draw on an aspect of humanity."

"Humanity?" I asked. "As in–humans?"

Xander smiled smugly. "Yes and no. Just because Astrales are immortal does not mean that we do not have humanity."

"So you're done with your technicalities and limited-question nonsense?" I asked, referring to the fact that he let my extra question slide. Not that it should have even counted to begin with.

"I'm feeling benevolent. But that will stop if you continue to interrupt me."

I screwed my lips shut, emphasizing that I was ready to listen.

Xander smirked in response. "Humanity is not a reflection of one's external self–it is in reference to the inner workings of their mind and soul, both light and dark. Soothsayers specifically draw on the darkness of human nature, using that energy to create various magics."

I pondered that concept for a minute, tossing it around in my brain. I struggled to fully grasp what he was saying, but the general idea did make sense to me.

"Okay, I see what you're saying." I was lying on my right shoulder now, looking up at him where he was still sitting. "Now, will you answer my question about his eyes?"

"Patience," Xander scolded, booping a finger on my nose and making me scoot farther away from him. "Some soothsayers have to take things another step further than that. It is not something that one is born with, rather something that they acquire over time–an inability to access that part of themselves...of their souls. They need a separate entity to bridge the gap between themselves and their Core."

"What do you mean? What part of themselves?"

"It is hard to put a single answer to that." Xander shifted so that he was half-lying on his side, leaning on an elbow and facing me.

Unwanted butterflies hit my abdomen.

"Some describe it as a lack of humanity. Others say that they can feel it, but it is at a distance. Like it is simmering below the surface, just out of reach. That is where the bridge comes in." Xander was quiet for a few moments, looking down at me like he was intentionally adding suspense to his lesson on Soothsayers.

"Did you know that water holds memories?" he finally asked, throwing me off guard.

I shook my head.

"Within each drop of water, there is evidence of the places it has been. And what is the largest component of blood?"

"Water," I murmured mindlessly, connecting the dots in my brain.

Xander nodded, looking out the window. I wondered what he was thinking about. "Because of that, your blood holds a part of you within it–the places you've been, the things you have felt. So, when a Bloodletter drinks a person's blood, that small part of their soul acts as a tether to their own humanity and allows them to access their Core once more."

I was quiet for a beat, trying to decide how I felt about the fact that I had just met someone who drinks blood. Xander was gauging my reaction, looking down at me with contemplation.

"So," I started. "Nygaard drinks people."

Xander was still laughing as he said, "First of all, that is not a polite way to phrase it. Gaar is a *Bloodletter*. Secondly, stop using his full name. It's weird."

"It's not weird," I protested. "I don't even know him. Why would I use his nickname?"

He rolled his eyes at me. "Yes, Gaar is one of the Soothsayers who has to bloodlet to maintain access to his Core. That might make it seem like he has lesser power than those that don't, because he needs a separate entity to activate it, but it is quite the opposite."

"How so?"

"Well, think of it like a dam in a river," Xander explained. "A free-flowing river typically has a strong current that is uninterrupted. This would imply that a river which is dammed has less of an impact, as far as currents go."

He reached for my right hand, startling me with his touch, and ran his finger over the juncture of my thumb and my palm absentmindedly, distracting me from his words.

"But think of all the pressure that is building up behind that dam. When a crack appears, the water breaks through with more velocity than the first river's current could ever hope for."

I was smiling by the time he finished. Xander looked over at me with a crooked one of his own. "What are you smiling about?"

"Someone told me that you have a knack for dramatics," I murmured. "I'm starting to see why."

"I am not dramatic! I am *emphatic*," he insisted.

"Mhm, sure," I murmured, forcing my lips straight and closing my eyes. "Keep telling yourself that."

I started to let sleep overtake me, slipping blissfully into that state of in-betweenness, when a thought occurred to me.

I looked over to see Xander still beside me, sitting up against the headboard of the bed with his eyes closed. His breathing was slow and even, but his face didn't resemble that of someone in rest. It looked somewhat pained, as if he was thinking about unfavorable memories.

"Are you asleep?" I whispered up to him.

"Yes," he grumbled, keeping his eyes closed.

"No, you're not," I countered.

He groaned and rolled his head to the side. "What is it?"

He may have sounded irritated, but his gaze was warm on me and made me feel something that I didn't want to focus on for too long.

"Are there bakeries here?" I asked him, and his face contorted in confusion.

"Yes, there are." He blinked at me. "Why do you ask?"

"I am craving carrot cake," I told him simply.

"A cake? Made out of vegetables? That sounds disgusting." Disdain filled his voice as he crinkled his nose in an annoyingly endearing way.

"Clearly, you've never had a carrot cake because if you had, you would never say such a thing. Especially if Archi were the one to make it." A sadness filled me as soon as I spoke the words, homesickness hitting me in the gut.

"Can I ask you something?" Xander adjusted so that he was leaning on his elbow nearest me. The movement brought those green eyes even closer to me, stealing all of my attention.

"Sure," I said slowly, a little on edge.

His eyes scanned my face as he posed, "Why 'Willow'?"

"Huh?" I asked, his question throwing me off guard.

"Why does Archi call you Willow?" Xander asked again, a definite sourness to his voice. "I'm not asking because I am jealous, if you were thinking that," he informed me with a smirk, but his eyes held a certain sadness. "Well, I was," he amended, "but it was because of the way you were looking at him. Like he was your family."

I remained speechless, my heart catching and then shattering a little when he added, "I've never had that."

He didn't have any family? At all?

I cleared the emotion away from my throat, anticipating him shutting me down if I tried to ask why. "We first met under a weeping willow–you know, the tree?" I asked, and he nodded. "He said that I reminded him of the branches because they were droopy and sad. I also refused to tell him my name and tried to ignore him, so he started calling me Willow."

Xander's face had the softest expression I'd seen on him yet, and I drank it in with my eyes. His brow smoothed out completely, his eyes relaxing as he looked off to the side, almost as if he were picturing the scene I had described.

But then he looked over and noticed me staring, and instantaneously strapped his mask back into place. He reached over and tucked my hair behind my ear–grazing my cheek lightly–before moving back to his original position against the headboard.

"Get some rest, little vixen," he commanded softly, letting his eyes fall shut again.

I did, but there was a cloud of sadness and unease over me as I drifted off.

What kind of hardships had Xander seen to make him end up this way?

$$\smile$$

XANDER

SOMETIMES, WHEN VIOLET LOOKED AT ME, IT WAS WITH an expression of such awe and admiration that everything else in the world slipped away, and all I could do was stare at her.

The first time that I saw it was also the first time that we met.

Before she knew anything about me or what I was there to do, she was staring at me like I was a natural wonder.

Her eyes drank in my size, as opposed to the way some people gawk and stare when first meeting me. And when they skirted up to my face and bore into my eyes like she could see right through them, all the way to my black fucking soul, I felt something inside of me shift.

I knew, in that moment, that I would do anything to see that look on her face again.

That was when she became my Angel, because of the serenity and admiration on her face when she looked at me.

Then, we got back to the Armoury and everything changed. Just like that, my Angel became a vixen with her sharp tongue and crass fucking attitude. It made me want to play with her until her defence mechanisms were all worn out, just to see that angelic expression arise again.

So, the other day–when I had my hold on her voice and was gripping her chin roughly, and her expression morphed from the previous fear and anger into that same utter peacefulness–I knew I was in deep shit.

My little vixen wanted to be dominated just as much as I wanted to dominate her.

Just the thought made my cock stiffen and strain against the waistband of my pants. I adjusted them and looked over at Violet, instantly regretting it.

She was lying on her side, facing me, the position making her generous breasts come close to spilling out of the tiny, strappy top she wore.

I groaned at the sight, pulling up the blanket to cover her before I did something stupid. I was careful to move slowly and set it down gently so that I wouldn't disturb her sleep.

I was enjoying watching her sleep more than I cared to admit. Her brown eyelashes fluttered lightly, brushing against her cheekbones and casting shadows there from the morning sun peaking through the blinds. Her face muscles relaxed completely, and those eyebrows that were raised eighty percent of the time finally settled into their natural position.

This was different to the last time I watched her sleep. That time she was fitful, tossing and turning constantly with worry etched on her face.

Now, she looked to be in utter peace and rest.

The sight stirred something primal inside of me. I would do anything and everything to ensure that she would always feel safe enough to reach this level of relaxation around me.

I used this opportunity to soak in everything about her without those sceptical eyes boring into me. Whenever my gaze lingered and Violet noticed, I could practically see the hair on her arms rising in defensiveness.

It was getting on my last nerve.

Everything about Violet looked so *soft*. Like I could sink into her and never want to leave.

Her shoulder-length, brown hair was spread on the pillow behind her, making the golden strands stand out among the darker ones. I looked to her left hand resting next to her head and studied the marking on her skin. It started on the side of her hand, near her pinky's knuckle, and moved up her wrist, wrapping around the side slightly. I followed the line of her arm up to her collarbone and studied another mark resting below it.

This one was much smaller, but I could not stop thinking about how familiar it seemed to me. The shape resembled something, but for the life of me, I couldn't figure it out.

Violet stirred, and I quickly averted my eyes in case she woke up. She'd already called me a stalker once, so I wanted to avoid getting caught while watching her sleep. She stayed asleep, but let out a small moaning noise in restlessness.

Oh. Fuck.

My entire supernatural sense of hearing zeroed in on the moan-like sounds coming out of her mouth, and my head swam.

I had to get the hell out of here.

I got out of the bed and grabbed some clothes to change into for the day, heading to the bathing room as quietly as I could.

I was about to fucking explode with the need to touch this woman, but I couldn't until I found some answers about if my Core would endanger her. Unfortunately, the only person who could get those for me was also the least likely to do anything to help me at the moment.

At that exact second, I felt Gaar's distinct presence pressing against the barrier of my mind.

Chills snaked down my spine.

This tended to happen a lot with Gaar. We would try to reach each other at the same moment in the day, or I would receive a message from him when I had been thinking about him a second earlier.

The thought sent a pang through me.

I opened myself up to him, knowing that he would want me to speak first, as per usual.

Yes, Gaar?

Your vessel has arrived.

And that was it. As soon as he'd arrived, he vanished.

I rolled my eyes at his pettiness, finishing buttoning my linen shirt before examining my hair in the mirror.

It was fine, albeit slightly dented, but that gave it an effortlessly-tousled look that I actually liked.

I peeked through the door and checked on Violet before leaving. She was lying there still, her chest rising and falling evenly and slowly as she snored quietly. I closed my eyes and imagined myself inside Gaar's shop, enjoying the bottoming out of my stomach as I switched planes.

That would never get old.

I used to be shackled, constantly kept in one place. While I was in captivity, there was a dimmer on my Core that limited my access to magic. I was never able to whisk until I was set free by Lilliana.

"You have those demons in your eyes again." Gaar's rich voice filled my ears and soul, pulling me out of that fucked up place like he had so many times in the past.

I smiled bitterly at him. "The only demon in this room is standing in front of me."

Usually, he would have at least cracked a small smile or snorted, but–if possible–his face closed off even more, reminding me of the space that existed between us now.

Gaar reached under the counter and pulled out the Memorium goggles before tossing them to me.

"That's it?" I asked, looking down at them. "Some super rare viewing vessel, and you just lob them across the room? They're not even in a box?"

"What do you want, a fucking bow?" he asked, scowling.

I shrugged. "I wouldn't mind a bow. They make things prettier."

I walked towards the door, wanting a cigarette before I left here.

"I know how you like pretty things," Gaar drawled, making me stop in my tracks. "Like that girl of yours. Although," he paused dramatically. "She doesn't need a bow to make her pretty, does she?"

I turned around slowly, promising him death with my eyes if he continued on this path.

"Stop trying to antagonise me," I warned with a low voice.

"Don't you remember?" Gaar asked, his lips curling into a sinister smile as he tipped his chin up and looked at me. "What's mine is yours."

"Not this time," I ground out. "Not anymore."

"Oh, is that so? And when exactly did you gain this new sense of authority towards me, hmm?"

"I will never share her. Not with you, not with anyone."

He smirked. "And if she wants to be shared?"

"You forget that I know how you like to take, and I know the way you do it. If you think you're getting anywhere *near* her..."

"Oh, you know quite well, don't you?" He stopped talking

and approached me. His slow, measured steps made my heart rate kick up a notch.

"You know what I think?" Gaar asked in a half-whisper. "I think that she *would* want my attention." He stepped up to me, trailing a finger along my jawline. "I think you've been so caught up in your incessant worries about your Core that you haven't even touched her yet. And I'd be willing to bet that she has begged you for it, if not with her words than with those big, big eyes."

My body stiffened.

"And you know what else I think?" he asked, leaning in to speak into my ear this time.

"I think that they would beg just as prettily for me, even if she *is* your *mate.*"

I growled deep in my chest, grabbing Gaar by the neck and slamming him into the ground below us. I kept him pinned with a knee digging into his chest and punched him across the face once before I pulled back, shocked to find him laughing.

"Oh, you are so predictable, Ponce. It's refreshingly linear."

I pushed off him, irritated that he'd gotten the better of me so easily.

Just the thought of him touching her, of him getting close to what is mine...I wanted to pound his skull into the hardwood floor.

Hearing those words spoken out loud did things to me.

My mate.

I wanted to go back to her and mark her as mine, but I wouldn't jeopardise her safety. Typically, us having different Cores wouldn't be a concern because of the fact that we are mates, but my Core isn't normal.

"Are you saying that I can touch her?" I asked him in a low voice, still breathing through my anger.

He sat up halfway, still chuckling a little bit. "I don't have the slightest clue. It's not like they made a rule book on your situation."

I scowled down at him, resisting the urge to kick him in the ribs.

"Just do it," he said dismissively.

A big part of me wanted to do just that, but I couldn't ignore my anxiety about the potential danger. Not when it involved her.

Gaar sighed. "Xander. Why would you be mates if your Core was going to hurt her? She is just a human anyway, so how could it?"

I kept quiet, not ready to unload everything that came along with that fact being wrong.

"Ah, I see," Gaar mused, standing up and brushing off his slacks. "The human isn't a human after all." He chuckled. "And so the plot thickens."

I grabbed him by his collar, hauling him to me. "Don't be a fucking prick. Just tell me what you think–you're the only one that I can ask who knows about my Core."

He looked down at my hands in a haughty way, telling me to remove them with his eyes. When I didn't, he grabbed my wrists and tugged them down before tossing them back at me.

"Figure it the fuck out," Gaar spat. "*'Not anymore'*...remember?"

His eyes gave me a final appraisal before he turned and disappeared into the back of his shop, leaving me staring at the space he had just occupied.

It seemed fitting that this was where it would end, considering that it was also the first place we had ever met.

I whisked myself out of the shop, leaving everything there behind as I went. I had something more important to focus on now.

My mate.

CHAPTER SEVENTEEN

VIOLET ~ AGE SIXTEEN

My chest felt hollow and swooping, like my soul was reaching out to something I would never be able to find. I craved fulfillment, but there was no way to know what would satiate me. It was a potent, restless uncertainty.

I wanted something, but I couldn't put my finger on what it was.

I was filled with so many potential answers–pottery, reading, writing in my journal, baking with Archi–but no matter what I tried, dissatisfaction filled me after a few minutes.

I was so discontent and miserable that I began to pace. I would probably look like a madwoman if anyone saw me, but I couldn't find it in me to care.

All I could think was:

When will this end?

I didn't want to feel this way any longer. I didn't want to be like this. I wanted to smile and laugh and enjoy the chance at life that I'd been given. But how the fuck was I supposed to do that when I was lacking in this way?

How could I use this opportunity to the best of my ability when my enjoyment of that ability was hindered?

How do I make it stop?

To be honest, I thought a lot about dying at that stage of my life. I wondered if that would be the solution to my answers, but I always came to the same conclusion.

What good would that do me now?

I knew that I was going to die eventually. Obviously–everyone does.

So, why should I have been in a rush to get there?

But on days like this one, when I felt like I could run every inch of the planet and still have a gaping, empty space in my chest...the waiting period felt like too much.

I left my bedroom for the first time that day, figuring that I should probably eat something. It was late afternoon, and while my stomach had been protesting its emptiness, I had this inexplicable inability to put food in my mouth when I was in the Void.

The second I did, it turned to ash and made me want to vomit.

I sighed, heading to the stove and seeing some eggs that had been scrambled by Archi hours ago, when he knocked on my door and told me that he'd left some for me. They were dried out, crumbling, and looked downright disgusting, but I wasn't about to make something else.

I mean, please. The *effort* that would take.

"Willow?" Archi asked in a quiet voice, approaching me from behind.

"Yeah?" I questioned.

"How're you doing?" His voice seemed timid, like he was approaching a wounded animal. The thought made me want to laugh, if laughing were within reach today.

"I'm fine," I assured him, not willing to expel the energy it took to convince him any further.

"Okay," he said, still in that careful way.

A few seconds passed, and I turned the stove on to heat the eggs back up.

"Those are hours old. Let me make you some new ones," Archi offered, reaching around me to grab the pan handle, but I jerked it out of reach.

"It's alright, Arch. It doesn't matter."

I stirred the eggs around with a wooden spoon.

"You'll get sick," he protested, reaching for it again.

"It doesn't fucking matter!" The words came out bitter and sharp as I snapped my head to look at him, hating myself as I watched him visibly flinch back and cast his eyes away.

Why am I like this?

He only wanted to help. But I couldn't explain to him the twisted logic behind not wanting to *be* helped.

I knew that I could be a bitch a lot of the time, but it was like something chemical would happen inside of me. I couldn't stop acting this way–lashing out at everyone around me, like they were responsible for the way that I felt.

Trust me–I tried.

I sighed, the knot in my gut growing with guilt. "I'm sorry, Archi. I just..."

"I know," he cut me off, stepping closer. "I understand, Violet. I just worry about you is all." His blue eyes were shining with emotion, locked intently on my face. "If I had seen half the shit you did, especially that young...I don't know how I would have turned out. You're the strongest person I know."

I swallowed back the words that sprung to mind, not wanting to have this debate with him for the hundredth time. I didn't feel strong, and didn't know how to tell him that every time he told me I was, it just made me feel like a fraud.

Strong people are those who rise from the ashes of their tragedies, not those who are barely scraping by, hardly finding the strength to force themselves out of their bedrooms to eat something. They're definitely not the ones who lash out at those they love most, digging their claws into them in an attempt to keep them close, but only ending up pushing them further away.

I put down the spoon and did something that I never did when I was in the Void. I walked over to Archi and wrapped my arms around him, bringing him in for a tight embrace.

"*Willow,*" Archi gasped out, but immediately returned my hug.

We stayed like that for a while, just supporting each other's weight. I tried to communicate to him without words that, even though it might not seem like it sometimes, I loved and appreci-ated him. I was eternally thankful for him, and the fact that he had wormed his way into my heart.

Even in the brief period when I tried to ignore his presence in the beginning, he still acted as if we had been friends our entire lives, talking until I was sure his voice would give out.

I even tried to ditch him once, like the fucking brat I was. I packed up my basket while he was asleep and tried to run away, but he somehow managed to find me, like always.

That was four years prior, and I still beat myself up over it regularly.

I squeezed Archi even tighter, knowing deep in my soul that if it hadn't been for him, I wouldn't have made it this far.

CHAPTER EIGHTEEN

VIOLET

I woke early the next morning to a symphony of loud, clashing noises, followed by a string of hushed obscenities and scuffling against the wooden floor of the room I was sleeping in.

I groaned and opened one eye to see Xander crouched on the floor, picking up an assortment of items he had evidently dropped.

"What. In. The. *Fuck.* Are you doing?" I asked him, opening my other eye to allow for the glare I shot his way.

"Well, good morning to you too," he responded while forming a pile of random shit on the small table next to the door.

There was a bag of apples, a small loaf of bread, three *rocks*—which were presumably what woke me up—a chunk of wood, some sort of eyewear, and a small humanoid figurine.

So fucking weird.

Why was he carrying all of this around?

"You'll get a 'good morning' out of me when you *don't* come crashing into my room, waking me up with less subtlety than a fucking *rooster,*" I muttered grouchily while sitting up slowly.

"I think you mean our room, Angel," he pointed out in an annoyingly bright tone.

Why was he so chipper?

"Anyway, while you were sleeping the day away—and snoring, might I add—I was out getting the missing piece we've been need-ing. You can thank me any time."

I scoffed and pushed the blanket off of myself, swinging my legs over the side of the bed and sitting. I've always had to do this in the mornings, waiting for a few moments before standing to prevent a head rush that sometimes caused me to faint.

"You've already been to see Nygaard?" I asked as I stood and walked over to him. "What time is it?"

Xander did that thing that he does when I say something that crosses him–his brows furrowed as he tilted his head back and scrunched up his nose–just a tad.

"I told you to stop using his full name. It's weird."

"You're weird," I snapped immaturely, not caring one bit. "Now, will you tell me what this thing even–"

I cut myself off as I saw the bag of apples out of the corner of my eye. Well, they weren't apples, actually.

"Are those peaches?" I asked a little breathlessly.

I hadn't seen peaches in years. Whenever my parent's friends would visit us, they would bring them as a gift. They had a son around my age, and we would always play together when they came to visit. He and I got along very well, constantly stirring up trouble that our parents would later chastise us for, but it never stopped us.

I looked forward to their visits and the peaches that always accompanied them. In fact, I loved them so much that my mother would slice and jar them so that I could enjoy them over months without the fruit going bad. My father even took to calling me 'Peach' as a nickname because of it.

But our friends stopped visiting us when I was around nine. Even after my parents died, I had no way to contact them, and I haven't seen them since. I wasn't ever able to find peaches in Armantrea, either.

It immediately pissed me off when I saw that Xander looked amused, but I stepped outside of myself for a second. He had no idea why I was reacting the way I was. It was unfair of me to hold that against him.

When Xander spoke, the smile was clear in his voice. "Yes. Would you like one?"

I hesitated for a few seconds and stared at the bag, unsure of what memories and emotions the taste would bring to the surface. There was no way I could turn it down, though. I would just have to deal.

I nodded and looked back at Xander, seeing that his expression had turned into one of curiosity and contemplation. He didn't voice whatever questions he had–just uncinched the sack and handed me a peach.

I took a bite out of it and closed my eyes, the sensations overwhelming me. I could practically see myself back at our old farmhouse, sitting on the porch and feeling the peach juice run down my wrist as it was right now. I could almost feel my mother's laugh traveling through me as the taste filled my entire being, transporting me to the past.

"This is a first," Xander stated, pulling me back to the present. "I've never witnessed an out-of-body experience brought on by fruit before."

"Happy to be of service," I muttered dryly.

I gestured to the pile of things he'd brought back. "What is all of that?"

"So glad you asked," he said, pointing at me. "I was momentarily distracted by the peach escapades. These," he started, gesturing to the rocks, "are apparatus stones. They each have different functions that I am not explaining to you right now," he added the last part just as I was opening my mouth to ask that very thing.

I promptly took another bite of the peach to cover it up, and tried to ignore the sensations so that I could listen to what he was saying.

"Bread." He held up the loaf, giving it a shake. "To eat."

He tossed it down and I rolled my eyes.

"Stop rolling those fucking eyes, little Angel," Xander

warned, a deep rumbling quality taking over the previously jovial tone of his voice.

"Stop calling me 'little', you patronizing prick," I leveled back.

Xander stepped forward–nostrils flaring–as his green eyes flashed viciously. I did my best to hide my smile at his reaction.

"Watch it."

I cocked my head. "Or what?"

My eyes tracked the way his tongue swept across his top teeth, his chest rising and falling in a slow, measured movement as he stared me down.

My heart began to pound.

Xander rolled out his shoulders, visibly shaking off the distraction. "The rest of the items are unimportant. But *these*," he picked up the eyewear from his haul and came to stand in front of me. "These are what we have been waiting for. The viewing vessel."

"Seriously?" I asked, unimpressed. "This is it?"

The vessel was a chunky, black garment with a strap that went around the back of your head and two entirely black lenses over the eyes.

"I know. I was unenthused too. You'd think that they would look less..."

"Frumpy?" I suggested.

Xander shrugged. "Sure, frumpy. No idea what it means, but that works. Now–where is the cube?"

I took the last bite of my peach and discarded the pit in the wastebin, washing my hands quickly to get rid of the sticky residue. I looked up at the mirror and groaned, seeing my hair in total disarray.

Whatever.

I didn't even bother trying to tame it before I fished the cube out of the small pocket within my bag and brought it over to Xander. He took it from me and turned the goggles over, slipping the cube into a small slot on the underside.

"Now what?" I asked, sitting down on the couch.

"When you put the goggles on, your entire vision will be cast into the encased memory. But you can only use a cube once, so we'll have to be methodical about this."

"Okay, got it." I reached into my bag and grabbed my journal and a pen. "Why don't you tell me what is happening as it happens, and I can write down some notes?"

"Oh, *I* won't be viewing the Memorium, Vi."

I stopped dead with my pen on the paper. "Excuse me?"

"You'll have to do it."

"And why is that?"

"Let's just say that the last time I tried to use a dated artifact, it didn't go very well. I personally think that they are resistant to extremely attractive and witty males, but it's definitely not something I care to repeat."

I marked the fact that he made a joke to smooth over actually telling me why he wouldn't do it.

I scowled up at him from where I was sitting, but didn't see much of an option. "Fine. I'll do it."

Grabbing the rather clunky pair of goggles, I settled myself into the cushions and took a deep breath.

It's just a memory.

I stole one more glance at Xander to find him observing me with his arms crossed. It made me squirm a bit in my seat as I searched for any logical reason to delay this.

Instantaneous migraine? Fainting spell?

"What's the holdup, precious?"

"Do not fucking call me *precious.*" I internally groaned when I saw the way his lips tilted and his eyes lit up.

Great.

He raised his annoyingly perfect eyebrows, awaiting an answer.

I didn't know what else to say, so the truth blurted out of me. "I don't love the idea of being completely vulnerable to you while I'm in this Memorium thing."

There was a long pause, and when I looked back at him, his

face looked open, like the facade had momentarily cracked and left him exposed. It was back within a blink, though.

"You are safe with me, Violet. I know you don't really know me, so it's not easy for you to trust my word, but there is no place safer for you than by my side."

I didn't know how to respond to that. Trust is not a concept that I've had much practice with.

Barring Archibald, there wasn't a person on this planet that I trusted enough to completely let my guard down around. I'd always suspected that my parents were hiding from someone when I looked back at it from an older age. They thought that we were tucked far enough away from the world that we were safe.

I learned from their mistakes.

There was also the fact that this man kidnapped me and repeatedly threatened me, all while refusing to tell me much of anything, that was holding me back a bit.

But, irrationally and irritatingly, my gut told me to trust him. That I would be safe with him. The first thing I learned when I began caring for myself was that I needed to trust my gut, so why would I stop now?

Unless he had some ability I hadn't learned about yet that could influence my instincts. There was still so much I didn't know about this world, Xander included.

His voice interrupted my contemplation. "I'll swear an oath."

"What do you mean?"

"In Cavell, an oath is a binding contract that can be officially written or verbal, though when verbal, it must be marked in a physical sense for both parties."

"Marked how?"

He shrugged. "However you please. Some people brand themselves, others are inked; very few intentionally scar their skin. As long as it is a physical marking that can be authenticated by a governor or governess, it qualifies."

"And what happens if you break an oath?"

"You die."

I swallowed thickly.

Surely, if Xander was willing to make a promise with these kinds of stakes, I could trust him to put on a pair of goggles in his presence. It couldn't hurt to be certain, though.

"Okay, yeah. What kind of oath were you thinking of?"

"How about," he cleared his throat and changed the pitch of his voice to be haughty and lofty. "*I hereby decree that Violet, the tiny, senseless, razor-tongued human, is under my protection?*"

"How about you go fuck yourself?"

He smirked, and his green eyes twinkled with mirth. "Only if you help."

I rolled my eyes even though my heart rate kicked up.

A memory of the way his mouth was curved into a smile as he adjusted my body against his abs sprung to mind.

He laughed a deep and hearty sound, as if he knew where my thoughts had gone, but then his expression turned serious.

"Truly though, jokes aside, I was thinking: *I swear an oath to you, Violet. To never harm you with malicious intent, and to disrupt the path of those who wish to.*"

I ran it over in my head a few times, making sure the wording checked out, silently thanking the plethora of fae novels I have read.

"And what exactly do you mean by the 'with malicious intent' part?" I asked.

His green eyes sparkled. "There are plenty of ways to have a bit of fun with pain, Vi."

Butterflies erupted in my stomach, both from his words and the suggestive tone he used to deliver them. I felt myself flush, but once I was sure I wasn't being tricked, I nodded.

"So, how do we officially write this thing?"

"Unfortunately, that takes a bit of time to organize," he explained, making me apprehensive. "It has to be done with the approval of a governess or governor, which requires the proper channels. We don't have the time for that, so it will have to be physically marked or we can proceed without the oath. It's your decision."

I stopped for a second, weighing my options.

Where was this even coming from? I'd slept in the same bed as this man, and now I wouldn't even put on a pair of goggles in front of him?

That's the thing, though—residual effects of trauma don't always make logical sense. Most of the time, they are rooted in specific scars on the soul, not specific circumstances.

"Okay, let's mark this thing then," I finally decided. "But I want ink—not a scar."

"I was hoping you would choose that," Xander said in an excited tone that had me raising my eyebrows. "What?" he asked. "I've been craving new ink."

"New?" I asked, unaware that he had any tattoos to begin with.

Xander smiled mischievously. "Oh, yes."

He unbuttoned his shirt quickly, and my stomach bottomed out when he let it slide to the floor.

Aside from the ridiculously chiseled muscles of his broad shoulders and arms, his chest was full and firm, drawing my eyes down to the ridges of his abdomen and the very distinct *V* carrying into his black pants.

Scattered all around his pale skin like patchwork were various tattoos, and my eyes skipped between them, trying to take in all of the different images and what they could mean.

There was one that seemed to be winding all around his body, a sort of dashed line that began on one wrist and wound up his arm, disappearing behind his shoulders and continuing down the other arm.

It seemed to unite all of the individual pieces, but one in particular—sitting directly over his heart—caught my eye.

It was a pair of shackles, united by a chain, that had small cracks running through them. The damage seemed to begin in the middle and funnel outward, slowly becoming less shattered as it reached the outside of the structure.

"You're drooling, Angel."

Xander's cocky voice jarred me out of my stupor, making heat rise to my face because of the way I had been unintentionally gawking at him.

"As if," I said half-heartedly.

What was with this man and his ability to reduce me to a blubbering mess?

"The blush on your cheeks suggests otherwise," he said with a laugh.

Xander reached down toward me and my body stiffened, anticipating his touch, but all he did was grab the pen sitting next to me on the couch.

"The *pen?*" I asked.

Xander shrugged. "Ink is ink."

He came to stand in front of where I was sitting, intimidating me with his height. "Where do you want it?" he asked me, his eyes skirting over my body.

I realized then that I had a lot of skin on display in my shorts and tank top. I probably should have changed out of my night clothes by now, but I couldn't be bothered.

"Here." I chose at random, pointing to the flat part above my elbow.

"Okay," he said, grabbing my arm and putting his thumb over the spot.

His other thumb covered the inside of his own wrist, the pen clutched in his grasp.

"Now put your other hand on me," he commanded. "We have to be joined during the recitation."

I placed my right hand on his thigh, which was the closest thing to me, and felt his muscles jerk at the contact.

I grinned smugly.

"Keep that hand fucking *still,*" he warned in a gravelly voice, closing his eyes.

As Xander spoke the oath aloud, I watched in wonder as the pen began to glow with a faint green light. The light funneled out of the spots Xander's thumbs were covering, and then I felt a distinct and bubbling *burn* on my skin before he released his hold.

I twisted my arm to look at the back of it, amazed by the intricate design that lay there now.

It was a winding and entwined shape, resembling the complicated macramé knots that I had seen sold at the market. The ink was black–thankfully–and stood out against my skin.

I grabbed Xander's hand and brought his wrist to me, comparing it to my own tattoo.

"They're the same," I observed out loud, looking between the two.

"It is customary that oath marks mirror each other. It symbolizes that we are both bound by this oath until the day one of us dies."

That was an intense sentence, reminding me of the seriousness of the situation.

Why did I make him do that when I had no intention of staying here?

I looked to Xander, who was staring down at our tattoos with a burning gaze, something shining on his face that I didn't understand.

Possessiveness?

It reminded me of our encounter with Shaed, when Xander snapped at him.

"Xander," I said in a low voice.

"Hmm?" he asked, still distracted by our markings.

"The goggles," I deadpanned.

"Right." He shook his head and retrieved the vessel and his shirt, slinging it around his shoulders but leaving it unbuttoned.

I consciously moved my gaze elsewhere.

He sat on the couch next to me, moving to put the goggles on my head but confirming with his eyes first that it was okay. When

I nodded, he slipped them on gently, stopping before they covered my eyes.

"I'll be here the whole time," he assured.

Then Xander brought the goggles all the way down, casting my entire vision in blackness before the image arose that would change my life.

Forever.

CHAPTER NINETEEN

VIOLET

The room was dark and unfamiliar.

It was a circular shape, with chairs lined up in rows, all facing the center of the circle. I looked up to see that the ceiling was made of glass, showcasing a sky full of stars. The room radiated an aura of solitude and peacefulness, leaving me puzzled by its emptiness.

What was the significance of this memory?

Xander's voice filled my head. *Be patient.*

I must've spoken that thought out loud.

A hushed voice echoed through the space. "Are you in here?"

My head turned on its own, looking toward an arched entryway. A woman walked through it and rushed to me, clasping my elbows and pulling me in for a tight embrace.

"I was so worried," she said, pulling back to look at me. "I got your message but thought you had already left."

The woman looked to be somewhere in her early thirties. She had tanned skin and her hair—so blonde it appeared almost white—was tied back in a tight ponytail, with the sides slicked down and the ponytail sitting at the nape of her neck. She wore a dress that was tailored perfectly to fit her body and shimmered slightly in the dim light.

"I am leaving Cavell—tonight." The male voice came from everywhere and nowhere all at once, scaring me before I realized that it was me speaking.

Well, not *me*, but the person whose memory I was inside.

"Is there not another way?" she asked in desperation.

"We both know that there isn't. She is the ticket."

"Please," the woman pleaded. "I'm sure that we can think of something else. Some way that you can stay here..." Her voice held a deep sense of hopelessness as she finished with, "This is your home."

The man let out a frustrated and pained sigh. "We both know what we want, and that there is only one way to get it." He ran a gentle finger over her cheekbone. "It must be made, and all other avenues have been exhausted. This is the only chance we will get."

She looked resigned, her face falling like she was about to cry.

Before she could speak again, the memory holder brought their foreheads together, whispering, "This is goodbye for now."

A moment later, the picture shifted, showing a quaint bathing room. I assumed the holder had whisked somewhere else. He was packing things into a bag frantically, moving as if the house was on fire and he needed to get out.

The holder suddenly stood and looked in the mirror before him.

The air inside my lungs fled in shock. My stomach churned.

The memory holder was my father.

CHAPTER TWENTY

VIOLET

I ripped the goggles off of my face, gasping for air and trying to understand what I had just seen and heard.

"Violet?"

I stood aimlessly, my knees and hands shaking, not knowing what to do with myself.

"*Violet*," Xander insisted, more harshly this time. He stood and grasped the sides of my face, angling my head up to look at him. "Breathe. Tell me what happened."

"Poppa." The name I used to call my father slipped from my lips in a whisper.

"You saw your father?" he asked softly, moving his hands down to my arms.

"The memory *was* my father's." I swallowed. "He looked in the mirror at the end. It was him."

I closed my eyes, the memory of his face sending a stabbing pain through my chest.

I had never admitted this out loud, but I didn't remember my father the way I remembered my mother. It was always like he was in the background of the few memories I had as a child. I remembered how I felt when I was around him—safe, loved, and determined to prove myself. But over time, his face had blurred in my mind. It was my mother's that I latched onto over everything else.

And I hated myself for it.

So now, seeing his face staring back at me was unlocking memories that I didn't even know I had of him.

Us standing on a mat in the yard while he walked me through the basics of fighting.

Me sitting in his lap as he read to me from a book.

Him smiling as Momma and I crafted a bowl, both of us covered in wet clay.

I've always remembered the similarities I had to my mother, mainly our eyes and hair. But how I had forgotten that I carried my father's stubborn jaw, too?

"Violet," Xander said again, jostling me slightly. "What else happened in the memory? Were you anywhere that you recognized?"

I shook my head distractedly. "No. It was just a circular room with a lot of chairs. The room was really dark, but the ceiling was made of glass. I could see the stars."

"I know it," Xander stated, his tone darkening. "You saw a room in the Astrolite headquarters."

My breathing felt too thin, like I couldn't get enough air suddenly.

"There was a woman there. She looked to be the same age as my father–early thirties. She was blonde."

I broke free of Xander's hold, suddenly needing to move. I paced to the couch and began grabbing clothes out of my bag.

My father was in the Astrolite district. Talking to a woman who was very much not my mother. About how he needed to leave.

As in, leave from the Astrolite district, assuming Xander was correct.

'She is the ticket.'

What did that *mean?*

"Violet," Xander quietly uttered, approaching me slowly. "I'm sure you have excellent cause to completely shut down right now, but first, I need you to tell me exactly what you saw. What did they say?"

I sat down on the couch, still holding a random pile of clothes, and told him everything that happened–front to back.

'This is your home.'

I flinched when Xander's thumb brushed against my cheek. He held it up to show me the wetness he'd gathered, and then brought the thumb to his own cheek, wiping my tears on his skin.

I looked at him, frozen for a second.

"That was a very strange thing to do."

"I think you've said, on multiple occasions, that I am a very strange person." His voice was soft and goading and strangely... comforting.

I laughed through my tears for a second before I remembered. I took a shuddering breath and looked at Xander; his intense, green eyes were focused on me intently.

"So, you know what this means?" he asked.

The breath I took went nowhere.

"My father was an Astrale."

"And?"

"*I'm*...an Astrale." It felt strange and foreign on my tongue.

"You're an Astrale," Xander repeated in a deep and rich drawl, his feelings on the matter clearly differing by a lot.

Well, fuck.

What was I supposed to do with that?

☽

XANDER

"Okay," I said, reaching down to grab Violet's bag. "Is this everything?"

She scanned the room before nodding once, her eyes faraway. I was a bit worried about her. That vacant look was encroaching in her eyes, and I had the feeling that I needed to move quickly if I wanted to stop it in its tracks.

I couldn't stop thinking about the memory of her brightened face and that gut-wrenching laugh as she bounced on the barrier.

It was like I was watching her inner child awaken, and it made me desperate to know what caused that part of her to be so bottled up.

What forced her to grow up so quickly?

I tucked both of our belongings in the pocket dimension, unsure where we would end up at the end of the day, and grabbed Violet's hand. Her much smaller one immediately clasped around mine, making me feel a sense of protectiveness that was new to me.

I guessed I would need to get used to that.

"Where are we going?" she asked me.

"To the Astrolite sector–Calliseo. Usually, we would need to get some clearance before showing up, but I have a sort of all-access pass."

Violet looked up at me sceptically. "What do you mean?"

"Part of my job for Lilliana is law enforcement, which sometimes requires travelling between sectors."

She seemed bewildered by that fact, almost like she was trying to gauge if I was joking or not.

"What laws do you enforce?" she asked.

"That is a long and complicated answer, Violet." I marked the way her face fell a bit, and my gut twinged. "Now, let me put the Soothe back on your voice."

I didn't need to touch her at all for it to work, but I did anyway, enjoying the way her pulse fluttered under my fingertips. After finishing, I told her, "We need to be methodical about this, so try to let me do the talking. This memory has to lead us to find answers about the Chalice and your father."

I cringed when she stiffened like a board. "The two have to be connected, Violet. Otherwise, Mr. Berger wouldn't have sent us to find that memory."

"But I don't understand what difference that will make," Violet remarked in a detached voice, the look on her face twisting something inside me. "My father is dead. My mother, too."

I'd guessed that was the case, based on the things she had said and the way she reacted to me looking at the photo of them, but this was the first time she admitted it to me.

"We are running off of very little information–anything will help."

Violet nodded, and I squeezed her hand, warning her that we were about to whisk. When we landed, Violet gasped, her eyes wide as she took in the palace before us.

It was a tall and spindly black structure with winding towers and sharp spikes at the tops. The stone, so dark it reflected sunlight off its shiny surface, appeared like stars even in broad daylight. The balconies and window trim were all chiselled out of pure gold, standing out among the darkness.

It was the gaudiest and most pretentious place in all of Cavell.

"This place is so tacky," Violet muttered under her breath, making me chuckle down at her.

She really was my mate.

Which reminded me, I still needed to find a way to have her Core tested. I was hopeful that she would be Astrolite because that happened to be the only Core that I *didn't* have, so there wouldn't be a concern about our Cores clashing. The only problem with that was, given how infrequently the testing was done nowadays, we couldn't do it under the radar. And the person who approved and oversaw testing sessions was the same one who could never learn of Violet's true heritage.

Lilliana.

She would exploit her to no end. If anyone knew that, it was me.

I still hadn't figured out how this was supposed to work in the long run. I couldn't exactly just quit working for Lilliana. But surely she didn't expect me to devote the rest of my life to her... did she?

The fact that Violet would inevitably need to leave her entire life behind in Armantrea had also been weighing on my mind. Even if she were to decide that she didn't want to be with me, it was now certain that she had Astrale blood running through her veins.

She wouldn't be returning to Armantrea. It was too dangerous.

But I also knew how hard that would hit her, and it filled me with dread.

We walked the short way up to the grand entrance, and I pressed the doorbell encased in a swirling gold frame.

"Hello there," the butler who opened the door greeted. "How can I be of help?"

He was a small and plump man. The too-small suit he wore did nothing to improve his appearance. His white hair was combed over and looked wet from the amount of product that was in it.

"We need to speak to Dmitri," I told him, getting right to the point.

"I am sorry to tell you this, but Mr. Endor is in the middle of an event. He will not be able to speak to you for some time."

"This is a matter of Cavell's safety," I advised, the tone clear in my voice.

I am not a person you say no to.

His eyes bulged, probably realising who I was. "Right—of course, Sir. I would be happy to show you to a room where you can wait."

"This is a time-pressing issue. We do not have the time to wait around for his majesty's schedule to free up."

"I truly am sorry, but that is the best I can do. Unless you would like to speak to his excellency's son?"

"No," I ground out. "He will not have the information we need."

"Then, by all means, Sir. Follow me."

He stepped to the side and allowed us to pass through the doorway, closing it behind us and promptly setting off. He led us around a corner nearby and into a hallway, not making any attempt at conversation.

Which I was happy about because I cannot fucking stand small talk.

"Xander, dear!" A familiar voice called from behind us.

I turned around to see Chelsea rushing down the hallway towards us with a glass of champagne in her hand and a smile stretching her face. Her blonde hair was pulled up in a high ponytail, making her cheekbones more pronounced. The pale skin that was so different from her brother's shimmered with that stupid fucking body glitter she always wore, making her look like a twiggy disco ball.

When she reached us, Chelsea wrapped her arms around my neck in an embrace, making me roll my eyes.

Will she ever fucking learn?

"Chelsea," I warned in a low voice. "How many times do I have to tell you?"

"Oh, shove it, Xan. You don't scare me." She pulled back and looked over at Violet, who was watching us with fire in her eyes.

Interesting.

I didn't know if an outsider would notice it because her body language gave off a bored and relaxed aura, but I knew she was feeling something. That fight was back in her eyes, clawing for a way out, and I felt like rejoicing at the sight.

She had just been veering into that other territory. That wouldn't do.

"Hello," Chelsea greeted in a warm tone. "I'm Chelsea."

She was the only member of her family that didn't fake their sunny exterior. It was just *her*–which made her the tiniest bit difficult to dislike once you got to know her.

"Nice to meet you. I'm Violet." Her words were in all the right places, but the evidence of her cold shoulder was very clear in the way she said them.

I repressed a smile at the little Angel's hostility.

Chelsea looked over at the butler who was escorting us and dismissed him. "Thank you, Martyn. I will take it from here."

He bowed his head. "Of course, your grace."

The little man looked at me once before scurrying off the way we came. Chelsea looked back to Violet, seemingly enamoured by her.

"What sect–wait, no. Don't tell me, don't tell me," Chelsea rambled, looking at Violet over the rim of her champagne flute and tapping her fingernail on the stem.

"Mmm. Mhm–you've *got* to be a Soothsayer," Chelsea nodded at her own statement, clearly deciding it was correct. "With that outfit and those eyes," she trailed off, clucking her tongue and appraising Violet with her eyes.

I couldn't tell if it was in judgement or attraction, either equally plausible coming from Chelsea. Both prospects made me feel a little violent.

I opened my mouth to respond, but Violet beat me to it.

"Wouldn't you like to know," Violet murmured, repeating my words from a few days ago while observing her painted nails with a bored focus.

I could tell by the erratic beat of her heart that it was a façade. She was anxious—as hell, based on the speed of it. I felt a burst of amused pride while watching her poker face in action.

"Ugh," Chelsea groaned, waving us off. "You two belong together with your abrasive vagueness."

I laughed at that, but stopped when Chelsea shot me a bewildered look. "I assume you are waiting for my father?" she asked.

"Yes," I answered. "We need to speak to him."

"You might be waiting for a while. He is knee-deep in his wine and dine stage of the evening." She rolled her eyes.

"Well, that's just lovely," I said dryly.

We'd likely be waiting here for hours. But what other choice did we have?

"Shaed is having a little get-together, actually. Just the regulars. Do you care to join us while you wait?" Chelsea addressed both of us, and I looked down at Violet to see her watching Chelsea with a cautious eye.

Was she always this distrusting towards people, or was it just Astrales?

"Beats waiting in a room with only this one to keep me company," Violet said at last, gesturing towards me.

I shot her an overly executed look of hurt, drawing a small smile to those plump lips.

Fuck. Me.

A few graphic images came to mind of those lips, making me groan inwardly. That was the moment an idea popped into my mind.

I needed to find Dom as soon as possible. She might have the answers I need about our Cores.

Chelsea laughed at Violet's statement. "Oh, you're good," she said, bumping their shoulders together. "Very good."

Violet smiled at her, seemingly less on edge than she had been before.

"Well, you know where to find us. I assume I don't need to worry about leaving you unattended?" Chelsea directed my way, looking at me behind lowered brows.

"It was *one* relic, Chelsea. And it was fifteen years ago. Honestly, when will you let it go?"

"I'll let it go when my grandmother returns from her grave to replace her diadem," she deadpanned at me.

Okay, honestly, breaking the diadem wasn't a complete accident. It just irritated me that this sector treated their leaders like royalty, and felt like a fucking bejewelled crown was only contributing to their self-importance.

So I eradicated it.

With that comment, Chelsea was gone, whisking herself to the Viewing Room. I would love to have done it as well, but the wards within the palace only allowed certain people to whisk within its walls.

And I was definitely not on the list.

I started down the hallway, not checking if Violet was moving with me because I knew she would be. She caught up to me quickly, her round eyes scanning our surroundings.

The walls and floor were hewn from the same stone as the exterior of the building, creating a black expanse. In keeping with the pretentious theme, the lighting fixtures in the ceiling were made from gold, as well as the trim along the ceiling. The reflection created a spectacle of the light rays, causing them to sparkle like real stars.

Someone, please, stab me in the jugular.

"An old fuck of yours?" Violet asked abruptly, attempting an indifferent expression but being betrayed by the edge to her voice.

It took me a second before I realised that she was referring to Chelsea, and I had to hold back my laugh. I wouldn't touch that preppy princess with a twelve-foot pole, but I did happen to enjoy the jealousy Violet was failing to cover up.

I shrugged, confident that my mask wouldn't reveal anything. Not in this lifetime.

"Perhaps at one point or another. I honestly don't remember."

Her shocked gaze shot to mine. "You've fucked so many people that you don't even remember?"

I leaned in closer, speaking softly as we continued walking. "I didn't know that you were in the habit of slut-shaming." I tsked, shaking my head. "Really isn't a good look, Angel."

Her eyes bulged. "I wasn't trying t–" She broke off, her face showing recognition of the fact that I was goading her. "You're a prick."

I laughed at that, the sudden urge to skip taking over me. I didn't, though, I just kept my same pace and looked down the hallway.

"You have no idea," I replied, the weight within that statement significant.

There was a lot–and I mean a *lot*–that Violet didn't know about me.

I couldn't help but wonder what she would think of me once she did.

CHAPTER TWENTY-ONE

VIOLET

I would like to have a conversation with whoever invented the phrase *'fake it till you make it'*.

Because how in the hell was I supposed to fake this?

I was standing in the Viewing Room, as Chelsea called it, surrounded by a bunch of Astrales, sipping lightly from a glass of champagne, and doing my best to keep a neutral expression while my heart tried to exit my body.

The room was entirely circular, the shape causing the voices of the gathered Astrales to carry and bounce off the black walls, creating a mingled mess of noise. Chairs were scattered through-out, but not arranged in circles like the last time I saw this room.

The memory. This was the room from my father's memory.

My brain was working overtime, trying to grasp the fact that my father had been an Astrale.

Was my mother as well, or was she a human? If so, did they run away together?

I couldn't stop trying to remember their voices. One thing I knew for certain was that, in my mind, their voices had human accents. But when I was in the Memorium, my father had an Astrale accent.

Was anything I remembered from my childhood true?

I did my best not to freak out, even though I was pretty sure that my feet were currently planted in the same exact spot my father's had been in the memory. The vantage point looked the same, even though there were slight differences in the room itself.

I looked up to the glass ceiling, clearly the reason behind the room's name, and watched the stars. It wasn't one static picture. The image kept changing periodically to show different portions of the sky–stars from places unknown to me. Some of them were shooting, while others were burning intensely in contrast to the limp and dim ones next to them.

I have always been enamored by the stars and their ability to keep shining. Even if there are clouds or smoke blocking the way, you always know that they are there, waiting patiently to show themselves again.

Beyond the room, I could see about twenty different Astrales mingling in small groups, and I really didn't know what was expected of me. Xander had left me as soon as we got in here, saying that he had to talk to someone named Dom. He told me to 'sit tight' until he came back, and to go to Chelsea if I needed anything.

Bastard.

Should I go and try to join in on a conversation?

I would probably make a fool of myself with how little I knew about this world. What could I even contribute to their discussions without giving myself away as an outsider? Then again, I was definitely giving off outsider vibes standing alone and staring at the ceiling.

So, tell me, mystery person–how in the *fuck* was I supposed to fake nonchalance in this scenario?

At that second, Shaed walked into the room through one of the alcoves that blended into the dark walls. He had a girl on his arm, whispering something in her ear that made her giggle. She was wearing a very low-cut gown and had her hair pinned up in braids. The look was elegant and regal, but it seemed out of place.

I scanned the rest of the room, realizing that *everyone* seemed a bit out of place.

Some people were wearing jeans and casual tops. A few others were wearing daytime dresses, while others were dressed as formally as Shaed's accomplice. It was strange–the mismatched attire and demeanors–but I kind of liked it.

If everyone stands out as different, is anyone really different?

"Well, well," Shaed bellowed from across the room. "If it isn't Xander's newest owner." He tipped his glass at me. "Where is the dog, anyway? Have you put him out to play?"

Some small chuckles rang through the room; most of the Astrales' attention now focused on me.

Damn you, Shaed.

"I don't know," I murmured. "I've heard you do a fair amount of playing yourself. Who holds the end of your leash?"

Shaed looked dumbfounded for a second as someone let out a choking laugh, bringing me satisfaction, before his charming smile was latched in place again. "You've met everyone, then?" Shaed asked, playing the perfect host. "Friends, this is Violet. I don't recommend touching her unless you fancy having her guard dog set upon you."

People laughed again, and I was beginning to feel irritation lacing its way under my skin.

Why did he keep referring to Xander as a dog?

Except–wait a second. I was pretty sure I hadn't actually told him my name that day in the forest. So how did he know it?

Everyone seemed to go back to their discussions pretty quickly, making me feel more uncomfortable than I had to begin with.

Had Shaed just ostracized me from them even further?

A woman approached me then–one dressed in casual pants and a top–and stuck out a hand in greeting.

"Hi, Violet. I'm Neerah."

I shook her hand and smiled, grateful that someone here seemed to have manners. She had beautiful, long black hair and dark eyes that radiated a welcoming energy. Her beauty struck me, and I found myself not wanting to look away.

"It's nice to meet you," I offered.

"You as well! I figure we better get to know each other, considering that our counterparts make a habit of disappearing to conspire together–as they have presently."

"Oh, uh, Xander isn't exactly..." I didn't know what to say–how to phrase it–after Shaed introduced me to the room as Xander's 'owner'.

"We are colleagues," I decided, remembering what Xander had said in Nygaard's shop.

"In that case," a male voice swooped in, and his body pressed against my side. "I'm Marj," he drawled, the attraction clear in his voice.

I looked over at him, finding a man with dimples on display and teeth so white they were practically sparkling. His sandy hair was slightly curled and flopping into his eyes, making him look endearing and harmless.

That glint in his eyes suggested otherwise, though.

"I'm Violet," I said sweetly. "And I am uninterested."

"Damn." The man's face fell. "The pretty ones never want me! Why don't they ever want me, Neerah?"

"Maybe because you lack all forms of subtlety?" she suggested kindly.

"Hmm," he mused, rubbing his chin and looking up at the stars. "You might be onto something there."

I laughed slightly, my chest feeling lighter than it did a minute ago.

"Anyway..." I directed my attention back to Neerah. "Who is *your* counterpart?"

She smiled, shoving Marj lightly as he walked away. "My wife, Domonique. I would introduce you to her, but she is off some-where with Xander."

I'd assumed Dom was a man when her name was mentioned, but clearly, I was wrong.

"Wait, you and Domonique were in Bosquera yesterday, weren't you?" I asked, suddenly remembering them as the couple in a passionate embrace on the barrier.

"Yes," she answered, her smile faltering. "We live near there."

"Oh, that's cool," I supplied lamely, trying to keep the questions running through my head at bay. "It's very beautiful there."

Why were they here if they were Terrala? Was it because Shaed's family is like royalty, so he is able to bypass the rules? Or are the rules not as strict as I thought they were?

"So, you're an enforcer as well, then," Neerah stated, changing the subject.

"Yes, I am new to it, though. This is my first mission, so Lilliana wanted Xander to show me the ropes." I didn't know how the lie flew so effortlessly off my tongue, but I was grateful for it.

"And are you in support of Lilliana's movements?" she asked too casually; the hidden meaning completely lost to me.

"I—um—"

"Violet," Shaed said, entering our conversation out of nowhere, "you'll have to excuse Neerah. She doesn't beat around the bush."

"I actually respect that about her," I leveled back at him.

He chuckled. "Why am I not surprised?"

I gave him a questioning look. He said that as if he knew me at all.

"Would you mind giving us a minute?" asked Shaed, looking over at Neerah. "I'd like to have a chat with Violet. Alone."

I decided that I really liked Neerah when she looked at me for confirmation first. I gave her a slight nod, my curiosity getting the better of me. I wanted to know what Shaed had to say.

When she walked away, Shaed gestured to one of the alcoves. "Will you join me in the Oracle's room?"

I nodded, unsure if I was supposed to know what the fuck an Oracle room was, and followed him through the doorway.

The room was much brighter than the one we'd just been in, causing my eyes to strain a bit. Where the walls were black before, they were now entirely gold, causing the stars in the ceiling to glint and reflect powerfully. A railing stood toward the center of the room, and I continued walking until I pressed up against it. I marveled at the sight below.

The floor fell away behind the balcony, creating a dropoff into an immeasurable depth. The darkness found there was home to a swooping array of stars, constantly shifting and moving, almost as if the ceiling was projected onto it. I could feel my eyes skimming over the view, not knowing where to look.

"Have you ever been in an Oracle's room, Violet?" Shaed asked me, making me jump. I'd almost forgotten he was there.

I felt like he was testing me somehow, so I stuck with the truth. "No."

Shaed approached, stopping at my side and looking over the balcony and into the abyss. "Quite a sight, isn't it?" he asked softly.

"Yes, it's beautiful."

He was quiet for a few seconds, and when I looked over at him, he was looking back at me with the strangest expression. "I wanted to offer you my aid," Shaed said quietly, all of the excessive warmth he usually packed onto his face gone.

"Why would I need your aid?" I asked cautiously.

"I am not saying that you do." He straightened, reaching into his back pocket and making me stiffen. But he just pulled out a small, round stone and placed it in my hand. "But, in the event that you might, turn this stone thrice in hand. It will signal me your location."

"And what makes you think that I would want your help in the event that I need it?" I asked coolly.

That smile made a reappearance on his face, coating my throat in distaste. "You may not, but it could be your only option."

"I'm not going to need it, but thanks for the offer," I replied, pocketing the stone, fully intending to throw it away as soon as possible. I didn't know this man's capabilities, and I wasn't sure what would happen if I were to reject him.

"You do realize that you are traveling around Cavell with our most lethal enforcer, don't you?" Shaed asked, his tone concerned.

Um...*what?!*

I tried not to let my shock show, but wasn't sure if I pulled it off.

"Obviously. Why else would I feel so confident walking into the viper's nest?" I asked him with a jeering tone and a smile that I didn't feel.

Not sure what possessed me to poke fun at a supernatural prince, but it might have had something to do with the fact that I could imagine Xander saying the same thing. He was pretty much my only base of comparison in terms of how Astrales interacted, but I was beginning to realize that he did not fit the mold of typical social interaction. At all.

Shaed let out a charming laugh, coming closer and putting an arm around my shoulder. "I think that I like you, Violet."

"Wow." My tone was as dry as the champagne they were serving as I pulled back. "My life now holds meaning."

"If you'd like to keep that limb attached to your body," Xander said from behind us, his deep, rumbling voice causing me to jump. "I'd suggest you *remove* it."

Shaed squeezed me tighter. "Come now, Xanny. We are all friends here," he insisted in a honeyed tone.

I turned to see Xander leaning against the doorway on one shoulder while his eyes narrowed on Shaed's arm. Suddenly, said arm was twisted backward at an unnatural angle, and Shaed cried out.

It bent even further, and right as I was sure it was about to dislocate, he conceded.

"Alright! I won't touch her, you fucking lunatic."

"I should hope not," Xander retorted, a regretful tone to his voice. "How could you possibly tend to Daddy's knitting without the use of one of your arms?"

Shaed scowled, straightening and shaking out his arm.

"Remind me, who invited you here again?" he asked in Xander's direction.

"That would be your sister," he replied, smirking as he made his way across the room.

"Damn her," Shaed muttered. "Thinking she can invite whoever she wants to *my* gatherings."

Wait.

Chelsea was Shaed's sister?

As in, the girl Xander may or may not have had sex with?

"We were already here, waiting on your father, actually," Xander interjected, and I wondered if he was trying to stick up for the princess I'd met earlier. The thought made me bristle.

"Why do you need to speak to my father?" Shaed asked, his face gaining a haughty quality.

"It pertains to our mission. And is classified," Xander answered, clearly enjoying keeping Shaed out of the loop.

"Does this mission have to do with the Eloko problem?" Shaed asked, looking between us both.

I glanced at Xander, trying to gauge what I should do, but his words told me all I needed to know.

"It's getting worse," Xander announced. "We are going to have to take more drastic measures."

"You see," Shaed mused, leaning in closer to me, "this is what happens when people think that they can play the Mother's part. They try to use their magic to create new beings, but just end up making *monsters.*"

The last part of his sentence was heavily weighted, telling me that I was missing something in this conversation.

"Right, well, it is not much fault of the being that has been created, is it?" Xander countered, inching closer to me. I felt his heat spread through my back and had to actively resist the urge to lean into it.

"I suppose not." Shaed looked contemplative. "But I don't think any being that is made instead of born is something to be trusted."

"That's a bit contradictory of you, don't you think?" I asked with a light tone, taking a sip of my drink.

"How do you mean?" Shaed asked, a crease appearing between his light eyebrows.

"Well, correct me if I'm wrong, but this entire race is a product of something that was made, is it not?"

I worried that my use of the word 'this' and not 'our' would give my position away, but Shaed seemed to be too dumbstruck to pick up on it.

"That *is* awfully true, isn't it, Shaed?" Xander asked, looping his arm around my chest and slowly pulling me back against his.

My stomach flipped, feeling like a group of butterflies had just set up camp inside it.

Why was he touching me like this now when he hardly had before?

Shaed looked like he didn't really know what to do with himself.

"I've grown tired of waiting on your father. We deserve to be treated with fucking respect. So tell his *majesty*," Xander said, smiling when Shaed's jaw clenched at his emphasis, "that I will be reaching out to set up a meeting."

And then he was whisking us somewhere; my body still pressed firmly to his. When we landed, I couldn't see much of my surroundings because it was so dark. The sharp contrast from the dazzling lights in the Oracle's room caused my eyes to strain with the need to adjust.

It didn't really matter, though, because Xander leaned down, still positioned at my back. His lips brushed against the shell of my ear as he spoke in a low, gravelly voice. "Remember what I told you about keeping my distance?"

"Yes?" My voice came out barely above a whisper.

"I'm thinking I can let up on that–just a bit."

His mouth traveled to my neck, dusting me with feather-light kisses in a downward trail, his breaths skating along my chest.

I inhaled sharply, overwhelmed by how quickly this had happened and dazed by how good it felt. "And why is that?"

He rounded me slowly, moving like a predator getting ready to pounce. "You just shattered the rest of my defenses."

Even though I wasn't really sure what they meant, those words left me breathless.

Xander's hand moved to the side of my head, entwining in my hair and tilting my face up. His mouth captured mine greedily and harshly, his body pressing down on me until all I could feel was him. My arms circled his neck immediately as I returned his intensity.

The kiss was as searing as it was crushing, seeming as if he couldn't get close enough...couldn't taste me enough.

I knew the feeling.

I opened my mouth to get more of him, and my core turned molten when he brushed his tongue against mine slowly, like he was acquainting himself with it. The taste of his last cigarette lingered there, the mystery herb's sweetness carrying on after the tobacco.

He groaned into my mouth and bent down, grabbing the back of my thighs and lifting me up. I circled my legs around his waist and gasped between kisses as he walked us backward, putting me down on a hard surface.

Xander seemed to be driven forward by the sound—his mouth cascading onto mine once more with much more force.

I was by no means a small woman; my figure was what Archi described as a 'tall, sexy pear.' I've had wide-set hips and thick thighs my entire life, and I liked it that way, but to be picked up as if I weighed no more than a bag of apples?

It sent a thrill traveling from my toes to a much higher place.

I pulled away, gasping, and he swept kisses along my jaw, lingering at the shell of my ear.

"Was that clear enough for you, Vi?" His soft whisper went through my entire body. Xander kissed my neck, dragging his teeth lightly across it. "Now, do you understand that you have been driving me insane with those sultry eyes and pouty lips?" He nipped at my shoulder and squeezed my hips. "With this fucking *body?*"

My heart thundered as I pulled back from him and grabbed the bottom of my shirt, yanking it off my body. All that remained was the tank top I had chosen to wear as a bra today, not wanting to deal with wearing a wire.

I was thankful for that decision now as I watched Xander's eyes widen. He ran a single hand down the center of my chest so softly, goosebumps broke out all over my skin.

He moved back down and bit the pulse point of my neck before kissing over the same spot, sending sparks down my spine and legs. My body reacted involuntarily, shifting my hips down closer to his. He groaned against my throat and grabbed my hips, roughly yanking me flush against him. I leaned back on my hands and rolled into him, letting my head fall back as he kissed a trail down my collarbone and chest.

"Do you have any idea how frequently I have thought about these?" Xander ground out, staring intently at the hardened peaks of my breasts pushing against the fabric of my tank top.

When I shook my head, he closed his mouth over one, grazing it with his teeth, and a moan escaped out of me.

He growled in response, clamping down on it and making me cry out before he spoke against my chest. "Those sounds might be the death of me, Angel."

Then he slipped his hand under my shirt and squeezed my other breast with his large, callused hand, causing a rush of warmth to flow down my body. Xander leaned into me, planting a hand over mine on the desk, but he pulled back suddenly, sucking in air through his teeth as if he was in pain.

"What's wrong?" I asked, struggling to catch my breath.

"You just burned me," he said in a tone of confused shock.

He used his grip around my back and hips to shift me over on the desk. A second later, a green glow escaped from Xander's hand, showing me the evidence of what he was talking about.

Two handprints burned into the surface of the desk.

CHAPTER TWENTY-TWO

XANDER

I fought and failed to hold back my grin as I looked down at the desk and the mark Violet's hands left on it. It was distinctly charred—her Starfire was so strong that the prints were set deeply into the wood. She had to be carrying a lot of dormant power for that to have happened, but only one Core could produce heat like that.

Astrolite. Just as I'd suspected, and hoped.

It made me wonder what the situation with her powers was, and how she hadn't noticed them until now. Her being over the mountain would have affected the strength of her abilities while she was there, but it wouldn't have nullified them altogether.

Only one thing could do that, and I'd stop at nothing to ensure she'd *never* experience it.

Corechain.

My fists tightened at the thought alone.

"Well," she said, breaking me out of my train of thought. "That was intense."

"What—the kissing, or your Starfire?" I asked, a grin spreading across my lips.

"Um, both."

I felt my cock throb at the sight of the slight blush spreading across her cheeks and her swollen lips.

Violet broke the staring contest she was having with her handprints and looked back at me, our gazes locking instantly. She held it for a second before those eyes skirted down to my lips, which I could feel were also swelling from the embrace. I hadn't kissed anyone like that in a long time.

If ever.

The connection we shared was raw and deeply rooted. I knew she had to feel it too. That instinct inside of our guts to do anything and everything possible so that we were never parted–to be there for each other until the very end.

The mating bond.

If I didn't talk to her about it soon, we would both start to feel the consequences.

When the bond goes unrecognised, it can cause some people to become overpowered by their needs and desires. This manifests in a lot of different ways, but they usually aren't good for either party. I'd heard stories about a man and woman who knew they were mates but decided to explore other options before marking the bond because they were so young.

The woman was content, going about her life in a typical way, though she thought of the man often. He, however, went a little… mad. He was obsessive, driven wild by jealousy and paranoia about his mate. He spent so long isolating himself and thinking about her with other lovers that he drove himself insane. The mental images he had concocted–entirely on his own–became so visceral that he couldn't cope any longer.

The worst part about it is that the woman, who had been with a few men in the meantime, decided that she didn't need to explore any longer. No one struck her fancy like her mate.

When she ran to find him and tell him her decision, he was lying dead in his bed, clutching the pearl necklace his mate had left behind when they decided to part. Guilt overtook her, and though she would have never committed suicide, it might as well have been the case. She lived the rest of her days as a shell of her past self, continuously replaying her mistakes in her mind and daydreaming about the life they could have had together.

The woman lived on until she was elderly, when she gladly

welcomed death with open arms. She could be reunited with her true mate once more.

I needed to talk to Vi about this as soon as possible. And now that I knew she had the Astrolite Core...

My worry was always that she would have the same Core as me, even though that seemed to make no sense, when considering the history with the plague.

But nothing they'd learned about the plague's origins applied to me, due to the way I was created. The plague was not the outcome that I feared.

My Core was a hand-crafted weapon of mass destruction–a combination of multiple syphoning abilities, and designed to take down anything that threatened its integrity. So, I'd worried that if her Core had the same magic as my own, there would be an uncontrollable battle for dominance that would put her in danger. But, maybe if it was introduced to a new sort of magic, my Core would welcome it.

Gaar's words came rushing back to me.

'Why would you be mates if your Core was going to hurt her?'

"Angel," I said, tipping her chin up and looking down at her face. "We need to have a little chat."

"Hmm," she mused. "Anytime someone starts a conversation like that, I'm immediately on edge. Spill."

I leaned down and nipped at her ear with my teeth, drawing out a little yelp. "That sounded like a command. I don't appreciate commands."

"Tell that to Lilliana," she muttered under her breath.

I narrowed my eyes on her. Slowly.

"What was that?"

"Nothing," she quipped, giving me an innocent, close-mouthed smile.

"Mhm, that's what I thought."

I checked myself, making sure that I was cooled down enough to risk seeing other people. Not that it was possible for my hard-on to go away completely after that, but it had at least improved slightly.

"We're leaving," I warned her before whisking us to the lake.

I felt my feet hit the grass and did a quick scan of our surroundings, glad to see that we were the only ones there. Because with Violet's body wrapped around my middle, her cunt pressed up against the ridges of my abs so tightly that I could feel how wet and ready for me she was, there was no shot at nonchalance right now.

Who was I kidding, anyway?

I blatantly slid Violet down the length of my body, my muscles convulsing the moment her centre slid along my cock.

"Holy fuck," she gasped, looking down at me with slightly bulged eyes. She glanced back up, her dilated pupils making my head *roar*.

"I am going to need that inside of me. Like, really fucking soon." The needy edge to her voice had me contemplating throwing this entire plan out the window and taking her right here on the grass.

"Oh, you'll take it. Trust me. We just need to discuss a few things first."

"Like what?" she asked, and I could tell she was distracted because her eyes had a sort of faraway look, like she was imagining what it would be like when we didn't have to wait anymore.

This would be the perfect opportunity to test it out. Even though every fibre of my being resisted the thought of attacking her, I had to do it. I needed to see her reaction time.

Without any warning whatsoever, I shot my hand out, reaching for her throat, but I never made it there. She swooped backwards out of my reach, and before I knew what was happening, she punched me in the side, something metal puncturing me and forcing me to my knees.

"Seriously?!" she yelled down at me. "What the fuck is wrong with you? You absolute psycho! Why did you do that!"

Violet's eyes burned with intensity, but I ignored her, looking down at the silver loop circling her knuckles. It was just big enough to fit around them and had three metal spikes jutting out, obviously intended for puncturing skin, as they had just done to me.

I put a hand over my wound, feeling free-flowing blood, and grinned up at my little Angel.

"Very nicely done." I nodded with my appraisal. "I think you might have even punctured an organ. Exquisite."

"You are so fucking demented." She looked down at me with distaste, her arms crossed now that the threat was neutralised. "What was that for?"

"I was testing your reaction time—which is very good, by the way. Very good." I was staring up at her, completely fixated, with a grin that I couldn't stop making an appearance.

"Aaand you needed to do that *because?*" she asked, and I resisted the urge to pinch her ass for her snide tone.

I stood up slowly, my wound already almost closed over because of my Sensinor abilities, and grabbed her hand with the weapon. The sight of them on her hand sent a pulse of energy to my cock.

Where did she get them? I turned her hand over, scanning for the seal of a blacksmith—anything to give me a clue.

"As Astrales mature, their gifts manifest in strange and unpre-dictable ways. Some people show forms of magic as young as five years old; others don't acquire a single gift until they are thirty—it always depends on the person. But, for those who develop their gifts at a different rate, their other heightened abilities take longer to develop as well. Hearing is an example of that, as is reaction time."

Her expression cleared out as understanding dawned on her face, her shoulders and posture loosening along with it. "So you were trying to determine what stage of development I'm at."

Although it wasn't phrased as a question, I nodded anyway, and brushed my thumb along her cheek. "Sorry if I scared you, but I obviously had to take you off-guard."

"You didn't scare me." She scowled, shoving my hand away. "You pissed me the fuck off."

I chuckled at her, moving a few strands of hair tangled in her eyelashes. "My sharp little vixen."

Her entire focus shot to me, her face showing a strange combination of shock, bewilderment, and...joy?

I was still learning the small tells and cues of her moods, but that seemed to be pretty accurate. Her eyes had that shining quality that I'd seen when we went to her apartment, and she was looking at Archi.

She shook herself slightly, whatever had been on her face falling away. "So, what did you get out of your little experiment, then?"

"I'm not sure what stage of development you are at. The signs are not consistent at all. First, you were able to create the Chalice, and yet–as far as I've seen–all of your physical senses are at a human level. But your reaction time is definitely not. You just showed Starfire capabilities, and damn strong ones at that, but no other gifts have manifested yet. It's as if something has blocked them."

I sat on the ground, tugging her down with me and positioned her at my side. "So, to sum it up–I have no idea what is happening inside of you."

Violet gave me a side eye, clearly not very thrilled with my deductive skills. "Cool, so basically you just give me a minor heart attack for nothing."

I didn't blame her for feeling that way. I couldn't imagine being in her place. Finding out not only that another species existed, but that she was a *part* of that species in only a few days must have been a lot to take in. She'd been taken into this foreign world, away from everything and everyone she knew. Now she had gifts manifesting, and everything about her past was beginning to unravel, including the truth about her parents, whose deaths still seemed to weigh on her.

No wonder she turned into that other version of herself sometimes.

"I'm going to need you to actually explain to me what is going on," Violet said, looking at the view of the lake instead of me. "Why did you go from telling me to keep my distance and glaring at me to whisking me away from a party so you could kiss me? And why does my stage of development have anything to do with us being together? The mixed signals are practically a fucking kaleidoscope at this point."

She sighed, looking up at the sky before turning back to me. "It's getting really old, Xan."

I sucked in a shrill breath, the sound of that nickname on her lips the sweetest melody to my ears. Her voice was on the lower range for a woman, slightly raspy at times but entirely silky at others. That's why even the slightest turn of phrase from her could send me into a spiralled frenzy.

Her words ignited a motivation in me like no one else's had before.

"I'm sorry, Violet. I really am." A pathetic way to answer her questions, really. She deserved so much more.

You're my mate.

The words were on my tongue. They were. I just couldn't push them out.

It wasn't fair to tell her that before I told her the truth about me—about how I came to be. If she learned we were mates, she might make a drastic decision or develop stronger feelings quickly, and then come to regret it once she understood me completely.

The thought filled me with an almost unignorable urge to make her mine before it was too late—before she could change her mind.

Bite. Mark. Claim.

But, no matter how strong that urge might be, I would never do that to her. I would never shackle her the way I had been for so many years.

"Is that it?" Violet asked, a disappointed edge to her voice. "That's all you're gonna say?"

"No–I just–" I sputtered off, suddenly feeling cornered. This was unprecedented territory, and I didn't know how to tell her what I needed to. I just wanted a second to gather my thoughts.

And I was so terrified she would hate me once she knew.

Violet scoffed and stood up, her irritation clear. I grabbed her hand firmly.

"Just wait, Violet," I said between my teeth, becoming impatient with her attitude. "Give me a moment."

"I've been waiting, Xander," she hissed back at me, undeterred by the warning in my tone.

"Will you just fucking–"

I stopped, hearing something coming from the woods behind us. It sounded like multiple bodies shuffling in tandem. It could've been animals out there, but with the Eloko problem on the rise...

"If I don't fucking *what?*" she asked mockingly, clearly not understanding why I'd stopped talking.

"Shhh," I quieted her, standing up.

"Don't you fucking shush–" Her words blended into a mumbling mess when I clamped a hand over her mouth.

"Be quiet," I whispered. "I am trying to listen."

She stopped protesting altogether, her body shifting and sinking into mine as her eyes skirted around the treeline. I heard it again, the distinct sounds of a multitude of bodies moving in unison.

They were much closer to us now, too. This couldn't be Eloko. They tended to travel alone, not in packs. My ears picked up a separate noise from the group, and it was alarmingly close to us. I shot my gaze around, trying to pinpoint where it was coming from, but the rapidly increasing sound of the group was muddling the other traveller. That, paired with the sound of Violet's pounding heart, made it impossible.

"Alright, fuck this," I decided. "We are leaving."

As soon as I spoke the words, the single most harrowing and infuriating noise I had ever heard in my life rang through the air–Violet's scream.

One second, she was there. The next, she was being ripped away from me by an invisible force.

"Xander," a booming voice called out. "Lilliana's most celebrated enforcer. Do you know why we have come here today?"

The voice was indiscernible, with a Soothe masking its origin and location.

I didn't give a fuck about it, though, my entire focus was centred on Violet. She was now standing about twenty feet away from me, breathing harshly and looking around at the artificially-empty clearing.

"You're going to help us," the voice said to me, the Soothe on it working frustratingly well. I couldn't begin to tell if it was a woman or a man talking.

"And in return, we will not hurt the woman you hold so dearly."

Violet was still in clear view, and while her captor was invisible, it was obvious that they were now holding her around the neck based on the way her chin was tilted up and strained. Panic crowded those unique, devastating eyes of hers, causing my magic to pulse through my veins violently, begging to be unleashed.

"If you think that *this* is the way to get me to help you," I drawled, doing my best to keep my tone nonchalant around the pulse pounding in my throat. "You're sorely mistaken. The only result you will get from harming her is the removal of your own head–maybe even a limb or two beforehand so you'll really get the point."

I shrugged. "You can decide that for yourself. You have three seconds."

"One," I called, skipping her way once. "Two," I drew the word out, taking a measured step towards them, a grin spreading over my face at the prospect of the fight. I knew that it might be a little tricky, considering that I couldn't see the attacker, but I had my ways.

They wouldn't harm a hair on her fucking head.

The person reacted idiotically, squeezing tighter on her throat and causing her eyes to bulge and her throat to gasp for air.

The expression made my vision turn red.

I decided they didn't get the fucking courtesy of reaching three and struck out with my magic, forming a harness around her neck and tightening it until I saw air enter her lungs.

The next events all passed in a blur.

I moved faster than I ever had in my life, reaching Violet in a millisecond. Her eyes scattered all around, unable to follow the superspeed yet, and I looped a hand around her waist, yanking her to my body.

The attacker's Soothe was disrupted by my magic's effect on their hand, bringing them into visibility. They seemed to have anticipated this because a black and silver mask adorned their face, the eye slits in the shape of crescent moons.

Bastards.

The Retaliators.

I didn't wait to see any more, now that I knew for certain who was responsible for this attack. It all made sense—the many heartbeats and steps I'd heard, the Soothes used to hide their positions, and the hidden voice. This was precisely their style; the spineless, havoc-wreckers that they were.

To attack behind the safety of a cloak? Fucking pathetic.

I whisked us to the one place that I knew, without a doubt, would be safe for us, my panic rising when I looked down to see how pale Violet was. Her skin had taken on a grey pallor and looked clammy, like she was about to faint again.

Fuck.

If she fainted while we were in between planes, she may never return from it.

Luckily—and thankfully—we landed back in my flat and Violet was still conscious, although hardly so. She swayed on her feet, and I immediately scooped her up in my arms, cradling her close to my body.

"Xan," she muttered, her voice weak. The new nickname she had taken to made my heart contract. "Why does this keep happening to me?"

And then she was out, her body going limp with unconsciousness. I tucked her head into my shoulder and moved to sit in the armchair, unwilling to let go of her yet. I needed to feel her heartbeat against my chest, the reminder that she wasn't gone, just unconscious.

"I don't know, Angel," I finally answered, even though she couldn't hear me. "But I'm going to find out."

CHAPTER TWENTY-THREE

VIOLET

The next morning I opened my eyes and immediately knew—the Void had found me.

My chest felt open and empty, like it was exposed for anything the world could throw at it. I rolled to my side and stared out the window of my room at the Armory, looking at the brick building across from me.

It was a bit like that wall, actually. Each time I entered the Void, another layer of bricks was added, separating me from the world around me. And as I got further and further into it, the grout was laid and given time to set.

It became a friend of mine, the barrier between myself and others. I never felt more complete than when I was in my own little bubble, because it was the closest I could ever get to *them*. The day my parents were ripped away from me was the same day I lost a part of my soul. So, by settling into that missing gap, I could almost imagine I was whole again.

Even if the bricks were beginning to cage me in.

Wait a second.

There wasn't a brick building outside my window at the Armory.

I sat up, looking around at my surroundings, to find an unfamiliar, studio-style apartment.

It was a home after my own heart.

Dim light filtered through the window I had just been looking out of, while thick, velvety curtains shrouded the rest of them in darkness. I didn't really care about the windows, though, as I got out of bed to stand in front of what had really grabbed my attention.

Floor-to-ceiling bookshelves made up the entirety of the longest wall in the apartment, sitting to the left of the bed. The books seemed to be organized perfectly, not a spine out of place in the arrangement of tallest-to-shortest.

My mind spun as I walked along the wall, too enamored to even touch the books, and I recognized some of my favorite authors on the shelf.

My favorite *human* authors.

Where in the fuck was I?

The creak of a door sounded, and I whipped around to find Xander ducking his head under the doorframe of what I assumed was the bathing room. I let out a relieved breath that it was just him.

"Had enough of your beauty rest there, have you?" Xander asked, that annoying drawl in his voice.

"I don't know," I joked. "You tell me."

"Oh, please," he said, making his way toward me across the room, the look in his eye bringing heat to my abdomen. "You don't need rest to make you beautiful."

I stood there for a second too long before saying, "I was kidding..."

"And I was not," he stated matter-of-factly.

Having reached me, Xander grabbed a fistful of my hair; his gaze locked on it. "But I will say, your hair rivals a tumbleweed after you have slept."

I swatted him away, resisting the urge to tame it down. I didn't really care what he thought of my bedhead.

He chuckled. "Are you hungry?"

"No," I answered immediately. I was never hungry when I was in the Void.

But, was I really in It? I definitely was when I woke up, that much was certain. But I didn't feel It now like I did then, and I couldn't understand that.

This had never happened before.

"Come on," he insisted, poking me in the side. "Not even for pancakes?"

"*You* know how to make pancakes," I repeated in a doubtful tone, physically unable to picture that.

"You'd be shocked how little you actually know about me, Vi."

I hardly noticed the nickname he'd used because of how idiotic his words were.

"Uh, no, actually. I would not be. You don't tell me shit."

I followed Xander as he walked wordlessly to the kitchenette, where there was a small stove and an oven. The fridge was tiny, reminding me of the first one Archi and I'd ever had. He flicked on a light and reached into it to pull out some ingredients.

"Where are we, anyway?" I asked, my eyes raking over the place again.

"This is my flat," Xander replied in a guarded tone.

"And you didn't think to tell me about this place until *now*?"

We had been staying at random inns the past few nights when he literally had an apartment of his own? Why would he want to waste marks like that?

"This is my private space. No one knows it exists—not Lilliana, not even Gaar or Roslyn."

I didn't even know what to make of that.

A few moments passed before I spoke. "Then why would you show it to me?"

For a second, I feared he would say that he had no choice, that the circumstances forced his hand, but his actual words felt like a gut punch; touching me in a way I wasn't familiar with.

"Because I trust you, Violet." They were soft and gentle, spoken in the direction of the mixing bowl on the counter, with his hands braced at either side of it.

I couldn't handle this back and forth with him. One second

he was snapping at me to stay away and abandoning me, and the next he was acting possessive and kissing me senseless, all while not communicating about any of it.

"It's so..." I took a pause, struggling to find the right word. "Dark. And warm," I finished, not even bothering to mask the awe in my voice.

I noticed an ornate gold pattern printed into the black curtains I had seen before, the foil glittering from the dim light coming out of a few lamps in the space. One was situated behind a deep loveseat that had velvet material and plump, lush cushions.

My legs practically melted with the desire to sit in that fucking chair.

I pushed the thought to the side, though, as I looked a little closer at the lamp that had initially caught my attention. It looked incredibly familiar, but I couldn't place why.

The shade was made from mosaic stained glass of all different colors, casting a colorful hue over the entire space. It gave such a cozy and homey feel that I slowly looked over at Xander, confused by the fact that this sanctuary was designed by the giant standing across from me.

Said giant was appraising me with his eyes, no doubt wondering what I felt about the space. The timid expression lying there seemed so out of place in comparison to the arrogant smile that usually did, and I felt like this was an opportunity to prove to him that he didn't need to have so many walls up around himself all of the time.

"I love it," I said honestly, rounding the counter to stand next to him and peering up at those beautiful green eyes. "Thank you for trusting me with it."

Something shattered within his gaze. He looked down at me like I was some great feat of nature, the adoration shining clear in his eyes. I leaned into him, and he immediately shifted to grant me better access, bringing one hand off the counter. Right as I was perching on my tiptoes to bring my lips to his, he spoke and broke the spell.

"As much as I would love to get lost in this for a while—and *believe* me, I would—we have a lot to discuss."

I tried and failed to stifle my disappointment, deciding to move away from him so that he could say what he needed to. I plopped down on the couch I was eyeing earlier, which did not disappoint in the slightest. It might've been the most comfortable thing I'd ever sat in.

I looked over at Xander expectantly, who had returned to his task of making pancakes. He added flour and sugar to the bowl, stirring it with a wooden spoon and avoiding my gaze.

"Well?" I asked, irritated. "If you need to speak, then speak."

Xander tsked. "There's no call for your hostility, Angel. I'm trying to figure out how to phrase it delicately."

"Um, where have you been the past few days?" I shot back. "I don't deal in delicacies. Just fucking say it."

"Very well," he said with a loaded look. "The man you call Mr. Berger is dead."

CHAPTER TWENTY-FOUR

XANDER

"*What?*" Violet asked in a shrill voice, her body jerking upright in surprise. "What did you just say?"

"I did some digging while you were unconscious. After speaking to my informant, I learned that Mr. Berger was an Astrolite deserter turned runaway. He fled to the human lands thirty years ago. His vanishing was kept quiet to discourage others from following in his footsteps."

Violet's body sunk into the cushions behind her, seemingly unable to hold her weight any longer.

My jaw tightened at the sight, especially because I was so far from being done. "This gave me hope that he may have found a way to evade the Retaliators–you remember that charming little group we encountered in the clearing by the lake?"

She nodded, her swallow audible. Fury slashed through my veins at her reaction, at the mental image of Violet struggling against her captor's hold; the memory reigniting my anger.

My voice turned harsh as I spoke about those spineless fucking *twats*. "The Retaliators are a rebel group working against the Astrale government: Lilliana and other officials, including Shaed's father–Dmitri. They are trying to upend any movements they support, including our perusal of the Chalice. I immediately suspected that Mr. Berger's disappearance was their doing when I saw the note on his wall–it had their name written all over it."

"You're going way too fast. I don't understand anything

you're saying." The raw ring to her voice made my throat constrict.

I was the absolute last person who should have been responsible for teaching Violet all of these things. She deserved someone more in tune with social cues and who was skilled in personable interaction, not someone who found it difficult to muster up the emotion required to console others on a daily basis.

Although, something told me that I would find no shortage of emotions when it came to this woman.

Violet's voice took on a harder edge, the irritation leaking into her words. "Why would these 'Retaliators' give a damn about Mr. Berger or the cup I made? He was entirely innocent in this. He was just trying to support my business."

"With all due respect," I started, doing my best to fill a role I never had before, "you need to accept that Mr. Berger was not just the elderly man you knew. He had to have played a bigger role than that. We just don't know what that was."

Violet pursed her lips and looked away, towards the window with its curtains drawn. She looked back to me, a closed-off glint to her eye. "So, what makes you think he is dead?"

Clearing my throat, I continued stirring as I spoke. "I paid a little unexpected visit to Shaed's father, Dmitri, while you slept. I grew tired of his lack of response to my messages and decided that this was worth revealing the fact that I can get past his wards."

I cursed myself for letting that last part slip. Not because I cared if Violet knew of my abilities, but because she wouldn't understand what that meant and didn't need excess information clouding her brain right now. Not on top of everything else she was trying to process.

"I questioned Dmitri about Mr. Berger, making it seem like Lilliana had me searching for stray runaways. He immediately knew who I was speaking of, even with very little information to go on. It seemed very odd to him that I was asking about the man he had just received a message about the day before."

I swallowed, knowing that this would be the hardest on her.

"One of the Astrolite guards found Mr. Berger's body outside the gates of the palace with a note tacked to his shirt."

I kept stirring the batter, unable to look up at Violet. I could smell the damp saltiness of her tears in the air and I didn't know how to stop them. I was not even slightly experienced in comforting others–especially women. All I knew was that she had hardly eaten the day before and then slept for almost eighteen hours. Her body needed sustenance.

That, I could take care of.

"What did the note say?" Her voice was pain-stricken, twisting a knife in my gut.

"*A consequence of your own inadequacies*'," I told her, the words still irritating me beyond all reason. "But more so than that, Dmitri told me that there was a substance sprinkled all around his body. A sort of soft power that left behind a layer of chalky residue when touched..."

Violet looked at me, her big eyes round and confused. My nostrils flared at the sight of her tears. "I don't understand," she whispered hoarsely.

"I believe that powder was the Chalice, destroyed and reduced to ash," I told her honestly.

She didn't respond to that, so I continued.

"Dmitri seemed perplexed by it all, but not enough to dig into the issue, apparently. He did show me the note, though. Otherwise, I would have a hard time believing it at all. Something about the way he buried the situation, keeping it strictly confidential, has piqued my interest. The only reason he told me was my status as a top Enforcer."

I forced myself to relax, the arrogance and selfishness of the entire Astrolite culture boiling my blood. But that wasn't my focus now.

Violet was.

I watched as the shock slowly hit Violet, her shoulders slumping to create a protective barrier around her as they shook with silent sobs. I abandoned the finished batter on the counter, turning the stove to a low heat to warm the pan before walking to her.

Slowly, I lowered myself to sit next to Violet and took her hand in mine, brushing my thumb over the fleshy pad below hers.

"I'm sorry, Violet," I said, because there was nothing else *to* say.

No words would make this situation right or take away her pain. All I could do was be by her side and try to comfort her.

"He was so *kind*," her voice broke on the last syllable, morphing into a sob as she crumpled into my side and began to cry in earnest.

I immediately lifted my arm and guided her down to rest her head in my lap, running one hand over the still-tangled mess of her hair and the other up and down her arm in a gentle touch.

"Fucking annoying at times, sure," she continued. "But so genuine and thoughtful. He didn't deserve this."

"Sometimes the world is the most cruel to the kindest of people," I replied in sympathy, unsure if the words would hurt or help.

She nodded and continued crying, the small sounds escaping her making my teeth grind together harder than I knew to be possible. I would find great joy in ripping the organs out of every last Retaliator for making her feel this pain.

We sat there like that for long enough that Violet's tears subsided and her breathing evened out, but she remained in the same position nonetheless. After a while, I began to worry about the stove being on, but right when I was about to turn the knob down with my magic, Violet stirred and sat up.

Her eyes were puffy around the rims, the blue spot in them shining brilliantly with the remaining glossiness lying there. I honestly expected her to be in that *other* state, but she appeared to be fully alert, albeit broken down and sad.

"The Chalice is destroyed?" Violet finally asked, visibly flinching at the sound of her strangled voice.

"That is just speculation, but I can't imagine what else would have been scattered around his corpse."

"But it doesn't make sense," she insisted. "Why would they leave that message for us to bring them the Chalice if they already had it?"

"Perhaps they didn't have it at the time," I offered, but I wasn't thinking about the Chalice. I was focused on Violet and the way I could hear her heart hammering inside of her chest.

"What else did you learn?"

I leaned in and brushed a kiss to her forehead, enjoying her slight inhale of breath at the act.

"It's okay, Angel. We don't have to cover it all right now. Let's eat."

I took her hands and stood us up, guiding her to the chairs facing the stove.

"I would rather get it all out in the open now," Violet said as she sat. "No sense in prolonging the inevitable."

I respected that about her. She didn't care for bullshit and pleasantries—just wanted to keep moving forward.

It almost reminded me of Gaar, but I quickly pushed the thought aside.

I sighed, pouring a dollop of batter on the too-hot pan. "I also inquired about your father. I was careful to give Dmitri his description without bringing you into it, claiming I didn't even know his name."

"And?" Violet asked, leaning forward.

"He knows something." I turned back towards her to find her eyes boring into me, hanging onto every word. "But he feigned ignorance. I could tell by the spark in his eyes and the way his spine straightened, though—he knew your father. Maybe even personally."

She swallowed audibly, and I tracked the way her throat bobbed with the movement, thoughts that were totally inappropriate for the circumstance jumping into my head. I turned back abruptly and flipped the pancakes, the little bubbles in them indicating that they were ready.

Every time I did this, I was reminded of when Roslyn taught me how to make them. Years before Ros deserted from Terrala, when she was still a girl, her mother taught her how to make the delicacy that was a part of her sector's culture. So, after she had to leave, it was a small part of home that she brought with her, then passed on to me when I joined civilisation.

I still remembered her words to me that night in the Armoury kitchen, so many years later.

'Sometimes, when life has gone to shit, when it all feels like too much, I come down here and make pancakes. They remind me of how far I have come, of everything I have survived, and put into perspective how small my current issues may be.'

I wasn't sure how that philosophy applied to the shitshow we were in, but I hoped that the fluffy goodness would at least bring a small smile to my Angel's face. She deserved a reprieve from the pain and confusion that had been battering her relentlessly.

The other side having cooked, I plated the pancakes and grabbed the hazelnut spread from the cupboard, sliding both across the counter to Violet. She looked up at me with a strange expression, pushing the gravity of our conversation to the side momentarily.

"You never cease to surprise me," she said in a laughing tone, looking between me and the meal I'd made.

"I do aim to keep you on your cute little toes," I responded, my chest feeling so much lighter now that her expression had cleared.

She laughed and grabbed the knife, spreading a healthy amount of the hazelnut on her pancakes before digging in with her fork.

I repressed a groan at the way her plump lips wrapped around the metal, feeling jealous of a fucking *fork* for the first time in my life. But then she moaned—deep and throaty—when the food touched her taste buds, and my already semi-hard cock strained painfully against the waistband of my trousers, even as loose as it was.

Fuck me. This girl might actually kill me. And I had hardly even touched her yet.

"Fuck *me*, Xander," Violet drawled after swallowing, mirroring my thoughts perfectly. "These are so damn good."

Then she was returning to her plate, shoving another bite into her mouth with so much excitement, I was surprised she didn't stab her mouth.

"I'm very glad," I said stiffly, turning back around to add more batter to the pan.

Those two words on her tongue kept looping in my mind. Even though I knew it wasn't a sexual advance, it sure fucking felt like one with that sultry voice of hers.

My chest was also swelling with a foreign pride; something primal stirring in my gut from her satisfaction. This must be the mating bond creeping up–the fierce need to provide for your partner and see to their needs.

Regardless of the cause, I would do this every fucking day if it let me hear her moans of pleasure. Maybe when she was done eating, I could melt some of the hazelnut spread she seemed to love so much and have a little fun with it.

I could picture it perfectly–Vi spread out on my bed, completely bare and exposed, writhing under my touch as I dribbled the chocolate substance–

"So, what else?" Violet asked, interrupting the turn my thoughts had taken.

I shook myself, forcing my mind back to the conversation we were having and away from the deranged thought process.

I mean, fuck. This girl had me hard from the sight of her *eating*.

"Dmitri's reaction to my description of your father was strange. It made me wonder how close–or estranged–they really were. Which also had me thinking...what if the woman you saw in the memory was actually Shaed's mother?"

Violet's eyes flashed, and I recognised the wheels spinning inside her mind. "That would explain a lot," she said, a contemplative edge to her voice. "When I first met Chelsea, I thought she looked familiar. Maybe it was because I recognised her mother's attributes?"

"That seems likely."

I plated the rest of the pancakes, turned off the stove, and moved to sit next to Violet. She eyed my plate, the attempt at stealthiness amusing me.

"Would you like some more, my ravenous little human?" I leaned in closer. "I thought you weren't hungry."

"No, I wouldn't." She tried to sound unaffected, but wasn't quite cutting it. "And I *wasn't*," Violet insisted. "But why do you insist on calling me that when we both know I'm an Astrale?"

I laughed, tossing two of the pancakes onto her plate. She was mad if she thought I'd intended on eating the entire stack on my own, anyway. I was only bringing them over to her.

I booped a finger on her nose. "You'll always be my little human."

Violet rolled her eyes, but her cheeks took on a pink tinge that snagged my gaze. I smiled as she dug back into her meal, the eagerness making me happy.

Making me *happy?*

I was further gone than I'd thought.

"So," Violet mused, "how can I get in front of Shaed's mother to confirm that she was actually the woman in the memory?"

"Well, that's the only problem. She's dead."

"Seriously?" Violet groaned. "Why is everyone we need to speak to dead?"

I gaped at her, a little dumbfounded by her bluntness.

She cringed. "Sorry, that probably sounded insensitive. It's just that we are, what? Like, sixteen days into this mission? With nothing to show for it?"

"Seventeen, actually," I corrected after swallowing my food. "You were out for almost an entire day."

"Well, that's just great." Violet pushed herself off her chair, grabbed her already-empty plate, and moved to the sink.

"You don't need to do that," I said when she started cleaning it.

She ignored me, using the soap to wash away all remnants of the food before grabbing the mixing bowl and doing the same. I tried to avoid staring at her full, delicious arse as she worked, even though it was beckoning me like a siren's call. I focused on my plate of food instead, even though it was much less appealing.

When Violet was done, she sighed and turned back around, looking at me from across the small kitchen.

"I need to get back to Archi. I need to know that he is okay." Worry was etched across her striking features. "Based on what you told me, over a month has passed for him by now. He has to be going out of his mind with worry, assuming that he has even been able to keep up with the bills. Please take me back, Xan. Please. Just to check in on him."

I swallowed the bitterness of bile that was creeping its way up my throat. Every fibre of my being wanted to give her anything she wanted, *especially* since she was begging me, but it was fruitless for her to go back there. Archi was undoubtedly fine, but she was unaware of why that was, so I understood her worry.

"I didn't just alter his memory of our visit, Violet." I used my skills of lying well, keeping some truth woven into the deception.

She stiffened like a board, anticipatory worry crowding her body language.

I continued, the words tasting like acid on my tongue. "I implanted the fact that you were going on a trip into his mind, like what you told your friend at the market. And I made sure that he had enough marks to last him a year–from my personal stores."

She visibly relaxed at the revelation, a metaphorical weight being lifted off her shoulders. The sight made a layer of guilt that I was unaccustomed to coat my insides. I didn't falsify that Archi was taken care of. He was.

But I also left a great deal out of my confession, and a lie by omission is still a lie.

"Okay," she said. "I'm trusting that you've looked out for him."

Fuck. There's that word again.

"Where are my things?" she asked, throwing me off guard. "I need to take a shower."

I gestured to where her bag was sitting in the corner of the room, and she walked weightlessly to it, moving to the bathing room with renewed energy.

As she closed the door behind her, I rested my forehead on my hand, feeling like a complete sack of shit for lying to her.

hazelnut

CHAPTER TWENTY-FIVE

VIOLET

"When are we going back to the Armory?" I asked Xander as I emerged back into the living space after showering and getting dressed.

I was wearing the last clean outfit that I'd brought with me and would need to get the rest of my things.

He looked over at me sharply from his position on the couch, where he lounged with a book propped on his knee. "What gave you the impression that we were going back?"

"Um...I don't know. I guess I just figured that we would?"

"Again," he muttered, his frustration clear. "Why are you asking?"

"I am out of clean clothes. The rest of them are back in my room there."

I shuffled on my feet a bit, feeling restless under his angry gaze.

Xander closed the book and set it to the side, standing up and stalking toward me. "Did I not tell you to gather your things when we left?"

"Well, yeah, but I thought–"

"I believe we have already covered that you are to listen to me when it comes to this mission." By the time he was done speaking, Xander stood before me, looming over me with a cold expression on his face.

I swallowed my protest, knowing that he was right but feeling frustrated that I was supposed to just throw aside the way I had functioned my entire life.

He sighed, brushing a soft hand down the soft knitted cardigan I wore. "It's alright. I will just have to sneak in and out undetected."

"Why does it have to be undetected?" I asked in confusion, a bit shaken by the abrupt change in his mood.

Xander's jaw hardened. "I'm not letting you anywhere near Lilliana."

"Uhh, what? Why not?"

Seriously, what was with this man? Was he not just chastising me for speaking poorly of her? And suddenly he didn't even want me in the same building as her?

"We cannot return to Lilliana before we've figured out more about where you come from and what your abilities are. I don't even know what our next immediate move is besides seeking out the Retaliators, but that will be like searching for a needle in a haystack." Xander's eyes shifted, almost like there was a curtain falling down within them.

"Besides," he murmured, moving in closer to me. "I am far less concerned about Lilliana needing the Chalice than I am about your...origins."

Why did the way he said that word sound so oddly sexual?

"We can buy some time by making Lilliana think that's where our energy is going and that we are too busy to return to the Armory. When in reality, we will be following this lead to the Astrolite sector and Shaed's mother."

I crossed my arms. "And why don't you think we should return back to her? I thought you trusted her more than anyone else? Wouldn't you want her to help us—to get her advice about this whole situation with Shaed's mother? Surely they knew each other."

"This isn't about my trust in her. It's about my trust in her when it comes to you." His voice was fierce and determined as his eyes shone down at me brilliantly.

My brow furrowed. "I don't really understand the difference between the two."

"If she knew about the abilities that have been revealing themselves...I don't even want to think about what she would do to you. She is ruthless when it comes to the safety of Cavell, and she will see you as a threat." He dipped his chin, moving closer to my face in emphasis. "Trust me, I know."

My brow pinched at the contradiction. "And yet you can siphon from more than one Core? Why aren't you a threat to her?"

As soon as the words were out of my mouth, I realized my mistake.

I'd been so careful not to betray Roslyn's trust, but with everything else we'd just talked about, it slipped past my defenses.

Xander took a small step back, his eyes and body language regaining the closed-off demeanor that they had in the beginning of our time together. "And just how, exactly, are you aware of *that*?" The words were slow, measured, lethal. That, paired with the pain flickering behind his gaze, made a panic rush to my throat, and words began pouring out of my mouth.

"It was just something Roslyn mentioned in passing. She didn't tell me outright–I put it together myself. Really, it isn't a big deal."

"Isn't a big deal?" Xander laughed mockingly.

I reached out a hand for his, but he retreated again and hissed, "You have no idea what you're talking about."

"Okay, right, maybe I don't," I started, and my voice raised with each word, my anger level along with it. It was unfair of him to treat me this way, regardless of the politics I might not be aware of. "But wouldn't that make me the best person to talk to about this? It's not like I'm going to judge you. I don't even know enough to be able to do that!"

He deflated a little, looking at me like he was considering his options. The sight filled me with hope that he might *finally* explain to me what made him so different from other Astrales.

"Please just talk to me," I pleaded in a tone I hardly ever used. "I just want to know you better. I just want to understand."

His features softened even more, and I knew that this was the perfect opportunity to strike. I moved to him, reaching a hand up and running my fingers through the soft hair at the nape of his neck. His eyes fluttered at the contact, and he leaned into my touch.

"How do you have access to more than one Core?" I asked gently.

He swallowed. "That's a very hard and complicated answer, Violet."

And that was it. I'd had enough of that fucking answer. I thought we were making progress on this front. I thought he was beginning to let me in, but apparently not.

Well, fine. If he didn't want to tell me anything about himself, I was done getting my hopes up. Done trying. I let my hand fall to my side and took a small step backward.

I wondered what he saw on my face as his own slipped into a pained sort of expression, as if he wanted to tell me but couldn't.

I didn't particularly care.

"So what's our next move?"

"Vi," he said softly, the nickname he so infrequently used threatening to melt my annoyance. "I'm sorry. There are just some things that I don't think you'd want to know, and others that are very difficult to talk about."

"Mhm," I muttered dryly, not even having the energy to repeat that he needed to stop deciding what I did and didn't want. That wasn't his decision to make, and yet, he kept making it anyway.

"What's the next move?" I repeated, making it clear that I was closing the conversation.

Xander blew air through his teeth and ran a frustrated hand through his hair, disheveling it a bit. "Well, if the events that happened at the lake yesterday are any indication, you need to be able to defend yourself. It seems that the Retaliators have put some sort of target on my head, and therefore yours, since you will not be leaving my side."

Something bloomed in my gut at the last part. I actively ignored it.

"You did appear to be somewhat trained, though."

I nodded.

My father began teaching me how to fight at a young age. Eventually, he told me that there were some bad people from my mother's past that might show up someday, so I needed to be able to protect myself. After he died, I did what I could to continue building my skill set–replicating it with Archi, and sometimes Imani–but I never had another formal instructor.

Xan grinned down at me. "I'm glad that you are. It will give us a good starting point."

"Starting point?" I asked with a bite to my tone.

If he thought his stupid grin was going to dissolve what had just happened, he was sorely mistaken.

"I'm sure that your skills are sufficient for defending yourself in Armantrea, but you need to be better equipped to fight off an Astrale."

"I seemed to do well enough with you by that lake–thank you very much."

Xander smirked, and my pulse picked up just from that tiny little curl of his mouth. "That is because you had the element of surprise and close proximity on your side. Sadly, those sexy little silver knuckles won't do you much good in a typical Astrale fight."

I bristled at the way he called my weapon 'little' when he had been the one bleeding profusely because of it.

"Where did you get them, anyway?" he asked, looking down at my hand as if he could still picture me wearing it.

"Well, for starters, it–not them," I corrected. "It's called a defense ring. My mother gave it to me."

I lifted up my right hand, showing the ring that I was wearing on my middle finger. It was just a gold band that didn't draw much attention, but I always thought that it was beautiful in its simplicity. I turned the ring once with my thumb, drawing out the moment the circle was completed, and watched Xander's face as the weapon sprung free.

I felt it snap into place around my knuckles and smirked at the expression of wonder that Xander was wearing. His eyebrows raised above widened eyes that skirted back and forth across my hand, clearly impressed by the ring.

"I'm guessing this reaction means that you have never seen a defense ring before?" I asked.

Xander shook himself out of his stupor, locking gazes with me once more. "No, I haven't."

"Strange," I mused. "So does that mean that it is a human invention or an Astrale one?"

"No idea, but I'd like to thank whoever it was. That might be the sexiest thing I've ever seen." His voice was loaded with arousal, the air in the room thickened along with it.

"Well, in that case," I said sweetly, pressing the release along the side and returning it to the plain ring.

Xander looked at me with narrowed eyes, making me flash-back to when he had my jaw clamped roughly in his hand, staring down at me.

"Get into a fighting position," Xander ordered, a harder tone to his voice now.

"Why?" I asked, but quickly complied when he shot me a look.

Xander didn't answer as he circled me slowly, making my heart race under his scrutiny. "You're keeping your weight too heavily on your dominant side," he observed.

"I am not," I protested, grounding myself even further to make sure that he was wrong.

"You are," he chided, coming to a stop in front of me. "The way you're positioned now, anyone could..." He shoved my left side, causing me to fall to the wood floor harshly. I stopped myself with a hand right before my head smashed into the unforgiving surface.

"What the fuck?" I asked, staring up at him in bewilderment.

The dickhead *shrugged*. "I was proving my point."

I gaped. "You could have hurt me."

Standing back up, I narrowed my eyes at him and did a full body scan to make sure nothing was injured.

"Well, it's a good deal you can heal yourself then." I could practically hear the smug smile creeping into his voice.

"What?" I asked, bewildered. "No, I can't."

"You can. I've witnessed it."

Xander grabbed my right hand and brushed his finger against my palm, the sensation familiar to me. "Remember in the woods? With the Manakoar? I sliced your palm to draw it near us before the whole ordeal happened. The cut was healed when we got back to the Armory," he paused for a second, gazing down at my hand. "I noticed it right away."

I stood there dumbfounded, my brain struggling to catch up to what he was saying. After a few seconds, I finally found my voice, and it was laced with irritation.

"Why haven't you told me about this yet?"

Xander brushed a few stray strands of hair out of my face from when I fell, and I felt like jerking my head away from his touch.

What was with his psychological need to withhold things from me? Did it have to do with the dark past he constantly hinted at, or was that just who he was as a person?

The answer to that question would definitely be a deciding factor for me.

"I wasn't sure what it meant at first," Xander admitted, still toying with my hair. "But then your Starfire revealed itself, and I realized how blind I had been all along.... Your pottery." He lifted my right hand to his mouth, dusting light kisses over my fingers. "You seeing through my Soothe in Armantrea." He dipped down to my neck, licking and nibbling the skin.

I panted softly against my will, trying with all my might to hold onto my anger as a thrill shot down my body.

He moved up and whispered the next words into my ear, his

deep, raspy voice causing me to repress a moan. "The way you broke through my barrier when I was Soothing Archi. And then, of course," he murmured, moving to speak against my parted lips, "when you burned me."

The words hung in the air as his lips grazed mine, not kissing, just hovering. My body felt torn–half of me aching for him, the other half wanting to throttle him.

The breath I took was shaky and didn't seem to go anywhere.

"I thought you wanted to train," I said, my voice much more breathless than I expected.

"Oh, certainly," Xander said, nudging my nose with his. "But I thought maybe you could use a warm-up."

"I *am* rather cold," I murmured, giving into the less-rational side of me that had been wanting from him since the second he showed up and blew apart my life.

Xander claimed my mouth instantly, groaning into it as I moved my tongue past his lips and slid it against his. He picked me up, setting me down on the counter behind us, all without breaking the kiss.

My heart rate increased, and my body was greedy for anything he was willing to give me. I slipped my hands under the hem of his shirt, marveling at how his skin felt–soft but firm, as his back muscles strained underneath.

He released my lips and stared down at me hungrily, his eyes boring into the crease between my thighs and my hips.

"You seem to like sitting me down. We have kissed twice and ended up like this both times."

"Oh, we're not ending like this, Angel," he promised. "Not even close."

The intent behind those words had my breasts tightening in excitement, and his eyes tracked that, too, his pupils constricting like it was his only focus.

"Tell me I can taste you," Xander said in a gravelly voice.

It sounded like a command, but I could tell it was more of an insistent request with the way he was restraining himself. His hands were bunched in the material of my tank top; thighs tightened like he was ready to pounce.

"Yes," I breathed, way beyond caring if I seemed needy or expectant. My thighs were pressed together tightly, my body clenching around far too much emptiness.

Xander didn't need any more approval than that, making me jump as he immediately picked me up and moved us to the bed in a blink. He laid me down gently before grabbing the waistband of my pants and pulling them off in one go.

I gasped, not expecting him to move so quickly, but it was like some sort of frenzy had taken over him. He was behaving like someone who hadn't eaten in days and was just presented with a four-course meal.

His eyes were as alert as I'd ever seen them, raking over the flesh he had just exposed. They traveled down my legs, drinking in the length and width. The hunger inside of them silenced any small insecurities I had about my birthmarks and stretch marks. All I could think of was the fact that he wasn't touching me, even though his gaze felt heavy enough to be one.

My entire body jerked when he grazed one finger over the center of me, the touch teasing in the best way as the lace of my underwear tickled my most sensitive area.

"There's that lacey number I saw before," Xander pointed out with a loaded tone. "It is even more divine on your body than it was in my fantasies."

He trailed that infuriating finger along the hem, up my hip, and then down again. I felt a pool of moisture gather between my thighs, struggling to control my limbs now.

He seemed to sense the shift because he dipped his head, speaking so close to my clit that I felt his breath skate across my panties. "I'd be willing to bet you taste better than I dreamed as well."

I whimpered, the idea of him fantasizing about me sending me spiraling toward someplace unknown.

"Should we see about that?" he asked, pressing down on my

bundle of nerves with his thumb and circling at a maddening pace.

I bucked my hips into his touch right as he retreated and lifted himself up. I was about to complain, but then he hooked his thumbs around the sides of my underwear and slid them down over my hips. I heard him inhale deeply, like it wasn't possible to get enough of my scent.

Slowly–too slowly–he lowered himself again, and I watched as his hungry gaze tracked every inch of my exposed cunt like he was committing it to memory. I was trying not to pant, the anticipation threatening to snap something inside of me.

"Doing alright up there, Vi?" Xander asked cockily, a grin pulling at his lips.

"Mhm," I moaned, every breath from him skating along the apex of my thighs.

"It seems like you might be struggling with something," he suggested innocently, acting like he didn't know damn well what I was *struggling* with.

I expected him to continue in his little game, but Xander dove down, drawing his tongue up my center in one clean swoop, purely tasting me.

"Fuck," he gasped, and my legs trembled slightly on either side of him. "You taste better than I ever could have imagined."

I whimpered, his words doing things to me I didn't even understand.

He moved again, tasting me and then focusing on my clit, circling it with his tongue before sucking it between his teeth. Sparks ignited behind my closed eyelids, and I already felt that distinct rush that told me my release was within reach.

He swept his tongue down again and groaned against my entrance, the sound reverberating through me all the way to my ears. I moaned at the sensation and rolled my hips forward, eager to get more from him. He complied, slipping his hands under my ass and lifting me so that my legs fell open even further.

Xander unleashed himself, the fevered movements against me

so intense that I couldn't even keep track of where he was or what he was doing. He moved up again and grazed the bundle of nerves with his teeth, sucking it between his lips.

"More," I pleaded, physically unable to form more words than that.

He chuckled against me, teasing me gloriously with his breath. "So needy," he chided, but plunged a finger into me at the same moment that he increased the pressure of his mouth on my clit.

Not bothering to ease into it, he fucked me with it hard and fast, just like I wanted. And after a few strokes, when he curled his finger inside me, hitting that perfect spot immediately—that was it.

I was *transported.*

Nothing existed around me. Not the apartment or the books, not the entire supernatural race I was surrounded by, and certainly not the Chalice or my fucking heritage.

The only thing that existed was Xander's finger, his mouth, and the tightening of my muscles around him as I rocked back and forth, aimlessly chasing a long-lasting orgasm.

"Fuck, Violet," Xander breathed out, and I moaned at the way my name sounded on his tongue. "You're so warm and soft. I can't wait until it's my cock you are spasming around instead of my finger."

I moaned again at his crass words, a mental image forming that I wanted to become a reality immediately. A soft hand slipped under my shirt, grazing from my neck to my belly button—feeling more like a proprietary touch than anything.

"You look fucking *magnificent* while you are coming for me, my little human," Xander rasped out, sounding breathless.

I reached out to him but froze when he withdrew from me, his green gaze penetrating and locked on my own as he brought his middle finger to his mouth, sucking every last drop of me off of him.

Xander had just fucked me with his middle finger.

Why was that so hot?

My toes curled as my body went slack, the pleasure and renewed arousal battling for dominance inside of me. But when he appeared at my side and started drawing lazy circles over the plane of my stomach with his fingertips, my muscles succumbed to the pleasant, post-orgasmic state.

"Your turn," I murmured, my voice sounding soft and distant.

Damn, I'd never had this strong of an aftershock before.

I turned my head, humming when Xander's hand skated up to my neck and he began stroking it lightly in sweeping movements.

"I just had my turn," Xander murmured, his own voice more gravelly than usual.

I looked at him more closely, noticing that his brows had entirely evened out. There was a dazed smile on his face as he lazily touched me all over, his eyes hooded but still intent on my naked, flushed body.

I've never really cared for nakedness after having sex, preferring to be alone as soon as possible once the act was completed.

But with Xander? And the way he was staring at me like he would never get enough?

I could have stayed there all day.

"You came?" I asked, not fully believing what he was implying. I could hardly believe I had finished so quickly, but I hadn't even touched him.

Xander made a low noise of agreement before nuzzling into my neck, the act so unexpected that it forced a giggle out of my throat before I could stop it.

"I like that sound," Xander said, his voice muffled against my skin.

He didn't move, staying tucked in there as his fingers moved into my hair, massaging my scalp. I moaned in response, both to his breaths skating along my skin and the way I felt my entire head release its tension.

"You smell so good," Xander gushed, inhaling deeply.

I flushed again. "No one has ever said that to me before."

"Then they're a bunch of fucking knobheads," he growled. "You smell like everything I could ever want."

"You're so fucking weird," I muttered behind a laugh, even though I felt a sense of giddiness take over me from his words.

He smiled, finally pulling back from me to look into my eyes. "Never claimed otherwise. Did I?"

"No, I suppose not," I answered, my smooth voice contradicting the way my heart was pounding inside my body. I'd never felt like this before. The desire to get closer, to attach myself to him like a small animal hugging a tree.

This level of intimacy.

I took my turn laying my head in the crook of his neck, his rich, woodsy scent of pine and smoke filling all of my senses. It left me feeling so whole, so complete, that I finally let the drugged feeling take over and drifted to sleep in my captor's arms.

And I'd never felt safer.

CHAPTER TWENTY-SIX

XANDER

There were times when I blacked out entirely.

I'd be doing one thing, and before I knew it, I was somewhere else entirely, doing something I didn't recognise.

At first, I chalked it up to trauma. Surely my brain was fucked-up beyond the way I craved violence. I believed that the way I was brought up might have led to me losing hours from my memory, possibly due to some sort of defect.

But it hadn't been happening as much around Violet. In fact, I could count on one hand the number of times that it had. Which was...strange. It made me think that there was something bigger at play than just traumatic effects.

I mean, there was always the possibility that because Violet was my mate, she kept my symptoms–or whatever the fuck I should call them–at bay. But that didn't seem very likely to me.

One of the few times I'd spaced out had just happened, and I was struggling to see past my worry this time around because it wasn't just about me.

Violet had been left defenceless.

After our gloriously inept training session, she'd started to doze off with her head on my shoulder. I understood her exhaustion after everything she'd learned and figured she needed to process and heal. So, I wrapped her up in my arms and cradled her close to my body, drawing small circles on the soft skin of her lower back. The last thing I remembered was drinking in her sweet scent that was almost like caramel, and then suddenly, I was standing outside the door to my flat.

The sun had gone down, the faint hue from the moon was shining through the hallway window. I looked down at my hands, confusion and dread wracking through my entire body when I saw the remnants of blood scattered there.

It wasn't the worst I'd seen them after blacking out, not by a long shot. But it was still very disconcerting. I'd focused my hearing to check if Violet was awake, but immediately heard her slight snore. In the interest of not waking her up, I whisked myself directly into the bathing room and washed up quickly, before moving to the sofa, where I was now sitting with a rare glass of whisky in my hand.

I glanced at her figure, lying on my bed and felt a swell in my chest at the sight.

She wouldn't be in any other bed again if I had anything to say about it.

Come to think of it, though, she had been sleeping an awful lot. Before, I had only been thinking about how she had been bombarded with new information and then climaxed very hard—much to my satisfaction—but that shouldn't have been enough to drain her when she had just slept for almost an entire day.

Something else was happening with her.

Was it that her body was acclimating to being in her homeland? Did it have to do with her dormant magic?

Or were those two things connected?

I drained my glass in one swoop, swallowing down the harsh liquid and enjoying the burn it left in its wake.

I wasn't sure what time Violet had gone to sleep, but it was definitely still light outside when she had, meaning that I must've been gone for more than an hour.

That was at least sixty minutes of her sleeping defencelessly in an empty flat. Even though it was heavily warded, someone could have found her.

The thought sent a wave of heat coursing through my veins,

my body reacting to the threat involuntarily. I stood and moved to the desk, staring down at Violet's handprints on the wood. Running a hand over the grooves, I tried to stifle the panic gripping me.

The mere idea of anyone hurting her made my ears ring with rage. I needed to find a way to stop these episodes of skipped consciousness from happening, but I didn't know how.

Maybe it was finally time to tell Gaar about them. If anyone would know what to do, it'd be him. I'd held off from telling him in the past because it never really bothered me enough to. So what if I space out sometimes?

Things had changed, though. I had a mate to look out for now—one who was not equipped to fight her own battles.

Yet.

I had every intention of training her to be the best Starfire wielder this nation had ever seen. Then no one would be able to touch a hair on her perfectly gorgeous head, tangled or not.

"*Xander*," Violet's silky voice reached my ears from across the room, the tone implying that it was not the first time she'd said it. "Are you doing some Astrale meditation shit, or what? Why are you so spaced out?"

"Sorry, love," I replied immediately and walked to her. "I was just deep in thought–I didn't realise you'd woken. Were you asking me something?"

Violet looked at me sceptically. "Did you just call me '*love*'?"

I tilted my head.

Well...that was a first.

"What of it?" I asked casually, not betraying my own shock at the endearment that'd rolled off my tongue so effortlessly.

"Oh, I don't know," she retorted with a dry tone. "Maybe just the fact that you called me it when you won't even tell me the first fucking thing about yourself?"

My teeth ground together in irritation. That attitude of hers was going to come back to her one day.

I could see her point, though.

"I like to sing," I offered at random, then cringed internally–a little more unsure of myself than I'd been in a while.

I mean, of all the confessions I could have possibly given her, *that* was what popped out of my mouth?

After I made it out of confinement, Roslyn showed me music for the first time. In all of my fifty-odd years of existence, I had no idea that it even existed. That's how hollow of a life I was forced to live.

So, after I discovered it, I never wanted to let it go.

Violet was sitting up now, seemingly less grumpy than she'd been a few seconds ago. My eyes tracked the way her top plunged low on her chest, showcasing her cleavage in a beautifully-confronting way.

I felt myself stiffening in my trousers.

"You can sing?" Violet asked, bringing me back to the conversation. Her voice was aghast, like she expected me to be lying.

"Well, I didn't say that I was any good," I clarified. "I said that I enjoy it. There is a clear difference."

She scooted to the end of the bed, and I came to stand before her, loving the way she looked up at me like I was a monumental landmark and not a semi-psychotic, murderous abomination.

Such a precious, oblivious little thing–my Violet.

"Sing for me," she pleaded, those big, big eyes working their way into my will like a Soothe would.

Regardless, there was no way that was happening right now.

"Absolutely not."

"Oh, come on. Please?" she pleaded, and with that voice of hers...

Yeah, I was fully erect now.

"You do beg very prettily," I told her, running a hand along her jaw and my thumb over her lips. "But still no."

She pouted that lip, her eyebrows scrunching up in stubbornness. I laughed lightly at the sight, the act becoming more frequent with each minute I spent with this woman.

"Come on, love," I said, reaching my hand out for Violet's.

She looked at me with suspicion again, but got up, taking my hand. "Where are we going?"

"The Mistral Festival is in two days, and you are coming with me. It will be a perfect opportunity to provoke the Retaliators a bit." There was a smile on my face by the time I finished, partly because of the prospect of having Violet on my arm in public–at my favourite event of the year, nonetheless. I couldn't wait to have her at my side, in front of the entire sector's eyes–even if we would be masked.

The other cause of my smile was that I might get the opportunity to cease the breaths of a Retaliator or two so soon.

"What is the Mistral Festival?" Violet asked, breaking me out of my train of thought. "And why would you want to provoke the Retaliators? Wouldn't that put us in danger?"

"You don't ever need to worry about being in danger when you are by my side," I all but growled, a fresh wave of protectiveness and rage surging to the surface. I put my hands on her hips, squeezing tightly to remind myself that she was right there. "I want to draw them out of their dirty little caves so that I can end their miserable existence, one broken bone at a time. After I get every answer that we need out of their rotting, peanut-sized brains, that is."

Violet was looking at me with parted lips, her eyes a little stunned. She didn't look afraid, just in a state of frozen surprise.

"What?" I asked her, jolting my grip on her hips.

She shook herself out of the trance, eyes darting to the ground briefly before looking at me from behind her lashes. "You're a little intense when you're pissed," she admitted.

I briefly wondered if she knew what that word meant in my culture, but pushed aside the thought as quickly as it came.

I hardened my jaw. "No one touches what is mine and lives to speak of it."

Her eyes widened again, and the pupils there dilated, a faint hue taking over the tops of her cheeks.

"I won't apologise for that," I told her firmly, having to resist the urge to lift her up, wrap her legs around my waist, and sink my teeth into her skin.

Shit. The clock was ticking.

I needed to tell her–soon.

I was suddenly very aware of how strong my grip was on her body, probably hard enough to leave bruises. *Fuck.*

I loosened them immediately and withdrew my hands, feeling a strange whirlwind of emotions taking over me.

The urge to mark her and make this bond visible for the world to see.

The desire to tell her everything, no matter how much I dreaded how she would react.

The uncertainty of how my words had just made her feel, worrying that I had been too forward.

Faster than I'd ever seen her move, Violet grabbed my hands and replaced them on her body.

Superspeed?

"I didn't ask you to," Violet murmured, her eyes slightly glossy and unfocused as they looked up at mine.

"You like being mine?" I asked, somewhat in disbelief. I stroked her hair out of her face, running the silkiness between my fingers.

"Yes," Violet whispered, almost as if she didn't want to admit it to herself.

My entire body felt like it was being picked up just from that one word.

"But," she started, and I deflated again. "I have a hard time saying that I *am* yours when you are still so closed off to me. I can't be connected to half a person, Xan." There was resolve in her gaze, letting me know that this was something she wouldn't budge on.

I leant down and brushed a kiss over her forehead before pulling back. "We will go now and get you some appropriate attire for the festival, as well as a few more clothing items to hold you over for the next day. I realised that Lilliana will be more than occupied during the event, so we will be able to slip into the Armoury and get the rest of your things then."

Violet nodded, a spark of excitement lighting up her beautiful, unique eyes. "Where are we going?" she asked.

"Inderton–the Hydroseis sector. Well, headquarters, to be precise," I told her. "Their magic deals with water."

The haze in her gaze had been replaced by an intense focus, clearly looking forward to another look at the Astrale society and its magic. Something in me calmed at the sight, her interest in magic made me feel like she might be more receptive to my situation.

"And when we return," I said, my chest feeling tight with anxiety, "I will tell you what you want to know."

When those big eyes locked on mine, the excitement within them deepened, and I emphasised, "I will tell you *everything.*"

And I would, I realised.

As long as she kept looking at me that way, I would tell her anything she wanted to know.

CHAPTER TWENTY-SEVEN

VIOLET

"Oh, my actual fucking god," I murmured under my breath, looking at the view in front of me in pure astonishment.

After I changed my clothes, Xander whisked us to the clifftop we were currently standing on, looking down at some sort of compound. It was unlike anything I had ever seen.

The building was *massive* and circular in shape, but the walls themselves were made of a material I had never seen before. It was a shining, light blue color that felt like it should be translucent, even though nothing was visible within the walls. In the center of the building was a great body of water that I presumed the citizens of Inderton used for swimming, based on the bodies I saw within it. We were so far away that they looked like tiny specks flitting around the expanse of blue.

"Let me ask you something," Xander's deep, rumbling voice broke through my focus on the building in front of me, causing me to look back at him expectantly.

He just stared down at me, so I said, "Well?"

Xander *tsked*. "Don't be impatient."

"Don't be irritating," I leveled back.

Xander's eyes narrowed, but he remained silent.

"Please, go on," I goaded dryly, sweeping my arms out in a mocking gesture. "We are all on the edge of our seats."

In a split second, Xander had my body pressed flush against his, my back to his chest, as he kept a hand clamped over my mouth. "I told myself that I would never take your voice away again," Xander spoke into my ear, a warning edge to his voice. "But you really make me question that decision in times like these."

I let out a grunt of frustration, the sound coming out all muffled and blurry. As annoyed as I was, there was something about the effortless way he handled me that was actually kind of... thrilling.

"Now that I actually have the chance to speak without you acting like a little fucking *brat*," Xander whispered, his breaths coasting down my neck. "Is it safe to assume that you worship this 'god' you are always swearing to?"

Xander's hand remained over my mouth for a few seconds before he slowly pulled it back. His other arm was still banded across my ribs, disallowing even the slightest of spaces between us.

I coughed lightly, the lack of breath causing my throat to dry out. "You're barbaric," I hissed at Xander, settling for glaring at the ground since his face was out of view.

"I've been called worse. Now answer my question." His voice was hard, unarguable, but softened with an added, "Please."

I was a little thrown by that last part, but I shrugged it off, refusing to turn into a puddle because of one word.

"No, I do not worship god," I told him in an exasperated tone.

He seriously went through all of this trouble for *that?*

"It is just a figure of speech," I finished and shrugged. "Everyone says it."

"But, generally speaking, your people believe in a god, yes?" His grip was less hard on me now as he ran a thumb along the strip of skin on my stomach that had been exposed.

"Yes," I answered, feeling tingles shoot all down my body where he was touching me. "Most people believe in some sort of god or higher power—one way or another."

"And you do not," Xander stated in a tone that suggested he was giving this great contemplation. I wasn't sure why he even cared so much.

He was closer to me now, if that was even possible. Everything about him overwhelmed my senses. His staggering height, the way his entire presence seemed to loom over me. His warm and woodsy scent.

It was everything.

"No," I said, my words coming out slightly breathless now. "No, I don't."

I couldn't bite back my disappointment when Xander disappeared from behind me. I turned to find him staring at me with a feral expression that made me flinch.

"Um," I uttered, literally perplexed by what had just happened. "Have I offended you in some way?"

"No." That was all he answered, continuing to stare down at me like he wanted to eat me alive.

"Okaaay," I drew out the word, looking toward the trees, the sky, literally anywhere else besides Xander and his penetrating green gaze.

I couldn't hold off any longer, though, and looked back to find him in the exact same position. Just staring.

"*What is going on,*" I hissed at him in a rush, frustratingly wet and perpetually confused.

The heat in his gaze increased somehow, and it looked like he was doing everything in his power not to pounce at me. I couldn't tell if he wanted to fuck me or attack me.

Honestly, maybe both.

"I'm trying to restrain myself," Xander admitted, his voice the roughest I had ever heard it.

"And why is that?" I asked carefully, my heart pounding in my chest.

Xander seemed to mark the change as his gaze shot to my neck. I swallowed under his inspection, his gaze so strong it may as well have been a touch. It shot back up and locked on my eyes. "Because I was just seconds away from ripping those clothes off of your body and marking my claim on you right here, right now."

His admission only made my heart rate increase as my whole

body seemed to clench. "Then why didn't you?" I was honestly impressed by how casually it came out, considering the overwhelming lust carrying through my body.

Xander let out a low curse to the sky before glaring at me again. "You. Are. Not. *Helping.*"

A small laugh escaped me, but I quickly reigned it in when Xander's nostrils flared and he ground his teeth together.

"I can already smell your fucking arousal in the air like it's beckoning me home," Xander said. "Don't make me endure your laughter as well."

"But why do you have to endure anything?"

"Are you saying you want the first time I fuck you to be in the woods?"

Oh. Right.

"Why don't you just whisk us back, and then we can come here after?"

Xander smiled wolfishly then, as if he were taunting his prey instead of hunting it. "Powerful as I might be," he said, that hunger still permeating his entire demeanor, "it uses a significant amount of energy to whisk us both across the continent. I intend on conserving every last drop of that energy for tonight."

I swallowed the reminder of what was to come when we got back to Xander's place. He promised he would tell me everything.

"Besides," he drawled, slowly raking over my entire body with his eyes before landing straight on my center. "Once I finally fuck you, I want you boneless and sprawled on my mattress. Not picking out clothes with other people's eyes all over you."

The images his words brought to my mind caused my core to melt again, needing them to become a reality. Like, *now.*

Xander moved abruptly and suddenly, stopping on the other side of me and facing away.

"The fuck are you doing now?" I asked incredulously.

"I need to be upwind of you," he snapped. "That scent of yours is maddening."

"Upwind?" I clarified while laughing, but quickly stopped when his entire body tensed up.

"Distract me," Xander ordered.

My chest shook with silent laughter, but I tried to think of anything that could take his mind off my scent.

Supernatural weirdo.

The idea came to me pretty naturally, as it was something I had wondered about on multiple occasions.

"Okay, so what about this Mother I keep hearing about, then? Do you worship her as your god?"

Xander looked over his shoulder at me as if I had sprouted two additional heads before turning back around. "No. She is exactly as she is referred to—the Mother and creator of all Astrales. We respect and give thanks to her, we cherish her, but we do not worship her. Nor would she want us to."

"How do you know that she wouldn't want you to?" I asked, noticing that a little of the tension had leaked out of Xander's body.

"The Mother created this life for us to enjoy, to improve our quality of life. She didn't do it because she wanted something in return."

"Okay, right. Well, how do you know she did it because of those things?" I pressed, not understanding his train of logic.

"Because she didn't create life. She gave us a way to *elevate* the life that already existed. And if she had created life, why wouldn't she have made that clear to Katerina when she visited her in a dream? It seems that would have been the perfect opportunity to garner the praise and adoration of our people, had she wanted it."

"Wait." The story that Lilliana told me popped into my mind. It felt like ages ago that I was sitting in her office. "Katerina actually spoke to the Mother? I thought that dream was symbolic."

"Oh, no. The dream was very real. Although, the way the story goes is that Katerina only received her message. It has never been suggested that she was able to speak back."

"Hm," I mused, deciding to keep my thoughts to myself.

That all seemed very...convenient. And who was this 'Mother' to decide that only a portion of humanity was to be helped? If she had the power to create this Chalice in the first place, why would she not use it to save the entire race?

"What's going on in that head of yours?" Xander asked, still facing away from me.

"Nothing you need to worry about," I replied sweetly, not in the mood to get into a debate with him over this. "Have you had enough of a reprieve?" I asked quickly, before he pressed me on it.

Out of nowhere, I was in Xander's arms again–facing him this time–as his hands found my hips. "I'm beginning to think there is no such thing where you are concerned," he said in a low tone that had thrills shooting up and down my spine.

He leaned down and kissed me deeply. The groan that rumbled out of his chest when my tongue met his made it seem like I was his salvation.

Xander broke the kiss just as quickly as he'd started it, speaking in a resigned voice. "But I suppose that will have to do for now."

I barely resisted the urge to demand that we forget the damned clothes and go back to his apartment, reminding myself that I needed something to wear to this festival. Even if we were to go get my things from the Armory beforehand, I didn't think anything I'd packed would cut it.

I took a small step back from him, trying to gather myself, but he began smoothing down my hair with both of his hands, pushing down on the strands like you would a horse's mane.

"Um, *no,*" I protested, swatting his hands away. He gave me a puzzled look.

"It's not a piece of fabric you're trying to get wrinkles out of! You have to be more gentle, or you will make it all frizzy. Like this," I grabbed his hand and lightly grazed the strands of my hair, enjoying the way his vision seemed to focus entirely on my hand guiding him.

He smoothed my hair again–much more gently this time–and I stifled a laugh at how cautious he was being now.

This man is an enigma.

"What about me?" he asked, striking a melodramatic pose. "How do I look?"

"Meh," I feigned an indifferent shrug. "You'll pass."

Xander reached out and pinched my side, just enough to hurt, and I shot him a glare. "Cheeky little brat," he called me. Though judging by the twinkle in his eyes, he was well aware that I was kidding.

It was ridiculous how good he looked. His hair was slightly tousled by the wind, but somehow ended up looking even better because of it. Those high cheekbones and full eyebrows served as frames for the most beautiful eyes I'd ever seen in my life. The dark gray shirt he wore today was cut a little bit lower, so I could see a hint of his tattoos poking out of it.

"*Nope,*" Xander pointed a finger at me. "Absolutely not. Don't go putting on your Angel eyes. I'm barely hanging on as it is."

I rolled said eyes and held out a hand to him. "Are we going or not?"

"Let's make this quick," he muttered, grabbing my hand and whisking us to the front door of the building.

I gasped when I saw the blue stone up close. Well, no, actually–it wasn't stone at all.

The walls were made out of water. It was continuously moving and yet somehow static, the structure seemingly sturdy.

I reached out a hand to touch the stone but was stopped by Xander saying, "I wouldn't recommend that."

"Why?" I asked, still hovering my hand a few inches from it.

"Just don't," Xander warned, glaring at my hand's position. I let it drop with an irritated exhale, shooting a side-eye in his direction.

We stood there for a few seconds before I said, "Are you going to knock? Why are we just standing here?"

"You might be the most impatient person I have ever met," Xander commented conversationally, but I could feel the darkness simmering under his words. "I already reached out to my contact Inmind. They will come and get us."

Bristling, I continued standing there and saying nothing. With each second that passed, my fingers itched to touch the surface even more. Right when I was about to give in to the urge, the door in front of us swung open.

I blinked back my surprise when two seemingly identical twins appeared in the entryway. They were the same height—much shorter than me—with deeply tanned, light brown skin. Both sets of eyes were a rich umber brown and focused on me; even their skeptical expressions matched. The only noticeable difference between them was that one had their hair cropped to their skull, and the other's reached their shoulders. Both of their features carried an unidentifiable quality, and I wasn't sure what gender either person was.

"Hello," they spoke in unison.

I tried extremely hard not to show a reaction, but that was very unusual for me to see. Twins were very rare in the human community. I had only met a set of them once, and they were not like the ones before me. So to hear them speak as one was unnerving.

"Batskii, Ren. How are you?" Xander asked them.

They gave each other a quizzical look before turning back to him.

"How are we?" the one on the right asked in a feminine voice. "First, you show up on our door with a woman—and a *stunner*, at that," their sparkling brown eyes flicked to me again, "then you ask how we are? Picture me gobsmacked."

"Something's wrong with it," the leftmost person said in a lower, bored tone. Their voice was much smoother than the first's, who had more of a husky quality.

Wait, did they just refer to Xander as an *it?*

"Or maybe," the first one grabbed my hand and yanked me through the threshold, before running their hands down my arms in a familial way. "Maybe you have just inspired a change in our dear Xander. Tell me, what have you done to turn him into a functional man?"

"Hands off, Ren," Xander commanded, moving toward us.

His advance was stopped by a wall of water shooting up in the doorway–not as thick as the walls, but enough to interrupt him.

"Well, it seems someone is a little territorial over you, my dear," Ren pointed out, leaning in to whisper conspiratorially. "I mean, really, you'd think he was your mate."

Mate?

As in, like, fated mates from the fantasy books I loved?

I brushed the ridiculous thought aside when I heard Xander's voice.

"You seem to have forgotten," Xan said, his signature tenor ringing in my ears, "that I cannot be bound by your little water walls."

"Fucking Enforcers," I heard Batskii mutter under their breath.

The water blocking his way parted for Xander like a curtain. He looked like a vengeful *god*, storming up to us and ripping me away from Ren's grasp.

"Aww, look at him, Skii–all grumpy and sour-faced. There's our Xander," Ren patted him on the shoulder, earning a distasteful look. "We missed you, friend."

"I am not your friend," Xander protested, looking affronted by their statement as he tucked me into his side.

What the hell? Why was he acting like this?

And why did I like it so much?

"Oh really?" the other twin–Batskii–remarked, giving Xander an unimpressed look. "Say that again the next time you want to get your clothing from the source and not at the merchant's like everyone else."

Xander flashed a charming smile. "Have I mentioned lately how much I adore you both?"

They rolled their eyes in unison before turning around and walking; each step synced with the others. I followed after them quickly, eager to see more of this building. Xander grabbed my hand and interlocked our fingers, pulling me into stride with him.

A jolt traveled up my arm, the act shocking me. It was so intimate, and the way he had done it made it seem like it was second nature to him.

It felt nice. Safe.

We walked through an archway that opened into a curved hallway, the sight causing all of the breath to flee from my lungs.

The water-filled walls seemed infinite. There were no corners or edges where the walls met, or a distinguished break between the ceilings and the floors, which were hewn from the same material as the walls. It almost felt like I was walking through a body of water, though the surface under my feet felt as hard as granite.

I looked up at the ceiling, marveling at the way it seemed to reflect and absorb light simultaneously, the way only water can. A flash of green in the corner of my vision had me looking over at Xander to find him observing me with hunger in his gaze.

"What?" I hissed at him.

He didn't respond—just clenched his jaw and flicked his gaze to my parted lips.

Oh.

"Aww, how sweet! Look, Skii, they're holding hands," Ren said in Skii's direction. They gave a *hmph* in response, not bothering to look.

My first instinct was to pull away from Xander, not used to this sort of public affection in any way, but he tightened his hold on my hand.

"So," Ren said, their hair bouncing as they began to walk backward, facing us. "I am assuming that you are in need of a garment for..." they trailed off, looking pointedly in my direction.

Right. Introduction is usually the first step in interactions.

"Violet," I announced with what I hoped was a warm smile. "It's nice to meet you both."

"Wow! The *manners* of this woman. Are you sure you want to be going around town with this one?" Ren pointed a thumb in Xander's direction, who glared in response. "Since he didn't see fit to do so himself, I'm Ren–the fun twin. That's my brother, Batskii. Don't mind him. He doesn't talk much."

He nodded in my direction once before turning back around.

Okay, so Batskii was male, but I still wasn't sure about Ren's gender. Not that it mattered either way, I just didn't want to offend anyone by misspeaking.

I smiled politely and explained, "I am in need of something to wear to the Mistral Festival."

"Ohhh," Ren gushed, eyes sparking. "We're going to have a lot of fun with this. What did you have in mind?"

"Uhh," I glanced at Xander, hoping for a little bit of guidance, but he just continued looking forward, his eyes boring into Batskii's shaved head. "I'm not really sure. I was hoping that I could have some help with the styling?"

Ren's eyes lit up like a fireplace, the excitement obvious within them. "Did you hear that? We get full rein."

"That is not what she said," Xander protested. "She said she'd like some *help*."

"Did you hear something?" Ren asked me, coming to walk by my side. "I didn't. Anyway, we were planning. I'm thinking a deep russet color–that would definitely accent your skin tone. Ohhh, or we could do a nice metallic silver that would shimmer as you walk. What do you think, Skii?"

"Blue," he answered without turning around. "To accentuate the spot in her eye."

I stiffened, unsure whether or not he meant any ill will by his comment.

When I was younger and traveling around rural parts of the continent with Archi, many people reproached me because of the fragmented color in my left eye. They thought that it was a *'devil's mark'* or a *'bad omen'* and that befriending me would be the equivalent of welcoming ill fortune.

The nicknames and whispered insults hadn't bothered me that much. What did was that the doubt of my character would spread like wildfire, infesting the minds of many people and turning whole villages against me.

"That's a great point," Ren said, jeering me out of my contemplation. "A light iceberg blue. Oh, it will be stunning on you. What shape did you have in mind, dear?"

"What would you suggest?" I cringed, hating how out of my element I was.

I had no idea if this was even a formal or casual event. Internally cursing Xander for his lack of foresight in preparing me, I tried to tug my hand out of his, but he held strong and shot me a look.

I shot him one right back, tugging on my hand again. Instead of squeezing tighter this time, I felt a small *zap* shoot through his fingers to mine, leaving a trail of tingles in their wake. Xander's eyes shone with some emotion I didn't understand.

The fuck? What was that?

Ren, seemingly ignorant to the silent battle happening between me and Xander, pushed forward. "I am envisioning a two-piece feminine suit, tailored to perfection, of course. Oh, and we could do a scalloped detail on the hem of the pants and the top, with a little bit of a flared leg to complement your height..."

Ren went on talking about the design and what it would look like, but I wasn't listening any longer.

The wall to our right opened up completely, apart from a black railing that transitioned the hallway into a never-ending, curved balcony. The view that it was showcasing was the body of water that I had seen from the cliff, but I was wrong initially. The people within it were not swimming. They seemed to be working.

I watched in awe as people glided through the water, each person moving their hands in a unique way. They looked to be manipulating the water in a very intentional manner, but from this distance, I couldn't determine what it was that they were doing.

I felt a small *tap* against my head and looked to my left, wondering why the hell Xander had done that, but he wasn't paying me any mind.

Strange.

"Well?" Ren asked me, coming to a stop in front of a door. "What do you think?"

Shit.

I had totally zoned out and missed the question.

"Um, yeah, I think that sounds great," I guessed, and seemed to have done a good job, based on their reaction.

Xander had an amused look on his face, like he knew exactly what just happened.

"Perfect!" Ren clapped once. "Skii will get going on the fabric, and I will begin sketching up the design. Are you available to come back tomorrow evening to pick it up and do a fitting?"

"Yes," Xander answered for me. "But do you think it could be ready by morning?"

"Do you know how rude it is to show up with such short notice for an event like this?" Batskii's cold voice filtered out. "And you dare to rush us on top of that?"

"Now, now brother," Ren said, placing a hand on his arm, "you know that Xander has done us many favors over the years. It is past due that we give him one in return."

The other twin simply scoffed and shot Xander a reproachful look before disappearing entirely, no doubt whisking himself someplace else.

"Well, I think that went better than last time. Wouldn't you say, Xander?" Ren asked, looking at him with amusement.

"I suppose so," he agreed. "There were no attempted drownings this time."

Ren laughed and opened the door, beckoning us to follow. I looked at the large body of water behind me one more time, wondering what the hell had transpired to make Xander and Batskii hate each other with such an aggressive passion.

⟩

ABOUT THIRTY MINUTES LATER, XANDER AND I WERE IN a private dressing chamber with copious amounts of shirts, shorts, dresses, skirts, pants, bras, and panties. Literally, name any garment ever made, and we probably had one in the collection.

"I do not need this many items," I told Xander for what felt like the thousandth time.

"Look, Ren *lives* for supplying peoples' wardrobes," he said, settling into an armchair and resting one ankle on the opposite knee. "So just placate her and try them on. No one is saying that you have to leave here with everything."

I groaned and began pushing the rolling rack behind the partition, which would allow me some privacy from the man that was currently irritating the hell out of me.

The Gallery Room, as Ren had called it, was a very large, expansive space with high ceilings and racks of clothing that seemed to go on forever. I had never seen so many different fabrics and patterns in my entire life, having only shopped at markets and some small clothing boutiques in the past.

The whole process passed in a blur of questions about my style and preferences, Ren throwing stacks of clothes into the arms of a begrudgingly complying Xander, and so many different garments that I couldn't keep track of it all.

Then, she–I'd learned that Ren was a woman–ushered us into this room and ordered that I try everything on before we purchased a single item.

"So, about that place where you are keeping all of my belongings," I said to Xander as I pulled a simple top over my head.

"What about it?" His response was slightly muffled by the partition.

I looked in the body-length mirror in front of me and made a face. This top was *not* right for me. All of the seams looked like they were in the wrong place, which made me feel like an over-stuffed sausage.

Next.

I continued on the stack as I spoke.

"Well, all of my money is with my things from the market," I said that loosely because there really wasn't that much there. Definitely not enough to pay for all of this and the garment they were creating for the festival. "So I'll be needing that back."

"I'll get it back to you, but you won't be needing it today," Xander replied, his tone unrelenting.

"Um, why not?" I asked.

I checked in the mirror again, pleasantly surprised to find that I didn't actually hate this one. It was a plum-colored dress made out of a simple fabric. It didn't necessarily hug my curves, but the cut of it definitely accentuated them in a flattering way.

"I will be paying for it," he explained matter-of-factly.

"Uh, *no*, you will not," I shot right back.

"And why might that be?" I could literally hear his smile as Xander spoke.

I peered around the corner, and sure enough, there was that damn grin plastered on his face. It fell away quickly, though, as he looked at what he could see of the dress–the scooping neckline and the color.

"I like that one. The color is nice on you," he said genuinely, eyes bouncing around my face and chest.

"Good thing I didn't ask you," I shot back, disappearing behind the wall before he could see the reddening of my cheeks. His compliment seemed so sincere it made little unwanted swells of warmth form in my chest.

"Have I done something to irritate you, little Angel?" Xander asked me from his position.

"Seriously?" I asked dryly, grimacing at the skirt I had on in the mirror. Skirts and I just didn't get along.

"Well, don't be shy. Let's hear it." It seemed like his voice was getting closer.

"Okay, well, how about we start with your irritating habit of withholding information from me," I said, recalling when he told me not to touch the walls. "And then there was the way you just threw me to the wolves out there without any preparation about this event we are supposedly attending, which I still don't understand the point of. And then you were acting all possessive over me when literally *two days* ago, you were snarling at me to '*stop looking at you that way*'–"

I broke off when Xander started laughing. He was definitely closer to me now.

"What's so funny?" I snapped, though it came out less menacing than I had intended.

"You really think I speak like that?" Xander asked, referencing my haughty and low-voiced impression of his voice.

"You do speak like that. Oh, and by the way, what was with that little zap you sent to my hand when I tried to pull away from you? Were you *trying* to piss me off?"

"That," Xander started, his rumbling voice devoid of all laughter now, "was a warning. Do not try and distance yourself from me in front of others."

"Well, if I am annoyed with you and don't particularly feel like touching you, I will pull my hand away. Simple as that."

"No."

"*No?*" I clarified incredulously, pulling a random garment over my head aggressively before rounding the corner of the partition.

Xander was standing right on the other side of it, causing me to slam directly into his chest.

I bounced back and glared up at him. "Who do you think you are to order me around?"

He didn't answer my question, too busy staring down at me

with a heated gaze, his eyes drinking in the black dress I wore. His full lips were parted and irritatingly captivating in that position, making me want to kiss him.

"Hello?" I asked, waving a hand in front of his face.

He snapped his own hand out and captured my wrist in his grasp, eliciting a sharp intake of breath from me when he yanked my body flush against his.

"You are *mine*," he let out in a harsh growl. "And I am yours. A little anger or irritation won't get in the way of letting the world know it."

"I think we've already talked about this, Xan." I tried to lessen the blow by using his nickname, but refused to budge on that matter.

I would not agree to being his before I knew more. And how would that even work, being his? He couldn't possibly expect me just to leave everything from my life in Armantrea behind.

Could he?

Xander's gaze shuttered slightly, and he released me, but didn't move away. "You are," he insisted in a low voice. "You might not know it yet, but you are."

I swallowed, my heart rate kicking up from his words.

Everything inside of me felt like what he was saying was true. When I was with him, things just felt...right. Even when I felt like slapping him across the face, I had never felt so comfortable with someone in my life. Especially this quickly.

Xander gave a pointed nod in the direction of the clothes. "You go ahead and try the rest of those. I will speak with Ren about payment and timing for the pick-up. Meet me outside when you're finished."

"Xander," I started, putting a hand on the crook of his arm when he began to turn away.

He looked back and gave me a hard look. "You're not paying for the clothes, Violet. You would have never had to do this if I hadn't shown up and disrupted your entire life. So *'shut the fuck up about it'* and say thank you."

I laughed against my will at him quoting Mikkie to me, balling up a discarded shirt and throwing it at his back as he left.

"Stalker!" I hollered at him as the door shut.

His laugh echoed off of the high ceilings in the room outside. I caught myself smiling as I turned around to continue on with the clothes.

CHAPTER TWENTY-EIGHT

XANDER

"So," I said, sauntering up to Ren's desk, "I noticed that you didn't discuss Violet's mask with her."

She hardly even spared me a glance, entirely absorbed in her vision as she sketched out the plans for Violet's garment on a large piece of canvas paper.

"You two are together, are you not?" Her question was more of a statement than anything else.

"Well yes, but no, not officially. Yet," I told her, perplexed at the fact that I was stuttering.

I didn't *stutter*. Ever.

"So are you telling me that I should go in there and have her design a mask for herself?" There was a challenge laced within her words.

"No," I levelled, meeting her challenge with my tone and placing my palms on her desk. "I was just commenting on the fact that you *didn't*."

Ren smirked up at me. "What kind of death wish do you think I have?" She laughed quietly and shook her head. "You show up here out of the blue with a woman on your arm, holding her hand, looking at her like she is the most precious thing to ever walk our lands–and you think I would give her the opportunity to wear an independent mask?"

I smiled down at her. "You're smart. I'll give you that."

"So," she mused, tilting her head to the side. "What were you thinking about the masks' design? I am assuming something over the top and eye-catching?"

"Would you expect any less?"

I sat in the chair opposite Ren's and told her about the design I was picturing in my head. I honestly couldn't wait to see how they turned out–how Violet and I would look wearing them together. This would be my first festival with an adjoined mask, and the thought of Violet accompanying me had my blood pumping to the surface.

I heard the door creak behind me and turned to see Vi emerging from the changing room, her eyes moving all around the room again. She seemed to be enamoured by the walls here.

She finally looked at us and made her way over. "What are we talking about?" she asked, glancing between us.

"Oh, I was just telling Xander that you guys can come and pick up your order tomorrow evening," Ren supplied seamlessly. "Everything should be ready by then."

"Great, thank you so much," Violet said with a smile.

"Seriously..." Ren looked perplexed. She whispered to Violet, "What are you doing with this one? You're as sweet as pie."

I scoffed. "Apparently, she is sweet to you, but don't worry. She's nasty to me."

Violet gave me a crass look. "As if you don't deserve it."

Ren laughed and pointed at her. "You and I need to have a meal together sometime. I like you very much."

"*Nope,*" I declared, pulling Violet to my side. "Not happening. You favour female lovers, and this one is mine."

"I am capable of being friends with a beautiful woman and not seducing her." Ren rolled her eyes. "I'm not a heathen."

Violet pulled out of my arms, and I let her, curious where she thought she was going.

"Sounds great, Ren. Besides," she said, giving me a side eye and walking towards the exit. "I'm not–"

"Do not finish that sentence," I warned in a low voice, matching her steps away from me.

"Yours," she finished anyway, flashing her middle finger at me. "Thanks again for all of your help Ren," Violet smiled at her, leaning on the doorway. "I left the clothes I liked on the right. The left rack has things that didn't work. I'll see you soon!"

"Yes. I'll see you then," Ren drawled, but Violet had already turned away and couldn't see the way Ren was gawking at her ass as she walked away.

"You like those eyes in your head, Ren?" I asked casually, moving into her line of sight.

She looked amused and shrugged. "Sure."

"Then I suggest you find a way to control them before tomorrow, or you will find yourself without them."

I turned on my heel to follow Violet. Ren's laugh followed me out the door. If she thought that I was joking, she was sorely mistaken.

I found Violet leaning against the railing, looking out at the workers in the pool. "What are they doing?" she asked when I approached her side.

"Waterweaving," I answered, leaning against my elbows on the rail and watching their process. "It is how the Hydroseis sector is able to produce clothing that the entirety of Cavell fawns after. Apparently, there is some big secret to their craft which allows their garments to last much longer than anyone else's."

Violet watched them with renewed interest, squinting her eyes slightly. It made me wonder when her *true* eyesight would kick in. Even the Astrales that have very limited magical capabilities have the same elevated senses as the rest.

"And have you found this to be true?" she asked. "That they last longer than others, I mean."

I loved her curiosity, even though it proved to be problematic at times.

"Oh, undoubtedly," I nodded, glancing over to find her looking at me. "I still have the first shirt that I ever bought for myself. It is in great condition, though I hardly wear it anymore."

Violet's eyes tracked along my face, her brows knitting.

Right. She wouldn't understand how I could possibly still fit in the first shirt I ever bought for myself.

"Come," I said, offering her my hand. "We have much to discuss."

She rolled her eyes but put her hand in mine. "So you keep saying." A silky tone crowded her words, giving me the urge to hum.

I whisked us back, with Violet's eyes locked on mine the entire time, making the heat rise in my chest.

"Do you fancy getting out of here for a bit?" I asked her, suddenly feeling like my flat was far too small to avoid ravishing her entirely. "We don't need to have this conversation here."

Violet looked like she was thinking it over for a second or two before she nodded. "We can go, as long as it is somewhat private. I don't like talking about intense, personal things around people I don't know."

It felt like someone had reached into my chest and plucked out a string of my heart with the way Violet's words reflected a thought I'd had so many times.

I yanked her to me aggressively, cherishing the beat of surprise shooting through her eyes before I sealed our lips together, kissing her the way I had been aching to do all day.

Seeing her in those fucking dresses and so many new colours had done a number on my sanity. And knowing that she was naked in the same room as me, only separated by a flimsy partition?

I was painfully hard at this point.

Violet returned the kiss with fervour, stroking my tongue with her own before running it along my bottom lip. I felt that pass like it was moving up my shaft and groaned deeply, using every ounce of my strength to break the kiss and pull away.

"Why'd you stop?" Violet asked instantly, her swollen lips and reddened cheeks making my thoughts blackout.

Fuck.

"Because if I didn't, I would have fucked you into oblivion. And we have–"

"Do it."

My entire body focused on her. Every single part of me zeroed in on what she had just asked–no–*commanded* me to do.

"Violet," I said in a warning voice. "You deserve to know what you are getting yourself into first."

My entire body was tense with the effort it took for me to say the words. To avoid fucking ravishing her.

"Okay, will you shut the *fuck up* about what I do and don't deserve already?"

My eyebrows raised on their own accord at her question and tone.

"Am I not a grown-ass adult? I can make my own decisions. I'm telling you right now, giving you any permission you need to turn off that little voice in your head saying this is wrong, or that you're taking advantage of me." She moved in even closer, pressing against me so that I could feel her nipples poking through the thin clothing over them, hard as ice. "I am giving you permission to fuck me *now*, tell me *later*."

I was breathing deeply at this point, Violet's words pushing me closer and closer to the edge, where all thoughts ceased and only need drove me.

"Please," she finished, the softer, silkier tone she used snapping any small remaining sense of control I had.

I grabbed Violet by her ass, picking her up and kissing her deeply, all hesitation gone. Her legs wrapped around my waist, and I whisked us to the bed, with me landing on my knees, still holding her up.

"Pick a word," I ground out between kisses, revelling in the way her breaths seemed unhinged and frequent. I laid her down under me, resting all of my weight on my forearms on either side of her head.

"What?" she asked breathlessly, moaning softly when I moved

down to her neck, taking in a full hit of her scent as I sucked on her pulse point.

I drew the skin there between my teeth, just lightly, but she gasped anyway, making my cock twitch against my waistband.

That's when I realised we were both wearing entirely too much clothing.

I sat up and pulled my shirt over my head, enjoying the way Violet was drinking me in with her eyes. They skidded between various tattoos, her pupils dilating and constricting as they moved.

"A safeword," I repeated, pulling my belt from its loops in one sharp movement, making it spring free with a small *snap*.

Violet's gaze was locked on mine now, burning with desire and excitement. "I've never needed a safeword before," she said.

"Well, you do now."

I hooked two fingers in the waistband of her loose pants, pulling them clean off her body in one go. She let out a gasp, her hands moving to run up the length of my arms. The sight of her exposed skin instantly sang out to me, making my chest hum and my tongue press against the roof of my mouth.

"Safe. Word." I growled between clenched teeth, physically trembling with the need to touch this fucking masterpiece of a woman.

"Hazelnut," she blurted out, her cheeks blooming red as soon as she did.

"*Hazelnut?*" I asked with a surprised laugh.

"I don't know–it just popped into my head. Does it matter?"

I loved the way she spoke to me sometimes, like I had every answer she could ever need.

"No," I growled, gripping her bra at the band with both hands and shredding it in two. "It's perfect."

"*Xander*," she scolded, crinkling her brow. "That was my favourite–*oh.*"

Violet's words cut off as I lapped my tongue over her nipple before biting it the way I had imagined so many times, noting that the smoky smell of her arousal kicked up a notch. I repeated it on the other side, and goosebumps cascaded down her body.

"Okay, fuck the bra," Violet said breathlessly, threading her fingers into my hair.

I grabbed the wrist of that hand and slammed it down to the bed above her head, doing the same with the other before she got any ideas about touching me again.

I had been thinking about this moment for far too long for her to *interrupt* me.

I continued holding them down and moved back to her body, relishing how displayed and open she was for me.

Fucking *finally*.

Her skin was so soft. It filled my head with all of the things I could do to rough it up. To leave my mark on it.

I ran a reverent hand down her side before cutting in my path, feeling down the ridge of her hip bone. Violet's breaths were coming in roughly. Her legs began to squirm in a jerky way, like she was trying and failing to keep them still.

Oh, that wouldn't do.

"Repeat that word for me, Angel."

"Hazelnut," Violet murmured, rolling her head to the side to look at me.

I stalked up her body, zeroing in on her lips.

"Good girl," I murmured against them with a small smile.

I sent out my magic to form a restraint around her hands, replacing my own. It locked in place immediately, the feeling so sweet I could sing.

Nothing in the entire world had ever felt as right as this. As fucking *welcoming*.

Sitting up, I positioned myself above her. Her eyes shot to mine, shining with a sort of untapped excitement, like she had no idea what to expect.

I brushed my thumb roughly across her lower lip, causing it to pull to the side before I released it. The little bounce that happened made my cock harden even more, if that was possible.

I moved again, trailing my pointer finger down the centre of her body slowly, tracking every plane of her. This was the first time I was seeing her entirely bare, and I wanted to fucking revel in it.

My hold on her hands made her generous breasts jut upwards, beckoning me towards them. I resisted the urge so I could look at every one of her birthmarks, committing the beautiful patches to memory. They made her so unique that no one would ever be able to mistake her for anything other than what she was.

Fucking *mine.*

I moved up the inside of her leg with that same single finger at the same time that I put my mouth back on her, dusting kisses over the spot on her collarbone. She was panting now–the breathy little sounds one of the most angelic things I had ever heard.

When I reached the apex of her thighs, I ran an exploratory finger right down the middle of her sex. Her arousal coated it instantly, making my mouth water.

"I thought you were going to *fuck me into oblivion?*" Violet asked, her tone making me pause. "What are you dicking around for?"

"Oh," I said, a slow, cat-like smile taking over my face. "You're going to regret that."

Fear sparked in her eyes at the same moment her heartbeat spiked, and I savoured it like it was my last meal.

I summoned that strange magic I had, the first one I'd ever mastered, and moved my hand to her right breast, gripping it so my palm lay centred on the peak. I bent down, keeping my gaze locked on hers, as I flicked my tongue over her clit at the exact same moment the shock left my hand.

Violet cried out as her entire body jerked, the stimulation to her breast doing its job. "Holy *shit,*" she said with a gasp.

I smiled against her clit, moving down so that I could get a real taste of her. I continued sending small shocks to her nipples intermittently as I worked her with my tongue, massaging and caressing them in between so that she would never know when to expect it. They weren't strong by any means, but enough to cause a harsh vibration.

Nothing compared to what I was capable of.

I moved up again, drawing her clit between my teeth before sucking on it deeply. Just as her entire body tensed up, her face cresting the way it had the last time I was between her legs, I pulled away again.

"Wha–"

I cut her off with my mouth, kissing her deeply. She welcomed me in, sweeping her tongue against mine with zero restraint, making me groan.

I didn't bother with any teasing this time, just moved my hand down and slid two of my fingers into her with no warning. I felt a bead of precum leak from me when her muscles clamped down on my hand, begging me to release their tension.

I worked myself in and out of her slowly and deeply, continuing to ravage her mouth and swallowing her loud moans. The vibration of them echoed through my entire body, and it felt like they were wrapping an invisible hand around my cock.

On my next stroke, I curled my finger, hitting that spot. Violet's back arched off the bed, her body wound so gloriously tight.

I left her again, my fingers feeling cold without her around them.

She groaned, the sound both frustrated and whiny. "Are you fucking *edging* me?" Violet asked with an appalled voice.

"I sure as shit am, you little brat."

I smiled when she tugged against her restraints, which were now securely fastened to the headboard with an extra length of my magic.

"What am I going to do with you now, hmm?" I asked, toying with her nipples, which were now painfully sensitive, the fact obvious with the way her body was jolting. "You weren't gracious enough to accept what I was giving you, so I am tempted to give you nothing at all." Cocking my head, I pretended to consider my options and internally smiled when her look turned to a glare. "Don't think I've forgotten about your little stunt with Ren back there, either," I growled, my fists clenching when she smiled.

"I have no idea what you mean," Violet said coyly.

"I suppose there is a way you could make it all up to me."

A small smile played on Violet's lips now. The things I would do to be able to see what was happening inside of that pretty head.

"Would you like that?" I asked while brushing all the stray hairs away from her face, kissing her jawline.

"That depends on what it is," Violet murmured, making a small humming noise when I moved to her neck.

"Oh, no, love. I'll be the one picking your apology. I was just wondering if you would like for this to be amicable or not."

A devious smile lit up her eyes, but her face was set in stubbornness. "I actually don't think that there is anything to be sorry for," she said, her raspy, breathless voice making my thoughts eddy out again.

I snapped the part of my magic that was holding her to the bed frame, but I made sure that her wrists were still secured. She lurched forward at the sudden loss of grounding, and I shifted to allow her a path.

"On your knees," I commanded, ticking my head towards the floor right beside the bed.

I was surprised when she moved quickly and without argument, kneeling beside the bed and falling back on her haunches. Her big eyes were moving along my chest and torso, glowing with intent, and ended on the waistband of my pants, which I realised were unbuttoned, but still around me.

I'd gotten so caught up in her that I hadn't even undressed myself yet.

I amended the issue quickly, standing before her and pulling them down. She watched with undivided interest; her neck craned all the way up so that she would be able to see. When my length sprung free of the clothes, Violet's gaze locked right on it, deepening into a look of pure want. It made the patch of blue in her left eye shine more brightly than I'd seen yet.

"The next time you think of yourself as *quite large,*"I quoted her, pumping myself once as my blood rose to the surface. "I want you to remember this moment."

I reached down and grabbed her jaw, brushing my thumb across it. "I want you to think about being bound at my feet, completely and entirely helpless, while I tower over you, stuffing that irritating fucking mouth of yours full of my cock."

Her cheeks bloomed the reddest I'd ever seen them, and her eyes glazed over with pure bliss. It was the difference between night and day–that look compared to the dead and void type of haze I'd seen in them before–and *fuck* if it wasn't the most beautiful thing I'd ever seen.

I pushed my hand into her hair at the back of her head and gripped it at the roots, pulling her up to kneel. "Can you snap your fingers with your hands bound?" I asked, running my tongue over my lip in anticipation.

I couldn't look away from her mouth, the way the full crest at the top formed two pretty little slopes. The way her bottom lip jutted out slightly, plump and begging to be fucked.

She snapped twice, presumably one with each hand, and I hummed in appreciation.

"You do that in place of your safeword," I told her, my voice serious. "Got it?"

She nodded her head, looking up at me beneath her lashes before looking back at my cock.

Waiting. Expecting.

She was probably anticipating for me to toy around with her, as I had been before, but I was well past having that level of restraint. I guided myself to her mouth, my thigh muscles clenching when those lips wrapped around the head and her tongue found the slit immediately, gathering anything I had to offer her.

I strengthened my grip on her hair and thrust my hips into her mouth, groaning through my chest at the feeling of hitting the back of her throat. Her breaths scattered along the base of me as she struggled to accommodate my size, and I shuddered at the feeling of her swallowing around me.

"You take me so fucking well," I told her, stroking an appreciatory hand down her cheek and feeling the weight of it against the side of my cock.

She moaned in response, the erotic sound travelling up my shaft in a soft vibration, and I *lost* it.

I began pumping in and out of her mouth, not bothering to move gently or to allow her to adjust, but she didn't seem to want that. Not as she bobbed her head with my movements and hollowed out her cheeks, seemingly unaffected by the tears gathering in her eyes.

She'd been watching my movements, appearing transfixed, but her gaze shot to mine when I released my hold on her hair. Instead, I gathered all of it up and held the entirety of it in one hand, using the stronger grip to my advantage and fucking her mouth even harder.

This was a little bit of a test, I'll admit. The force had to be causing some pain, and I wanted to see how she would respond to it.

It was better than I ever could have imagined.

Her thick fringe of lashes fluttered closed, causing the tears to spill over onto her cheeks. It was so beautiful, the way that they painted my very own trail across her skin.

"You're doing so well, Vi. Your lips feel so good wrapped around me."

But what got to me more than the tears was her fucking *scent*. It filled the air impossibly, every fucking thing in the entire world losing meaning in comparison. It was almost as if it had been crafted with my very soul in mind, the way that her aroma invaded every morsel of my being.

Fuck. There was that urge. The urge to claim her.

I tugged on her hair before demanding, "Eyes on me."

At the same moment that she did, Violet swirled her tongue around the tip, and I felt myself throb against her. It was like she was communicating with me, talking even as she had my cock in her mouth.

I grunted and pushed deep again, my thighs twitching in anticipation of release. Violet's brow creased, confusion dancing across her face as her own scent of arousal was pulsing at me.

She thought I was going to finish and then be done with her. As if coming down her throat *once* would ever be enough.

"What?" I asked, my voice more breathless than I'd heard it in a long time. "You think that you're the only one who is allowed to come more than once?"

I tugged on her hair, tilting her chin up so that I wouldn't miss a single beat as I began to come. Nothing had ever felt as good as the fluttering of her tongue against me as I spilt down her throat.

I gripped myself and pulled out until the tip rested against her lips, which she immediately wrapped around it again. With me still inside of her, Violet swallowed down every single drop, the tightening of her mouth as she did so exquisitely *depraved.*

I released my restraints on her wrists and moved in a second, picking her up and throwing her down on the bed. Violet's eyes were wide as she watched me prowl towards her, pure surprise riddling her features.

I wasn't sure what sort of stamina she was used to with her human lovers, but there would be no waiting. I needed to be inside of her.

Now.

I moved up the length of her leg, keeping my lips close enough to brush her skin, as I reacquainted myself with the close proximity of her sex.

It seemed like Violet didn't really know what to do with her hands now that she could control them. They were constantly moving without an anchor, and I was more than happy to oblige. I gripped both of her wrists with one hand, holding them against her chest. The position caused her arms to press roughly against her overly sensitive nipples, and she moaned at the contact.

"You are fucking *incredible*," I growled, biting the skin on her hip hard, the urge to mark her coursing through my veins.

She cried out and muttered something unintelligible, no doubt close to snapping from the slow torture I'd been subjecting her to.

"It's okay, love," I coaxed, enjoying the way she whimpered. "I'm going to take care of you now," I assured her, pressing a few kisses to the red, angry mark my teeth left behind.

I moved down and brushed my lips against her sex in the softest kiss. I relished the way her whole body shuddered at the contact and did it again before repeatedly stroking her with my tongue. Her knees slackened entirely, giving me the signal I had been waiting for.

She was ready.

I slid my tongue into her slowly, methodically, and showed her just how much I fucking cherished her taste. After a few strokes, I circled it inside of her. Violet bucked her hips in response, pushing me further into her. I followed suit, picking up my tempo a bit, and knew the time had come when she rolled into me even harder.

I pressed my thumb to her clit, circling twice while sending another vibration—and that was it.

Violet came with a shriek, her legs coming up to clamp around my head with the force of her climax. I brought my hands around her thighs and squeezed, not to ease the pressure, but to fucking *revel* in it.

I felt like I could suffocate between this woman's legs and actually die happy.

She continued rocking, and I licked and kissed her through the wave, massaging her plump thighs on either side of my face as I did, and watched her. I tracked every single shift in her face as she came—the gaping of her mouth, her chest rising on an inhale, the way her forehead creased with pleasure in a way I'd never seen.

It was everything. She was so achingly gorgeous, even more so as she came apart on my tongue. But too quickly it was done, and I realised then that Violet had just become my newest addiction.

One that would never be satiated.

When her movements ceased and her legs slackened into my hands, I knew that she had come down from it.

"Have I ever told you that you are undoubtedly the most beautiful creature I have ever laid my eyes upon?" I asked breathlessly, still able to feel the sensation of her trembling against my face.

Her cheeks were the most exquisite shade of red, and something inside me sang at the sight of it. I expected her to remain where she was, but she sat up immediately, pulling me to her by my biceps.

Violet kissed me with urgency, pulling me down to get me as close to her as possible. I complied, giving her more of my weight, and my semi-stiff cock lined up to her entrance on its own. I felt her heat permeate me, her arousal slide over me, and instantly hardened against her.

"Fucking *hell*, Xander," Violet finally spoke, her voice raspy and rough from panting. "That was absolutely insane."

"Oh, my sweet little Violet," I murmured in a low voice, smirking when her lips parted. "That was just the beginning."

Watching the way Violet's throat bobbed and remembering how that movement felt around my dick, I thrust my hips forward, burying myself inside of her sweet, decadent heat in one go.

CHAPTER TWENTY-NINE

VIOLET

The moment Xander was fully sheathed inside me, I knew that I was completely and utterly screwed.

Nothing would compare to him. Ever again. And here I thought that he felt large when his cock was in my mouth. This was on a whole new level.

I'd never felt so complete. So entirely and utterly *conquered*.

Xander let out a shaky breath, and I couldn't tell if he was feeling the same sort of shift inside himself, or if he was just struggling to show restraint so that I could adjust to him.

Maybe a little of both.

"I'm a bit torn right now," Xander admitted, shifting so that he could brush the hair out of my face. His movement caused a maddening sort of friction inside of me, because it wasn't enough.

"Why?" I asked on a breath, feeling frustrated that he wasn't just *fucking me*.

Apparently, where Xander was concerned, it wasn't just sex. It was an entire entourage of activities.

"Because, you are so perfectly fucking cut for my body, it's like you were carved just for me." Xander pulled out to the tip and thrust back in, the impact making me cry out as tingles exploded all over my body. He groaned. "And you keep making those fucking *noises*. They make me want to tie you up again so that I can spend days categorizing all of them in my brain."

He released his hold on my hands and gripped one of my nipples harshly at the same moment that he rolled his hips.

I literally yelped at the onslaught of sensations. No one had ever handled me like this before, as if he was trying to find the limit at which I would break.

Little did he know, I was not one to break easily.

"Mmm." He ran the tip of his nose along my hairline. "That noise in particular. I like that one very much."

My breathing picked up, each of his thrusts bringing me closer and closer to the edge. It didn't help that his hands were currently roaming all over my body, caressing, grabbing, pinching–anything he could reach was shown attention. And then there was the way he was staring at me, like I was the most delicious thing he'd ever seen.

I could feel another orgasm building, which I wouldn't have even thought possible this soon after the first one. I had never orgasmed that hard before.

But still, I could feel my body winding up, the endorphins rushing through my blood like crazy.

As if he could sense it, Xander hauled my body up and moved to his knees. He supported my entire weight with his arms, holding me so that I could wrap my legs around his waist as he entered me again. The new position made him hit spots in me that I didn't know existed.

I moaned, "Oh, my fucking–"

"I wouldn't finish that statement, Angel." Xander leaned forward to grumble in my ear, "Highly unadvised."

"But, I was just–"

I broke off as Xander flipped me around, forcing me to my hands and knees and brutally thrusting inside of me from behind. It made me moan so loudly that my cheeks flamed.

He wrapped his hand around my hair again–short as it was–and pulled my head back so that I could look into his eyes.

"When I am inside you," Xander shifted his hips to emphasize his point. I panted. "You call out to no one but me."

He grabbed my ass with his other hand, squeezing hard as he reached an even deeper point inside of me. Then he changed his rhythm, hitting that spot repeatedly, brutally, with small strokes that had my vision blacking out.

"You worship at my altar, or you worship at *no* altar. Your choice, love."

Love.

I never expected that word to cause such a reaction in me. But hearing it from Xander's lips was...wow.

I shoved my face into the bed so that I wouldn't embarrass myself any further with the inhumane sounds coming out of my mouth. I could feel myself getting wetter and wetter against him and knew I was close.

"Oh no, you fucking don't," Xander scolded, pulling my head up from my cushion of sanity. "You don't get to muffle the sounds I force out of you. Weren't you listening before? I am making a catalog of them."

He sounded so affronted that I laughed breathlessly.

"*Shit*," he spat. "I felt that laugh like it was your tongue stroking my cock."

I did it again as I arched my spine, backing up into him, and he let out a deep, rumbling *purr*. It was a distinct reminder that this man inside me was a supernatural being.

So are you.

Xander became unhinged, moving behind me with more force than I'd ever known. The sound of our bodies connecting was echoing through the air, and it was just fanning my flames further.

But then he leaned down and whispered, "Come for me, Angel. I want to feel this cunt giving me the praise I deserve."

I was done for.

My body clenched impossibly, my muscles clamping down around his dick like they never wanted him to leave. I literally saw stars behind my closed eyes, the little spots of light like nothing I had ever experienced before.

"Look at you, Angel," Xander said with an awestruck tone.

"So clean and slick against my cock, glistening with pleasure. I think it's time to mess it up a bit, wouldn't you say?"

I could only moan and nod in confirmation, my orgasm still rocking through my entire body. It felt like he had touched every part of me with the way my entire limbs were tingling.

"*Fuck*, you feel so good spasming around me like that. I could get lost inside of this cunt." He moved his hips in a twirling motion, drawing out every second of my pleasure.

"I am going to come inside of you now," Xander's voice rumbled, the roughness of it curling my toes. "And don't even think about using that word. This is non-negotiable."

I reached behind me and pulled his hips flush against me, showing instead of telling him that I *wanted* him inside of me. To feel his cock throbbing with the release that my body had brought him.

Xan growled, slamming into me with zero restraint, his movements wild and untamed. I intentionally squeezed down on him inside of me and was rewarded by the shudder that coursed through him.

I felt him begin to throb before an exquisite warmth spread inside of me, his cum blazing a trail right through me. I panted at the sensation, feeling more satisfaction than ever before at my partner's release. It was only intensified by how I could feel Xander's arms shaking, him having moved closer to me, like he couldn't bear for any parts of us to be disconnected.

"No one has ever finished inside of me before," I told him in a voice that was unrecognizable to me, once I caught my breath.

It was breathless and vulnerable; definitely not the way I'd ever wanted to come across when it came to sex.

So why did it feel so right with him?

He pressed a tender kiss to my neck. "And no one else ever will," Xander stated as a concrete fact. Something that would never be brokered with.

He slipped an arm underneath my upper body and turned me

on my side, all while staying inside of me. He curled his whole body around mine and tucked me into him.

I felt goosebumps spread across my arms at the closeness I was feeling.

Xander trailed a finger down one of them, reminding me how this all started. "I love when you get these little bumps," Xander said, his voice soft and lazy. "It's like I get to peek inside your brain."

More of them exploded over my whole body for some reason, and Xander nuzzled in, smiling against my neck.

"Do you have a neck fetish?" I asked him somewhat seriously.

He did spend a *lot* of time there.

"No," he nipped the skin there with his teeth. "I have a *you* fetish."

CHAPTER THIRTY

VIOLET

I totally would have expected to be a pile of loose limbs and fatigue after the world-shifting orgasms Xander had just pulled from me, but I surprisingly wasn't.

After he begrudgingly got up to grab a damp washcloth for me, Xander cleaned me up. Then he immediately laid back down and pulled me on top of his chest, both of us still completely naked.

I spent a few minutes lying sprawled across his body and running my fingers through his silky hair. I actually felt more energized than I had in days.

I sat up on my knees, resting back on my feet and looking down at Xander. He wrinkled his brow at me, those luscious lips pulling down in a frown.

"Why'd you go?" Xander asked, turning over and resting his head on my lap.

Holy shit. Why was he acting so...precious?

"Oh, you know," I started. "This guy keeps going on and on about some huge conversation we need to have, and I apparently have a date set up with him to do so. So I'd better be going."

Xander growled and pounced on me, bringing me down on my back while he towered over me, glowering. "I did not enjoy that."

"I was literally talking about you, you fucking psycho," I said while laughing.

He nipped at my cheek with his teeth. "You said 'some guy'. I am not *some* guy, I am *the* guy. No other *guy* will be lucky enough to have your attention again." Xander hardly took a breath before continuing on. "What is with that word choice, anyway? I think I am befitting of a much better one. 'A devilishly handsome suitor', perhaps? Or 'a man so charming, he seems more like a god'?

"Yeah, that totally sounds like something I would say," I dead-panned, rolling my eyes.

"It's a marvel those beautiful eyes of yours have never gotten stuck in your head with the number of times you roll them a day," Xander stated in an observational, sarcastic tone.

"Oooh, sarcasm. How original," I shot back.

He blinked at me. "You do realize you've just used sarcasm in saying that, yes? And in the sentence before mine?"

I shrugged. "Well, I was born with it free-flowing through my veins, so I get a pass."

That grin appeared–the full, genuine one–and my thoughts ceased to move for a beat as I stared at it. He was so achingly beau-tiful; I suddenly wished I had the ability to paint like Archi so that I could capture it.

In a blink, Xander was off of me and standing next to the bed, pulling his pants back on.

"That was abrupt," I commented lightly, looking around the room for where he discarded my clothes.

"Well, you insist on looking at me with that fucking *expres-sion,* and it does things to my impulse control. We have many things to discuss, so give it a rest."

I did no such thing, taking a second to look into those eyes that never ceased to make me melt, knowing full well that it would only bring it out more.

"You fucking temptress," he growled, threading his hand in my hair and pulling me up to stand before him.

He held me two inches away from his face, and I could feel his breaths skating across my lips and down my neck, waking my body up all over again.

His eyes tracked down my body slowly, calculating. "Get dressed," he directed once his eyes found mine again.

I rolled my eyes but did as he said, finding my clothes in a pile by the foot of the bed. I went to the bathing room to fix myself up a bit, and when I emerged, Xander was putting something into a basket on the counter.

"What is that?" I asked, walking up to him.

"It's food. You know, that thing that allows you to keep breathing?" He gave me a remorseful look.

"Oh, give it a rest. I eat plenty."

"Mhm, sure," he muttered, closing the lid and grabbing my hand. "Ready?"

I nodded in confirmation, squeezing his hand. As I saw the familiar array of colors as we whisked, I felt a knot form in my stomach.

It was finally happening. Xander was going to come clean about everything.

We arrived at a cozy hillside, the green, rolling hills speaking to me in a way I couldn't explain.

"Wow," I breathed, looking around. "This is gorgeous."

"I think so, too," Xander said, pulling a red blanket out of the basket and spreading it out below a tree. "I've always found it to be very peaceful here."

I looked down at the blanket and sandwiches that Xander pulled out. He glanced up at me and smiled.

"What?" he asked.

"This is a *picnic*," I observed.

"And?"

I shook my head and sat down. "You're just full of surprises."

I grabbed one of the sandwiches and bit into it, my traitorous stomach instantly growling at the taste. Xander gave me a pointed look as if to say, *'See?'*

"So," Xander said once he settled in next to me. "What do you want to know first?"

I wanted to ask about his past immediately, but wasn't ready to dampen the mood quite yet.

"This may seem random–"

"And how utterly *shocking* that would be," Xander chided sarcastically.

"Anywho," I went on as if he hadn't spoken. "So, with your elevated senses, can you smell like…" I stuttered, not really knowing how to word it delicately, and then all of my questions bubbled out at once. "Everything? At all times? How long of a distance can you smell things over? And does it affect your sense if there are a lot of different scents going on? Or if your other senses are overloaded?"

I looked over at Xander to see him staring down at me with amusement written all over that annoyingly perfect face. His eyebrows were raised high on his forehead, making creases appear there that actually added to his attractiveness, as backward as that may seem.

"Oh, is that all?" he asked with amusement.

I gave him a look, and he laughed.

"Well, most of those questions do not have cut-and-dry answers. In regards to the first one, no—I cannot smell *everything*. That would be impossible." He looked toward the sky, the corners of his eyes crinkling in a gesture that I was beginning to recognize as contemplation. "I guess that the best analogy I would have for you is that it is similar to your sense of hearing. When you are out on a busy street, you can physically hear everything around you, right? But your brain doesn't pick up on small, unimportant things like a bird chirping or someone dropping their marks.

"It is similar for me. I *can* smell everything around me, but my brain subconsciously picks up on high-trigger scents. Like your blood, for instance. The second I smell it, my nervous system is on alert for any potential danger."

My heart caught on that.

"Or–conversely–the smell of cinnamon rolls baking. That one is a high trigger for sure."

Xander let out a contented sigh, which forced a small laugh out of me. "What?" he asked, his gaze shooting to me quickly.

"Cinnamon rolls?" I asked.

"They're delicious," he defended, giving me a cross look.

"I mean, yeah...just a random thing to use as an example," I said, still laughing.

He smiled briefly. "What else would you like to know?"

I sat up a little more. "Will you tell me about you? How do you have access to more than one Core? What is this darkness that you've alluded to? And why is it all so damn secretive?"

I intentionally closed the flow of my questions because if I hadn't, it would have gone on for a while and only delayed him finally telling me the truth.

"Well, my incredibly gorgeous little human," Xander said, leaning in and rubbing a thumb over my cheek, which turned red from his words.

"Not a human," I interjected.

"Semantics. Are you planning on interrupting me this entire time? Just so I can be prepared, of course." Xander was clearly mocking me, but I couldn't help but smile at how he looked at me with so much warmth in his gaze. I leaned in closer, kissing him softly and feeling his smile against my lips.

I went to pull away, but his hand wrapped around the back of my head, bringing me in again. But when he pulled back, his expression was more somber than I expected, making my stomach drop.

"I'm not sure if you are going to look at me the same way after you hear this," Xander admitted, his voice sounding wrong. It shouldn't have that unsure, apprehensive tone. "I love the way you look at me now," he added in a whisper, looking deeply into my eyes with a quiet sadness in his own that I had never seen before.

It made my throat close up. I grabbed his hand.

"I can't promise you that I won't have a reaction," I said before reaching to smooth out his forehead creases in a light touch. "But I can promise to hear you out, to do what I can to see this from your perspective, and be receptive to what you tell me."

Xander gave me a strange look and glanced down at our intertwined fingers, like the gesture seemed foreign to him. He continued looking at them for some time, and I didn't press him, gathering that he was taking a second to prepare.

"This story goes back many years, to before my birth."

I swallowed around my heart pounding in my throat, adrenaline coursing through my legs.

"It follows a woman. I still do not know her first name. I have only ever known her as Dr. Kavara. This woman was an absolute mastermind Astrale. She belonged to the Mistral sector–Myrana."

I realized then that Xander hadn't told me much about the Mistral sector. Was this why?

"While she did have great power, her biggest asset was the power of the mind. She was an experimenter like no other, the source of many great Astrale discoveries." Xander looked out at the view we were facing, his eyes stagnant on the flow of water through the river as he spoke. There was a strange bitterness hanging on his features. "But, after living for decades on end, her accomplishments began to fade in importance and excitement. She began to crave *more*. She wanted power. So she started experimenting in different ways, trying to create a weapon that would give her the power to rule. Not just over Myrana, but over all of Cavell.

"Dr. Kavara knew that the mixing of different Cores after magical development was toxic–and deadly–but she had a thought: what if they were mixed earlier on in life, or even before birth?"

Xander looked over at me, the most daunting expression I had ever seen on his face. It was full of deep-rooted disgust, shame, and an anger so strong that my breathing ceased momentarily.

"You can imagine what lengths her experiments took her to," Xander said, his voice a promise of death. My stomach bottomed out at what he was implying. "She tried to shock young Astrales' systems with Corepower—the concentrated essence of a person's Core. It can only be extracted when said person is close to death, and only by someone who is very experienced with that sort of magical extraction."

I felt a wave of nausea roll over me and wanted to be sick from the mental images his story brought on.

"These experiments were not successful, though. All of the people she tried it on died gruesome deaths, their bodies overloaded with foreign magic. After failing repeatedly, Kavara knew she needed to change tactics, and she was willing to submit her own body to do so."

Xander's voice took on a rough edge. "She found her ideal donor and saw to it that she became pregnant with his child, unwilling as he may have been. But Kavara had lost all sense of morality and empathy in her many years of existence and in her perusal of power.

"In her eyes, those Astrales' lives were given up for science. They were just sacrifices that needed to be made—her child's father included. And so, as the child was barely forming in her womb, she did...things. Unnatural and barbaric things to ensure that the child would be everything she needed it to be and more. It was her last hope."

It felt like pressure had been added to my chest, hoping against all odds that this story wasn't going where I thought it was. I squeezed Xander's hand, realizing that there were tears in my eyes as his figure blurred.

His eyes tracked along my face. "When he was born, she cared for him. The way that one would care for a good sword or even a dog, doing all of the necessary things to keep it alive. But she did not care for him like a mother would her child.

"She kept him in a blank, white room with nothing on the walls, one small horse figurine being the only toy in sight. She forced him to activate his magic at an age that was far sooner than he should have, causing great pain and suffering for him. He hated her, and tried to fight her at every stage. But that wasn't her biggest problem for long."

Xander laughed bitterly then, making my mouth dry out. "No–her problem soon became how to *contain* her weapon. His magic became stronger at an exponential rate and increasingly more difficult to handle with each passing day. She hadn't considered that this weapon she was creating might actually have feelings of its own. That it would resent her and the way she brought it to life."

Xander's voice took on a haunted quality, the quiet timber making chills shoot down my spine. "Kavara resorted to many... unfavorable methods to try and weaken him, to put a damper on his power. Starvation, physical torture, mental warfare, bleeding him out–"

He stopped abruptly and frowned, his hand reaching out to wipe the tears off my cheeks that had fallen. "Why are you crying?" he asked.

"Because you are the boy from the story." I ended with a sob, bringing my hand up to my mouth to hold back my disgust and shock. My entire body was shaking.

Xander blinked, looking a bit taken aback. "Do not cry," he requested in a soft voice, wiping at my cheeks again incessantly, like my tears were the main focus of his thoughts right now.

"Xander," I whispered, a fresh surge of tears flowing over me without restraint.

I yanked him to me, hugging him deeply and resting my cheek on the crook of his neck. He froze, like he was in shock, but he quickly wrapped his arms around my back and sank into the embrace, inhaling shakily.

"I am so sorry," I said, and that was all because I didn't know what else to say.

Here I thought I'd had my share of trauma. I couldn't even begin to imagine the atrocities he'd faced growing up.

"I do not want your pity," Xander said quietly. He remained

sealed to me, though, his words muffled against my shoulder. I pulled back to look into his green eyes.

"I do not pity you. My heart is broken for you and the horrible things that you have been through. I am *angry* at the woman who did this to you. I am crying in sympathy for the pain you have suffered."

His expression softened, and it felt like my chest was glowing. Xander wiped my cheeks again with his thumbs, transferring them to his own as he had done once before.

I shook my head through a laugh. "You're so fucking weird."

"Mmm, you like it. Admit it," Xander goaded cockily, nudging my chin with his nose.

"Maybe," I shrugged, but couldn't help the smile pulling at my lips. It quickly fell away, though.

"Tell me that the person who did this to you is dead…"

I couldn't bear the thought of her being alive. It filled my gut with a burning rage that I had never known before. My mind was taken over with images of the unfavorable things I would do to that monster if I ever had the chance.

Maybe there would be one upside to her being alive.

Xander leaned back, a reminiscing look overtaking his eyes as he smiled wistfully. "Oh, she is very much dead. Lilliana made sure that I would have the opportunity to end Dr. Kavara's life in whichever way I saw fit."

"Lilliana?" I asked.

"Lilliana was the one to find Dr. Kavara's facility. She staged a coup and broke me out of confinement. I was the last subject alive."

So many things Xander had said made sense now. All of the times he defended Lilliana to me…of course, he would feel strongly about respecting her since she was the one to save him.

What Shaed said that night in the Oracle's room came rushing back to me then.

'I don't think anything that is made instead of born is something to be trusted.'

That absolute sack of fucking shit.

Fresh tears surged to the surface when I remembered Xander's reaction to it, the way he stiffened behind me like he was waiting for my opinion. The way that he hugged me closer when I unknowingly defended him.

I wiped at my cheeks, glancing around to make sure we were still alone. "Okay, I am officially a crying mess. Was this enough of a field trip for you? Can we return now?"

"Violet," he murmured, low and deep. I loved the sound of my name on his tongue. "If we go back there, I will be inside you–one way or another–for hours on end. And we have only covered the tiniest portion of—"

I screamed as Xander's body shot ten feet backward. He landed roughly on his back and stayed down, his body entirely limp.

"Xander?!" I called out, but he didn't respond.

I stood and began sprinting toward him, but strong arms grabbed me from behind.

"*XANDER!*" I shrieked, thrashing to get free, but my captor whisked us further back into the clearing.

Xan stirred, sitting up groggily before shooting to his feet. His eyes locked on me immediately, flaring so violently that I felt myself relax.

He would save me.

CHAPTER THIRTY-ONE

VIOLET

"I am not sure why I'm surprised," Xander called out as he raised his arms at his sides. "You are a bunch of fucking cowards that hide behind masks and Soothes to do your bidding. Why wouldn't you be so low as to use a moon jinx on me?"

"Let's try this again, shall we?" It was that strange voice—same as last time.

I whimpered in shock when I began to lift off the ground, my body levitating five feet into the air.

"Xan," I called out, my voice shaking.

"What the fuck is it that you want, exactly?" Xander asked the empty field, no actual person visible this time either.

"Lilliana must be stopped."

I watched as Xander's entire body stiffened, though his face showed no reaction to the words.

"You are the only one who can help us take her down. All you need to do is agree to hear us out, and we will let Violet go."

Chills skated down my spine when they said my name.

"And I assure you," the voice continued, "you will want to aid our cause when you learn what we know. "

Xander laughed bitterly. "The only thing that I *want* is your head on a bloody spike. And I have a little secret for you," he spoke in a loud whisper that carried through the wind, echoing all around me.

Suddenly he was standing below me, and a green mist spread from him in every direction, bleeding out into the entire clearing in a rapid crawl. I watched in fascination as it began to stick in random places, quickly forming into humanoid shapes.

"I'm not quite as easy to blackmail as most."

I was still floating in the same position, my limbs locked at my side, when Xander thrust a hand out, and his figure blurred, moving around the clearing faster than I could see. A bright green stream of energy followed his path, shooting from him and striking the figures down.

I balked in horror at the very real, very *dismembered* body parts now taking their places.

One of them must have been my assailant because the hold on me snapped. I fell through the air so fast that I didn't even have time to scream, but I didn't need to. Xander caught me easily, like this had been his plan all along.

He put me down quickly and stepped forward, scanning the bodies with his eyes. Counting, I assumed.

It had to have been at least fifteen Astrales. And Xander killed them all in a matter of seconds.

Actually, I wasn't sure killing was the right word. He obliterated them.

"See?" Xander said, shooting me his murderous grin. "I told you that you never have to worry."

I widened my eyes and nodded. "Mhm, yeah. Noted."

The next few seconds happened as if they were in slow motion.

Xander yelled and reached out to me, his face contorting into a horror-filled expression. A strange noise pulled my attention to the right, to find what looked like white flames shooting at me in midair.

I looked back at Xander and screamed as a searing pain engulfed my entire midsection and lower belly. He let out the most deathly roar I had ever heard in my life. It was more animalistic than anything, and so loud that my head swam as the pain overtook me and my knees buckled.

He caught me easily with an arm around my back, but my vision began to black out sporadically.

We landed in Xander's apartment suddenly, my feet completely unsteady. I swayed and instantly hissed, the movement causing the blinding pain to flare and my vision to blacken again.

"Fuck! Violet?" His voice sounded so panicked.

It made me anxious enough to pry my eyes open, finding myself lying out on Xander's plush rug. He was kneeling beside me, his face two inches away from mine, with his hands on either side of my head. All I could see were his eyes.

"*Fuck,*" he repeated, sighing and closing his eyes. "I almost lost you. You almost fainted in the fucking Between."

I tried to understand what he was saying but only felt my eyes drooping closed again, the pain too much to handle.

"*No.* Come on, Vi. Open your eyes."

I did when he shook my head, one strong hand on my jaw.

His eyes were shining intensely, jolting me awake a bit. "You can heal this. I know you can. You just have to stay awake and do as I tell you, okay?"

I couldn't nod, but I kept my eyes open and on his.

"Good girl," he murmured, brushing some hair out of my face.

"Really?" I croaked, surprising myself by speaking. "Now?"

He smiled. "Always."

Xander's face turned serious. "The ability to heal yourself is one that most people master quickly. You can do this." His fingers brushed the hair out of my face. "I am going to remove your shirt, okay? Don't try to move or look at it—just remain still and keep your eyes on me."

"Okay," I said as well as I could, the battle to stay conscious getting harder and harder.

Xander continued looking into my eyes as he spoke. "Imagine the thing that brings you the most peace."

I screamed at the sensation of the air hitting my burn as my shirt was removed, but Xander kept speaking to distract me.

"Think of a time when your mind felt like it could just take a pause, and your body was safe and comfortable."

I closed my eyes and immediately thought of being with my parents.

A memory sprang forth–all of us cuddled up together under a blanket, gazing at the stars.

I remembered my dad tucking me into one side of his body and Momma on the other, squeezing us both. I felt tears streaking down my face. Both at the memory and the fact that I had previously forgotten all about it.

Another flashback that had somehow been blocked from my mind.

"Violet, love, I don't really think you understood my instructions...you're not supposed to cry," Xander's voice sounded both relieved and amused. "But whatever you're doing, keep doing it."

Tears were free-flowing now as images of my father played in my mind. Him trimming flowers to give to my mother. The way he would pick me up and spin me around.

A tingling sensation began to overtake my midsection, the pain lessening by the second.

"Is it working?" I asked, my voice sounding closer to normal.

"Er...yeah. You could say that." I couldn't read his tone.

"What do you mean?"

"This is incredible," Xander spoke quietly. "I've never seen somebody heal this quickly."

"Really?" I asked, forgetting Xander's advice and craning my neck to see for myself.

He pushed me back down by my forehead. "You're a horrible listener," Xander scolded, but there was a renewed energy about him now.

I laughed, expecting the act to hurt, but was surprised to find that it didn't.

"It's already healed," Xander breathed, running his fingers over the plane of my stomach.

I leaned forward, peering down at it, and saw that it was good as new, save for a shiny substance I quickly looked away from.

Xander slipped one arm under my knees and picked me up with the other around my back, promptly moving to the bathing room.

"What are you doing?" I asked, curling my arms around his neck to stabilize myself.

"Running you a bath."

"Xander, I'm healed. I can walk and bathe myself."

His voice became more firm. "I know."

But he proceeded to set me down on the countertop gently before starting the faucet on the bathtub.

I spun around to look at myself in the mirror, specifically at my stomach. I couldn't understand how it was possible that I wasn't feeling any pain. I didn't even feel fatigued in the slightest.

The hit had landed right where I knew a birthmark to be, but as I looked in the mirror, I saw that it was still in place. When I healed myself, the mark came back.

Strange.

"Are you wondering why the birthmark on your stomach remains?" Xander asked, drawing my eyes to him in the mirror.

He was now standing behind me, staring at the mark with intensity in his gaze.

He moved so quietly sometimes, it was impossible to know when he might be lurking. I didn't know why, but that made me think of what he said in the alley.

'There is nowhere you can run and hide where I won't find you. Ever.'

It felt like months ago that I was running to get away from him, but I honestly wasn't even sure how long it had been.

"Angel?" Xander asked.

"Hmm?"

"I asked you a question."

"Oh, right." I shook my head to clear it. "I was wondering that, actually."

I looked back at the mark, and suddenly, Xander was sliding his arm around my waist, wiping away the nasty residue with a warm, wet washcloth. I closed my eyes at the sensation, butterflies fluttering in my lower stomach.

"I was wondering the same thing," he said into my ear in a low voice.

"I'm a little shocked that you realized there was a birthmark in the exact spot as the burn, to be honest," I admitted. "You've only seen my bare stomach once."

"Twice," he corrected with a side-eye. "And, of course I noticed."

He carried me over to the tub and sat me on the ledge. "Do you honestly think," he started, his finger skating along the bare skin of my back as he moved to unclasp my bra. "That I could see you naked, and it *wouldn't* be burned into my mind in exquisite detail?" Xander leaned down and nipped at my shoulder with his teeth, drawing a gasp from my mouth.

I was fully naked now and pushed forward into the hot water. My muscles instantly relaxed, and I sighed happily, loving the way the heat warmed me to my core.

"Your lack of faith in me is irritating," Xander mused before reaching for a bottle of soap.

"That the only thing irritating you?" I asked, trying to figure out what caused this shift in demeanor.

He poured a healthy amount of the soap into his hands before running it over my arms, chest, and back. "I'm resisting every urge in my body not to go after the Retaliators right now. A burn that size could have immobilized you for months if you weren't a Sensinor, and we didn't have access to a healer." Xander was seething, and the primal, unhinged rage I could hear in his voice was traveling straight to my center.

"You couldn't have healed me yourself?" I asked, tipping my head back to look at him.

My entire thought process blanked at the expression I found

on his face. It was vengeful, menacing. Like he would gladly kill the first thing he came across, just to take the edge off.

"No." He left it at that.

Okay...seemed like we were back to the non-answers then.

I sighed and looked forward again, drawing my knees up to rest my chin on them.

"It is a very rare gift to have the ability to heal another person," Xander explained, surprising me. "One that I do not have. My specialty is in ending lives, as you've become quite familiar with." He pushed my body forward gently and tipped my head back to rest on some sort of cushion. "Most of the Astrale healers hail from the Terrala district. Which makes sense because their magic already stems from nature and gives many the ability to cultivate life through crops."

He must've had some sort of basin or pitcher because he began pouring warm water over my head, saturating my hair. I closed my eyes, feeling more pampered than I had in a long time.

Xander began to work shampoo into my hair, massaging in slow, firm circles around my scalp as he spoke. "There are many Terrala healers that travel throughout the continent, filling in gaps where they are needed. But it can be a lonely life for them, going home only on occasion. Many of them eventually find a life partner in their travels and complete the ritual, deserting from their home sector."

I was honestly struggling to keep up with what he was saying; the head massage causing my ears to muddle with pure bliss. Xander began to rinse my head with more warm water and I moaned, feeling like it was washing away all of my stress.

"Maybe I should keep being held hostage if this is the type of treatment I get afterward," I said happily.

"*Wrong*," Xander said, flicking my cheek.

I shot him an amused, surprised look.

"Unless that is because you enjoy watching me end the lives of those that touch you," he said in a drawl, a smile finally overtaking his features.

I turned around to face him, smiling as well now, and found myself leaning against nothing. "What...?" I asked, looking at my arm resting in midair.

"It's an air cushion–Mistral magic. A bit like the barrier in Bedruke."

"Aww, you made a cushion just for me?" I poked him in the chest as I said it, earning a dry look.

"Turn around and let me finish, smart arse."

I did as he said and smiled as I sank back into the cozy embrace. It somehow seemed more comfortable now that I knew Xander had made it for me.

He worked in the conditioner next, and I suddenly understood why his hair always looked so good. I'd never known a man to use a conditioner before. Then again, the only man I'd lived with was Archi, and he always kept his hair cropped close to his skull.

Xander's hand appeared before me, and it turned out that he was not using a pitcher to rinse my hair. A stream of perfectly heated water was flowing from his hand, seemingly out of his fingertips. It was strange, though, because there was a definite gap between his skin and the start of the stream.

"Is this how you were able to get through that wall of water with Ren and Batskii? Because you have Hydroseis magic?" I asked, watching as he rinsed all of the soap off of my arms and chest.

"Yes and no," Xander said.

I actively resisted an eye roll at the number of times he had used that phrase with me.

"There are certain parameters set for Enforcers so that they can bypass wards. This law was established to prevent us from being locked out during emergencies, but it has become a privilege that many Enforcers take advantage of."

"So, you would be able to get past any ward, even if you weren't an Enforcer?" I asked him, beginning to realize why it was such a secret that Xander was...different.

"For the most part, yes. There is one Core that I do not have access to, though. Some of their wards actually hold against me, but others are as flimsy as the rest. Now stand."

I stood up, suddenly very aware of the fact that I was entirely naked and he was clothed. Xander began to lather up my stomach and moved down, bringing the soap to my legs. I inhaled sharply when he casually brushed past my clit, sparking a fast-growing heat inside me.

He ran the suds all over my legs before wrapping his arms around me, moving to my ass cheeks.

"I wouldn't want to miss anything," Xander said cheekily, giving me a knowing look.

I rolled my eyes, and he kneaded the muscles hard, causing my knees to weaken. It felt achingly good, tension I hadn't even realized was there seeped out of me.

I tried to hide my pout as his hands left me, but saw him reaching for the soap again. "Um, I think I am thoroughly clean," I insisted, gesturing to the stuff covering my entire lower body.

"Nonsense," Xander scolded, putting the tiniest dollop of soap I had ever seen between his pointer and middle fingers.

"What is that fo—*oh*," I ended in a sigh as Xander brushed those fingers along my bikini line so softly, I thought I might combust.

"As I said," Xander emphasized with a smirk, pulling away from my body after he had spread the soap very minimally with featherlight strokes.

It felt like my entire body had woken up under his touch; every place he had teased now ached for more.

Xander snapped his fingers, and the water below me was crystal clear again, any remnants of old soap and dirt gone. He guided me back into the water with a firm grip around the back of my neck, kneeling so that we were eye to eye. I got lost in his signature green for a second, the intense color calling out to me.

I wanted to ask him why he had insisted on us waiting to have sex until he told me about his origins, but he finally looked a little less murderous, and I didn't want to bring his mood down again.

But had he thought that I would feel differently about him after learning how he came to be? Did he think that I would be disgusted by him or something?

"Go on," Xander nudged me with his nose. "Ask whatever question you're thinking about."

"I'm not thinking about any question," I lied, wrapping my arms around his neck and getting his shirt wet.

"Mmm, you're lying," Xander's tone was sultry and dark, making my pulse kick up. "Now I really want to know what it is."

I remained silent, shrugging as I continued stroking his shoulders.

"I could always coax it out of you..." Xander warned, pushing me back gently to lay in the tub.

"You could sure try," I said, though when his hands began to travel over my body, I knew it would be a losing battle for me.

Xander's dark laugh rumbled through the room, bouncing off the hard tile everywhere and skating down my neck. "Is that a challenge, little vixen?"

I cocked my head. "I don't know, is it?"

"Oh, you are so," Xander squeezed one of my breasts, keeping it in his grasp. "Gloriously," he continued, reaching for the other. "*Fucked.*"

As soon as he said it, Xander sent a shock to each of my breasts, the strange sensation causing me to cry out and arch my back instinctively.

He released me and moved his hands down, caressing my stomach in a loving way that made me melt. But then, one hand skated even lower, brushing against my center softly. I shifted my legs, his touch on me was too minimal, especially with the added sensation of the water moving.

He continued teasing me with one hand and rinsed the conditioner from my hair with the other. The water was trickling all down my chest and against my nipples, making my breaths come in short bursts.

"Are you sure you don't just want to tell me what it is that you were thinking about?" Xander asked me, brushing a thumb over my cheek.

"I already told you." I smiled against his hand as he ran that thumb over my lips. "I don't have any questions."

He narrowed his eyes and increased the pressure of his finger, running it upward until he reached my clit. He remained still for a moment, watching me with an observational expression.

I let out a sound I had literally never heard before when his finger sent a brutal wave of vibration directly to that bundle of nerves, sending tingles throughout my legs.

"Oh my god," I panted.

"I thought we talked about that irritating habit of yours," Xander said, his tone warning me of danger.

He did it again, and the shock felt stronger this time. Much stronger.

"What even is this?" I asked around my moan. "I am literally underwater. Are you going to electrocute me?"

Xander laughed again. "No, little human. It is a very specific concentration of my Mistral magic. A Windforce, if you will."

"*Wind?*" I asked incredulously.

Xander picked me up abruptly and whisked us to his bed. My entire body was dry by the time we were there, but my hair remained wet.

He toyed with the strands, running his fingers along the wet ends. "I suppose we should finish our conversation," Xander said in a resigned tone, still messing with my hair.

I rubbed my legs together, my entire body turned on after his game in the bathtub. "Or we could...you know...finish it later?" I supplied hopefully, the aching between my legs intensifying by the second.

"Tell me what you were thinking, and I'll consider letting you come, you beautiful little vixen," Xander said deviously, giving me a full smile.

I'd thought he was going to keep torturing me with his Windforce, but apparently, my torture was now a *lack* of touch. Xander pulled away from me completely, leaving a definite gap between us.

I glanced down.

"Or I could just take care of it myself..."

I slid my own hand between my legs, instantly relieved when I ran a circle over my clit. I groaned in frustration when Xander ripped my hands away immediately, his fingers circling my wrists.

I glared at him, and he chuckled. "You're so adorable when you're frustrated. Now tell me what I want to know."

I felt a presence skate up my legs, Xander's hands still occupied with holding me, and I looked down to see his green mist spreading around my calves. It felt similar to that portal in Mr. Berger's apartment–like the touch of a cloud.

A small noise escaped me when it wrapped around my legs entirely, not trapping them, just embracing them in its soft touch. That feeling began to move upward even more–getting dangerously close to where I needed it–before stopping its advance.

I whimpered, my cunt actually throbbing with need and neglect.

"Tell. Me," Xander commanded in a hard voice, his eyes stuck on mine with intensity.

I realized in that moment that Xander had every capability to actually force the answer out of me. He could be using his Soothsayer abilities to make me answer, but he wasn't.

"I was wondering why you didn't want us to have sex before I knew about your...upbringing," I finally blurted out, the realization I'd just had combined with my need for release getting the better of me.

Xander cocked his head, looking at me strangely. "That is not why I wanted to wait," he told me.

"Then what?" I asked, completely thrown off but ready to be done talking.

"Well, would you like to know now?" Xander asked with a leading tone, shifting to speak into my ear. "Or would you like me to make you come around my cock while I fuck you into oblivion?"

I clenched around nothing at his words, trying to move but failing as his magic kept me in place. "Second option, please," I said politely, trying to manage my frantic energy so that he wouldn't sense it.

A fruitless endeavor, really.

"Mmm," Xander mused, moving into my space again. He brought his thumb up to my bottom lip and swept it across in one slow, sweeping motion. "Such a pretty word from an even prettier mouth."

I felt myself blush, remembering the last time he had paid my mouth such undivided attention.

"Open," he commanded.

I did as he instructed, and Xander slid his thumb into my mouth. My lips closed around it immediately, and he stroked my tongue, the sensation so erotic that I felt myself get even wetter.

I felt his mist travel up farther and gasped as it brushed against my center. It felt so foreign and soft that it was *torturous*. It was way too much and not enough at the same time.

Xander was gripping my chin with the rest of his hand, his thumb still against my tongue. "I can feel your entire body trembling beneath my magic, little human." He sounded delighted. "Tell me, is that because you are afraid? Or is it just your body begging for release?"

I moaned against his hand, unsure how exactly he expected me to respond to him. He must have seen the answer in my eyes, though, because he brought his other hand to my hip and spoke softly into my ear.

"It's okay, sweet thing." He pressed a kiss to my temple. "I will give you what you need."

Xander moved again, thrusting two fingers deep inside me, and I cried out against his hand keeping my mouth shut. His hands were seriously massive.

"Oh," he shuddered, "that noise was my favorite yet. So depraved, little Angel, the way you are drenching my hand with your arousal from being entirely dominated."

He picked up his pace, working me even faster, and I felt myself spiraling.

"Are you preparing to finish already?" Xander asked with a taunting laugh. "You turn into such a pliable little whore beneath my touch, you know that?"

His words *engulfed* me, and I didn't even have time to consider how wrong that might be because he abruptly removed his hand from my mouth. I missed his hold instantly, but wasn't even sure why. The thought was gone in a second, though, when he braced that same hand around my throat, putting pressure on the sides.

I panted, the feeling of his large hand being there, able to cut off my breath at any given moment, intensifying every sensation in my body. Xander continued fucking me with his fingers and brought his thumb to my clit, pressing down roughly. I tried to yell, but he tightened his hold on my neck, cutting it off.

"Be a good girl and come for me so that I can bury myself inside of you and show you just how much you're affecting me right now," Xander commanded.

As soon as he finished speaking, he sent a burst of vibration to my clit, lighting my nerves on fire. My body reacted to his words and magic on its own, cresting and exploding as my release finally found me. The orgasm overtook me as Xander drew out every second of that bliss, stroking and fucking me through it.

Right when I thought it was done washing over me, Xander removed all of his clothes in a blink and sheathed himself fully inside of me.

I moaned, deep and throaty, at the feeling of being so gloriously full of him. It was like he had been designed to fit me perfectly, just big enough to eddy every other thought out of my head but the feeling of him.

"So."

Thrust.

"Fucking."

Thrust.

"Perfect," Xander growled, pounding into me with a fevered energy.

I began to meet his thrusts with movements of my own. My hands roamed all over his body, touching every bit of skin I could reach. I arched my back, pushing my breasts against his chest and my neck further into his grasp.

"*Fuck,*" he rasped.

Xander repositioned us so that he was sitting against the headboard and I was on top of him, my knees resting on either side of his legs. He pulled me flush against him and grabbed my hips in a bruising grip, slamming me down on top of him.

I cried out at the deeper fit this position gave and began panting as he continued moving my hips up and down, meeting my body with small thrusts of his own.

I may have been the one on top, but Xander was undoubtedly the one in control.

He leaned forward and brought one of my nipples into his mouth, swirling his tongue around the peak. The other side got the same treatment, and I was coiled tightly by the time he was done.

He rested his head in between my breasts and continued bouncing me as he spoke against my skin. "I could spend the rest of my life between these breasts. They're fucking magnificent," Xander's sentence ended in a groan as I rolled my hips, steering his cock to the spot I needed him most.

He kissed the top ridge of my breast before sucking the skin into his mouth harshly, keeping it in place between his teeth. I screamed at the pain and the pleasure that followed closely after, feeling my arousal coating Xander beneath me. He sucked even harder, bringing more pain, and I realized that he would definitely be leaving a mark on me.

Why the hell did that turn me on even more?

I felt like I wanted to cry. And not in a bad way, or from too much pain, but because I had never experienced this kind of overwhelming pleasure before.

The sounds coming out of me were entirely unhinged now, and Xander pulled up to look at my face, his expression turning into one of soft admiration.

"Look at those pretty tears in your eyes, taunting me." He ran a reverent hand over my cheek. "Let them spill, and I'll let you come."

I felt his mist work its way around my midsection and up to my breasts. The slight coolness of it made goosebumps spread all over my body. I completely froze, my body giving in to the overwhelming sensations running through it as I went hurdling over the edge.

"So beautiful," Xander whispered, running one thumb down each of my cheeks, right over the streaks of tears. "You are so beautiful when you are coming undone around my cock."

He leaned in and kissed me then, his mouth capturing mine in a different way than before. It was searing and intense, but soft and warm and so *intimate* that I felt my entire body melt into his embrace. He took everything I had to offer him, not slowing his pace one bit as he held up my weight with little effort.

It was like I could feel the lines of our souls blending and molding into one with each brush of his full lips against mine, with each catch of my breath or flutter of his impossibly long eyelashes against my cheekbone.

But then he wrapped his large hand around my throat again, applying pressure to the sides, and I felt myself tense in tandem with his hand. Any romantic thoughts I may have had left me as my body prepared to come again.

I panted, drunk on the feeling of Xander controlling my

breath, and he pitched forward to suck the skin below my collarbone between his teeth.

His thrusts turned urgent, desperate even, and I returned his intensity, eager to give him the same pleasure he was giving me. Xander was staring at me with so much admiration that I felt like my soul was completely bared before him.

"What?" I asked breathlessly, moaning as he moved his hand from my throat to the back of my neck, pulling me forward so that our foreheads were joined.

"Don't you feel that?" He groaned, grabbing my hips and slamming them down, holding them in place as he began to spill inside of me.

"Your cunt is gripping me like it never wants me to leave."

"Maybe it doesn't," I said, trying to be coy, but Xander brought his hand to my clit and let out the longest burst of Windforce yet.

I cried out fully, the orgasm whipping through me with more force than a tornado.

"That's it, Vi. Let it out," Xander crooned, leaning me back so he could kiss a trail across my chest. "Show me how much you want me to stay."

I whimpered, my body spasming and my cunt pulsing with release. Xander held me through it, murmuring praise against my skin as he continued kissing me all over.

When I finally came down, I reached my hand up and softly brushed my fingers along the delicate skin behind his ears and down his neck. His muscles seemed to ease from it, our embrace becoming more relaxed.

"I know that this is all very new," Xander said after a beat of comfortable silence and heavy breathing. "But I want you to know...I have never, in all of my existence, felt for a person the way I do for you." His words were spoken softly, sounding completely genuine, and held an undercurrent of surprise.

This was uncharted territory for him, and that filled me with a rush of satisfaction that I could be a sort of first for him. Especially because it was a sort of first for me, too, to be this open and verbal about how I was feeling. To feel this deeply connected to someone in the first place.

"I feel like I know you, but not enough," I admitted, scared to even speak the words aloud. "Every time you show me a snippet of yourself, I want to know more. I want to know every part of you."

He hugged me close to him, peppering kisses all over my right shoulder and neck as his thick biceps held onto me tightly, not a single part of our bodies disconnected.

I sank into it all–the safety of his embrace, the warm feeling taking over my chest, the post-orgasmic bliss.

And I realized that I never wanted to let go.

CHAPTER THIRTY-TWO

VIOLET

A few hours later, Xander and I were lying in his bed, leisurely exploring each other as if we had all the time in the world to do so. My head lay on his chest as I ran my fingers over the ridges of his abs, and he was making small purring noises in his chest at the sensation.

His hand was doing some exploring of its own, making its way down the expanse of my bare back and skating over the curve of my ass, paying that area some very *undivided* attention.

As I soaked in the sensation, I took notice of the lamp across from us again, the one behind the couch. It was seriously so damn familiar, which I was beginning to realize was a very common thing I'd been feeling in Cavell.

The patterns on the fabrics yesterday, the people that I'd met, the peaches—were they all just things from my childhood that I'd experienced because of my parents?

That lamp was different, though. Even the scalloped shape of the bottom of the glass shade was like something I'd looked at a thousand times before.

I shot up so fast that my vision blackened slightly. I blinked it away and looked down at Xander, who seemed disheveled and quickly joined me in sitting up.

"What is it?" he asked in a panicked rush. "What's the matter?"

"Where did you get that lamp?" I asked him and pointed at it, unsure whether I should laugh or yell.

His expression swerved into utter disorientation. Clearly, he had no idea that was what I was thinking about. "You almost gave me a *heart attack*," Xander quipped, clutching a hand to his chest dramatically. "And Astrales can't even have heart attacks."

I ignored his obvious diversion.

"You did *not,*" I couldn't help laughing as I said it, the incredulity winning out.

"I have no idea what you are talking about," Xander claimed, and he laid back down, a smile of his own showing up.

"Xander!" I chided, smacking him on the shoulder. "Why would you steal a lamp from Clarif's?"

He rolled over on his side, facing me, and closed his eyes. "I didn't steal it. I *obtained* it. And if I happened to have dropped a fair amount of marks on my way out, no harm done, right?"

"But why?"

I couldn't stop laughing. This was so ridiculous.

Xander looked back at me with a boyish type of grin on his face. "I wanted a souvenir from our first date," he admitted, his tone implying that it should have been obvious.

"Date?" I asked. "If you think that qualifies as a date, I'd better go."

I made to get out of bed jokingly, but Xander grabbed me by the hips and hauled me up. I giggled as he plopped me down on top of him in a straddling position and locked an arm around my back, trapping me in.

"Oh, you're not going anywhere." His warning was clear in the tone he used.

"Good," I placed kisses on his jaw and whispered, "because I don't want to."

Xander hummed appreciatively, seeming to enjoy my lips against his skin.

"So, what are we doing today?" I asked between kisses.

"Well, in a perfect world," Xander said, striking out and nipping the skin of my neck with his teeth, eliciting a small yelp from me. "We would do nothing but this."

"Mmhm." I arched into him, loving the way my skin tingled and burned where he had just bit it. "That does sound pretty appealing."

He sat up and pulled away, toying with the ends of my hair. "Indeed it does, but sadly, we do not live in a perfect world. We live in a world where there are fucking recluses that try to harm you to get to me. So today, we will train."

"Train how?" I asked apprehensively, moving to sit next to him.

"We are going to get that Starfire to show itself again," Xander explained, booping me on the nose and standing up. "And hopefully make some strides with you being able to wield it."

"But I thought you said last night that our conversation wasn't over?" I pointed out, moving to the edge of the bed.

"It's not, but you need to be able to defend yourself. That takes precedence over everything."

I groaned but stood up, knowing he was right. Yesterday could have ended a lot worse, and I never wanted to be in a position like that again.

"Oh, by the way, I laundered all of your clothes for you while you slept," Xander told me, walking over to a neatly folded pile of my clothes that I hadn't even noticed yesterday.

"You did my laundry?" I asked in shock.

He raised an eyebrow. "And why is that so surprising to you?"

"It's just very domesticated, is all. I'm also wondering why you insisted on me buying so many new items when you could have done this all along." I began to pick through the clothes, pulling out leggings and a compression bra to put on.

"I can be domesticated," Xander insisted, looking affronted. "Did I not make you pancakes? Was that a figment of my imagination?"

I rolled my eyes. He had a point, though.

"You needed to have something made for the festival, so I figured you may as well get a supplemental wardrobe as well. It's not like you brought all that much with you, and we don't know how all of this is going to end. Where you'll end up. "

There it was. The subject I'd thought about so many times but had never brought up.

"How do you hope it'll end?" I asked, avoiding looking at him.

I wasn't even sure what I was hoping for him to say. That he wanted me to stay? To move here permanently?

Or maybe I was just hoping he would make it easy for me to move back to Armantrea when it was over and put all of this behind me.

He tipped my chin up with two fingers, forcing me to meet his eye. "I want you here. By my side. For good," Xander said with a passion that surprised me.

I looked into his eyes for a few moments and knew, deep in my soul, that I could happily do it forever.

"I can't say goodbye to Archi for good," I trailed off for a second, just the thought of it being too painful to bear. "But I do think that I need to stay here a while longer. I need to learn where my parents came from...where *I'm* actually from. I don't see how I could do that across the mountains."

I took another breath as guilt and concern for Archi wedged their way up my throat.

I ached to know how he was doing. I knew that Xander had given him enough marks to hold him over, but for how long? Was he already struggling? Or could he be thriving without me there to burn through all of our firewood and piss through all of the excess cash, as he always complained about?

Xander was watching me, marking every change on my face.

"Plus, there is the whole Chalice situation," I continued. "What is Lilliana going to do once she learns that it is gone? Or... what if it wasn't actually destroyed and they were just trying to throw us off track?"

"The Retaliators have an agenda–that much is certain," Xander said immediately, his voice changing the same way it did whenever they were brought up. "I would be willing to bet that they were only interested in it because they heard that we were, which makes me think that they have somebody on the inside of Lilliana's team. She has kept this whole situation under lock and key."

"How do we figure out what they are up to?" I asked, irritated that this was the first time Xander had shared his suspicions with me.

"I have a plan. But that is not our focus today. You need to train."

I looked at him for a moment and left wordlessly, heading to the bathing room to get changed.

Sometimes it felt like he was finally opening up to me. But that conversation made me realize that there was still so much he wasn't telling me–namely, this plan he apparently had in the works–and that really bothered me.

I brushed my teeth and finished getting ready, my heart feeling so much heavier than it had when I first woke up. Images of Archi were playing in my mind, and I ached to talk to him about all of this. I wanted to tell him about the new memories from my childhood that were resurfacing and the fact that I was apparently a fucking *magical being*. He would know what to say about this whole situation with Xander, because Archi always knew somehow. It was like he had some sort of internal compass that read other people and told him if their intentions were good or bad.

I sighed and returned to the living area, only to find that the bed was gone. The room was open now, some sort of mat laid out where the bed had been. However, the most eye-catching change was the placement of a shimmering green forcefield between the bookshelves and the rest of the room.

"Ready to get your Starfire–"

Xander cut off as he turned around and looked at me, his gaze turning hungry as he took in my leggings and bra.

"What was that?" I asked innocently, putting a hand on my hip and cocking my head.

"You have no business looking that fucking delicious, Angel," Xander growled, looking at me like he wanted to punish me.

"This is what I wear to train at home." I shrugged. "If it distracts you, that seems like a personal problem to me."

I walked onto the mat and stood below him, challenging him with my eyes.

He narrowed his back at me, appraising me from head to toe. "Your Starfire has already shown itself once, so we know it is in there," Xander said after a few seconds, breaking our staredown.

"The question is how to draw it out again. I find it interesting that it hasn't reemerged in any similar circumstances to the first time," he added with a cunning smile.

My body temperature kicked up at the reminder of that night. Our first kiss.

But I was in no mood. So I remained silent.

"I want to try something else today," Xander said, moving off the mat.

"Sit down," he commanded me, and I listened.

"Now close your eyes," his voice sounded from behind me. "And think about a time when you were angry. I don't mean a time when someone made you mad trivially. Conjure a memory from a time that you were truly, to your core, furious."

I closed my eyes and did my best to remember a time like that. There was the day that Archi got so high that he thought it would be funny to mess with a bunch of my projects while they were drying. The memory brought back a sense of irritation, but I didn't feel anything significant stir inside of me.

I tried to recreate the way I felt when I was watching Xander put his Soothe on Archi, but I couldn't feel as enraged about it now that I knew he wasn't hurting him. I dug in deeper, trying to channel that wave of determination to break Xander's hold on me, and felt a slight tingling in my right hand. The moment I noticed it, though, it was gone.

I sighed. "This isn't working."

"You have given it all of five minutes. Keep at it," Xander instructed.

An idea occurred to me then.

I refocused my thoughts on the past, but tried to remember a time that I was angry with myself. It came to me immediately–a renewed slice of pain and regret cutting into my heart.

There was a period of time when I was totally lost as a person. It felt like I could never find my footing in life, like I would never find a place where I fit in after losing my parents. That oftentimes made me lash out, taking my pain out on anyone around me, which happened to be Archi most of the time.

I summoned that pain, reminiscing on all of the times I would lie awake at night, replaying every rude comment and snippy tone. I thought of all the times his hurt expressions would play back in my memory, making me want to reach out and strangle this *thing* living inside of me. The thing that grabbed me in its clutches at the most random of times, sucking out my personality and replacing it with something much colder, much more menacing.

The Void.

A burning emotion crashed through me then–a mixture of anger, resentment, and hatred. A venomous feeling toward the cloud that overtakes me, souring every part of my being until I feel like someone else entirely.

In a small corner of my brain, I recognized the fact that my hands felt strange. It was like they were on fire, but not in a painful way. Almost like they had become the thing that burns, not the victim of it.

No, all I could focus on was this *feeling* inside of me. And how badly I wanted to purge it out.

"Magnificent," Xander breathed, his voice much closer to me now.

I opened my eyes to find him before me, staring down at my hands. I looked to see what he was referring to and gasped, my eyes bulging out of my head.

Flames engulfed my entire hands and forearms. From the tips

of my fingers, breaking off right before my elbow, were unmistakable flames, licking and shifting as I moved my hands. It looked like the fire I had seen shooting at me yesterday–a brilliant white color that hurt my eyes. Even though my irises burned, I couldn't tear my gaze from it.

"Well, that took much less effort than I was expecting," Xander said in a light tone, clearly trying to soften the mood. "Let's see if you can concentrate the fire into an external medium. That way, you will be able to wield it as a weapon from a distance."

The memory of fire shooting at me played in my mind, and I decided very quickly that I wanted to be able to do that as well. If these Retaliators insisted on using me as their hostage, I would be prepared next time. Show them a little fire of my own.

"Picture your Starfire in your mind's eye," Xander instructed, coaching me again. "Once you have the image of it solidified, reshape it. Form it into something that could be used against another person."

I took a shuddering breath, feeling entirely overwhelmed.

I had been so focused on Xander the past few days that I hadn't spent much time thinking about myself, or coming to terms with the fact that I had this magic at all.

What if I couldn't learn to control it and ended up hurting somebody?

I focused in, pushing the worries from my mind. I didn't know how long I'd spent trying to get a mental picture of it, but it felt like many minutes had passed by the time I could see it in my mind, covering my hand and arm like a lethal protector.

Recalling Xander's advice, I imagined the white flames forming into a sphere above my hand, moving all of the flames until they were contained in the circle.

"Very good," Xander murmured into my ear, making me jump and shriek.

I looked down to find all of my flames were gone.

"You dickhead!" I exclaimed, ready to fight him. "You totally broke my concentration."

"That was the point, you foul-mouthed vixen," Xander said, flicking my forehead.

I leaned away. "Would you stop fucking *flicking* me? And what do you mean that was the point? I thought that the point was for me to train."

He laughed and moved in closer, erasing the distance I'd just gained. "We are training. You formed a sphere perfectly, and it held strong. Now comes the harder part–being able to do it while distracted."

"Oh," I said simply, feeling a little embarrassed about my outburst.

Xander shook his head and moved away. "So feisty."

I didn't wait for his instruction, calling on my Starfire without closing my eyes this time. It was definitely harder with the visual distractions around me–namely the giant man in my peripheral vision–but I was eventually able to call it forward.

I pushed harder, focusing it into a ball, and grinned like a fool when one great orb formed above my outstretched hand, spinning and glowing.

"You are a wonder," Xander announced, and the ball went away again.

I gave him an irritated look.

"Again," he demanded.

We continued like that for a while, me forming the fireball and him throwing me off course. While his methods may have been annoying as hell, they did prove to be effective. Each time I formed the weapon, it became harder and harder for him to disrupt my focus.

"Let's escalate this, shall we?" Xander asked, and I sighed internally, already exhausted.

"What did you have in mind?" I asked before taking a swig from the water bottle he'd given me.

"Clearly, wielding your Starfire is not going to be an issue for you. Let's see how much of a punch you can pack with it." I could hear Xander's smile in his voice, and looked at him questioningly.

"Like, throw my fire at you? In here?" I asked incredulously, not wanting to cause any damage to his home.

Xander's shield around his books shifted then, encasing the two of us on the mat. I had forgotten about it as I worked on strengthening the pathway to my Starfire, which was a shock considering how brilliantly it was shining.

"This face?" he asked me, gesturing to himself. "As target practice? Absolutely not."

I snorted.

"We'll have you aim here," Xander nodded in the direction of one shimmering wall where a darker green circle had formed.

"And I'll add a little twist for your motivation." He crossed his arms, giving me a provocative expression. "Every time you hit the target, I will answer one of your incessant questions."

I groaned. "Is this like the last time we played your stupid question game? Where every single thought is somehow deemed a question?"

"Well, Vi," Xander sauntered over, towering above me. "That wouldn't be the case if you didn't insist on making every statement into a query."

I formed my Starfire instantly out of frustration, thrusting my hands out aggressively and sending the sphere hurtling across the space. It completely missed the mark, crashing against Xander's wall before it absorbed the fire entirely.

A strange shuddering sensation crawled over my body when it happened, but I didn't understand why.

"Mmm," Xander hummed from behind me, making me jump. I hadn't realized he'd moved there. "Your fire tastes divine."

"*Tastes?*"

"Are you telling me you felt nothing when our magics interacted just now?" Xander asked, suggesting that he already knew the answer.

"Well, yeah...but I wouldn't describe it like that," I clarified. "Fucking weirdo."

"I heard that," Xander snapped, pinching my ass.

"Congrats," I quipped back. "I said it loudly."

"Ohhh," he gushed, a rumbling warning in his tone. "Your tongue is just begging for a fucking leash."

I bottled up my reaction, channeling it as motivation to hit the mark with my next shot. I pictured my flames crashing into the barrier, perfectly centered in the middle of the target. They listened to me without much of an effort, soaring through the air and landing right where I'd wanted.

Xander took a step back with the force of the blow. I struggled to hide my smug smile, feeling rather proud of myself for catching him off guard.

I felt like asking him a mocking question just to be a brat, but I didn't want to waste a single opportunity to gain information.

Turning around, I found him staring down at me with a feral hunger in his gaze that shook me to my core.

"Why did you want to wait to fuck me?" I asked, a little breathless from the exertion of energy.

Xander's face remained open, but I marked the way his eyes shuttered. "That question has multiple answers. I will give you one." He raised his chin, making his jawline pop.

I may or may not have felt a little tingle at the sight.

"You know a bit of my history now, but trust me when I say that it would take weeks to brief you on everything that happened in my adolescence. And some of those things are not worth sharing. They're better off left in the past." Xander swallowed visibly, his eyes shining when he looked back at me.

I grabbed his hand, letting him know that even though he was irritating me, I still supported him. I was still on his side.

"So, needless to say, I was beyond grateful to Lilliana when she, er–" he cleared his throat. "Freed me."

It was strange to witness Xander stumble over his words. So at odds with his usual cockiness and ability to deliver a punchline.

He continued, "But she didn't just free me and send me on my way. She took me in, gave me a place to live, a space to grow in." Xander's voice turned softer, reminiscent. "At that point, I'd hardly ever interacted with other people. I didn't speak much, if at all, and she did her best to guide me through that. She introduced me to Roslyn, who talked *constantly*, by the way."

I laughed at the way he spoke of her. It was a familial type of resentment usually only reserved for siblings.

"Ros taught me many things, but most of all, she helped me learn what it meant to be a member of society. To be a person, not just an experiment gone wrong."

I choked on bile—actually choked—hearing the way Xander once viewed himself.

Or did he still?

"Once it was clear that I was adjusting, Lilliana began to tell me more about who she really was, what she did. I'd thought that she was just a businesswoman with a kind heart—I had no idea that she was the governess of Myrana."

The sudden urge to sit down took over me. The mental image of Xander at that stage overwhelmed me with sadness and rage. He must have felt so lost. So alone.

I remained standing, though, and interlocked our fingers. He looked at our hands strangely again, sweeping his thumb across my knuckles.

"I learned that she serves as the head of the Enforcers, a group that was put together when the sectoral lines were drawn. The goal of this group was to stop any potential resurges of the plague. The decision was made to designate the Mistral Core as the nation's best line of defense due to its Astrales' ability to harness wind magic in a wide variety of ways."

His tone shifted from informative to reserved. "Lilliana saw an opportunity with me, a way to increase efficiency. She never pressured me to work for her, but she was very candid with me about how much it would help her. There was a big problem at the time: a huge influx of rogue Astrales. When the reports of them became more and more frequent, I stepped in."

Xander gave me a firm, serious look. "I don't want you to misunderstand me, Violet. I became an Enforcer entirely of my own free will. I have committed horrible acts on Lilliana's behalf—things I am not proud of. But I'm not some tortured soul who was led astray by a person or a set of circumstances. I chose this life for myself. And I felt as though you should know that about me before we took that step."

A slew of emotions traveled through me.

"But, I also want you to know: I've never acted on my own beliefs. I haven't killed innocent people because I thought that they were a danger to society, or were beyond reasoning with. I did it because I owe Lilliana more than I could ever hope to pay back. And nothing ever mattered more than that."

Xander reached up, flicking away a tear I hadn't realized had fallen. When he spoke, his face held a quality of uncertainty and something else, something...warmer.

"Until you."

CHAPTER THIRTY-THREE

XANDER

Violet was looking up at me with quiet hesitation, her eyes scanning all over my face like she was searching for any hints of trickery or mockery.

It made me a little angry that she didn't accept what I'd said with open arms, but I could understand her reluctance to trust me right away. I had no problem proving my merit to her, either. I intended to show her every day how much she was ingrained in my soul now, if that's what would make her trust me.

But right then, she needed to be thinking about other things.

"Try again," I told her, nodding in the direction of the target.

Violet looked at me a second longer before turning around, forming a ball, and hitting the target with minimal effort.

Shit, she was learning fast.

Now, something that I hadn't told her was that I practically had no idea what I was doing. I mean, I was well-versed in learning how to control your gifts, that much was certain. But I didn't contain the Astrolite Core myself, so everything that I'd advised her to do was born out of a gut feeling and well-informed guesses.

But it seemed to be working pretty damn well, if I do say so myself.

Violet gave me a self-satisfied look that made the blue spot in her eye sparkle, and the sight made me want to meet her challenge.

"Go on," I encouraged her. "Ask your question, and then we are kicking this up a notch."

She groaned. "I'm already tired. We've been at this for so long."

I tsked. "Retaliators won't care if you're tired, and neither do I."

Violet shot me an especially menacing glare, and I hid my smile.

So hostile.

I knew I was pushing her hard, but I hadn't expected her to advance so quickly, so it felt justified. I also couldn't stop replaying the panic I felt when I saw her eyes roll back while we were in the Between.

I could have lost her. Forever.

I took a deep swig from the water bottle, trying to help my suddenly dry throat.

Once we mastered this part of the training, I had all sorts of ideas for ways that she could wield her Starfire defensively. Then, hopefully, she would never be in that position again. Plus, I had a feeling this little vixen didn't break easily. She could handle the pressure, and the hard work.

"How long were you and Nygaard dating for?" Violet asked out of nowhere, making me choke on the liquid I was swallowing.

I coughed, my throat burning even more now, and took a moment to recover.

"My situation with Gaar was...complicated. But we were never in a relationship," I explained, a touch incredulously. "What the hell ever gave you that idea?"

Violet looked at me like she was calling out a lie. "There is no way on this planet you two weren't fucking. Do you think I'm stupid?"

"I never said we didn't fuck," I said, getting irritated. "I said that we weren't in a relationship. It was more of a..." I paused, looking for the right description. "Mutually benefiting arrangement."

"Okay, well, how long were you in an 'arrangement' for?" Violet asked with a bite.

I ground my teeth together. "That's not of importance."

"Fuck that." She pointed at me venomously. "You said I got to ask you any question, and you haven't answered it yet. How long?"

"I did technically ans–"

"Xander," Violet cut me off with a tone that called me out on my attempted diversion.

"About…fifteen years? Give or take?" I ran a hand over the back of my neck, wincing a bit.

Had it really been that long?

Violet visibly swallowed the information, her whole presence looking taken aback.

She turned around abruptly, looking back at the target. "How did you want to escalate the training?" she asked.

"Violet," I started, feeling at a loss for words. *Again.*

"Do you want to talk about this?" I asked, stepping closer to her.

"I'm processing," she admitted, her tone making me tense up. "Just let me absorb this for a second. Let's get back to training."

I turned back to the wall and focused on my magic for half a second, redesigning the target so that it would begin to move.

Her head moved as she watched it shift, tracking every new position it found. "So, you're wanting me to hit the moving target," Violet said, not as a question, just a clarification.

"Yes," I told her, crossing my arms to keep from reaching out to her. "Same rules apply."

I was definitely not a fan of the way things felt colder, more closed-off between us now. I was enjoying our back and forth before she went and asked me that stupid fucking question. What good would it do to bring that up now?

Although, I supposed she thought she was just asking me about an ex-boyfriend, and not…Gaar.

If only things with him were that simple.

I watched as she attempted to hit the mark, failing multiple times. She was trying to use the same methods as before, but her trajectory wasn't fast enough for that yet. What she needed to do was record the patterns of movement so that she could predict where the spot would be next.

I thought about voicing that, but decided that it would be more beneficial for her to reach that point on her own.

Violet kept trying–and kept failing–until finally, she let out a deep-throated yell and pushed both hands out in front of her. A *massive* beam of Starfire streamed out of them in a concentrated rush, barrelling right towards the wall in front of my books.

I felt my eyes bulge out of my head and shifted the shield until all four walls were concentrated into that one area, using all of my strength to absorb Violet's power.

The hit was hard, much harder than I expected, and it brought me down to my knees with a surprised grunt.

Violet whipped around and looked at me, her hand drawn up to cover her mouth. She dropped to her knees in front of me, trembling like a leaf with panic-ridden eyes.

"Hey," I said, closing the distance between us. "It's alright. No harm done. I just wasn't expecting a blow of that size, so it surprised me. Next time, I'll be more prepared."

I was lying through my fucking teeth to try and get that fear out of her eyes.

The only fucking thing that is allowed to scare her is *me.*

But I honestly didn't know if I would be able to contain her training this way. She had so much more power than I had ever known, or been around. This was all uncharted territory.

"Violet," I murmured when she didn't answer.

"Yes?" she whispered, finally looking at me.

I braced my hands on her hips, suddenly needing to touch her. "You are truly miraculous."

She was looking up at me with such an innocent expression, I felt myself tensing up with the need to protect her.

"Most Astrolites can't even conjure external flames at all," I told her in amazement. "You are just getting started, and it is very rare for Starfire to be physically wielded this way. With a stream of that size...your potential is immeasurable."

I saw the panic grow in her eyes then and realised that I had been misunderstanding the cause of her stress. She was afraid of herself—of her abilities.

"This is a good thing," I assured her, nuzzling into her neck briefly. "Now, you don't need to worry about being in danger for two reasons."

She smiled then, albeit in a slightly perturbed way.

"Let's take a break," I said, deciding that we were done for the day.

I needed to bury myself inside of her until there wasn't space in her thoughts for anything but me.

But first: food.

I didn't wait for her response, just scooped her up and kept her in my arms. She looked down, noticing the fact that I had covered her body with one of my black cotton shirts.

She pinched it between her fingers and lifted it, looking at me with a dry expression. "Really?" she asked.

"Well, I can't exactly bring you in public wearing only that bra. Then I would have to murder every person we come across for looking at your bare skin, which would really get quite tedious after a few minutes." I purposely made it sound like I was describing making small talk instead of ending lives. "Unless you *enjoy* seeing me spill blood for you," I suggested with a devious smile. "In that case, I wouldn't mind at all."

"You are maniacal," Violet choked out, her demeanour slowly going back to normal. Relief coursed through me.

"Don't pretend like you don't love it," I murmured, leaning in to kiss her at the same moment I whisked us to the food district.

As we landed in the middle of the bustling street, I put Violet down, thinking that she probably wouldn't appreciate me carrying her around in public. Even though I, on the other hand, would be absolutely thrilled by it.

Her unique eyes began skittering around the different food vendors set up: tents and tables, and restaurants with walk-up windows–all occupied by at least one customer.

"This place is incredible," Violet said in amazement.

"Yes, it's all so wonderfully life-changing and new," I teased, pulling the tin from my pocket and knocking out a stick.

I lit it with my Corefire, watching as Violet studied the small green flame. I hid a smile, occupying my lips with the cigarette instead, and began walking down the street.

Violet caught up to me. "Why do you always start walking as if I am automatically going to follow you?"

I raised a brow. "Well, you did. Did you not?"

She huffed a breath before eyeing my cigarette, and it occurred to me to ask her about an observation I had made. "I noticed something," I started, stopping and pulling Violet into an alley between two buildings.

"Oh god," she muttered, her eyebrows rising a bit. "Do I even want to know?"

I laughed around the cigarette, pulling her body closer to me. I took a drag between my teeth before snatching it away with two fingers. Leaning forward, I pressed my lips against Violet's and waited a second, so that she would know what I was about to do.

When she didn't pull away, I blew the smoke into her mouth, my cock instantly hardening against the waistband of my pants as her lips brushed against mine on her inhale.

Fuck.

"Let's eat quickly so we can go home," I suggested, momentarily dazed by the sight of her before me, her eyes locked on mine with dilated pupils.

Her lips quirked in amusement, those eyebrows still resting high as she exhaled the smoke. "What is it that you noticed?" she asked in a light tone, bringing me back on track.

"I have not seen you use those herbs you bought in Armantrea–not a single time. What's the deal with that, Vi?" I nudged her nose with mine. "Did you just want an excuse to go to the market and try to slip away from me?"

I wasn't expecting much of a reaction out of her apart from her usual glare or scoff, but she jerked back, her eyes going unfocused as she began to think about it.

"Woah," I said, trying to pull her to me again. "I was just curious. It's not a big deal."

"Sure," she forced out, smiling forcefully. "No big deal."

"Unless it is..." I looked at her closely, hearing her heart hammering inside her chest. "What's going on?"

"It's not really something that I want to talk about here. Can we just eat?" Violet asked.

"Of course," I said straight away, regretting bringing it up at all. "What do you fancy?"

"I don't really give a fuck," Violet muttered before reaching over and ripping my cigarette out of my grasp.

She drew it to her lips and I gaped, completely taken aback by her thievery.

"What?" She levelled me with a look, letting the smoke trail out of her mouth. Those very full, very erotic lips looked even more sinful with my hand-rolled cigarette between them.

"Yep," I decided. "Definitely eating quickly."

She rolled her eyes before eyeing the cigarette between her fingers. "What is this herb, anyway?"

"It's a blend. Mostly tobacco," I told her. "Nothing too barmy."

Her lips quirked. "Barmy?"

I chuckled. "You know—mad, crazy, foolish. It won't intoxicate you, if that's what you're asking."

She nodded and took two more drags before putting it out, the stick having reached its end.

"You can finish it, by the way," I said dryly, giving her an amused look.

"You're the one who literally blew smoke into my mouth," she protested, and I suddenly realised the mistake I had made.

I'd been so distracted when we left that I forgot to put the Soothe on her voice. I corrected it instantly, unnerved by the thought of what could have happened if I hadn't remembered.

I grabbed her hand and tugged her out of the alley, directing her down the street towards my favourite stall.

"You're going to love this," I promised her. "It's the best smoked fish I've ever had in my life."

"Uh, I don't usually eat fish," Violet said, looking uncomfortable.

"Xander?" A voice called out from behind me.

I stopped dead in my tracks.

No.

Fuck.

"Lilliana!" I turned around, my best charming smile strapped in place.

Why hadn't I considered that she might be here before we came, damn it?

She walked up to us slowly, her blonde hair hanging loose. Her petite frame was covered in a casual dress that hung down to the sandals she wore, masquerading the extremely powerful being that she was.

"How are you?" Lilliana asked casually, giving Violet a polite smile.

I knew that smile–it was undoubtedly fake. Calculated.

"Good, yes. We were just taking a break from our work to get something to eat," I half-lied, my muscles tightening in preparation to make a quick exit.

Lilliana looked down where my hand was still interlocked with Violet's, her expression shifting into a mild shock that was too slow...too rehearsed.

I expected Violet to pull back the way she had in front of Ren, but she squeezed my hand even tighter, giving Lilliana a neutral, respectful expression.

That sight alone had me ready to faint in shock.

Lilliana looked back to me. "I expect that there has been

progress with finding the Chalice, even considering this," she gestured between me and Violet, "development?"

I narrowed my eyes, her entire demeanour feeling off.

To my surprise, Violet was the one who spoke. "We have encountered a few hiccups," she said carefully. "But we're following a new lead now."

A Soothe on her voice, Lilliana said to me Inmind. *Smart.*

I didn't respond, my stomach filling with dread.

Lilliana nodded at Violet. "Hopefully, that will pan out, then. Enjoy your meal. I'll see you later." She smiled before departing, whisking away entirely.

"Something's not right," I muttered, my thoughts spinning in overdrive with all of the things I'd overlooked the past few days.

Like the fact that Lilliana hadn't reached out to me at all. Not once did she check in, or speak to me Inmind to see what the latest was with the case.

What was more strange than that was the fact that she hadn't given me any assignments whatsoever since the day Violet and I left the Armoury. This was the longest off-period I'd had since I became an Enforcer.

"Um, care to explain?" Violet asked, struggling to keep up with my strides as I pulled her down the street.

"Not here," I told her, eyeing the crowd around us.

How could I have been so stupid? So fucking reckless?

Well, I knew the answer to that, actually. I'd been *distracted*.

I knew that something bad would come from letting our mating bond go unmarked. We had been so caught up in each other, in our own little bubble of isolation, that the outside world had faded away. The need to touch, fuck, and conquer her had overcome me so completely that I hadn't even noticed when Lilliana went silent.

I looked over at Violet to find her watching me, her brows pulled together and one of her cheeks tucked into her teeth.

I tried to form a pathway between our minds so that we could speak without being overheard. I still hadn't figured out if Violet was capable of Inmind communication, a gift that is seemingly random with whom it is given to. I reached out to her but felt a wall blocking me out–the same that I'd felt when I tried this before.

It didn't feel the same as when I tried to reach out to others who didn't have the gift. Then, it was like I was reaching out to nothing. There was a distinct and clear force keeping me out of her mind.

It was fucking *maddening*.

We made it to the stall and I ordered food for carryout, already more than satisfied with our excursion out of the house and itching to get Violet back to safety. That way, we could eat in my flat while I tell her about everything I'd just realised, and make a game plan for moving forward.

I was certain of one thing–Lilliana had something up her sleeve. She was the living, breathing embodiment of a mastermind, every step taken in the direction of a bigger picture.

But there was another thing that I'd realised the moment I saw Lilliana walking towards us.

I would kill her before I'd let her touch Violet ever again.

CHAPTER THIRTY-FOUR

VIOLET

"Why do we have to bring the food back?" I asked Xander, looking around at the city center before me. "We've been in your apartment for days. I'd like to at least eat a meal before we go back."

I hoped that it didn't come across like I didn't like his place, because I did. That didn't mean that I was in a rush to get back there, though.

"Vi, I'll explain it to you when we get home," Xander said in a frustrated tone, bouncing his knee incessantly as we waited for the food to be ready.

I couldn't help but notice that this was the second time he'd said 'home', like it was both of ours. But it was only half a thought because I was too absorbed in his demeanor.

I'd literally never seen him act like this. He looked anxious.

I put my hand on the crook of his elbow, stepping closer to him. "Breathe," I told him under my breath. "You look like you're about to have a panic attack."

He didn't answer, just continued staring forward and grinding his teeth together.

"Stop that," I scolded, cringing at the force he was using. "You're going to file your teeth down to nubs. How will you ever bite me, then?"

I accomplished my goal as Xander's head whipped to me, a shocked expression on his face.

"What?" I asked coyly, shrugging.

A slow grin started spreading across his face, but it halted when the woman behind the counter called his name. She held out a paper bag for him to take and he did, offering her a smile and thanks.

He grabbed my hand again and leaned down, his lips brushing against my temple in a kiss. He whispered, "Don't worry, Angel. There will be plenty of biting to come."

My blood heated at the rich, flirtatious rasp of his voice.

Xander squeezed my hand. "We can stay and eat here if you like, but I really think that it would be best for us to go home."

I nodded with a genuine smile. "We can go back; it's okay."

I was definitely ready to after feeling his lips against my skin again. But more importantly, if Xander was worried about something, I should probably be worried too. He was the one that had experience in all of this, and clearly, I'd missed something in our conversation with Lilliana.

Xander tipped my chin up and met my lips with his own, whisking us the moment that they touched.

I loved it when he did that.

I felt my feet land in his apartment in some distinct corner of my brain, but was too wrapped up in the kiss to really care. I wound my arms around his neck, deepening it now that we were in private. But he pulled back in a jerking motion, and I had to blink a few times to see that he had moved back a step.

"Xan?" I asked in confusion.

I looked at him with concern, his entire body was rigid and alert. He wasn't looking at me, but across the room, with a blank, stoic expression.

"Xander," I repeated, stepping forward.

"You did perfectly, my boy."

Everything inside of me froze.

My thoughts ceased to move. My shoulders pulled up defensively and stayed there. I don't think my heart was even beating inside my chest as I looked up at Xander's face, silently screaming at him to look at me.

But he didn't. He continued staring forward, looking at the person I now knew to be standing behind me.

Lilliana.

And then the Void.

I whimpered as my viewpoint shifted, turning chaotic and mismatched until it came into focus again. I was no longer in Xander's apartment. I was someplace new.

The room was completely blank, barren, and white. All of the walls, the floor, the table in the middle of the room–everything was stark white in color.

"It is quite a shame that you weren't able to locate the Chalice before the Retaliators did. That would have saved us all of this trouble," Lilliana said with a tsk, nudging my limp body with her foot. "Oh, sit up already. I don't care for dramatics."

"Dramatics?" I repeated in rage, pushing myself up on shaky arms.

"Boys," Lilliana murmured, inclining her head.

My brow pinched in confusion, but I felt my consciousness begin to sway at the onslaught of emotions I'd been attacked by the past few minutes.

I cried out when something heavy latched into place around my neck, making a definite locking noise. The second it was in place, I felt like something vital had been ripped away from my soul. I was hyperventilating by the time I brought my fingers up to touch the collar, screaming in pain once I did.

It was like the thing had burned my hand, but I didn't feel the heat against the skin of my neck.

"The fuck are you going to do to me now?" I asked in a low, grave voice that I didn't even recognize.

Lilliana beamed a full, shining smile then, looking at me with a manic light in her eyes. "Now," she said, looking behind me once more. Her eyes locked on mine again as I was hoisted up by my armpits and held off the ground.

"Now, we have some fun."

Part Two

VIOLENCE

CHAPTER THIRTY-SIX

VIOLET

"I already fucking *told you*!" I screamed as the pain laced throughout my body. "I have no idea how I made it to begin with. I can't just do it again."

A fresh bout of Lilliana's magic slammed into me, this time pressing down on my chest so hard I was sure it would collapse.

Apparently, Lilliana's idea of *'fun'* was chaining me to a chair by my ankles and attempting to torture me into creating a new Chalice. She'd had her minions confine me in this seat a while ago before a slab of clay and a wheel appeared in front of me. I couldn't believe that was her endgame in all of this.

Lilliana let up her hold on my chest, and I gasped for air, tears streaming down my cheeks.

I didn't speak, nor did I make any move to unwrap the clay in front of me. I just maintained eye contact with Lilliana, trying to communicate with my eyes just how deeply she was going to regret this one day.

I had no idea how or when, but I *would* be escaping from here. And when I found her again, she'd regret the day she came into my life.

"Boys," Lilliana said, addressing the two other Astrales in the room. "I think our dear Violet is failing to grasp her lack of choice in this. Shall we show her the way a human would?"

The two men rounded the table, and I couldn't help but laugh at the fact that she referred to them as boys. One of them was on the shorter side but had the largest and most defined muscles of anyone I had ever seen. It looked like he spent his days lifting boulders and carrying them around for fun. His skin was a deep russet color, his knuckles already holding the evidence of someone else's abuse.

The other man could only be described as slimy. While he was lankier than the first, his brown eyes held an unnerving gleam of malice and bloodlust. The color was offset by his pale skin, which had a gray, lifeless sort of quality to it. His sharp nose hooked out when he smiled, the sight so disturbing that I wondered what sort of things happened in his imagination.

The buff one ripped my chair out from the table abruptly and tipped it back so that I was looking up into his hazel eyes. Those eyes were too beautiful for such a soulless monster.

"You sure you don't want to just do as she asks?" he asked me, but his eagerness for me to say no was clear in the way his eyes were shining with excitement.

"Go to hell," I spat at him.

He flashed all of his teeth at me before releasing his hold on the chair, causing it to crash to the ground. My skull bashed against the unforgiving surface, making my vision go hazy and my ears ring. Someone was talking, but I couldn't hear what they were saying, my consciousness fading in and out from the hit.

"But you just *got* a turn," I heard the slimy one whine.

"Fine," the buff one huffed.

A bloodcurdling scream tore through my throat as a foot collided with the ribcage on my right side. I heard a definite crunching noise and clutched my side with my hand–the pain was unbearable.

Apparently unsatisfied with his first blow, the man punched me in the same spot, directly over my hand, and I felt those bones snap against his assault as well.

I lost touch with the sounds coming out of me. The only thing I was aware of was the pain overtaking my senses. My vision blacked out as my head rolled to the side.

When I came to, my chair had been righted, but wasn't

pushed back up to the table. I blinked repeatedly, trying to force away the blurriness that was clouding the three Astrales' figures.

My shattered hand was resting limply on my lap and swelling by the second. I tried to conjure a memory to trigger the healing process, but it felt like I was grasping at straws. I couldn't get my thoughts to focus for a second around the pain.

When my ears finally stopped ringing, I heard Lilliana chastising the one who'd attacked me last. "How is she supposed to create a new Chalice with a broken hand? You useless, brainless, *waste* of fucking space. It will be hours until Roslyn is back, and she is the only healer we can trust."

I could feel Lilliana's frustration through her words, and it brought me such great joy that I let out a laugh. Well, as close to a laugh as I could muster in that state, which ended up being a wet sort of chuckle that funneled into a cough.

"What exactly is so funny? I don't think you're in any position to be laughing, my dear," she finished, a smug sort of smile on her face.

"I am just enjoying watching you scramble as you realize that this plan is never going to work." My voice was more croaky than I would have liked, and it caused great pain to speak around my injuries, but I continued nonetheless. "You may as well kill me now, Lilliana. I am never going to give you what you want."

Lilliana came into focus more, a pinched, maniacal look to her face. I thought at that moment how strangely satisfying it was to see such a beautiful face finally reveal the vile creature I'd always suspected was lurking within.

"Oh," she mused, stepping up to me and leaning down so that we were eye-to-eye. "There are plenty of avenues we have yet to explore. For example," Lilliana cocked her head to the side, looking up at the buff one. "Dhan, didn't Xander tell us about a certain human best friend, just waiting for his sweet Willow to return home?"

The buff one–Dhan, apparently–grunted in agreement, his huge arms crossed over his chest.

My stomach bottomed out, the blood draining from my face as the threat to Archi hit home. At the sound of his nickname for me on her lips.

There was only one way she would have learned that name.

"You fucking *touch* him, and I'll–"

"You'll what?" Lilliana mocked. "You'll hit me with your untrained Starfire? Go on," she stepped back and held her arms out in a waiting gesture. "Give me your best shot."

The sound of her shrill laugh is what finally sent my rage bubbling over, something inside of me snapping. I reached into myself, trying with all my might to summon my Starfire the way I had in Xander's apartment. I visualized it engulfing my hand and flying through the air in an unrestrained, chaotic manner, latching onto the three people in front of me until they were nothing but ash.

But nothing happened; not a single spark of that white fire emerged.

"Did I forget to mention?" Lilliana said in a regretful tone. "That nifty little collar was forged out of concentrated Astrolite Corepower. It nullified any Starfire in your veins the second it was placed around your neck, as well as any Sensinor abilities."

I fought the tears crowding me with all my might, trying to hold on to any scrap of dignity I had left, but I had never felt so hopeless in my entire life.

Lilliana seemed satisfied with herself because she turned to address the slimy one. "Jax, please escort Violet up to her chambers–we will have her wait for Roslyn there." She gave him a distasteful look, her resentment clear. "And do be sure to stand guard outside her door. No one enters the room besides me, Xander, or Roslyn."

Lilliana looked at me with gleeful malice. "I'll see you soon," she promised,

☽

. . .

I looked around my room at the Armory, feeling an emotional numbness overcome me that was so potent, so deeply-rooted, I wasn't sure it would ever go away.

Jax had whisked us to my room before dumping me on the bed. He left immediately, closing and locking the door behind him. My entire body hurt, and I was using all of my willpower to stop myself from pulling at the collar still around my neck.

All of my belongings were on the desk. The duffle bag from Xander's apartment was sitting there, staring me in the eye and reminding me of his betrayal. I thought that he must've been the one to bring my things back here, but then again, it really could have been anyone. For all I knew, his 'secret' apartment was really just a ruse to get me to trust him.

What had I been thinking? Taking the word of a man who had kidnapped me, all because of some faulty oath he had made.

Even though I told myself that was what made me feel totally safe around him, I had to admit that I already had a gut feeling that I could trust him before he'd taken it. More often than not, my instincts served me well, but this wasn't the first time they had royally fucked something up. It just happened to be the first time they'd resulted in me being tortured.

I got out of bed painfully, muttering curses at myself for forgetting my true place here all because of him. A man I barely even knew, regardless of how it felt when I was around him.

I needed to get home. Now. And there was only one option that I could see for how to get there. Something that I remembered when Lilliana mentioned the Astrolite Corepower.

I moved to the desk, using my uninjured hand to unzip my bag. I reached into the small pocket and grabbed the oblong stone Shaed had given me.

Feeling more than slightly silly, I turned it thrice in hand, as he'd instructed.

There was a light rapping at my door—no. Not *my* door. Nothing about this frigid and unfamiliar space was mine.

I pocketed the stone and clutched my shattered hand to my chest. When the knocking came again and louder, I hoped the signal had gone through and Shaed would show up soon.

"The door is locked, moron!" I yelled to whoever was out there.

"Jax gave me the key, brat."

My blood went cold at the sound of his voice. At the fact that he'd actually called me that after everything.

"You better not fucking come through that door, Xander," I warned in a low voice.

My heart rate began to pick up as I realized I had absolutely no idea how long my message would take to reach Shaed, or if he could even get into the Armory.

Xander walked through the door anyway, that same detached expression on his face.

"Violet." His voice was oddly strained and grainy. "You are hurt," he stated in that same strange way, his entire body tense and his green eyes focused intensely on my hand.

He seemed rooted in place, and I eyed him wearily, feeling the need to back away from him for the first time since I'd met him. He seemed unhinged. Dangerous.

"Can you please," I breathed out, my hands shaking. "Just get the fuck out."

Xander was before me in a second, making me jump and consequently yelp at the pain that shot through my rib cage, doubling over in pain. He tried to help me, but I jerkily moved out of his reach and away from him. Xander was staring at the collar still on my neck with unnerving focus.

At that moment, Shaed appeared right behind me, so close that his body was pressed against my back. I winced in pain at the contact, and he immediately moved a small step away.

"Violet," Shaed breathed out, relieved. "What can I do?"

Xander's cold laugh filled the room. "You seriously think *he* will bring you to safety?"

"From where I'm sitting, anywhere is safer than here with you psychotic fucks." My hands were still shaking as I turned to Shaed, surprised that I was actually relieved to see him and his stark blond hair. "Will you please grab my bag?" I asked quietly, wondering what Xander would actually do when we tried to leave.

"Trust me, Violet," Xander insisted in a low voice. "You don't want to involve yourself with the Everton family."

"Trust. *You,*" I repeated slowly, dumbfounded. "After you did this?"

Yanking my sleeve all the way up, I pointed to the Oath mark on my arm. "I mean, what was the point of it?" I asked, hating the way my voice shook. "Did you just want to lower my guard? Or did you want to brand me like I was some sort of prized cow in your possession?"

Xander flinched, something about his demeanor shifting. Then he was in front of me, gripping my chin and forcing my gaze to lock on his. "You have to listen to me, Violet. There has never been a safer place for you than by my side since the day we met."

"You're insane!" I yelled, pulling my chin out of his grasp. "You're genuinely, certifiably, in-*sane*. You handed me over to her." I choked on a sob, covering my mouth with my hand as images ran through my mind from that room.

His voice turned deadly quiet. "What did she do to you?"

"You're so full of shit. You are the one who told me she isn't afraid to get her hands dirty. You are the one who said I shouldn't be around her. And yet you delivered me to her, told her about everything that has been happening to me, and now you're trying to tell me I'm *safe* with you?"

His brow furrowed painfully, like he couldn't get the words out. "I took the oath, Violet. And I am alive."

"Oh really?" I deadpanned, "Is this you disrupting the path of those who wish to cause me harm?" I thrust my shirt up, exposing the brutal bruising deepening by the minute on my ribs.

I watched Xander's eyes widen and then turn to ice as his nostrils flared, and he took in the early evidence of my abuse. Even though it couldn't have been more than half an hour since I was dumped back into my room, the ribs along the right side of my body held deep purple splotches, and my breath hitched if I took one too deeply. I was pretty sure they were broken.

He stepped into me, grabbing both of my elbows, and all I could sense was his closeness. The smell of pine filled my nostrils, and that deep rooted feeling of familiarity took hold in my gut.

"Who was it." Xander's voice was deep and full of dark promise.

I tried to wriggle out of his grasp but didn't budge. He moved his hands to my shoulders and squeezed lightly.

"That's enough," Shaed tried to interject from behind us, but Xander didn't pay him any mind.

His eyes were shining with an animalistic rage and focused solely on me. "Tell me who raised their hand against you so I can tear it from their fucking body," Xander growled.

"What does it matter whose hand it was when *yours* was the one that delivered me to them!" My vocal cords felt like they were going to snap after so much yelling, and I felt the energy leaving my body by the second.

Xander flinched again and released me before taking a full step back. He blinked a few times, his expression a contradicting mix of haze, confusion, and burning intensity.

When he spoke, it was no more than a whisper. "*My* hand?"

"Let's go, Violet," Shaed said, placing his hand on my shoulder.

Xander's whole body tensed again, his eyes locked on Shaed's hand. "Touch her again, Shaed, and I will rip your throat out before you've even fucking blinked."

At that moment, Roslyn entered the room frantically, like she had been running to get there. "What," she started, freezing as she took in the scene before her, "in the *hell* is happening?"

"I'm leaving, Xander," I said with finality, stepping back to stand beside Shaed. "If you want to stop me, you're going to have to kill me."

Xander let out a frustrated sound and inserted himself between me and Shaed. "Angel," he whispered, leaning down so that we were eye-to-eye. "Do not go with him. Please, stay with me."

I felt a crack lace its way up my heart as I looked into his eyes, and knew in that moment, I would never be the same again.

Xander had changed the very essence of my soul—once when he made me fall for him, and again when he showed his true colors.

Roslyn stepped forward and put a hand on Xander's elbow, not so much as flinching when he whipped a venomous gaze toward her. Every part of his body language warned against her getting involved, but she didn't seem to care.

"Xander," Roslyn spoke softly. "Keep her here, and you are no better than those you despise so deeply."

I watched as the message sank into him and, despite everything, felt myself crumble at how broken and panicked his face looked when it turned back to me. But then I remembered what he had done. I felt the bruises pulse as if in response to my thoughts.

"Let's go," I said, turning to Shaed and refusing to look at Xander again.

Shaed nodded and whisked us out of the Armory, most likely bringing us to the Astrolite sector.

The destination was unimportant to me as I listened to the echoing of Xander's bellow in my ear—the last thing I heard before a beautiful darkness came and swept everything away.

CHAPTER THIRTY-SEVEN

LILLIANA

I took a healthy gulp of the pink wine in my glass, feeling a tingle through my fingers and legs. It could have been the effects of alcohol, but it was more likely excitement.

The time had finally come.

I sent out the mental ping, knowing both responses would come immediately. They did.

We are ready, I told them both, skipping any greetings or pleasantries.

The satisfaction from the words was sweet on my tongue, even though they were spoken Inmind.

It turns out all he needed to mature fully was to meet his mate, I explained to them.

Do you think that if they would have marked the bond, he would be uncontainable? His response came in, and it was strange to hear his voice after all this time and not be able to see him at all.

This new life form he'd taken on was...unnerving.

It is hard to say. This is so unprecedented. I pondered what he'd asked for a moment. *But I think that it is very likely that the Corechain wouldn't have worked on him any longer if they had. Both of their magics are far too unique for anything external to bind them, if they were bonded.*

Enough of the hypothetical jargon, the female voice interjected with irritation, and I bit back my retort.

Someday, she wouldn't have the authority to speak to me that way anymore.

Someday.

Let's get to work, I told them both before cutting off the connection.

And so we did.

CHAPTER THIRTY-EIGHT

XANDER

Something was wrong.

Something within me was deeply and inherently wrong.

My mind felt like it had been split into two, both sides fighting a losing battle for dominance.

I couldn't get my bearings with what was happening–it felt like I was trapped inside of a night terror where someone else was in control of my body.

All I knew was that I had just seen a very injured, very *scared* Violet, and I had no idea how she ended up that way. It was ultimately her scent that made me break free from that strange haziness, the tang of fear on it tangible. When I finally did, she started talking about things I didn't understand.

She showed me the evidence of her abuse.

And then she left. With *him*.

Roslyn was saying something to me, but I didn't have the capacity to listen to her right now. I needed to leave.

I whisked myself to my flat, desperate for the solitude and peacefulness that it always brought me. I landed in front of my armchair and immediately collapsed into it, my body feeling like I hadn't slept or eaten for a week. My head spun like a top, and I clenched my eyes shut to try and stop it.

"I thought you might come back here," a familiar voice called out, making my spine straighten to a point.

A strange sensation overcame me then, as the realisation of what had been happening all this time hit me.

It felt like the chills that gather at the notch where your neck meets your back. When they grow and swirl until you have to consciously nudge them downwards so that they fizzle along the entirety of your body, sparking electricity in your blood and making little bumps pebble across your skin.

It was one of those moments when you realise that the truth has been there all along–a dormant, unacknowledged thing waiting beneath the surface to be unleashed at last.

"*You,*" I said with boiling rage, standing to my full height and staring down at Lilliana.

She was sitting politely on one of my barstools, as if she were just there for afternoon tea. I moved within reach of her and squeezed her throat with my hand harshly, stopping any air from entering her lungs.

"You are the reason I lose time," I snarled between my teeth, my entire life feeling like a lie.

"How did you get in my fucking head?" I growled and tightened my hold, but was ripped away from her by two people who had come up behind me.

I knew what was coming next, so I did everything in my power to get away from them, but it was too late. I felt the shackles lock into place around my wrists–a panic like none other overcoming me from the sensation that still plagued my worst nightmares. My access to my Core began to fade away by the second, no matter what I did to try and anchor myself to it.

I still had my physical strength and size on my side, though.

I swept one foot out, knocking Dhan flat on his back. "I always knew you were a fucking coward," I spat down at him.

Jax yanked against my shackles from behind me, and I bit back a yell from the pain that brought me to my knees. The strange material squeezed tightly on my wrists, the specific pain so familiar to me that I almost welcomed it.

Lilliana walked towards me, cocking her head like she actually was sad to see me like this. "I'm sorry, my boy. It had to be done.

This was all a part of the plan." She smiled at me warmly, like she was happier than ever.

"What plan?" I stopped moving, the cuffs suffocating my wrists so tightly that my fingers were tingling. "What the fuck are you getting at, Lilliana?"

"My whole reason for creating you. The grand plan," she said simply, making my heart stop.

Lilliana raised her hands like she was showing off her greatest accomplishment.

My entire body went cold.

"You–" I took a breath. "You what?"

"Yes, my dear." She reached out to me, placing her hand on my cheek. I wrenched my head back, wincing as the shackles tightened even further.

"There is no need to jerk away. I am your mother, after all."

CHAPTER THIRTY-NINE

VIOLET

I'd been in Shaed's home for two whole days, but I hadn't seen much of anything outside of the guest suite he'd shown me to.

It was more luxurious than any place I had ever stayed before, so I felt completely out of my element. The bed was held up by a gold four-poster frame that had sheer fabric hanging from it, the sheets on it were softer than butter. The overall decor of the room matched the black and gold theme that seemed to make up this entire palace.

It made me feel a little sick to my stomach, if I was being honest.

After Shaed brought me here, he immediately removed the collar from my neck and incinerated it. Apparently, he was one of the few Astrolites who could wield very strong Starfire, if that fact was even true.

I had no idea what to believe anymore.

I told Shaed numbly that I needed time to process everything that had happened. After making me thoroughly assure him that I was a Sensinor, he gave me space, not pressing the issue and leaving immediately. I hadn't seen him since.

In fact, the only people I had seen were a few workers who brought me food and offered to launder my clothes. Chelsea hadn't even come, which made me wonder who Shaed had told that I was there.

I made sure that the lock on my door was in place multiple

times a day, even though it probably didn't do me much good in the fortress of supernatural royalty.

I spent a lot of my time spiraling and feeling hopeless, worried that Lilliana would come to retrieve me at any given moment.

It unnerved me that she seemed to have just let me go. Surely she would have a way to know when people come and go from the Armory, especially someone from another sector.

There was also the fact that Roslyn had witnessed Shaed leaving with me, and Lilliana definitely made it seem like she was a trusted ally.

But why had Roslyn encouraged Xander to let me go then?

The constant wondering from the past two days sent me into a new sort of Void. It kept shifting, moving me from panic to dissociation and everything in between within minutes. I felt like I was walking on a tightrope, just waiting to fall over the edge into full-blown insanity.

I had managed to heal my injuries shortly after I'd arrived, the process was much more difficult this time without anyone to guide me through it.

After a little bit of moping, I realized that I needed to continue to learn how to defend myself regardless of what had happened. I was still trapped in this foreign land with no known allies and no way home.

So, I spent hours summoning my Starfire until it hardly took a thought to do it. I had to admit, it made me feel really powerful and...whole. Like I was connecting with something that had been ripped away from me.

I began to wonder what else I could do. If I was a Whisken, surely I would've known by now, right?

Regardless, I spent countless hours trying to move myself across the room but ended up just staring at nothing really hard for a ridiculous amount of time.

I didn't know what to do. It wasn't like I could ask anybody here how to figure out if I had dormant abilities. It would raise suspicions, and I couldn't afford that.

There was one thing working in my favor. Xander must have forgotten to remove the Soothe from my voice, so I was still speaking with the Astrale accent. At least I didn't have to add that to my pile of things to worry about.

I sat on the bench at the foot of the bed, sighing dramatically and laying back, staring at the ceiling.

How could Xander have been playing me that entire time?

I'd done everything in my power to avoid thoughts of him in my time here, but that was proving to be impossible. I still woke up from my dreams sobbing, remembering the things he had said to me and the way he made me feel.

Safe. Appreciated. Desired.

But that was all gone now, replaced with the harsh reality.

Everything he said and did was just to gain my trust.

I felt a tear roll down my cheek and sat up abruptly, wiping it away aggressively. I was so *sick* of crying over him, of thinking about his betrayal. He didn't deserve my energy, my time, and certainly not my fucking tears.

A knock sounded on the door and I walked over to it, fully expecting it to be my lunch. It was, but Chelsea was the one holding the tray, a beaming smile on her face.

"Hello, Violet."

"Hi," I responded, totally thrown off and suddenly worried about my appearance.

Chelsea looked gorgeous as ever, dressed in a beautiful blue dress that elongated her legs. Her blonde hair was flowing freely, the shiny locks reaching all the way to her midsection.

"May I come in?" she asked.

"Oh, of course." I stepped aside quickly.

She breezed through the doorway with an elegant grace that only a princess would have, though I wasn't sure if their family officially carried any titles. The way she moved didn't seem like it was forced or intentional, though. She just seemed to carry that energy with her.

Chelsea set the tray down on the table that was set up near the window and took a seat, swinging her body around to face me. I stayed put, leaning against the dresser by the door and feeling completely out of my element.

"So," she started, "I hear there is a little trouble in paradise with you and Xander."

"Yeah," I huffed. "You could say that."

"Would you like to talk about it?" Chelsea asked.

She seemed so genuine that I was tempted to take her up on it.

I walked toward the table and took the seat across from her. "Honestly, it's all I've been thinking about the past two days, so I would much rather not."

"Oh, perfect!" she exclaimed and clapped her hands, startling me. "I am having a party tonight. Shaed said that there was no chance you would want to come, but it seems like you are looking for a distraction! Right?"

"Well, I guess so," I started. "But I'm not sure–"

"No! Come on, it'll be fun," Chelsea promised, whisking across the room and throwing open the doors to my dresser.

"Um, *excuse me*," I called out at her invasion of my privacy, but she was already leafing through the clothes I'd packed.

"Really?" Chelsea goaded, holding up my favorite pair of jeans. They were black and distressed around the knees and cuffs from years of wearing them. "You seriously need a wardrobe remodel. I mean, I know that you're an Enforcer, but that doesn't mean you have to dress like one." She gave me a drab look.

"I like dressing comfortably, thank you very much," I told her, marching over and ripping my jeans out of her grasp.

"Okay, whatever, but none of this is going to cut it tonight. *I* got to organize the event for once, so it is formal attire only," she said, and I could literally feel her excitement radiating off of her.

I had to admit, it was a little infectious.

"We can find you something from my closet that'll work," Chelsea offered kindly.

"Actually," I interjected, "I placed an order with Ren recently, it should be ready to pick up now. You know Ren, don't you?"

She gasped. "Of course. Ren and Batskii are two of the most famous clothing designers in all of Cavell." Chelsea practically squealed, bouncing on her feet.

"Right, of course," I sputtered. "Do you think you would have time to bring me to them before tonight? I am not a Whisken."

"Ah, I actually cannot. I have to finish preparing for tonight. Shaed should be around, though. I'm sure he would be able to take you. Let me ask."

"Oh, no, that's okay–"

Chelsea cut me off with a finger in the air, her eyes gaining that unfocused quality I'd seen when Xander was talking to Lilliana Inmind.

The thought brought along the memory of his face, sending a stab of pain shooting through my chest.

She looked back to me a few moments later and clapped again, clearly excited. "Shaed will be here in ten minutes to take you there! Come knock on my door when you get back. I will help you decide what to wear tonight. Oh, how exciting!" Chelsea spun and moved to the door with a pep in her step, her energy level overwhelming me.

I began moving to the bathing room to get ready, but Chelsea's voice stopped me.

"I will say one thing about Xander and then leave it be." My whole body tensed up, but she continued, "I don't know what happened between you two, but I do know one thing. In all of the years I have known Xander, I've never seen him look at anyone the way he looks at you. Like he would rearrange the Edithian mountains themselves if it brought you happiness. Nor have I known him to be so quick to laugh."

It felt like someone was reaching inside me and making small incisions in my heart, one at a time.

"That being said," she amended, giving me a wicked smile. "If he did do something to hurt you–something unforgivable–let's just say I have a few tricks up my sleeve when it comes to dealing with horrible men. Just say the word."

I smiled at that, the first genuine one in days.

"Noted. Thank you, Chelsea," I acknowledged, feeling a pang of guilt.

I had misjudged her the first time we met, purely based on her looks and her familiarity with Xander. In hindsight, I just felt insecure and wanted to bring her down a peg. That was petty of me.

"Don't mention it. I'll see you in a bit," she said happily before striding out of the room.

$$\mathrm{)}$$

EXACTLY TEN MINUTES LATER, I HEARD A KNOCK ON MY door.

I finished putting the belt end through the loops of my pants and opened the door. Shaed was standing there with one hand wrapped around his opposite wrist in front of him. He was smiling subtly, the sight totally unnerving. His previous smiles had been overbearing, manic even. This one was quiet, harmless, but it felt much more out of place for some reason.

"Hello," Shaed said, and I realized that I hadn't spoken for a long time.

"Hi."

"Are you ready?" he asked politely.

I stepped inside, allowing him to enter my room and closing the door behind him.

"Thank you," I blurted out before I lost my nerve, my cheeks reddening against my will.

Shaed looked at me with wide eyes, and I cleared my throat.

"For coming to get me," I clarified. "Thank you."

He stayed put, looking at me curiously. It was the same look that he gave me in the Oracle's room, like he knew something I didn't.

"Why are you looking at me like that?" I asked slowly, narrowing my eyes at him.

"I am just wondering why you seem surprised that I answered your signal when I am the one who offered my aid to begin with." Shaed was speaking with a casual elegance, like a true born-and-raised diplomat.

"Um, maybe because I do not trust you with any sense of the word?" I suggested, immediately regretting my words the second they left my mouth.

Why did I seem to make a habit out of provoking these people?

Shaed just laughed, though, the sound echoing off the marble floors. "I've already informed Ren that we are coming," he said, moving closer to me. "She will be expecting us by now. Are you ready to go?"

I nodded, sticking my hand out for him to take us.

He arched an eyebrow, looking between it and my face. "Are you wanting to hold my hand, or...?" Shaed asked, holding back a laugh by the looks of it.

"Don't you need to touch me for this to work?" My tone held an attitude, but it was only because I was shitting myself.

I wouldn't last through the day without exposing myself to these people.

"No," Shaed looked contemplative. "I suppose it's possible that some people need a tether to bring others with them. I have never heard of that, though."

I cleared my throat awkwardly. "Shall we, then?"

He whisked us to the Hydroseis headquarters, but all I could focus on was how different this was to when I would travel with Xander. There was no explosion of color, no strong arms holding me, or gigantic hands wrapped around mine. It was just a blank, gray view until the familiar blue walls were in my vision again.

I choked back bile, emotions pushing their way up my throat that I didn't have the capacity to deal with right now.

Ren was already waiting for us at the entrance, leaning against the open doorway with a suspicious gleam in her eye. She gave me a big smile, though, greeting me with warmth. "Violet, love, how are you?"

I didn't want her calling me that. Only one person ever had before.

While entering the building I replied, "I am well. And yourself?"

She nodded, shooting a strange look in Shaed's direction. To his credit, he looked deeply uncomfortable. At least he could tell when he wasn't wanted somewhere.

Ren turned around and headed the same way we went last time, but at a much faster pace. I met her stride and busied myself with looking at the waterwalls, their beauty still as profound to me as the first time I'd seen them. I could hear Shaed's footsteps behind us, but I couldn't tell how far back he was.

"Where is Xander today?" Ren asked in a casual tone, though there was nothing innocent about it.

"With Lilliana, I suspect," I said coolly, an acidic feeling coating my stomach.

Ren gave me a side eye, her brows pinching in concern. I ignored it, focusing on the curved hallway before us.

She didn't speak the rest of the walk, which I was grateful for. I really didn't want to answer any more questions about Xander. I just needed to get my clothes and leave.

Shit. The payment.

My heart began to hammer in my chest as an old feeling resurfaced. That deeply-rooted panic of not knowing how I would pay for the food I was eating, or the bed I was sleeping in that night. Memories from a time that felt like eons ago.

We made it to the doorway of the Gallery Room, cutting right through it to get to the entrance to Ren's studio. It was exactly as I remembered it last time–the high ceilings and walls all made of water. Ren's desk was still littered with papers and pencils, though the sketches themselves all looked different.

I refused to look at the door to the changing room I had used last time, though it felt like *it* was looking at *me*.

"Violet," Ren said in a low voice, having moved behind her desk. "What's wrong?"

"Nothing," I answered, putting all my energy into making the smile I forced look real.

"Okay." Ren seemed unconvinced, glancing at Shaed. "Sure."

"I'll just give you a minute," he said from behind me. "I'll be waiting outside."

Ren watched him exit with narrowed eyes, and I wondered if she was thinking about him escorting himself out. I probably would be if I were in her position.

Once she decided he was out of earshot, Ren turned back to me and crossed her arms, managing to totally intimidate me even though she was half my size.

"Okay, spill," she demanded. "What in the actual fuck is going on?"

"Look, if it's all the same to you, Ren, I'd really rather not talk about it."

"No," she replied haughtily, "it's not all the same to me. Why didn't Xander bring you here? And of all the people to ask instead, you chose *Shaed?*"

I pinched the bridge of my nose, a headache pounding at my skull. "Xander and I are no longer involved. Okay?" I said, deflating with exhaustion. "Now, can you drop it? Please?"

She looked totally taken aback and blinked a few times before she sighed. "Alright."

"Great," I said with little enthusiasm. "How much do I owe you for the clothes?"

Ren flicked her hand through the air, like she was physically shoving my question aside. "Xander told me to put it on his account, no matter what," Ren remarked, reaching under her desk to pull up a large, wrapped package. "I am actually not in the mood to be decapitated today, believe it or not, so I am going to stick to that."

What the hell did that mean, *'No matter what'*?

Did he expect that I might have to get the clothes myself, after he betrayed me?

That didn't make any sense, though, because wouldn't he have expected me to still be under Lilliana's roof after he sold me out? Why did he even want to pay for them?

Ren rounded the desk, carrying the package by a thick strap around it. She passed it to me, and I accepted it, shocked by how heavy it actually was.

"This is massive," I observed, adjusting my grip on it. "Thank you for wrapping it for me."

"Oh, that's nothing," Ren scoffed, leading me back toward the entrance. "You should see the size parcel I need for Xander's clothes."

"Why am I not surprised that he buys so many items?" I asked, bristling.

"Oh, no. It's because they are large, not the quantity," she corrected, giving me a knowing look.

"I'd never really considered his clothes in respect to his size before," I mused, wondering how that was.

I sure as shit thought about his size enough for it to be ignorant of me not to.

"That's why Xander has to get his clothes from me," Ren said in a soft voice. "Most merchants don't have a need to carry clothing in his size."

It felt like someone had added a weight to my heart, but I forced myself to push it aside. So what if he had difficulties navigating society? It didn't change anything.

I opted out of replying, looking at the Waterweavers instead. It was so interesting to watch them work. The way that the water seemed to be flowing into and out of their fingers simultaneously as they moved, showing a glimpse of something beautiful in the place where the two directions met. But it was as if the second I saw the creation, it was transported somewhere else. They must be creating the fabrics, as Xander had explained to me, and they were sent to some other place as they were being formed.

Wait a damn minute.

I stopped walking and felt my eyes widen as my pulse jumped to dangerous heights.

"Violet?" Ren asked, stopping with me. "Are you alright?"

"Yeah—yes," I said, smiling and walking again, keeping my eyes trained forward.

I folded my hands behind my back to cover up the fact that they were shaking.

I could see them. Every small detail of their hands and work was in harsh focus, unlike the last time I was here, when I could hardly make out the shapes of the people within the water.

So, just when the hell had my Astrolite sight come in, and why was I only noticing it now?

"You are acting very strange, Violet," Ren pointed out. I could feel her stare on me as we continued down the hallway.

"With all due respect," I told her, trying to calm my nervous system. "You don't really know me well enough to say that."

Ren seemed unconvinced but let it go, and we walked in silence until we reached the exit.

I cleared my throat. "Thank you again for everything, Ren. I appreciate it."

She nodded, giving me a kind smile. "Whenever you decide you want to talk about what is happening between you and Xander, my door is always open. I mean it."

I smiled appreciatively but thought there was little chance I would ever be taking her up on that offer. Then again, I never expected to take Shaed up on his, either.

Ren opened the door to reveal Shaed sitting on a bench nearby. He immediately stood and walked to us, his face much more closed off than it had been in my room at his house. It held that arrogant quality again, like everything and everyone around him was less than.

"All set?" Shaed asked, stopping at the bottom of the stairs.

I didn't respond; just walked down to meet him.

"Chelsea is hosting a party tonight," Shaed said, looking at Ren. "You and your brother are welcome to join."

I was shocked by his invitation, and I looked back to find Ren holding back a grimace. "I believe Skii is already planning on it," Ren replied disapprovingly. "But I will certainly not be in attendance."

I choked on a laugh at her tone, stifling it as soon as it arrived.

"Very well," Shaed conceded, and immediately whisked us back to his palace.

I blinked away the disorientation, the move having come before I expected it.

"Sorry," he mumbled. "I wanted out of there quickly. I should have warned you first."

"It's alright," I said, looking at him strangely.

He seemed to be upset about something; his jaw clenched tightly and his light-colored eyebrows pinched. There was an air about him that suggested he wanted to say something but was holding it back.

"If there's something you want to say, just say it," I spat with more venom than I'd intended. I was just desperate for a moment alone to digest everything that had just happened.

"Exactly how aware are you of Xander's responsibilities for Lilliana?" Shaed asked me with an overly casual tone to his voice.

I had been expecting him to ask me about Xander, but more so about the fight that he'd overheard. Not about *that*.

Instead of answering his question, I asked, "Why?"

"I would not expect you to be okay with his line of work," Shaed admitted, and my attention sparked.

"You speak about me sometimes as if you actually know me at all," I observed, looking at him skeptically.

He gave me his most dazzling, most artificial smile. "You're right, of course. Forgive me for overstepping. I'll just go see if Chelsea needs any help setting up for tonight."

Then he was gone, making my confusion rise even higher.

I didn't think about it for long, though, deciding to nosedive into my bed instead. I only had a few hours before I was expected to socialize and talk to people, so I desperately needed to recharge.

I settled into the plush mattress and sighed contently, feeling like I had been hugged by the softest cloud. It wasn't long before my eyes grew heavy and I drifted to sleep, silently thanking whatever entity had created the concept of sleeping.

Whether it was a god or some other magical being, I didn't care. I was just thankful they had provided me with the bubble of peace that sleep always gave me.

That was my last thought as I drifted into a dreamless sleep.

CHAPTER FORTY

LILLIANA

I stood by the window in my office, looking out at the view of my city, as I had done so many times before, and prepared myself for what was about to happen.

It wouldn't be pretty. In fact, I was almost certain that it was going to cause me a great amount of pain to actually do it, but I hadn't come this far–dedicated so many years of my life–to back out now.

I needed to see it through.

A light rapping sounded at my door, and my three most loyal subjects walked in, responding to the Inmind message I had sent out about a minute ago.

"Thank you all for coming so quickly," I greeted, moving to sit at my desk.

Jax, Dhan, and Laura all sat in the chairs I had set out for them. They were all much shorter than mine, a strategy that I had learned long ago.

It helped people remember their place when I was speaking to them.

"We need to discuss our situation with Violet."

The three people nodded, and I noticed Laura's eyes shining with a sort of excitement. I knew that look–it was the one she got when she was anticipating violence.

"Let me make one thing clear," I said pointedly, looking each of them in the eye. "Violet is to be kept alive–at all costs."

Laura let out an audible huff of annoyance, and I pinned her with a look.

"The things we could do with her creations would be completely world-altering. Believe me, I would prefer her to be a loose end that we could tie up now, but unfortunately, she is not."

"What is it that you need from us, Madame?" Dhan asked like the doting apprentice that he was. "You want us to be a protection detail?"

"I appreciate your initiative, but that would be impossible without raising suspicions about our involvement with the girl," I told him regretfully.

I looked towards the other man in front of me. "Jax, do you still have a reliable contact within the Astrolite sector?"

He flashed his most skin-crawling smile. "Yes, Madame, I do. Would you like for me to contact them?"

"Yes," I answered immediately. "We need to tread lightly with this. To find a way to make sure that she stays in place, but also out of harm's way."

I sighed, bringing a hand to my chin. "We also need to work quickly with Xander. If he finds out she is capable of seeing through his eyes before we are able to complete the binding, we will be royally fucked."

"But I don't understand why that is, Madame Lilliana," Jax questioned, his high-pitched voice making my temples ring with irritation. "What could she possibly do? She hardly even understands her magic yet, from what you've told us."

"If Violet learns that Xander did not actually betray her to me and she finds a way to get him out of here, they will mark their mating bond. And if that happens, there will be nothing we can do to stop either of them.

"That is far too many *ifs* for me to be comfortable with," I said strongly.

"The closer they are to each other, the higher the probability of him learning that is," I told them all before I locked eyes with Jax. "You need to keep in frequent communication with your contact at Dmitri's and report back to me on her status. We need her far away, and we need her alive. Is that clear?"

I waited until all of them acknowledged that last statement before continuing on.

"As soon as we have the Xander situation under control, we will retrieve her again and get her to make us another Chalice. In the meantime, she needs to stay far away, stay breathing, and protect those Chalice-making hands."

The three Astrales nodded in unison, clearly accepting my orders without question. They were all such loyal apprentices, and I appreciated their dedication to me more than I ever let on.

"Okay." I gestured to the exit. "You are free to go. Meet me in front of Xander's room in exactly one hour—we will begin then."

They all stood and left. The second they were out of the door, I let my body relax and slumped in my chair, closing my eyes and mentally preparing myself for what was undoubtedly going to be the most challenging thing I had ever done.

Stealing the soul away from my son.

CHAPTER FORTY-ONE

VIOLET

About two hours later, I sat in a chair, trying not to scream while Chelsea fretted over what color pigment to put on my eyelids.

Chelsea was standing before me in a beautiful black gown that hugged her figure and flowed all the way to the floor. The material was a sort of matte black and made the tanned tone of her skin appear even darker. Two thin straps held up the dress and led down to the deeply cut V that went well below her breasts, framing her cleavage in a very confronting way.

"Are you sure that I have to go to this thing?" I asked for what felt like the hundredth time.

Chelsea whacked me on the head with the end of her makeup brush. "*Yes*, you have to go," she insisted. "You have been moping around for two days. Getting dolled up will help to get your mind off things, and some social interaction will do you some good. Now, close your eyes," Chelsea demanded, tipping my chin up.

I sighed but complied, giving in to the fact that I wouldn't be getting out of this party.

Right after she showed up, Chelsea went through the things that I'd bought and immediately started fawning over the pantsuit that Ren had designed for me.

I had to admit, it was very beautiful. The color was a clear and crisp light blue, like the shade of the sky on a cloudless day. It was three pieces in total: the pants, a sleeveless top, and a jacket to wear over the top.

All of the hems had a wide scalloping detail, and I actually really liked the way the top fit me. It was a stiffer fabric than I had worn before, which ended up making the garment much more flattering and supportive. It did wonders for my cleavage, too, which was quite a feat considering the way my breasts seemed to hang a little lower from their significant weight.

Going to this party might not be the worst thing if it meant that I could actually wear this outfit. Clearly, I wouldn't be going to the Mistral Festival anymore, and I wasn't sure where else I would wear it.

Chelsea finished with my eyeshadow and passed me a tube of mascara. "It's so freaky to me, applying other people's mascara," she whispered, like she was spilling a secret she'd been keeping in.

"I don't mind." I laughed, and leaned closer to the mirror to do it myself.

"Okay," Chelsea started, standing up and ticking off different objectives on her fingers as she spoke. "You are dressed, makeup is done, hair is styled, shoes have been selected. I think we're all set!" she finished with a squeal, clapping her hands excitedly.

"You are going to need to lower your decibel if you want us to get along, Chels," I commented, wincing.

I jolted internally as I realized that the nickname had rolled off my tongue so effortlessly. Clearly, I was becoming attached to her very quickly.

Had I not learned my lesson yet about forming emotional bonds with these Astrales?

Although, I supposed that I should probably stop referring to them as different to myself in my mind, considering the Starfire that I'd spent the past few days mastering.

"Noted. I will keep my squealing to a minimum," Chelsea said lightheartedly, clearly unperturbed by my grouchiness. "Now put your shoes on!"

I laughed lightly and complied, making sure that the clasps on my pumps were fastened securely.

The heels weren't very high by any means, but I did love the way the front of them formed a point, which stuck out from my pant legs. I thought that it added a little bit more dimension to the flowing cut of the pants, elongating my legs even further.

I stepped up to Chelsea, and she said, "Ready?"

"As I'll ever be," I murmured, but my reluctance was almost entirely feigned at this point.

I couldn't have her thinking that I was actually *excited.*

Chelsea gave me a knowing smile and whisked us in front of a set of doors. I looked around myself, realizing that this was a part of the palace I hadn't been to before.

It had a similar style to the rest of it, but something about it seemed a little bit more minimalistic, like they weren't trying as hard to flaunt their wealth in this corner of the house.

Chelsea led us through a set of tall double doors, which opened for us automatically when we got close enough to grab the handle. I tried to mask my amazement, focusing instead on the room we were walking into.

This was much different than the last party I had been to in their home.

Everyone in sight was dressed in formal attire–gowns, suits, a few jumpsuits. While the Astrales appeared much more fancy, their demeanor was still littered with a comfortable grace, like this was a group of true friends.

People gathered in small groups and pairs, conversing and sipping from the gold-rimmed flutes that were being passed out by servers. They were all wearing full white suits with shiny gold ties, their figures obvious within the large group of guests.

"Well?" Chelsea asked, practically bouncing with excitement. "What do you think?"

"It's very beautiful," I told her, looking around the space again.

Chelsea beamed, gushing, "Thank you."

This room was much more grand than the Viewing Room. The ceilings, for starters, were much higher, giving it a more elegant feel. Where there were stars before, there was now an incredible mural spanned across the ceiling. It seemed to tell a story—one side of the room showed the sky in daylight, fading gradually into a starry sky on the opposite side.

There was one long table on the left wall with countless dishes laid out, and my stomach instantly growled at the sight.

"You alright if I go make the rounds?" Chelsea asked, putting a hand on my arm affectionately. "I mean, you're welcome to come with me if you'd like. But I didn't think you would want to deal with countless introductions right now."

"Go ahead, Chelsea. I can handle myself," I finished with a reassuring smile that I didn't feel.

"I'll find you as soon as I'm finished," she promised, dropping a farewell kiss on my cheek that took me by surprise.

I chastised myself for blushing, knowing that she hadn't meant anything by the gesture. She was just one of those people who communicated everything with physical touch—it was nothing more than that.

But she looked every part the regal princess tonight, so I couldn't help but feel *something*.

A server passed me and offered me a drink, his smile bland and clearly pasted on.

"Thank you," I said as kindly as possible, wondering what these workers' lives looked like.

Did they live here, in the castle? Did they have families?

His smile turned warmer then, and his eyes crinkled around the corner. "My pleasure, ma'am," he acknowledged kindly, and I went to move past him.

In true form, I wasn't paying much attention to where I was stepping and came close to smashing my hand against the corner of the table next to me.

The waiter's free hand shot out, blocking the space between the back of my hand and the sharp edge perfectly.

"Thank you," I breathed, shocked by how quickly he moved, even though I knew he was supernatural.

"Don't mention it," he replied quickly before scurrying away.

I took a sip of the champagne, savoring the way the bubbles traveled through my body. As I walked down the expanse of the room, I listened to the conversations happening around me and confirmed something I had been noticing for the past few days. The Astrales in this sector seemed to have a slightly different dialect to Xander. The vowels were less drawn out, making the words seem more curt.

It wasn't surprising to me, considering that the human dialect differed slightly by region, but it did make me realize that I didn't actually know how big Cavell was. For all I knew, it could be double the size of our continent.

As I continued moving through the space, I noticed that this room was like the last one in the fact that there were many alcoves tucked away along the walls, providing private space.

I practically sprinted to one as soon as I realized it, excited by the prospect of taking a beat. My heart was racing, the reality of my situation weighing heavily on me all of a sudden.

How in the hell would I ever get home?

The only possible solution I saw was to come up with a believable story to tell Chelsea and hope that she would take me without asking too many questions.

That didn't seem very likely, though. She seemed like the type to always want to know more, which wasn't a bad quality, but it made my situation more difficult.

I rounded the corner of the alcove, relieved to find that it was empty. There were two stylish chairs facing each other, clearly designed to allow for comfortable conversation.

I sank into the one facing the entrance so that I would know the second someone entered the space. The chair was more attractive than it was comfortable, but I was just thankful for its existence as I allowed my guard to drop the slightest bit and took a deep sip of my champagne.

There was a painting hung on the wall in the middle of the seating area. It was very interesting, and I shifted my body to face it. The image showed a woman's face, but it was blurred and distorted; several different outlines of it overlapped. It almost looked like it was done with chalk, but I could tell by the texture of the canvas that it was painted.

"Beautiful, innit?" a jovial voice asked, and I turned to see a familiar male Astrale.

I smiled at him. "Marj, right?"

His eyes sparkled as his smile kicked up a notch. "So you do remember me! Can't fault you for that."

"How could I forget that charm?" I asked sarcastically, rolling my eyes.

I looked at him more closely, seeing him in an entirely different light than I had at Shaed's party. Maybe it was because of the fact that he was wearing a full navy suit, or that his golden-blonde hair was slicked back with gel. It made his pronounced cheekbones stand out much more, and I wondered if he was wearing a contouring powder.

Whatever it was, it was really working for him.

Suddenly, Marj's eyes were rolling back into his head as his knees buckled and he hit the ground. Hard.

The fuck?

"Now, now" a familiar, deep voice drawled from behind me, making me tense up. "What do we have here?"

I took a breath and turned around, feeling my stomach bottom out as I looked into Nygaard's red eyes once more.

CHAPTER FORTY-TWO

VIOLET

Nygaard was standing in the entrance of the alcove, staring at me with an unnerving light shining in his eyes despite the casual boredom his posture was giving off.

His hair was not tied back as it had been the last time I'd seen him. It was hanging in loose curls that looked like they had to be natural, reaching just past his shoulders. The white pieces framing his face were trimmed perfectly, making his jawline somehow more prominent than it had been before. The suit he wore tonight looked identical to the last one I'd seen him in, except that this time his undershirt was a deep olive green.

"What exactly are you doing here—dressed like *that*—without Xander attached to your side?"

Nygaard hadn't moved, glowering at me from the entrance of the alcove. I looked down at myself. Literally, the only skin showing was my chest—including a bit of cleavage from the cut of the top. But I was wearing full pants and a jacket...

And he had no right to comment on something like that.

"It is no longer Xander's business where I am and what I do," I retorted calmly, having gained my composure. "Nor is it yours."

Nygaard looked at me suspiciously, like I was lying to him or something.

I scoffed and stood up, fully intending to walk past him, but he stepped forward to meet me, passing over Marj's limp body on the ground.

"What is going on, Violet." It was more in warning than inquisition.

"I really don't think that's any of your business," I snapped, trying to move past him again.

He grabbed my elbow, yanking me back in front of him. "I'm not going to ask you again," he growled through his teeth, digging his fingers into my arm to emphasize his point.

"Xander would much prefer to be Lilliana's lap dog than have any sense of loyalty toward me," I said, trying to swallow down the emotions that saying the words out loud brought on.

The only part of him that moved was his eyes; they narrowed in on me, only thin slits of red visible now.

"What do you mean by that?" he asked, still gripping me.

"Let go of my arm, Nygaard," I demanded calmly, trying to keep my voice level.

He released me immediately and moved back slightly, looking at me with distaste. "Don't use my full name," he demanded. "It's odd."

I felt like he had punched me in the gut because Xander had said almost the exact same thing. But the message felt different coming from him.

I nodded and stepped back, clearly making space between us.

"What are you doing here, Violet?" Gaar asked in a different way, like he actually wanted to know the answer this time.

I didn't know if I should trust him, but I figured based on the fact that he was so close with Xander, the answer was probably no.

"I was invited," I explained casually, feigning nonchalance. "That is usually how parties work, isn't it?"

"Don't be a little shit," he hissed, his red irises flashing as his hands fisted at his sides. "I can help you–just tell me what is going on."

I thought about it for a second before deciding that I couldn't risk it, not with his involvement with Xander for so many years.

So, I simply raised my eyebrows and took a sip of my champagne, all while keeping eye contact with him.

He took a deep, frustrated inhale, making his nostrils flare. "I'm beginning to lose my patience," Gaar said between his teeth, glowering at me.

I scoffed. "This is you being patient?"

"Everything alright here?" a haughty, fastuous voice called out from behind us.

Gaar let out a curt, mocking laugh. "Everything is fine, princeling. Why don't you run along and see if Daddy's tea needs tending to?"

Shaed gave Gaar a drab look, like he wasn't concerned with him or his comment. "Violet?" he asked, stepping closer to me and eyeing Marj's body on the ground.

"I am *fine,*" I snapped, exasperated. "Both of you, let me make one thing clear. It is not your responsibility to take care of me, dote on me, or make assumptions about my well-being. I appreciate the thought, but if you would–just fuck off. Kindly."

I looked between them slowly, making sure that there were no protests. Gaar was watching me with the calculative expression he seemed to be fond of, and Shaed appeared to be holding something back.

I nodded, satisfied that my message had been received, and began to leave the alcove.

Gaar stopped me with a hand on my elbow, leaning in to speak softly into my ear. "When the time inevitably comes that you find yourself seeking sanctuary," his low, rumbling voice was an intense thing to hear at this proximity, forcing me to listen intently. "My door will be open for you," he finally finished before brushing past me, exiting the alcove without a glance in Shaed's direction.

The latter scoffed, turning back to face me fully. He didn't say anything for a while, and I considered moving past him too.

But then he said softly, "You look very beautiful tonight."

I jolted back, shocked not only by his words but also by the way he held that same casual, laid-back demeanor that I'd seen earlier.

"Thank you," I replied, but my tone indicated a question.

I decided that I was entirely done with this bullshit, and moved past Shaed to leave. I drained the rest of my glass on the way out the door, finding a server to grab another as soon as I could.

I've never been a big drinker, but I just felt like I needed a night to escape–to forget about the shitshow that my life had become.

I looked around the party, searching for any familiar faces, and immediately perked up when I saw Neerah standing in the corner, talking to another woman. Neerah looked stunning. The orange dress she was wearing brought out the warm tones within her eyes and complimented her brown skin. Her long, black hair was styled in two braids that had been wrapped around her head in a sort of crown, making her look elegant and regal.

I approached them somewhat hesitantly, unsure whether or not Neerah would even remember me. We had only talked for a couple of minutes, after all.

But it seemed that my worries were baseless, because as soon as she saw me, Neerah rushed forward and gave me a hug that shocked me with its intensity. "Violet! It is so wonderful to see you," she gushed, the decibel making me wince with how close she was to my ear.

"*Neerah*," the other woman scolded, pulling her back by the arm with an incredulous expression. "Please excuse her," she said to me. "She has already drunk her weight this evening, I'm afraid."

I laughed lightly, looking at Neerah again to see that her cheeks were blooming an intense red, the effects of the alcohol clear in her complexion.

"That's okay," I dismissed with another laugh.

"Violet, this is my *wonderful* wife, Dom. Isn't she so beauti-ful?" There were stars in her eyes as Neerah gazed at her wife, the love shining through in her expression. Dom rolled her eyes, patting her wife on the arm affectionately.

"Thank you, my love, but we've talked about this. You must stop introducing me that way."

"It's nice to finally meet you," I cut in before Neerah could chime in, her expression looking like she was about to go on a drunken rant.

"You as well," Dom murmured, her blue eyes tracking up and down my body. "Xander has told me much about you."

I stiffened like a board but kept my voice level. "I am here on my own tonight."

Her expression pinched, but she nodded and didn't press the issue, and I appreciated that someone was finally able to read the room for once.

"We were just discussing who is the hottest dressed tonight," Neerah informed me with a slight slur, leaning her weight against her wife. "My vote is on Ana. She's the one over there in the purple suit, talking to Batskii," she said as she pointed their way.

I saw that Batskii had a similar, blank expression to the one he'd had when I first met him. He was dressed in a stylish, pinstripe suit that elongated his legs, making him appear taller. The woman he was talking to was stunning–her ivory skin offset by her coils of red hair and the deep purple shade of her pantsuit, which looked a little bit similar to mine. I wondered if Batskii had designed it for her.

"They are *so* going to bone tonight," Neerah quipped in a giddy tone, watching the two Astrales talking to each other.

"No way," Dom countered. "Skii is undoubtedly gay."

"*Dom!*" Neerah chastised. "You can't go around saying that like it's a fact!"

She just rolled her eyes. "It is. Someday, you'll see."

We continued standing there for a while, laughing and drinking while we talked about different people's outfits and potential couples that were emerging. I chimed in when it felt natural, but mostly stayed quiet so that I could absorb all of the information they were giving me.

I learned that Batskii and the woman named Ana had been seen together a lot lately, and there were rumors as to if they had gotten together or not.

Apparently, someone named Dana was newly single and on the prowl tonight, her dress cut short and clinging tightly to her short, yet robust frame. I wondered if Marj was aware of her situation, having seen him walking around the party while we were gossiping. They were both so beautiful that it seemed obvious they should get together.

Marj appeared to have recovered from Gaar's...whatever it was that he had done. When I last saw him, he was facing me while talking to a man I didn't know, but he hadn't even blinked in my direction again.

Couldn't say I blamed him.

Gaar, on the other hand, was nowhere to be found after our altercation, which I thought was strange.

Had he only come here with the hope of seeing Xander?

I looked around again, trying to see if I could find him, but my eyes landed on Shaed instead. He was seated on a bench with his arm around a woman. She was wearing a long gray dress that had a very deep slit up the side, which was made visible by the position of her leg as it was draped over Shaed's knee. Her hair was braided in many small sections, which had all been collected into a beautiful updo.

"Who is that woman Shaed is with?" I asked, interrupting whatever conversation they'd been having while I was distracted.

"Oh, that's Esodelle," Neerah said with a hiccup. "Her and Shaed have been off and on since they were sixteen."

"Very toxic relationship, that one," Dom commented with a weighted tone.

I looked back to them, realizing with clarity that it was not the same woman I had seen Shaed with at his last gathering. I couldn't remember if I had seen her there or not, though, not with how much was going on at the time.

"Violet, there you are!" Chelsea all but shouted, running up to us out of nowhere. "I'm so sorry that it took me this long to come and find you. I don't know how time got away from me so quickly."

"It's okay," I assured her with a smile. "Dom and Neerah have been making this evening very entertaining."

"Oh no," Chelsea said, looking between us. "I'm a little scared about what that means."

"Don't be so quick to assume, Chels," Neerah slurred. "We *are* capable of making good company without proposing a threesome."

My eyes bugged out of my head at the realization of what Chelsea had meant, and my cheeks tinged pink of their own accord.

"Yep," Dom said in a final tone. "That would be my cue to get this one home."

"Nooo," Neerah pouted at her wife. "Don't make me leave already."

"Don't worry, you have plenty of fun awaiting you at home." Dom winked at her before shooting me and Chelsea an exasperated look.

"Thank you for hosting us, Chels," Dom said with a smile. "It was a great time. And Violet," she turned to me, "it was lovely to meet you."

"You too," I replied, and I meant it.

Dom nodded once before whisking them both out of the palace, Neerah's shout of dismay barely audible before it cut off altogether.

"Isn't the palace warded against people whisking in and out of it?" I asked Chelsea, remembering something that Xander had once mentioned.

She nodded as she finished chewing the dessert she'd just taken a bite out of. "Yes, there are. But on nights like tonight, we are able to adjust them to allow for more convenient travel. The wards are only down in this part of the palace, though, and only those on the guest list are able to enter."

I hummed appreciatively, not having considered that they would be able to adjust the wards so specifically.

"Did you get anything to eat?" Chelsea asked me out of nowhere.

I narrowed my eyes on her slightly. "I haven't yet. Why?"

She shrugged casually. "Shaed might have mentioned that the servers reported you haven't been eating very much of your meals the past few days. I just wanted to check on you."

I sighed through my clenched teeth. "What is it with these men monitoring how much food I consume?" I asked, gesturing to my forehead. "Do I have a sign on my face that says, *Please, comment on what you think is an adequate amount for me to eat'?*"

Chelsea held her hands up. "Say no more–it will not be commented on again. By me *or* by Shaed," she promised. "I'll make sure of it."

I looked at her for a moment, still shocked by how much I had misjudged her.

"Thank you," I said in my warmest voice, feeling the strangest urge to hug her.

For some reason, she reminded me of Archi at that moment, with the way she just jumped to my defense without any hesitation at all.

I settled for hooking my arm through hers, steering her in the direction of the bar. "Now, let's get so drunk we'll hate ourselves tomorrow," I suggested pleasantly, already feeling like I was on my way to that point.

"Oh, Violet," Chelsea gushed, speeding our advance toward the liquor. "You may just be what has been missing from my life all along."

CHAPTER FORTY-THREE

XANDER

I sat at the edge of the bed, which was the same bed that had been here when I'd left this place, just staring blankly. It was still surreal to me that I was back in this place again, staring unseeingly as I had for so many years. I couldn't believe that I had actually trusted Lilliana when she told me that she had burned the facility down.

Just the thought of her name sent a new wave of pure, undivided *rage* shooting through my veins. I wanted to end her. Slowly. Painfully.

I'd woken up in my old room a while ago. It felt like it had been five hours, but there was no real way to tell. There were no windows, no way to judge how much time had passed.

Everything was the same in my cell, like no one had even touched it in the many years I'd been away. The walls and floors were still stark white in colour, with every piece of furniture matching it. Even the clothes someone had dressed me in were the same white cotton shirt and pants that I wore throughout my adolescence and early adulthood.

The only splash of colour in the room was my shackles, the strange material shining with the same green as my magic.

I felt my chest constrict at the memory of them being made. The lengths that they had to go to get me within the brink of death were extreme. But only then could they extract my specific Corepower to form a weapon capable of restraining my magic.

It had taken me weeks to recover from it, with countless healers working on me every day.

I stood up in a rush, unwilling to let these memories of the past plague me any longer.

"Lilliana!" I bellowed as loud as I possibly could. No response.

"*Mummy dearest,*" I mocked, letting out a harsh, brittle laugh. "Your darling son wants to talk with you!"

The metal screen on my door slid to the side, revealing the barred gap that was there. Lilliana already stood outside the door, looking at me with a kind expression. I wondered how long she had actually been out there, or if she had some sort of alarm system to notify her of my movements.

"It is so nice to have you home, my love," Lilliana said to me, coating my tongue with distaste. "It is even better to finally have you acknowledge me as your mother after all of these years. It feels like a breath of fresh air."

"Oh, I can see why," I sneered emphatically. "What a fucking *heartwarming* family reunion." I lifted my arms in emphasis, my shackles immediately tightening around my wrist with the movement.

"This was always your purpose, Xander," Lilliana levelled at me with a condescending tone. "You were always going to end up back here."

"What the fuck does that mean, Lilliana?" I spat out, moving right up to the door so that I could glare straight into her eyes. "Why did you pull this whole ruse of letting me live a free life? And if Dr. Kavara wasn't my mother, who was she?"

"Her name was Amelia," Lilliana uttered softly, her eyes gaining a softer quality. "She was my sister, and was as equally devoted to this cause as I was. That is why she was willing to give up her life so that we could advance to the next stage of your development."

"Your sister..."

I didn't know how to feel about that.

"So it wasn't actually my mother who tormented me my entire life. It was my *auntie,* who was moving on my mother's orders. Much better," I sneered in a low voice, feeling my anger simmering within me, begging to be unleashed.

I moved away from the door, standing in the middle of the room and lifting my bound hands up.

"Well, you have me, Lilliana," I sang out, taunting her. "What do you plan to do with me now?"

A small door in the wall opened then, and before I even had a chance to flinch, I was blasted with a stream of water so strong it felt like someone was stabbing me repeatedly. The force knocked me on my ass, but the water didn't let up, the stream hitting directly in my chest so that I wouldn't be able to breathe around it.

And then came that fucking noise–the bell that rang anytime someone was opening the door to my cell. My chest tightened painfully, wishing that it was Gaar's bell I was hearing instead.

I wondered if I would ever hear it again.

The door's hinges creaked as someone entered, right before I felt that familiar click of additional shackles being added to my ankles that always came after they blasted me with the water stream. It was only intended to disorient me enough for them to restrain me even more, which meant that something unfavourable was coming.

Lilliana's heels clicked on the white, tiled floor as she made her way across the room and knelt down beside me. She stroked my cheek with the back of her hand, and I forced myself with great effort to stay still for a moment.

When I was sure that her guard was slightly lowered, I snapped out as far as my restraints would let me, biting down on her wrist as hard as I possibly could. She cried out as my teeth cut easily through her flesh, and I smiled around it, which regrettably loosened my hold on her slightly.

Another stream of water poured out of the gap in the wall again, breaking Lilliana free of me completely. Blood was streaming down her arm as she held her hand up, inspecting the teeth-shaped wound I'd left there.

"What do you say?" I asked in a jovial tone, raising my eyebrows in a quick movement. "I'd give it at least an eight out of ten for effort and execution. Maybe even a nine."

She just looked down at me, the same way you would look at a dog that pissed on your floor. "You asked what I am going to do with you now," Lilliana said in a dark tone, grabbing a cloth that Jax offered from behind her.

I noticed that Dhan was also in the room now, as well as Laura—another one of Lilliana's lap dogs.

"We realised towards the end of your last stay here that it was imperative for you to go out into the world," she informed me, beginning to move around me in a sort of circle, like she was inspecting every part of me.

I refused to try to fold into myself as I used to, recalling the things Gaar had taught me about resisting those urges and holding my ground. As soon as he had, it was like something flipped inside of my brain, and I refused to cower, to show weakness to anything or anyone.

Except for him.

But being back here, back in this room and in these clothes...it was hard to remember how I'd felt that way before. The trauma from my past was no longer a memory—it was here, everywhere around me, staring me straight in the face.

"You were created for one sole purpose, Xander, and that is for *me*," Lilliana stated matter-of-factly, giving me a pointed look. "You probably don't have much memory from the last month of your time here. There was a large portion of the time that you spent entirely unconscious because we were trying to move on to the next stage of your contribution to the cause."

"What cause?" I asked, letting out a harsh laugh. "The cause of you gaining even more power? Or was that just another lie that I was told about the reason for my creation? Is everything that I knew about Dr. Kavara true, just applied to you?"

"Everything that you've heard in this building is true, apart from Amelia being your mother," Lilliana said, moving to sit in a chair at the table. Her arm had stopped bleeding by now, and I cursed the fact that she was a Sensinor.

"Small details may have been changed, but that is because it was not safe for you to know the truth at first," she insisted, bringing me back to the conversation at hand.

"Unsafe for me?" I asked. "Or for you?"

"Unsafe for everyone involved," she levelled. "I needed to be sure that you were entirely matured–and your magic stabilised–before I told you that you were my son. Just so that we could be sure that there would be someone to reign things back in if anything went awry with Amelia."

I looked at Lilliana with a blank stare, unsure if she was insinuating what I thought she was.

"You had your sister stand in your place as a diversion, just in case I found the means to finally kill her. And then you staged a fake coup, freeing me and giving me every freedom to kill her in any way I pleased?" I asked, for clarification.

"Yes," she answered simply, and the casualness of it made my hair stand on end.

"Amelia was always fully aware of the position she held, and she was more than willing to give up her life if it meant finally achieving what we had spent most of our lives striving after," Lilliana explained plainly, a nostalgic sort of look on her face.

"I miss her every single day. But I think of her every time I see your sweet face," Lilliana said, looking at me warmly. "You both got our mother's black hair. I took after our father with the blonde."

The way she spoke was like it should have provided any explanation I needed, and I started to realise that she was far more psychotic than I ever gave her credit for.

"Anyway," she pushed forward, shaking out of her reverie. "We've gotten a little off track. I was telling you what is going to happen next."

Lilliana stood, and I noticed her arm was entirely healed and cleaned off. "The whole intention behind creating you was to create a link between us, so that I would be able to use your power as my own."

I felt all of the blood rush out of my face as her words hit home, realising for the first time that I might not be seeing the outside of this prison ever again.

"But, back then, after it was clear that your magic had stopped developing, I was still unable to establish a strong enough bond between us that I could truly syphon from your Core. I had enough of a connection to your mind—thanks to the work I did when you were in the womb and in your earliest days—that I was able to see through your eyes, but that was where my abilities halted.

"After a lot of deliberation, Amelia had the realisation that it was probably your lack of overall development that was stunting my ability to connect to you. We learned long ago that magic doesn't just stem from your Core, but also your *soul*."

I felt like the walls of the room were closing in on me tighter by the second, my breaths feeling more laboured now.

"We knew that you had to become a complete person on your own before I would be able to truly draw on you, and the only way you could do that was for you to go out into the world on your own," Lilliana said, as if it should have been obvious, and I felt rage pulse to the surface. "Of course, we needed to be able to monitor you closely still—hence making you an Enforcer. It was just an added bonus that you are particularly skilled in killing."

I growled and lunged towards her, pulling against my restraints with all of my considerable strength.

Even though I knew it was going to happen, I still yelped in pain when they tightened against my wrists and ankles so much that I felt them grind against my bones.

Lilliana made a regretful noise. "You know full well the consequences of trying to fight us, Xander. Why must you insist on hurting yourself?"

"Why don't you come over here so I can let out my anger without hurting myself?" I asked in a low, gravelly tone.

"Moving on," Lilliana dismissed me, leaning her weight against the table now. Her three minions were standing in a semi-circle behind her, clearly ready for anything that I pulled. Which made me think that there *was* something I could do to get myself out of this. I just needed to figure out what.

"As time has gone on with your liberation, I have slowly been able to connect to your soul more and more. In the beginning, things only improved after you started spending time with Nygaard. Which, by the way, was an absolutely appalling time for me. I can't always control when I see through your eyes, and I saw some things that had me temporarily considering blinding myself."

I felt bile pushing its way up my throat at the fact that she had literally been invading every facet of privacy I'd thought I had.

"After you'd worked through a fair share of your trauma, my connection began to strengthen. It even went as far as me being able to control your actions altogether!" she exclaimed, like she expected me to be proud of her. "I tested it the best way I knew how—by forcing you to fulfil the missions that you had turned down."

Even more bile rose to the surface because I knew exactly what kinds of missions she had apparently completed on my behalf.

Pregnant women and children.

They were always where I drew my line, absolutely refusing to murder such a defenceless form of life, regardless of their magical state or mixed bloodline.

"But, over the past ten or so years, something strange has been happening," Lilliana explained, making even more dread gather in my stomach. "There have been times when I have tried to access your mind, but there has been something distinct blocking me out. At first, I feared that I had let this leg of the experiment go on for too long and that you were beginning to form defences against me.

"But then I realised," she started, a mischievous smile forming on her face. "I was having trouble getting in because somebody else was already there. A parasite had found its way inside your brain, getting herself wrapped up in something she had no business meddling in."

"*No*," I growled, pulling again at the chains holding me.

"Yes, my dear," Lilliana said with insistence. "Your mate is the one who was blocking my way, but she was also the thing that would allow me to connect with you fully–merging our souls and our Cores into one.

"After you met her, you began to change in certain ways–didn't you? You stopped thinking as much about yourself and your past, and began to consider her in everything you did. You opened up your heart and soul for her, and therefore for me, by taking the necessary step to complete your development at last."

My heart thundered in my chest.

"And what now, Lilliana? What do you plan to do to her?" I asked slowly, glowering at her from my place on the floor, my wrists resting on my knees.

"I wouldn't be worried about her, my dear," Lilliana suggested, looking concerned. "She won't be touched until I am through with you, and what we are about to do is going to be very unpleasant for you."

I let out a sound of warning that was rooted deep within me, informing her of exactly what would happen if she tried to harm Violet.

"There is no sense in fighting this, my dear," Lilliana said, like she actually cared about the ramifications it would have. "It will only make things harder."

Then a pain so great, so meticulously targeted at my soul, overcame me, and I let out a scream that made my eardrums feel like they were going to burst.

And then everything went dark.

CHAPTER FORTY-FOUR

VIOLET

Chelsea and I had been drinking and eating for some time, chatting about complete nonsense while we stuffed our faces with everything the party had to offer.

I found myself genuinely enjoying her company and the way she seemed to tell me about everyone that was here without ever badmouthing them. It was like she had this ability to gossip in a positive light, which I had never known someone to do before.

I took a sip of the spiced rum I had switched to a while ago. The champagne seemed too dry and carbonated after a few glasses.

Chelsea was telling me a story about Neerah and Dom, her arms moving around in an animated way as she spoke. I'd been listening intently, but something strange started to happen. My ears were buzzing slightly, and my eyes felt like they were going in and out of focus.

I set my glass down on the table, steadying myself against it as the room started to spin.

"Violet?" Chelsea asked, putting a hand on my back. "Are you alright?"

"Just dizzy," I said, my voice sounding far away. "I think I need to lie down."

A panic swelled in my chest as the view in front of me shifted immediately, revealing my private room. I felt relief wash over me and immediately moved to sit on the end of the bed, putting my head in my hands.

I heard the sound of Chelsea's heels clicking, and she appeared in front of me a second later, holding a glass of water.

I accepted it graciously, knocking back the whole thing in one go.

"Better?" she asked, and I could hear the concern in her voice.

"Yes," I assured her, nodding. "It's not uncommon that I get dizzy spells, especially when I've been drinking. I just need to sleep it off."

Chelsea visibly relaxed, her shoulders dropping down on an exhale. "Oh, good. Your face went so pale, I was worried you were going to faint in there," she said, and I felt my hands go clammy. That would have been terrible.

"It's okay, really," I assured her. "I am just going to go to bed."

"Can I get you anything before you do?" Chelsea offered.

"No, I'm alright."

She gave me a warm smile and turned to leave, but I stopped her. "Chels," I called, and she turned to look at me. "Thank you for tonight. I had a good time."

She gave me a devious smile. "Well, you don't have to sound so surprised, Violet. But you're welcome."

"I am a little surprised," I admitted with a laugh.

She raised her light eyebrows in a challenge. "Well then, stick with me, and you might just find yourself being surprised quite often."

I couldn't help but smile at that, even though I still felt like the room was spinning around me.

"Night, Violet," Chelsea bade before whisking herself out of my room, presumably heading back to the party.

I stood slowly and moved to the dresser once I was sure I'd be safe. I made quick work of changing into pajamas, making sure to hang my new outfit up with care. I dug through the loose items that were left in my bag, trying to find the herbal supplements Mikkie gave me for dizziness, when my hand closed around a very familiar frame.

I pulled it out and sighed heavily. My parents were staring

back at me, curled up on a blanket under the tree in our yard. They both looked so *happy*.

If only I could just travel back in time and talk to them. Ask them questions about where they came from and why they left Armantrea. For all I knew, my mother could have been human and my father had to run away from Cavell so that they could be together.

My ears started buzzing again, and I wanted nothing more than to just be in my bed, lying down.

I let out a startled yelp as my body landed roughly on the mattress, as if someone had thrown me across the room.

Had I just...whisked myself?

I remained very still, staring up at the ceiling as my heart hammered in my chest.

Unless I was suffering from short-term memory loss or hallucinating, I had definitely just whisked myself across the room without even trying.

I felt like I was going to freak out, my breaths coming in short and fast as a sort of panic gripped my soul and made me want to scream. I wasn't even sure where it was coming from because it's not like I had never considered that I might be a Whisken before.

All I knew was that I felt trapped, like my heart was literally trying to beat its way out of my chest.

A thought occurred to me then–a habit I had subconsciously cut out of my life during my time here.

'I have not seen you use those herbs you bought in Armantrea–not a single time.'

I tried to whisk myself back to my bag, but nothing happened.

Groaning, I forced myself out of bed and dug through my belongings until I found the tin of pre-rolled cigarettes. I grabbed my matches as well, but put them back when I remembered that I literally had fire running through my veins.

Jumping back into bed, I thought momentarily that I should probably ask someone about their smoking protocols in the palace, but I honestly couldn't even bring myself to care. So I took one out of the case and lit it carefully, only allowing the tiniest flame to emerge from my fingertip, and actively resisted the memories that sprang up.

As I took a drag from it, I relished the familiar tingling in my throat as the smoke went down. The K almost had a cooling effect; its blend of different herbs instantly made my heart rate calm.

I laid back on the pillows and sighed contentedly before taking another hit, wondering why the hell I hadn't been relying on this all along.

I focused all of my efforts on not considering that Xander was a big enough distraction to make me forget about needing this herb, and I *definitely* didn't think about the fact that he had made me feel so safe and grounded that my cravings disappeared.

After a few minutes, I felt drowsy enough that nothing else mattered besides going to sleep. I threw the cigarette into the glass my water had been in, hearing it sizzle as it met the drops of water still sitting in the bottom.

As I drifted off to sleep, I wondered again where that sense of panic had come from and why it felt so specifically abrasive.

☽

I WOKE UP HAPPILY, SMELLING XANDER'S DISTINCT scent before I even opened my eyes. I reached over and felt his chest against my hand, stroking it and snuggling closer to him.

Then I jolted, everything that had happened rushing back at me at once.

I sat up, opening my eyes, but suddenly found myself inside the room that Lilliana had tortured me in. It looked slightly different, though—this one was a bit bigger and felt more like a room and less like a cell.

"*Violet,*" the muffled voice yelled out to me, the tone of panic and exasperation breaking through to me.

I groaned, confused by what was happening and feeling like my chest was going to cave in. I couldn't get any air in, and my lungs were on fire.

"For the love of fuck, Violet. Wake up! *WAKE UP.*"

I was violently forced awake, the air being sucked into my lungs in viscous gasps and my spine straightening, springing me into a sitting position.

The first thing I noticed was the smell of a fire.

The second thing was that I was on the floor, on top of a substantial pile of ashes.

Shaed was kneeling next to me, breathing heavily. He seemed to be wearing night clothes, and his hair was tousled like he had been sleeping.

"What happened?" I asked, my voice strained.

"You were having a nightmare," he answered, looking disoriented. "Well, actually, you looked to be in more of a trance. But I heard you screaming, and I smelled smoke. I tried to knock, but you obviously didn't answer, I came in when I heard the bed collapse.

"Then I saw you." His voice turned haunted as he looked through me, like he was remembering what it had looked like.

"You were lying completely still, on your back, surrounded by the most significant display of Starfire I have ever seen in my entire life."

I felt like my eyes were going to pop out of their sockets, and stood up abruptly. Shaed immediately tried to help me, but I walked over to a chair on my own and sat down, putting my head in my hands. I took deep breaths, trying to calm myself down.

But what the *fuck*.

Xander had never told me what to do if I suddenly started *lighting myself on fire* in my sleep.

I finally looked up at Shaed, who was sitting in the chair across from me, watching me with a patient expression. He seemed entirely unconcerned about the fact that I had just turned his bed to ashes.

"I need to tell you something," I finally said, not seeing another option after what had just happened.

"You are untrained," Shaed assumed with an open expression, like it was an obvious fact.

I didn't know what to do with myself, wondering if I had made the right call or not.

"I'm not sure what you've heard about me from Xander," he said in a low voice, making me tense up. "But I assure you—that is only one perspective of the situation. And I am not entirely convinced that you would be so eager to trust him over me once you hear what I have to say."

"Okay, look, this is not about trusting one of you over the other," I explained, trying to stay composed. "This is about *me*. And going to him for help with this is not an option."

I took a breath. "Will you give me your word that you won't tell anybody what I am about to tell you?"

Shaed adjusted to sit up taller and gave me a proud look. "Of course," he agreed with a nod.

"I am not an Astrale. Well—I am. An Astrolite, actually. But I wasn't raised here," I clarified. "I was raised as a human."

Shaed's eyebrows shot halfway up his forehead, almost to the line where his hair was hanging down. His lips were parted in shock, and he looked like he was doing some sort of mental calculation.

"Well?" I asked. "Are you going to say something?"

"I—erm," he stuttered, and I realized that I had only ever seen him do that when we were alone. "I was not expecting that at all. When I guessed that you were untrained, I thought it was because of struggles with your family or an unfortunate upbringing."

I swallowed thickly, worried that I had just made a terrible mistake.

"I'm just trying to absorb it, Violet," he assured me, no doubt having picked up on my anxiety. "You have nothing to fear from me."

I felt like laughing at that last part but thought it might be a little bit stupid to provoke him when he now held my life in his hands.

Why had I even told him this to begin with?

"I do wonder, though," Shaed added, making my blood pressure rise. "How exactly did you end up in the Enforcers' care?"

I took a deep breath and ran my hands over my hair, realizing that it was a tangled mess.

After gathering myself, I just started telling him everything. How Xander had shown up at the market and brought me to Armantrea. The whole situation with the Chalice and Lilliana sending us to go out and find it.

I told him all about Archi, and the Soothe that Xander put on him to forget everything he'd learned, and make him think I was just on a vacation. I didn't know whether or not to trust what Xander had told me about Mr. Berger's death, so I told Shaed that too, figuring that he would have heard about a body being left outside of his estate.

Now that I was finally telling this to someone–actually getting it off my chest–all of the details started flying out of my mouth at a much faster pace. The exact scenario in which my Starfire had emerged stayed a secret, but I did tell him about the way that Xander taught me how to wield my magic. I also explained everything that had happened with the Retaliators and how Xander thought it was essential that I was able to protect myself.

Keeping my explanation of what had happened with Lilliana brief, I told him how Xander delivered me to her and a little bit of what happened before I signaled him with the stone.

The only thing I left out of my recounting to him was everything that had happened between Xander and me on a personal basis, because that really had nothing to do with this in the bigger picture. It was also none of his business.

The fact of the matter was, I just needed a way to get home to Archi.

By the time I was done, I felt physically exhausted from how long I had been talking. I slumped back in my chair and looked across the small table at Shaed, who was alert and perked up, having absorbed every detail that I told him.

After a few moments of silence, he cleared his throat.

"What is it that you are wanting me to do with this information, Violet?" Shaed asked, making me worry that I had put him in a terrible position.

Was he legally required to report me? Was there even any precedence for this situation?

"I just need someone to bring me home," I half whispered, unwelcome tears springing to my eyes.

Shaed looked like he wanted to come to me but thought better of it. He tilted his head to the side, giving me a pitying expression that made my irritation surge.

"You know that I can't do that, right?" he asked softly, glancing at the pile of ashes. "It wouldn't be right to just plop you back into your old life, not when you have untamed and untrained magic at your disposal. You could hurt someone...kill them, even."

The tears began to flow as I realized just how right he was.

I couldn't go back there and just pick up where I had left off. Selling at the market, talking to so many people every day, putting all of them in danger. It wouldn't be right.

But...Archi.

"What about Archi?" I asked, not even caring how desperate I sounded. "He is the only family I have left, and I don't even know for certain that he is alright. All I know about his current state is what Xander has told me."

Shaed sighed heavily, running a hand down his face. "What if I went to check on him for you?" he asked, his golden features crowded by exhaustion and apprehension.

"Like alone?" I asked, sitting straight up. "If you're going, I'm coming with you."

"Look, whisking across the mountains is something that takes a great deal of strength to do alone, never mind with another person," Shaed told me, and I remembered Xander mentioning the same thing.

"Please," I pleaded, the word tasting acidic. "I need to see him."

Shaed looked at me deeply, like he was weighing something in his mind, before standing with a nod.

"Get dressed. We leave in ten minutes."

CHAPTER FORTY-FIVE

VIOLET

I stood beside Shaed outside the door to my apartment, feeling like I was going to be sick from the anxiety wracking through my body.

He'd shown up to my room and whisked us across the mountains without saying much of anything. All he had done was ask me what street we lived on, having brought a map of the human lands with him for us to use. It looked like he was preoccupied with his thoughts, his eyes carrying a distracted haze that worried me.

I think it was a combination of his strange demeanor and the fact that I was about to see Archi that had me so worked up. Maybe there was something else contributing to it as well, because I felt like I was about to have a full-blown panic attack.

"Okay, you wait out here. I will yell for you if I need you, but if not, please don't come inside," I asked, politely as possible. "I don't want another reason to have to lie to him."

Shaed's eyes softened, and his lips pulled down into a pitiful frown again.

Maybe it was the anxiety or the sudden agitation that was wearing on me, but I reached my hand out quickly, pushing my pointer finger and thumb into his cheeks, forcing the corners of his mouth upward.

"Stop giving me that pity-filled frown," I demanded, giving him a distasteful look. "I'm sick of it."

His muscles flexed beneath my fingers with a genuine smile, and he spoke with a muffled voice. "Message received."

"Good," I said, releasing him and stepping back.

I turned on my heel and grabbed my keys out of the pocket of my jacket, pushing the right one into the slot. I took a deep breath and turned it, strangely relieved when I heard the deadbolt click open.

Why had I been anticipating that it would fail?

I opened the door slowly, half expecting something to jump out at me. When it didn't, I closed the door behind me and leaned against it, sighing.

It immediately felt like home.

But then I noticed a few things, and my head started to spin.

The decor on the walls was entirely different, and I didn't recognize any of the paintings or hangings.

I didn't see any of my shoes in the entryway, and I definitely had at least five pairs lying out when I left.

Maybe Archi had just put them in my closet while I was away?

"Archi?" I yelled out, taking off my boots before walking through the archway.

I screamed as someone slammed my front into the wall, holding me there with a strong forearm pressed tightly against my shoulder blades. My head was forced brutally to the side from the pressure, my neck straining at the unnatural angle.

The scent, though…it was so familiar, and stronger than I'd ever smelled it before.

Eucalyptus and peppermint–the distinct blend immediately springing me back to memories from my younger years.

"Archi," I choked out. "It's *me.*"

There was a moment of silence before I felt the distinct kiss of a metal blade being pressed against the side of my throat, and panic surged through me instinctively.

"And I'm supposed to have any idea who the fuck you are?" Archi asked.

My stomach bottomed out. All thoughts seemed to slow.

'All I did was Soothe him into forgetting about everything to do with this mission.'

In his own conniving little way, he had actually told me the truth about this. I just didn't hear it at the time.

Xander erased me from Archi's mind completely.

CHAPTER FORTY-SIX

VIOLET

"Archi," I choked out, and he pressed harder with the knife, silencing me.

"How in the fuck did you get in my apartment?" he asked in a voice I hardly recognized.

I was actually thankful for his arm pressing me into the wall now, because without it, I was sure that my legs would have failed me from the shock.

"Step the fuck back," a deep, warning tone called from the entrance.

Shaed.

Archi swung my body around, holding my back against him now as he pressed the knife to the front of my throat. "Don't come any closer," he warned.

Shaed laughed, full and mocking, looking at Archi like he was gum on the bottom of his shoe.

"You have no idea that, while you are trying to threaten me, you have one of the most dangerous weapons in the entire world in your arms," Shaed said, like it was the most amusing thing he had seen in a long time.

It felt artificial, though, like this was some sort of show put on to disarm him. I thought that I knew what he wanted me to do, but every morsel of my being retaliated at the idea of hurting Archi.

Striking while the opportunity was there, I used all of my effort to try and heat my hand without actually producing any flame. I didn't want to injure Archi; I just needed to do something to break his hold on me.

I grabbed his arm with that hand, hoping to fuck that it would work before he slit my throat. He cried out, jumping back from me and cursing.

I sprinted across the space toward Shaed, marveling at the fact that he had somehow become my safety net in all of this. I remembered a time when I flinched at his touch. Now, I was running away from my brother–for all intents and purposes–and toward him.

"Wait!" Archi yelled when I reached Shaed. "Who are you?"

I stopped and looked at him closely–I mean *really* closely–and felt a twinge of something sour in my gut at what I beheld.

Archi looked better than I had seen him in a long time.

His frame had filled out, indicating that he was eating regularly. I knew by now that this was a sign of lower drug use, because when he uses them frequently to aid his painting, he gets so caught up in the work that he forgets to take care of himself.

The previously cropped hair on his head was longer, falling onto his forehead in soft curls that I had never seen before. I never even knew that his hair was naturally curly. Even when we were living as nomads, moving from place to place, he'd kept it cut close to his skull. The new look suited him, making his blue eyes and freckles stand out from his features even more.

There were no purple smudges under his eyes, which meant that he was sleeping well, and the clothes he was wearing were nothing I had ever seen before. That told me that he was doing well enough financially to be able to afford buying new clothes, something that wasn't a common occurrence for us in the past.

"You seem well," I said at last, a tone to my voice that sounded both sad and proud.

He took a step forward, looking at me like I was some foreign creature standing before him. "What position are you in to tell me that I seem well?" he asked, and there was a bite to his words that I recognized as a defense mechanism.

He felt threatened, and rightfully so. I was a stranger to him now, and I had just walked through his front door.

I took a look around the space, seeing that the whole apartment was swimming with things that were just so very *Archi*. Some of the paintings in this room were the same as before, but there were new ones now too. I knew without any doubt that he had been the one to paint them because of his unique style and the signature he added to the bottom left corner. He always said that signing it there made his pieces more original because everyone else signed them on the right side.

My countless fuzzy blankets that he always complained about were nowhere to be found, replaced with the thin, cotton quilts that he preferred. I wondered how much of a difference that had actually made in his life and if he was happy now that there wasn't fuzz littering the apartment.

The door to my bedroom was sitting open, and I noticed with a stab to my chest that it had been made into an art studio–just like he always wanted.

Archi complained frequently about how cramped his bedroom was with all of his art supplies in there as well, and always talked about how we should find a bigger place with a spare room.

Paint cans and canvases were all over the floor and propped up against the wall, erasing any evidence that I had ever lived there at all.

My worries in Cavell hadn't been entirely baseless, it seemed.

Archi was thriving without me. He looked to be in a better place than he ever had been when I was around. Even though it was going to kill me to do it, I knew what was best for him. What had to be done.

I looked back at him, a wave of grief so strong crashing over me, I wasn't sure I would ever come back from it.

"Be safe, Arch," I whispered, choking on the words, and nodded in Shaed's direction.

He grabbed my hand in a supportive gesture, no doubt seeing

the pain written all over my face. As he whisked us away, I kept my eyes locked on the crystal blue ones that had been my home for as long as I could remember. There was confusion lying there, but I just gave him a broken smile.

When the blue was swept away by the swirling gray of the Between, I finally let out an ear-crushing scream, knowing deep in my soul that this was the last time I would ever see Archi again.

I felt my soul crumble at the realization and let the pieces go, not particularly caring to hold onto them any longer, anyway.

CHAPTER FORTY-SEVEN

VIOLET

I woke up slowly, groggily, in a state of confusion.

My body felt like it was detached from my mind and soul, and I struggled to figure out what was happening. The last thing I remembered was saying goodbye to Archi; the pain from it still potent in my heart.

So when did I go to sleep?

Upon opening my eyes, I noticed a sky full of the biggest, fluffiest clouds I had ever seen. I rolled my head to the side, my body feeling too limp to move.

I saw what looked like a never-ending expanse of nothingness.

I couldn't even put a name to the color that it was, but it looked like a blend of black, purple, and gray, and stretched as far as I could see. The floor, the air, everything but the fluffy clouds was that strange color.

"Hello?" I called out, hearing my voice echo around me.

My body began to feel more attached, the strange disconnectedness fading away. I sat up wearily and looked to the other side, just finding the same long offshoot as before. Panic began to set in then, forcing me to my feet.

I spun in a circle more times than I could count, seeing utterly nothing.

When nothing new arose, I just started running. I chose a direction at random and went with it, slamming my feet into the ground as fast as I could.

I didn't know if I was trying to run toward something or *away*, but I didn't stop to think about it. I just moved.

I ran for what felt like an impossible amount of time–until my breathing was labored and my feet were aching. I bent over with my hands on my hips, failing miserably to catch my breath.

"You know, it only causes more strain on your lungs when you bend over that way," a strange male voice called out from behind me, making me scream and literally jump into midair.

I whipped around to find what looked to be a male figure standing behind me, but I couldn't say for certain because they were heavily cloaked. It was a black material, flowing from their body and masking everything but their general size.

I noticed with some shock that they seemed to be as tall as Xander, if not a little more. They appeared to have a leaner physique than him, though; their entire frame slimmer.

The head that was hidden behind a deep hood cocked to the side, and it was so unnerving that I took a step backward.

"You flinch away from me," the definitively male voice spoke, but it was more observational than anything. "Safe to presume that you are not a new Angel, then?"

"What..." I choked out, my voice feeling thin and inadequate.

"How exactly did you get here, little girl?" he asked curiously, and I bristled at his condescension.

"I have no idea," I answered as calmly as possible. "I just woke up here."

The man took a step closer to me.

When I tensed, he advised, "Do not worry–I sense a kinship with you. There is a reason you ended up in my plane."

"Your what?" I asked, looking at him wearily.

Was I in some sort of drunken dream?

"My plane of existence. The dimension in which my Angels reside," he explained plainly, coming closer to me again. "Although, we are in a sort of waiting area right now. It is where new Angels await my ruling."

"What do you mean by 'Angels'?" I asked, unsure if I actually wanted to know the answer to that question.

"You know," he said conversationally, sweeping a hand through the air. "Angels of death: guides to the next stage and all that."

I think my soul left my body at that point.

"Am I dead?" I asked in a panic.

"No," he stated immediately. "Definitely not."

"Why am I here, then?" I asked, an irritated edge to my voice.

"That is what I was trying to ask *you*, if you recall," he told me, laughing.

What in the actual fuck?

"I have no idea what's happening," I admitted, and he cocked his head.

I was in a different plane altogether?

"So do all...Angels of Death–" My voice gave out on me, my throat felt like it wanted to close up. "Do all of you reside in this plane?"

"Oh, my sweet. *I* am not an Angel." He laughed, and unlike before, it seemed true and genuine. And dark.

"I am Death." His voice was soft, subtle–which only made it more chilling.

I felt my heart jump to my throat, panic crushing me from the inside out.

"There is nothing to fear from me, dear girl," he assured me, no doubt seeing my reaction to his admission. "I told you, I see a kinship within you."

"Oh, yeah," I quipped sarcastically. "It is super reassuring that I share a kinship with Death. I'm totally calm now."

He laughed again, but in a lighthearted way this time. The sound was rich and smooth–downright intoxicating. "You are quite amusing," Death said while stroking his chin, and I noticed that he had a different accent to both Astrales and humans. It was more clipped and curt, but with a rolling sort of quality to the consonants.

"I see my Mark on you," he admitted, and all thoughts about how nice his voice was flew away from my mind.

"Your..." I stammered, still coming to terms with the fact that I was apparently talking to fucking *Death*. In his dimension, nonetheless. "Your Mark? What does that mean?"

"You have a Mark of Death on your soul," he stated plainly, like he was talking about the weather.

Death paused, drawing down his hood. I blinked in surprise at the face that was revealed–it was nothing like I had expected.

His face showed signs of a grueling life; the years lived were immediately apparent in the wrinkles around his eyes and the laugh lines deep in his cheeks. But it didn't necessarily make him seem aged. It was more like *experienced*.

He smiled then, showing off two rows of perfect, white teeth and the dimples responsible for the markings etched into his face. His eyes were a deep brown color that radiated warmth, and his long hair was black, tied back in a neat bun at the nape of his neck.

"You know," he continued with light dancing in his eyes, silencing any potential question I could have asked. "There was one day that I was out on the Search, gathering souls as they passed on, and I was working on a particularly nasty job. The woman's soul was in the utmost anguish, a deeply rooted betrayal permeating her recent death. I was already exhausted, beyond ready to get back home, to my dimension," he trailed off for a second, making my anxiety rise.

"But then I felt a presence calling out to me, begging me for help."

All of the air left my lungs in response to his words.

"Now, normally," the man said to me conversationally, as if he were just telling me any old story, "when I feel souls reaching out to me, I don't take any notice. But something about this one was...different."

No. I tried to voice it, but I couldn't.

"It was something I had never quite seen before–such a

unique creation that I paused. I felt intrigued. But do you know what happened when I approached it?" he asked.

I barely shook my head, too filled with dread to do anything more.

His perfectly shaped, black eyebrows pinched together in a sort of contemplative look. "In the time it had taken me to decide, someone else had already placed their mark on her. Therefore, my Mark, because it had been one of my Angels–but, semantics."

I felt like my heart should be beating out of my chest, but I couldn't actually feel it beating–at all.

"I think that mysterious presence was you, little girl."

"I don't care if you *are* Death," I growled between my teeth. "Fucking call me 'little girl' one more time, and I swear to–"

His harsh laugh cut me off, and I felt my irritation rage even higher. "Were you really just about to threaten me?" He sounded more amused than anything.

"What do you want from me?" I asked, trying to change my approach.

"Right now?" he asked, with a guarded look. "Nothing."

I tried to hide my anxiety, but wasn't sure if that was even possible.

"But you will want something in the future?"

He shrugged. "There is no saying when and if I might want something from you. But for now, I think you have much more pressing issues to be dealing with, hmm?"

I started to ask him what he meant by that, but then he was directly in front of me, having moved so quickly that I didn't even register it. He was so close to me that I could see flecks of pure *orange* within his brown eyes, something that I had never seen before.

"I will see you soon, dear," Death bade, and then he placed his cold hands on my shoulders and pulled me to him.

I jolted in surprise that he was trying to hug me, but this was no hug.

My body turned to ash as I traveled *through* him—the sensation was like none other, and almost impossible to describe.

It felt like I had died and been reborn again; every physical sensation ripped away and slammed back within a split second. My heartbeat returned to me as well, startling me with its ferocity.

I was gasping frantically when I opened my eyes, my body springing into a sitting position. The air was too thin and my lungs too small as I tried to acclimate to being back in my body.

"Violet," a relieved voice gushed from beside me, causing me to jump back in shock.

CHAPTER FORTY-EIGHT

VIOLET

Shaed was sitting in a chair next to the bed I was in. His hair was standing on end and looked like it had just been tugged on relentlessly. His eyes scanned my face and body in double time, looking for any signs of injury or illness.

I looked around, realizing that I was back in my room at the Astrolite Palace.

"What the fuck happened?" I asked once I could find my voice.

"I have no idea," Shaed answered, his eyes filled with exhaustion and relief. "I was whisking us back into Cavell, and then suddenly, you just went limp. I held your weight until we were back here, but it was like you were having a fit." His voice sounded haunted.

"Your eyelids were fluttering, and you were entirely unresponsive for over half an hour. I didn't know what to do," Shaed rambled, still sounding flustered. "I obviously thought about calling a healer, but I was worried about what I would tell them. How to explain where we had been, or warn them about the untamed Starfire burning in your veins. I was just about to call Chelsea in here when you woke up," he finished, sighing and sitting back in his chair.

It wasn't getting any easier to breathe. If anything, it was harder now.

I got out of bed in a rush, pacing the room as my heart tried to hammer its way out of my chest.

"Violet," Shaed said in a warning tone, standing and approaching me with his hands out. "You need to try to calm down."

"Are you a goddamn idiot?" I yelled at him, pacing even faster now. "You don't fucking tell a woman to calm down–*especially* when she is already upset–unless you are in favor of becoming *dead*."

I vaguely recognized that the last part didn't really sound right, but I could feel my cheeks burning up, my body struggling to maintain the rate at which I was breathing and thinking.

Archi didn't know me. He didn't remember me at all.

No, more so than that, he had threatened to kill me.

I had a Mark of Death on my soul, apparently.

Where were all of my belongings that had been in our apartment now? Would I ever see them again?

Would I ever see *Archi* again?

What was I supposed to do with my life now? Live in the Astrolite sector forever?

And, given that I was an Astrale, how long was my life actually going to be?

Xander had told me once that he was sixty years older than me, but he didn't look to be a day over twenty-five. So how did the Astrales' aging actually work?

Oh, and did I mention the fucking *Mark of Death* on my soul?

"Okay, I think you might be having a panic attack," Shaed pointed out unhelpfully.

"Oh, really? You fucking think?" I snapped, feeling so flustered that I wanted to crawl out of my skin.

Shaed approached me the same way you would a wounded animal, and I had to physically fight the urge to punch him in the face. "Take a deep breath," he instructed slowly.

"You can shove your deep breath bullshit right up your undoubtedly virgin ass."

The satisfaction I gained from his expression was short-lived because a great pain started shooting through my chest. I dropped to my knees, heaving great breaths as I tried to calm myself down, knowing that it was unhealthy for my heart to be racing this fast.

Or was it, actually, since apparently I had a supernatural heart?

There was so much that I didn't know about myself, and it made me feel more alone than I had in a long time.

Out of absolutely fucking nowhere, Shaed grabbed both sides of my face and lunged forward, sealing our lips together in a kiss.

It was uncalled for, unwanted, and extremely disgusting.

I shoved him away from me in a volatile manner, sending him rocking back on his ass.

"What in the holy fuck was that?" I asked slowly; my chin lowered and my muscles tightened in anticipation of a fight.

"I was just trying to distract you," Shaed said, raising his hands.

"Try that again, and I will murder you," I said in a deadpan voice, letting him know just how serious I was.

His expression turned slightly amused, but his brow was still etched with concern. "Peach, look, I–"

"What–" I started, but my voice gave out. "What did you just call me?"

Every thought in my head died out, and my heart rate definitely wasn't an issue anymore because I was almost certain it had stopped beating altogether.

Shaed's face paled more and more by the second, and his eyes were the size of gold marks.

"What did you just fucking *call me*?" I repeated with emphasis, standing up.

Shaed's head dropped with a sigh before he stood, his face looking resolute and resigned. "Peach," he replied simply, and all of the dots connected at once.

It was like a smokescreen lifted from a deep, buried corner of my brain where my childhood memories had been long hidden away. Memories of my parents' friends and the son that they would bring along with them.

The peaches.

I choked on my breath as the realization hit me.

"You knew. This whole *fucking time* you knew exactly who I am?"

I felt a rage I had never known before overcome me, and a deeply-rooted embarrassment, as our past interactions played through my mind in succession. The way he watched me fumble over my words and try to blend in with their society.

"Violet, you don't understand," Shaed said gently. "I–"

I cut him off, slamming my fist into his face as hard as I possibly could.

His entire head and shoulders kicked back at the force, and I felt a small satisfaction settle in my gut. He looked back at me immediately, his eyes burning intensely.

"Guess I deserved that," he admitted, poking gingerly at his cheekbone once. "You don't understand, though, Violet."

"Oh, bite me, you entitled fuck," I spat and turned away from him, unsure where I was even trying to go.

Anywhere far away from him would do.

He caught my wrist and scrambled to say, "I have known who you are since the moment I saw you, but you obviously had no idea who I was. I didn't know what to do because I had no idea why–"

"You had no right to keep this hidden from me," I interjected, my voice rising. "You have let me pretend to know what the fuck I'm talking about and doing. You pretended not to know me when *yours* was the family that used to visit our farm for years?"

Memories sprang to mind, but they were different now. I'd thought that the faces of our friends had simply blurred in my mind over time–because I was so young when they stopped coming–but apparently, this had been yet another block put in my mind.

It was Shaed. My childhood friend was Shaed.

But...who had blocked him from my mind?

"And then you put on that grand performance when I told you I was raised in Armantrea? *Really?*" I was fully yelling by the time I finished, the urge to punch him again was strong.

"Violet," he said in a warning tone, charging forward and grasping my arm. "We have been looking for you since the day your parents died."

I ripped my arm back.

"Oh, really? It's not like I was in fucking hiding. Why should I believe a word you say now, anyway?" I scoffed, my blood boiling. "Xander told me not to trust you. I should have listened."

"Fucking hell, Violet, *Xander* is who we were trying to *protect you from*," Shaed screamed back at me, the level of his voice making my arms hairs rise. "Lilliana and her whole group of fucking Enforcers–they are why your parents were in hiding, who they were running from. When Lilliana learned of your location, your parents were dead within the hour. We tried to find you, but there was something stopping the tracking spells. Someone put a sort of cloak over you to keep you hidden."

"I don't believe you," I choked on a sob, too overwhelmed to accept what he was telling me.

Even though I knew deep down that it could very easily be true.

"Violet," he whispered, looking distraught.

"Go to hell, Shaed." My voice sounded hollow now; apathetic to the display of regret and dismay that was radiating off of him.

I didn't have to think very hard about what to do next. It just happened instinctively. I willed myself to be in the only other place that I knew I could go, completely unbothered by all of my belongings in the room.

I just needed to be gone.

One moment, I was looking at his white-blonde hair and tanned face, ringing with devastation. The next, I was staggering backward toward the exterior wall of Gaar's shop.

My back hit the building, and I sank to the ground, landing

with a thud. It was freezing outside and storming, but I felt nothing as my leggings became soaked and the cold raindrops pelted my face and neck. I sat there, staring up at the storm clouds above me, and the sobs began to rock through my chest.

Images of my mother and father dancing in the living room of our little cottage flashed behind my eyes. My mother's beautiful face was beaming with a smile, her golden-brown hair gleaming in the firelight. My father was looking down at her like she was the most magnificent thing on the planet.

It was the last memory I had of my parents before that bright light exploded. Before the darkness came, and my parents were ripped away from me forever.

I called out to that darkness now, begging it to take over me and spare me of this pain.

To my surprise, it obliged. My body slackened, and I slumped sideways, crashing into a puddle and losing consciousness.

CHAPTER FORTY-NINE

VIOLET

I woke up slowly and comfortably, letting out a soft sigh of contentment at the feel of the silk sheets beneath my fingertips.

Silk?

I sat up abruptly, bringing a hand to my head when it began to spin. After it passed, I looked around and felt utter confusion.

The entire room was black. The floors were glossy black marble that stretched halfway up the walls, which were also painted black. The few sets of doors within the room were all a jet black type of wood, as was every piece of furniture. Even the silk sheets I had woken up in were a deep ebony color, reflecting the light radiating from the gold sconces on the wall.

The only thing that *wasn't* black in the room was the head-board of the bed. It was a deep red color, the fabric was tufted and very regal-looking.

Where in the hell was I?

The events from the night before all came rushing back–my encounter with Death after fainting in the Between, my whole altercation with Shaed, and ending with me whisking myself to Gaar's shop.

So this must be his house, then.

I stood up and opened one of the doors, finding a huge walk-in closet. The next revealed a bathing room, which I quickly used before heading to the last door. After opening it, I saw a large apartment with the same styling as the bedroom. This time, everything in the space was black except for two red loveseats sitting in the middle of it, facing each other.

It was very strange, but also a little bit seductive, in a dark and alluring kind of way.

Very much like Gaar, I realized.

I walked around a corner to find the kitchen, which Gaar was currently in, sitting at a table and eating something out of a bowl.

"Aha," he muttered, setting down his spoon. "The human girl is awake."

I scowled. "You know I'm not human."

He raised his eyebrows, making his eyes widen, and I noticed that they weren't quite as red as the last time I'd seen him.

Strange.

"You are a testy little thing, aren't you?" His question was murmured in a quiet tone as he raised a mug to his lips.

That was somehow much more menacing than any other delivery would have been.

I cleared my throat. "I'm sorry that I just kind of showed up here last night. It was honestly a complete shitshow, and I didn't know where else to go."

"I must admit, finding you lying unconscious in front of my shop–in the rain–was probably the last thing I expected."

He paused.

"But why not go to Xander?" Gaar asked carefully, placing his coffee cup down.

"We've been over this already," I said with irritation. "He and I aren't involved anymore."

"Okay, it's time that you and I had a little chat," Gaar uttered in a resigned tone before nudging the chair next to him toward me with his foot, inviting me to sit in it.

I walked forward and sat down slowly, suddenly very aware of the fact that I was extremely alone with this man. The same man that Xander warned me had a vicious dark side.

Lovely.

"What is it exactly that transpired between you two?" Gaar asked, the deep timber of his voice putting me on edge.

I adjusted in my seat.

"He sold me out to Lilliana. Basically, he was just spying on me the entire time we were together and reporting back to her on my status. And then he hand delivered me to her to be tortured."

Gaar looked unconvinced. "And how did you gain this information?"

"Lilliana made it very clear. She made sure I knew *before* her lackey beat the shit out of me, though, just to be sure I wouldn't miss a beat."

He didn't seem very phased by the fact that I had been abused, which was a little disheartening.

"Did you speak with Xander after this altercation?" he asked.

"Yes. He acted really strange–as if he had no idea what I was talking about. He also turned into a maniac when he saw the bruising on my body." I couldn't help but recall the way his entire face morphed into a fiery rage when he saw them.

"There is no other way that Lilliana could have known the things she did without him having told her, though," I reminded him, but also myself. "He is either scarily good at acting, or truly didn't think that Lilliana would actually hurt me."

Even as I said it, I knew that last part couldn't be true. With the way he emphasized that he didn't trust her to be around me anymore, it didn't add up.

Gaar didn't respond to that. He just sat there, tapping his finger on the table, mulling over the things that I'd told him.

After what felt like a solid *minute,* I couldn't hold it in any longer.

"Well?"

He shot me a look that had me checking my impatience.

Gaar rubbed his jaw, his eyes looking far away. "I have had my suspicions about Lilliana for many years. She is a conniving little bitch who knows exactly how to spin a narrative in her benefit. That woman does not have one selfless bone in her fucking body, so I have always wondered why she would go to the effort of getting Xander out of his...previous situation."

Gaar looked at me then, a startling fury in his eyes. "I'm presuming you know about that? Of his origins?"

I swallowed thickly and nodded, still appalled by what Xander went through, even though I was harboring a lot of negative feelings toward him.

Gaar looked contemplative. "I never voiced my suspicions to Xan. He was already having a hard enough time acclimating to the real world. I couldn't add that weight to his shoulders."

I wondered what things Gaar had seen and heard about Xander's past. What insights he could give me into some of the things Xander had hinted at.

"But I have had my eye on her for years," he continued, bringing me back to the conversation, "watching every move that I could, and she is definitely working on something outside of the public eye. But I haven't been able to figure out *what*." That last part was let out with a frustrated growl that had my arm hairs rising.

"So you think that she has some secret project going on. What does that have to do with this situation?" I asked, frustrated and not liking the direction this was heading in.

Gaar tilted his head to the side and looked at me so deeply I felt like I was under a magnifying glass. I shifted, a little uncomfortable from it, but maintained eye contact with him.

"So, you were raised human, but have since found that you are Astrale. Correct?" Gaar asked in clarification.

"Yes. I grew up in a small farming community in the human lands with my parents, who are now dead. I have shown strong Starfire capabilities—according to Xander—and I am a Sensinor. Oh, and apparently, I am a Whisken as well, if last night was any indication."

Gaar raised his eyebrows, looking slightly amused by my rambling.

I narrowed my eyes. "Why do you ask?"

"And everything that you know of our world was told to you by Xander?" He pushed forward, ignoring my question.

"Apart from the things Shaed," I bristled at his name, making Gaar's lips twitch, "and Chelsea have unintentionally taught me the past two days, everything has come from Xander."

Gaar rubbed a hand over his jaw, looking the most uncomfortable that I'd ever seen him.

"What?" I asked, becoming irritated by his dramatics.

I could see why he and Xander were so close.

Gaar grabbed his mug and took a casual sip. "Has the topic of mates come up at all?"

"Mates?" I asked, recalling when Ren had joked about it. "I mean, I know what it is in a fictional sense—like in books and stuff. But I'm not sure what it means to your people."

He cleared his throat before speaking. "There is a bond that exists between some Astrales. When accepted and marked, it is a lifelong tether between their entire beings; body, mind, heart, and soul. It is a force stronger than any other."

So exactly like in books, then.

"The power that comes from two bonded mates is boundless, their very souls calling out to each other in a way that strengthens and unifies their magic. It is also incredibly rare and mostly unheard of at this stage of civilization. They used to be more common in our history, before the plague changed the way our societal constructs are laid out."

Gaar shifted in his seat, bringing one ankle up to rest on his opposite knee.

"I have been alive for a hundred and fifty years, and have only known two sets of mates. But both times, I knew within moments of being around them that they were companions at a deeper level than those who are married or committed in a typical way."

I marveled at the concept–two people who are so attuned to each other that their souls actually become *one*.

"I'll let you in on a little secret," Gaar said, leaning in to whisper. "I have the ability to see into others' minds."

I felt my eyes bulge out of my head, my heartbeat pounding in my ears.

Gaar chuckled, deep laugh lines appearing in his cheeks. "There is no reason to fear that. Honestly, after all this time, I hardly notice it unless I am actively trying to."

Gaar leaned in slightly, making sure my focus was entirely on him. "Of course, if you tell anyone this, I will have to kill them— and then you. That includes Xander."

He relaxed back into his chair and sighed.

"So you can literally read my mind right now?" I asked, gulping.

"Yes. Although to be honest, I actively try to avoid your inner monologue. It's quite grating."

Ouch.

Gaar's lips tilted in a smirk at that, and I couldn't stop the one pulling at mine, regardless of the insult.

"We've deviated from the point, though," he announced and cleared his throat. "Back to my story. Their emotions were so tied up and intertwined, it was almost as if an act against one was an act against the other. Both sets of mates had things in common. They talked about the fact that they felt this inexplicable need to protect their mate from the first moment they saw them. They also recognized the fact that there had been a level of comfortability with their partner from the very beginning that was atypical to their other relationships."

The air I breathed suddenly felt inadequate as I picked up on what Gaar was trying to tell me. "In one case, the couple reported being able to see through the other's eyes while they were dreaming. In the other, it was found that the two people were unable to fool their mate with a Soothe, for one could not hide any part of themselves from their mirrored soul."

"I think I'm going to be sick," I interrupted, contemplating if I should start running to the bathing room.

'You sound human as ever.'

'The idea of hearing your human phrases with the Astrale accent is quite amusing.'

Gaar looked at me with distaste before standing up to grab a small waste bin and placing it in front of me. He continued standing and looked down at me with crossed arms, making his biceps swell.

"So you understand what it is I'm getting at, then?" he asked, raising a brow.

"I think I know what you're implying," I replied, doing everything in my power to convince myself it wasn't true. "But what about what you said about mates needing to protect each other? Clearly, that's not the case."

"This is exactly my point," Gaar stated matter-of-factly, like he had been waiting for me to catch up to his logic. "There has to be something else at play here."

I shrugged. "I think you're wrong."

"Oh no," Gaar exclaimed mockingly. "The not-so-human-human thinks that I am wrong. Whatever will I do?"

"Is there any coffee around here?" I asked in exasperation, my head suddenly pounding.

He went to pour me a cup, but only after giving me an unimpressed glare.

While he was bustling about, I looked around the kitchen, noticing for the first time that there were no windows to be seen anywhere. The walls in this room were the same as the others, that black marble stretching up from the floor until it met the black-painted plaster. Even the cupboards were black and shiny, reflecting the light sent out from the fixtures.

"Are we below ground right now?" I asked Gaar as he walked back toward me.

"Yes," he confirmed, passing me the mug. "We are directly underneath my shop."

I nodded and took a sip, unsurprised to find the coffee

extremely bitter and unsweetened. I resisted the urge to ask for sugar, not wanting to be a bother.

"Okay," Gaar said, deciding I'd had enough of a break, "if you insist on staying in the dark about your and Xander's connection, let's talk about what happened last night. How did you end up here?"

My eyes darted away from him. "I'd rather not."

I jumped as Gaar's mug slammed down on the table, his face completely devoid of its previously collected expression. Irritation and impatience littered his features now, and they were directed entirely at me.

"*Enough,*" he hissed out, leaning two hands on the table and moving in closer to me. "Your period of leniency and adjustment is officially fucking over. Xander may have been more understanding of your incessant naivety and denial, but let's make one thing clear. I am not Xander."

The red within his pupils was swirling and dissipating, splotches of black showing through in between.

Fuck.

Did that mean he needed to feed? Or bloodlet, as Xander called it?

"Let's try this again," Gaar ground out, his voice rumbling. "What happened last night."

I took calming breaths, not out of fear, but anger. "Apparently, my father and Shaed's were quite close. Close enough that they used to visit us in Armantrea."

Gaar leaned back in his seat, still simmering, but paying close attention to every word.

"Shaed has known this entire time that I grew up human, but he waited until I was desperate enough to get back to Armantrea that I would be forced to tell him myself. So I did, after the party yesterday, and he took me back, only to find out that Archi—my best friend—has no recollection of me at all. None." I swallowed back the tears, doubting that Gaar would appreciate them.

I told him about how Xander had wiped me from his mind,

how all of my belongings had been cleared away—any evidence of my previous life completely obliterated.

"It wasn't until we got back to the palace and I was freaking out that Shaed slipped up. He was trying to calm me down and called me the nickname that my father used to use for me. Just like that, it was as if a screen had been removed from my memories. I could remember him coming to our farm when I was a child. I remembered them bringing us peaches from Cavell. I remembered how I was always afraid of his father but never of him. We were friends."

I closed my eyes as the memories resurfaced again, feeling like a fool.

"But then," I pushed on, "they suddenly stopped coming one day. I can't remember when it was. I didn't even remember what they looked like until Shaed called me Peach. I'd always thought their faces had just faded from my memory, but then he used that nickname, and it was like my memory was restored." I sighed, sitting back in my chair. "None of this makes any fucking sense."

I looked back at Gaar to find him staring at me, blinking evenly.

"And you came here as soon as you learned of this?" he clarified.

"Well," I started, cringing slightly. "I kind of, um...punched him. And then came here."

His face did a weird, twitchy thing, and I wondered if he was trying to contain a smile.

"Let me get this straight," he started, leaning toward me. "Shaed offered you his aid—should you need it—and you took him up on it. He then brought you back to his home and watched over you, saved you from dying on multiple occasions, and brought you to see your little human friend?"

"Yes?" I said, frustrated.

"And then you punched him in the face?"

I nodded, wincing slightly. When he put it that way, it seemed like an overreaction.

Gaar's laugh burst out of his chest with so much power that I flinched back involuntarily, the deep bellow echoing loudly off the marble around me.

"Wow," he said after a minute, wiping his eyes dramatically. "That's the best story I've heard in years."

"Why do you all hate him so much, anyway?" I asked.

"He's a spoiled little prick–why else?" Gaar sounded casual, but I marked the way his posture stiffened and the humor dropped from his eyes.

"Oh, come on–"

"I believe you have some more important things to be focused on, hm?" That chill was back in his voice again, and I promptly shut my mouth.

He raised his chin, evaluating me. "Someone has obviously been tinkering in your mind. I can go in and investigate it myself, but it is likely that everything you have known about your life has been a lie."

He paused, a heavy silence falling between us.

"Are you ready to come face-to-face with that?" Gaar finally asked.

"Um, do you think that this is new information to me?" I asked, suppressing an inappropriately-timed laugh. "It has become painfully clear that my entire childhood was constructed by lies. But what do you mean?" I asked with apprehension. "As in, you going *into* my head?"

"We need to find out what kind of blocks have been placed on your memories because they could very well have been placed on your magic as well."

Gaar's eyes swept over my body as if he could look right through it and see my inner workings. I honestly wasn't entirely sure that he couldn't.

"But this will not be an easy process, and it will not be without pain. Is that something you're prepared to handle?"

I bristled at his condescension. "I can handle pain, jackass."

"Ohhh," Gaar said through a cold laugh. "I would *not* recommend irritating me right before I start digging around inside that bitter little head of yours. It would be very easy to…" Gaar made a *popping* noise while flicking a finger, and I thought I actually felt my soul leave my body.

"I'm kidding," he assured me, though his tone suggested otherwise. "I am not stupid enough to harm Xander's mate. He would skin me alive."

Chills ran over my entire body from hearing myself referred to that way.

"Well, he'd surely try," Gaar amended with a sadistic smirk.

I gathered myself, feeling unsure in every sense of the word about what I was getting ready to say.

"Okay." I took a breath and nodded. "You can look into my mind."

Gaar's eyes sparkled with delight, making me wonder what he got out of this whole situation. I didn't have to wonder for long, though.

"This will not come without a price."

"What kind of price?" I asked slowly.

"I presume you're aware by now of my particular fuel source?" he asked with a loaded tone.

"Uh…yeah. I am."

"I won't be able to do this without it."

Wait. Was he waiting for me to offer him my blood?

I blinked, dumbfounded. "You want to drink my blood?"

"It is not a painful process if the Bloodletter knows what they are doing," Gaar informed me with a soothing, convincing tone.

The decibel of it made my muscles instantly relax, tension that I hadn't even realized had gathered fading away.

"And, trust me," he spoke in that same way. "I very much know what I am doing."

"I don't doubt that," I said, my voice the calmest it had been in days.

But, wait…why the hell was I so tranquil all of a sudden?

"Are you doing some sort of Soothsayer juju on me right now?" I asked.

"Just a little something to ease your nerves," Gaar assured me with a smooth tone. "Your temper was becoming redundant."

"Can you please do this for me every day?" I asked blissfully, feeling like my limbs were featherweight.

"Did you just say *please?*" he asked in a bewildered tone. "Fuck. Maybe I went a little heavy for your first time."

"Don't be a bore," I teased, shoving his shoulder playfully.

His hand whipped out, and I giggled when he caught mine midair. "Oh, there will be none of that," Gaar declared, giving me a hard, askance look.

"None of what?" I asked.

"*Touching* me," he explained like it should have been obvious.

My brows creased, and Gaar sighed like a father dealing with his child's temper tantrum.

"Hey!" I shouted way too loudly, a thought occurring to me at random. "Where is Briella? I want to see her."

He looked at me like I was a menace. "She is up in the shop, waiting to alert me if any visitors arrive."

I gasped. "You can communicate with your dog?!"

Gaar pressed his lips together in a way that seemed like he was both annoyed and trying not to laugh. "No. She will *bark* if someone enters."

I nodded deeply in understanding, and Gaar made that face again.

"It's okay, you know," I assured him. "You can smile—I won't tell anyone."

"Alright, get up, you little shit," he demanded, tugging me up by my wrist.

As I followed him back into the living area, I could've sworn I heard him mumble something about me and Xander being too much alike, but I couldn't be sure. Gaar led us to one of the red loveseats, sitting down and indicating for me to join him, but I eyed the limited space and decided to sit on the other couch.

"How, exactly, do you expect me to bloodlet from you when you're sitting all the way across the room," Gaar deadpanned, looking at me critically.

"Oh...right," I said, feeling like I was slowly returning to my typical state.

He must have stopped whatever Soothe he'd put on me.

When I didn't move, Gaar heaved a great sigh and whisked himself to sit next to me. I flinched back a bit, sobering up by the second as I realized what was about to happen.

My heart rate kicked up, right on cue.

"Oh. Great. Now your blood is going to be riddled with adrenaline." Gaar looked put off. "I should have kept the Soothe going."

I stuck out my wrist in front of his face, sick of the anticipation and just wanting to get it over with.

Gaar gave me a smirk, looking at my wrist with amusement. "I'll have you know," he said, leaning in closer, "I've never given anyone the courtesy of choosing the spot I drink from."

My anxiety spiked even more, worried that he was going to want to drink from my neck the way vampires do in novels.

"But I will for you," he amended. "For Xander's mate."

My heart caught, and I wondered how deep Gaar's feelings for Xander actually went.

Was he in love with him?

Gaar grabbed my hand, drawing my wrist closer to him. I adjusted my body to try and get more comfortable but gave up quickly.

There was no way to make this any easier; it was best to just get it over with.

"Just try to relax your muscles as much as you can," Gaar instructed me in a soft voice, his eyes locked on the veins of my wrist. "It won't take long."

I nodded words far beyond me at this point.

Gaar dipped his head, and a few white strands broke free from his bun, hanging around his face like a cage.

With very little warning, Gaar slid his teeth into my skin with expert precision. It was such a smooth and fast movement that I hardly even felt it, though my skin was pulsing and throbbing as his mouth worked around the cuts, sucking and probing with his tongue.

A strange whirlwind of emotions took root inside of me. The first was utter shock at the fact that this was even happening right now—I felt like I was living out a scene from one of my favorite books.

I was also very disturbed by how...*undisturbed* I was by the act. It made me question everything about myself because I wasn't revolted. I wasn't waiting for this to be over.

No, I was...enjoying it.

How fucked up was that?

Regardless, with every brush of his lips against the soft skin there, my thoughts became more and more muddled, veering off into a blissful sort of blankness.

Gaar released his mouth from my wrist sooner than expected, and I saw blood instantly pool, which he licked away like it was melted ice cream.

Fucking strange, these Astrale men.

I focused my energy on healing the wound and did so with minimal effort, the marks from his teeth only having gone deep enough to puncture the skin.

When it was closed up all the way, I looked over at Gaar to find him staring at me like I was wearing seven hats.

I didn't really pay attention to it, though, because his eyes were a booming red and took all of my attention. The color was far more intense than I had ever seen it, the fresh blood was obviously doing its job very quickly.

"I think you forgot to mention something, Violet," Gaar snapped with a rumbling, irritated tone.

"What?" I asked, still groggy and disoriented from that strange state of mind I'd been in while he was bloodletting.

"You didn't tell me what happened before you learned of Shaed's involvement in your childhood."

"Oh, right." I sighed. "That."

"Yes, *that*," Gar hissed, standing up. "How could you not have told me that you are Marked?"

"Um, pardon me for being a little bit mentally fried after the fucking hellhole of the past few days." My voice was littered with sarcasm, my nifty defense mechanism springing to attention.

"Oh, spare me the sob story."

"I don't even understand what it means, and have been a bit preoccupied bringing you up to speed on everything else that has happened. Is this going to be a problem?"

Gaar sighed. "Not presently. But down the road...yes," he said, walking to a bureau set up against the wall and pouring two glasses of amber liquid. "You're right, though. We have more important things to be focusing on."

I did my best to shove all thoughts of the Mark on my soul aside, though it seemed almost impossible after his warning.

He came back and handed one of them to me. I brought it to my nose, wrinkling it when I smelled the contents. "Really?" I asked.

He gave me a side-eye. "Some people might say, *thank you*."

"It's morning," I protested. "Wait–it is morning, right?"

"More like mid-afternoon," he corrected, tipping his chin up. "You do a lot of sleeping, hmm?"

I rolled my eyes, taking a sip of the liquor.

Gaar was sitting next to me again, leaning back against the corner of the couch and regarding me. He swirled the liquid around once in his glass before kicking it all back in one swoop.

I took another small sip, gathering myself for what was about to come.

I'd given him my payment–my blood–and now there was only one thing left to do.

Let the most unnerving man I'd ever met dig around inside my brain.

CHAPTER FIFTY

VIOLET

"Okay," Gaar said, taking my glass and putting it down next to his. "When I enter your mind, we will still be able to communicate. There is no telling whether you will be present for what I see or not–it is different for every person."

I sent out a prayer to whatever being would have a say in this, wanting more than anything to be able to see what was hidden from me inside of my own head.

"In the event that you can, just remember that I will be there the entire time," Gaar assured me. "We can stop at any point to take a break if you need it. Just say the word."

I nodded my understanding, trying to calm my nerves with my breathing.

"Lie back," he commanded in a soft tone.

I did as he instructed, relaxing into the couch and resting my head back against the soft cushion of the back.

I closed my eyes and almost instantly felt something inside of me shift, a sort of door opening on its own accord. From there, it got even weirder, the sensation that something foreign was entering my system was so potent that I could feel myself tensing up.

Relax, Violet. Gaar's voice wasn't coming from his mouth. It was sounding *inside* my head.

Forcing myself to ease up, I mentally repeated over and over that I was safe and nothing would go wrong.

Something clicked–I'm not sure what–but I knew without a doubt that Gaar had successfully entered my mind.

I'm in, he confirmed.

"I'm still awake," I commented.

Can you see anything? Gaar asked.

I opened my eyes–well, I *tried* to open my eyes, but I saw nothing.

It wasn't like the Between, or trying to look out into darkness.

There was literally just...nothing.

Gaar, I said in a panic, but I didn't hear anything actually come out that time. I wasn't even sure that I had spoken at all until his response filtered in, sounding like it had to travel through many layers to get here.

It's alright, Violet, he assured me, his voice far away. *The block seems to be fragmented...part of it has been destroyed already. It's a mess in here.*

Wow. Thank you so much, I muttered dryly.

I felt–more than heard–his chuckle. *It seems that your subconscious is trying to show you something. Until it does, I won't be able to remove what is left of the block.*

I took a deep breath, steadying and preparing myself.

As soon as I accepted that there was something I needed to see, a memory formed in front of my eyes very quickly.

I was young–about four years old, from the look of it–and gripping the edge of the kitchen counter as I watched my mother slice up a peach for me. She was looking down at me with a loving expression, her eyes crinkling around the corners from her smile.

I was blown away by how similar we looked. Seeing her like this now that I was older felt completely surreal.

The scene in front of me dissipated, morphing into another.

I was a few years older and peeking around the corner of a wall, watching my parents. I sucked in a breath at seeing them this way–clear in focus and very much *alive.*

They seemed to be having a sort of argument, their body language radiating hostility and anger.

"I don't understand. Why won't you just make the peaches grow here?" my father asked in a cruel tone. "You know how much she loves them, Mali. She asks for them every single day."

"And what then, Reid? Somehow find a way to explain it to the neighbors? *'Hello! We planted a brand new species of fruit tree that has never been seen on this continent before! Just found the seed lying about!'*" My mother threw her hands up in exasperation. "I mean, really, Reid. We may as well just hang a fucking *banner* from the roof!"

"They will find us eventually, Mali," my father hissed out, moving closer to her as he did. "You know they will. Which is exactly why I need to start training her. Violet needs to be able to defend herself."

"I agree that she does, but *not right now*," she countered, her eyes burning with passion. "She is only seven years old, for fuck's sake, Reid. Our daughter deserves to have a few more years of happiness before she spends every day looking over her shoulder."

"Mali, her magic is going to emerge soon, and she could be hurt if she is not prepared for it. And that is only compounded by the fact that we have no idea which Core—or *Cores*—she possesses... my Astrolite or your—"

Their figures and words fizzled away in a blur before I could hear the end of his statement, transitioning to a memory of me and my father training in the yard a year or so later.

"You must stay focused, Peach," my father said sternly, watching over me as I balanced on one foot.

"But Poppa," I whined, "how is balance supposed to help me win a fight?"

"You must master your mind before you can master your body. It takes a great deal of focus to be able to command your body to move at the speed of a fight, so this is where you'll begin."

My younger self's brow furrowed in concentration, doing everything possible to keep myself still even though my muscles were burning with the effort it took.

"Good," he murmured, his brown hair catching in the light.

That was the last thing I noticed before the image faded out again–the one that took its place made my stomach bottom out completely.

It was the night my parents were killed.

My twelve-year-old self brought the bow down to the strings of my violin right as a loud *boom* rang through the air. I watched in shock as an explosion that was unmistakably Starfire blew an entire wall off of my house and saw my small body go flying across the room.

"Violet! Violet, where are you, my baby?" my dad bellowed, but I couldn't see him with the white light crowding the room.

There was the sound of many footsteps approaching at a rapid pace, men and women alike shouting with distinct Astrale accents.

"Where's the girl?" one yelled.

"You have nowhere to go. Just give her to us now, and no one gets hurt," said another.

"Don't you fucking touch her, you weasely little bitch!" I heard my mom spit, her voice closer to me than the others.

There was another loud noise, and then she emerged from the smoke and light, looking around frantically and landing at my side in a split second once she saw me.

It was strange to watch her move with superspeed, and it made me wonder how much my childhood memories were actually tampered with.

"I'm sorry, baby. I am so, so sorry that I never got the chance to explain any of this to you," she said, running her hands down my hair. "But I have to leave you now."

My mother's voice broke into a sob, and tears flowed freely down both of our cheeks.

I began shaking my head fervently, not wanting her to go, but she clutched my cheeks and stopped me by saying, "You are ready. It's far too early, and you are too young, but you will grow to be the strongest of any of us. I know you will be okay."

Her voice hardened then, turning into a firmer command. "You can do this."

"But why can't you come with me, Momma? I want you to stay."

Her face crumpled, but she just said, "I love you with my entire heart, Violet. I would stay if I could."

I sat up and hugged her. "I love you more, Momma."

"Now, before I go," she pulled back, looking at me pointedly. "There is one thing you need to remember, okay? Listen closely."

"The world will try to make you believe that the depth of your emotions is a weakness. Do not listen to them, Violet. Your intensity will be your saving grace. Use it, always."

She placed a kiss on the top of my head, and then the image shifted again.

I was up in the treehouse my father built for me, looking down as my house went up in a shining white flame. I screamed and started pulling on the door latch, banging on the window, trying to find a way to get out of there and go save them.

But I was trapped–there was no way out. Now I knew why.

My mother had whisked me up there and must have put some sort of ward around it so I wouldn't be able to get out. She protected me. She saved my life.

This true, unclouded memory told me something else too.

She'd known they were coming.

There had to have been some preparation involved for my escape. Why else would there have been food, water, and spare clothes waiting for me in the treehouse?

No–she was anticipating the attack.

My vision went black again, and I blinked with disorientation, but quickly brushed it aside when a new image arose.

It was a dream that I'd had a while back–the one with the woman in the dark alley. She was begging for mercy, trying to tell me that she was pregnant, but I stabbed her anyway.

I expected the image to change again, wondering why in the hell I was seeing this random dream, until my perspective shifted.

My brain failed to process what I was seeing. I felt like I needed to vomit.

I was no longer the person holding the knife. I was standing a distance back, watching as he stood above the woman's body, wiping blood from the blade with a cloth. His face held that same dispassionate expression that I had seen the last time we were together–the one that made him look like a stranger.

Xander.

Xander was the one who'd killed that woman.

My surroundings changed again, and this time, I saw Xander standing at the top of a hill, looking down at something. He still looked catatonic, like all of the feeling had been leached out of him and replaced with a bitter nothingness.

I followed the direction of his gaze to find a family on the hillside. The parents were sitting on a blanket together while their daughters played in the field, and I felt a sense of dread pool in my stomach.

He couldn't be about to do what I thought he was. There was no way.

Xander took a step forward–toward the family–but suddenly was being forced down to his knees, the scene behind him shifting to show his apartment.

His green eyes were burning with an emotion so strong that I sucked in a gasp. It turned into a horror-filled sound when I realized what was actually happening.

Xander was on his knees with shackles on his wrists now, reminding me of the tattoo that I'd seen on him once.

No...

With that thought, the memory ended again, shoving me back into that all-white room at the Armory.

Except, it wasn't the room that I was tortured in. It was the room that I had seen in my dream. The one that ended in flames and being woken up by Shaed.

This time, though, my vantage point was from above. I was looking down at a scene that made me so angry, so deeply *infuri-*

ated that I felt my Starfire pulse to the surface, begging to be let out.

Easy now. I heard Gaar's voice enter my mind again and realized I'd forgotten he was even there.

I ignored him as I watched Xander fight against the restraints on his wrists. He was screaming, trying to break free from them, when a spray of water came out of the wall, totally incapacitating him.

Stop it! I tried to yell, but nothing would come out.

I watched as that slimy motherfucker, Jax, and Dhan entered the room, followed by Lilliana and another woman I didn't know.

Lilliana was watching Xander with an expression of regretful resolution, like she was sad to see this happening but had already decided she wouldn't put a stop to it. She was speaking now, but I couldn't hear anything she was saying. I could only look at Xander.

He hadn't betrayed me—not for a second. I knew now, as I watched her circle in on him, that it was Lilliana all along. She had to have been forcing her way into his mind and controlling his actions somehow. That was why his face looked so different in our last interactions.

This new expression was much more harrowing, though. Rage intertwined with betrayal and a helplessness he was obviously trying to mask.

It made me see red.

But that was nothing compared to what overtook me when I heard him scream. When I saw his body crumble to the floor.

The sound was so raw, so primitively painstricken and broken, that I let out a war-cry of my own. I felt it tear through my body with the force of a thousand winds, snapping something within my mind, body, and soul that had been holding me back.

I sat up gasping for air, my hands seeking an anchor around me as I adjusted to being back inside my body, inside Gaar's living room.

Everything felt like it was tingling, a new sense of awareness making itself known all along my limbs and in my chest and gut. I squeezed my hands into fists, overwhelmed by the sensations coursing through me.

For once in my life, my mind felt completely and entirely clear. And there was one very distinct objective at the center of it all.

I looked at Gaar beside me on the couch, his bright red eyes shining with dark violence so potent, I could almost pluck it from the air.

I met his stare with one of my own, doing my best to emulate that I felt the same rage he did.

And I was ready to act on it.

I stood up, giving Gaar an expectant look.

"Where are we going?" he asked as he stood with me, his body already perched for a fight.

I gave him my most devious smile then. One that I was sure showed my thirst for retribution–the way that I craved the feeling of Lilliana's neck snapping between my hands.

I spoke loud and clear with zero hesitation. Not a single doubt in my mind.

"We're going to rescue my mate."

To be continued...

ACKNOWLEDGMENTS

To Cameron~ for always being a FaceTime away. Whether to discuss plotline ideas, listen to me ramble incoherently about the publishing process, or obsess over Billie Eilish with me, you have been my rock and sounding board. You've quite literally been there since day one, and believed in this story when it was still an inkling of a seed in my mind. Thank you.

To Genna~ I've never known such unconditional acceptance and mutual understanding in my life, and I am so thankful that our lives crossed paths when they did. Your constant support–no matter what–has kept me going, and kept me (relatively) sane. I love you 9 million. P.S. for nicknaming dear ole Xanny.

To my editors~ your patience and dedication throughout this project were my support beam, and helped turn a convoluted first draft into something I am proud to put my name on. I admire each of you and am so thankful to have met you.

To TGC~ I have never felt more at home with a group of people than I do with you wonderful weirdos. You've been by my side daily, kept me laughing, and grounded me throughout this journey. For that and so much more, I cannot thank you enough. I love you all. #teamtails #tatedmates5ever

To my indie author friends~ each of you continues to inspire me daily and share every resource at your disposal with me. I've learned so much from you, and I appreciate you so much!

To the IG besties~ the support, friendship, and encouragement you all have given me during this journey is not something I will soon forget. I look forward to many more years of electronic laughs and tackle-hug gifs. Love you bitches.

To the Bad Bitches Book Club~ for rekindling my love of reading when I needed it most. Love you long time.

To my alphas–Cris, Fern, Cam, Hannah, Taryn–and betas– Ashley, Sam, (wife) Sam, Kali, Katie, Vanessa, Steph, Brit, Di,

Laura, Carolyne, Fabienne, Sabriba, Abby~ your encouragement and support through this journey have been unwavering, and propelled me forward when I needed it most. I can't thank you enough for your reactions, excitement, kindness, and suggestions. You read this book in its raw, unfiltered form, and played a massive role in making it what it is. Thank you.

To Taryn~ for completely and entirely corrupting me. Not only were you the reason I joined Bookstagram in the first place, but you helped me through the darkest period of my life–and I'm honestly not even sure you knew you were doing it at the time. I appreciate that and our friendship more than I can put into words (ik, if only Ingramspark offered invisible ink).

To my parents~ for giving me the opportunities I have had, and your undying faith in me. For teaching me that family comes before all else. For being the kind of people who not only accepted my decision to deviate from the traditional path of life, but *encouraged* me to. You cheered me on every single day throughout this process, and for that, I can never thank you enough. And, finally, for inviting me to live in your corner of paradise while this book was born. It is a time I will never forget. I love you.

To Hannah & Billy~ for showing me the value of staying dedicated to your future, while simultaneously making a shitshow of it. I am so proud to be your sister, and I look up to both of you every day.

To Caiden~ for my daily "It's 12:00" text. While it started as a joke, it became a handy writing tool. I'm not sure I've ever told you how deeply I value our friendship and how thankful I am to have you in my life. So, there you are. Oh, and for naming Briella.

To my family as a whole~ for always, without fail, making me laugh. I love you all endlessly, and cannot begin to describe how grateful I am for your unconditional support and unconventional way of life.

To Kelly~ for teaching me to manage and navigate my traumas, and offering me a guide back to myself when I needed it most.

To Di~ for planting the seed in my brain that blossomed into a world of literature and fiction. I wouldn't be the reader/writer/person I am today if you hadn't been my fourth-grade teacher, then a role model, and eventually a friend. Say it with me…*"It's a beautiful day to save lives."*

To Jess~ for everything you did to help me get this book out into the world. The last stages of the publication process have always felt the most daunting to me, and I am incredibly grateful for your insights and support!

And to you~ you've taken a chance on me, and that means more than you will ever know. Thank you. I hope my story found you well, and maybe even allowed you to escape reality for a hot minute. If you've made it here, you've already supported me in a monumental way. And, if you feel so inclined, please head to Goodreads and Amazon to leave a review. It makes a world of difference to an indie author. <3

ABOUT THE AUTHOR

Alice Stanco is a full-time writer who has spent most of her life between the pages of fantasy books. When not obsessing over fictional characters, she can usually be found celebrating Christmas at any given time or frolicking in proper ADHD fashion.

While a born-and-raised Minnesotan (American), Alice is also half English. This can be seen in her writing, as it explores the many cultural differences in a fictional sense.

Mental health representation is also a strong focus in Alice's work, and is a passion that will ring true indefinitely.

Visit her website, www.alicestanco.com, for merch, signed copies, and more info! Find her on social media: @alicestanco.